Her Punishment Was Passion

"I think I should have let my friends kill you," she said quietly.

Logan smiled. It did not reach his eyes. "You only think it?" Raising one hand, Logan lifted Katy's chin. When she tried to move away his fingers tightened marginally. "What I have in mind will make you sure."

Logan bent his head. His mouth hovered near Katy's so that she could feel the warmth of his breath. There was the faint but unmistakable scent of brandy. A moment later she was tasting it on his lips.

"Go ahead. Fight me."

"I can't." Katy's mouth parted on a sob. It was no good telling herself that she wanted to reject him. She couldn't do it. This is what he meant, she thought helplessly: desire in the face of all good sense, all good reason. It was her punishment.

She hated him. *She did.* But she wanted him now as much as she had when she was a girl. Perhaps more.

Fire was licking at her insides. Each time he touched her she thought she would be consumed in a flash of heat and light.

"Tell me what you want," he said.

There was a long silence, so long Logan thought he had lost her. Then, "You." There were tears on her cheeks, despair in her voice. "I want you."

THE BEST IN HISTORICAL ROMANCES

TIME-KEPT PROMISES (2422, $3.95)
by Constance O'Day Flannery

Sean O'Mara froze when he saw his wife Christina standing before him. She had vanished and the news had been written about in all of the papers—he had even been charged with her murder! But now he had living proof of his innocence, and Sean was not about to let her get away. No matter that the woman was claiming to be someone named Kristine; she still caused his blood to boil.

PASSION'S PRISONER (2573, $3.95)
by Casey Stewart

When Cassandra Lansing put on men's clothing and entered the Rawlings saloon she didn't expect to lose anything—in fact she was sure that she would win back her prized horse Rapscallion that her grandfather lost in a card game. She almost got a smug satisfaction at the thought of fooling the gamblers into believing that she was a man. But once she caught a glimpse of the virile Josh Rawlings, Cassandra wanted to be the woman in his embrace!

ANGEL HEART (2426, $3.95)
by Victoria Thompson

Ever since Angelica's father died, Harlan Snyder had been angling to get his hands on her ranch, the Diamond R. And now, just when she had an important government contract to fulfill, she couldn't find a single cowhand to hire—all because of Snyder's threats. It was only a matter of time before the legendary gunfighter Kid Collins turned up on her doorstep, badly wounded. Angelica assessed his firmly muscled physique and stared into his startling blue eyes. Beneath all that blood and dirt he was the handsomest man she had ever seen, and the one person who could help beat Snyder at his own game.

Available wherever paperbacks are sold, or order direct from the Publisher. Send cover price plus 50¢ per copy for mailing and handling to Zebra Books, Dept. 2958, 475 Park Avenue South, New York, N.Y. 10016. Residents of New York, New Jersey and Pennsylvania must include sales tax. DO NOT SEND CASH.

PASSION'S SWEET REVENGE

Jo Goodman

ZEBRA BOOKS
KENSINGTON PUBLISHING CORP.

ZEBRA BOOKS

are published by

Kensington Publishing Corp.
475 Park Avenue South
New York, NY 10016

First printing: April, 1990

Printed in the United States of America

Also by Jo Goodman:

Midnight Princess
Tempting Torment
Scarlet Lies
Violet Fire
Velvet Night
Seaswept Abandon
Crystal Passion
Passion's Bride

Chapter One

April 28, 1863 — Washington, D.C.

"Mama, tell her to come away from the window!" Megan McCleary winced as her mother tightened her corset strings. The stiff whalebone stays made deep breathing a luxury.

"Whining becomes no one," admonished Mrs. Allen. "There. You're quite finished." She glanced at the window. "Mary Catherine, do as your sister says." When there was no response, Rose's soft, singsong tone became stern. *"Mary Catherine McCleary,* come away from the window. There's no need to gawk. He'll see you."

Instead of obeying, Mary Catherine flattened her nose against the cool window pane and peered down at the sidewalk. The narrow path to the house was partially obscured by a rose trellis and the mist of her own breath. She pulled back only long enough to clear the condensation with her sleeve.

"She's deaf, Mother!" Megan wailed. "Look what she's doing now! She's going to ruin everything!"

Rose Allen's mouth tightened. "And you're going to alert all of Washington," she said impatiently, her voice never rising above a harsh whisper. "Have a

7

care what you say in this house. What if the colonel himself were to hear? We're not supposed to know he's expecting anyone."

Mary Catherine's forehead wrinkled at the mention of the colonel. Her tawny brows creased over a pair of large, expressive brown eyes. Anger made the shards of gold in them a little brighter. "I think he *should* hear," she said, answering in her sister's place. "He'd divorce you and we could go home." She finally turned away from the window and sat heavily on the bench beneath it. Her dress twisted around her waist and legs but she didn't bother to right it. Mary Catherine, in spite of the signs that she was on the precipice of womanhood, had a thirteen-year-old's disdain for posture and social grace. She swung her feet back and forth, liking the flash of her red patent leather shoes. "I want to go home, Mama. Back to Stone Hollow." She stopped kicking and lifted her eyes in appeal. "Please? Can't we go home?"

Megan covered the distance between herself and her younger sister in seconds. Grasping one of Mary Catherine's honey-colored braids in her fist, she pulled hard. "Ninny! Don't you care how you hurt Mother? You have to stop asking for what can never be. Stone Hollow is gone for us. Gone! Do you hear?"

"Megan!" Rose stepped beside the girls and gently removed Megan's hand from Mary Catherine's braid. "Finish dressing now," she told Megan. Rose sat beside Mary Catherine and placed an arm around her daughter's slumped shoulders. Rose's eyes were drawn to their reflection in the cheval glass across the room. They were a study in contrasts. Rose's skin was as pale as cream, her hair jet-black. Her younger daughter was a changeling. She possessed neither her father's red hair and flashing green eyes as Megan

8

did, nor the striking Black Irish features of Rose's side of the family. Mary Catherine, with her golden fall of hair and faintly exotic slant to her eyes, was a lioness. The child didn't know it yet, but she was the beauty of the family.

Rose's cheek rested against Mary Catherine's hair. She smiled at her daughter's grave reflection. "You miss the Hollow, don't you?"

Mary Catherine sucked in her lower lip. She wasn't going to cry. She already felt terrible for hurting her mother. "Not so much," she lied bravely. Then, because she felt just as bad about lying, she hedged, "Sometimes. I don't like Colonel Allen."

"I know you don't," Rose said gently. "Sometimes he can be a difficult man to get along with."

"But you married him!" It was less a statement of fact than an accusation. "You have his name and you let him kiss you and—" She bit back her next words because she saw she had hurt her mother again. Rose's dark eyes were bleak and it was as if a mask had been drawn over her face. And he's not Papa, Mary Catherine wanted to say. He's a Yankee and you let him touch you just as if he were Papa . . . and sometimes he touches me in a way Papa never did. Mary Catherine shivered as her mother's arm tightened around her. Had she spoken aloud? No, it was still her secret. Her secret and Colonel Allen's. She had promised not to tell and she wouldn't. Not ever.

Megan jerked her dress over her head and flounced over to her mother. "I can't believe you let her say things like that. Papa would slap her face."

"If your father were alive," Rose began quietly, "Mary Catherine wouldn't have this complaint. Turn around, Megan, and let me fasten your gown. The green silk is an attractive color for you. You thanked the colonel, didn't you? The material was hard to come by, even for a Yankee officer."

"Yes, Mama," Megan said dully. "I thanked him."

Rose's fingers paused on the cloth-covered buttons. "I'm sorry things aren't the way they used to be. Perhaps I wish for the past even more than either of you, but I can't bring it back. None of it. Not your father, not the Hollow, not any of the young men who used to race thoroughbreds down Stone Lane and across the pasture. Things have changed, and I'm determined the McClearys are going to survive this damnable war."

"Won't Papa hate us?" asked Mary Catherine. "You have a different name now. What if he doesn't know you? When he sees us from heaven in this Yankee house, won't he think we've forgotten him? He might think we're traitors."

"No!" Megan whirled on her sister. "Don't ever think that! We're *using* Colonel Allen and his Yankee friends and Papa knows what we're doing! We haven't forgotten whose side we're on."

"Megan!" Rose interjected softly. "You forget yourself."

"I'm sorry, but she makes me so mad. How could she think we like any of it or that Papa might think we would?"

"Mary Catherine's a child, Megan. You're five years older. It would be best if you kept that in mind. There are some things she doesn't understand. Her questions are honest ones." With a light touch on Megan's waist, she turned her daughter and finished buttoning the gown. "Perhaps it would be better if you waited in the garden. Mr. Marshall will be here soon and I think it would be nice if he saw you there. Sit near the dogwood. You'll look lovely with the blossoms behind you."

10

Mary Catherine stared at her hands. Her nails were ragged and torn where she had bitten them. She didn't look up until Megan was gone from the room. "I'm not a child," she said with quiet dignity.

Rose looked at her daughter carefully. The expression on Mary Catherine's oval face was serious. The full lower lip of her wide mouth was pushed out slightly, but her manner was thoughtful rather than petulant. "No, darling, you're not really a child any longer, are you? You haven't been one for quite some time." Rose realized she had no idea when it had happened. When had Mary Catherine's eyes become so old, so knowing? When had her chin developed that little determined thrust or the pared line of her nose taken the shape of arrogance? The dimples at the corners of her mouth, always in evidence at the Hollow, had disappeared. When was the last time her baby girl had smiled?

She tried to coax one now with a memory. "Do you remember when you used to play at being queen of all Virginia?" asked Rose. "The stable loft was your tower room. Young Neddie guarded your pony."

Mary Catherine nodded. "But that was silly. Virginia doesn't have a queen."

"No, you're right about that. It was just pretend, like a play. That's what Megan and I are doing now. Just as if we were actresses in a play. I married Colonel Allen because he can help us and there are times I pretend that I like him. Megan pretends, too. We're acting, Mary Catherine. Your Papa knows that. He knows that we're helping the same cause he died for. There are secrets to be learned, secrets that the Yankees want to keep from us. When Megan and I discover one, we tell the right people and it helps our soldiers. That's why we have to stay in Washington. That's why it's important to live in Colonel

11

Allen's home and not go back to Stone Hollow."

Rose did not say there was nothing left of their home. Mary Catherine had slept while the main house and outbuildings burned to the ground. The Hollow, caught in an all-day siege between Rebel and Yankee forces, was the last victim of the bloody struggle. She fell, not to the Yankees, but to the Rebels who did not want the enemy to have her. Animals that could not be taken were recklessly slaughtered. The grain sheds were set ablaze. From a position on a knoll just east of the farm, Rose and Megan watched an indifferent wind direct fire to the roof of the stable, then to the summer kitchen, and finally to the main house.

A Yankee scouting party from Colonel Allen's forces found them huddled beneath the soft, sparse boughs of some loblolly pines. Shortly after they were taken to headquarters, neighbors came in search of them, offering shelter and support. Rose would have none of it. She made no secret that she wanted revenge on the army who had left her homeless. Her shocked neighbors thought she was turning against her own kind. No one understood that Rose Mc-Cleary did not blame the men who burned her house and destroyed her land. She blamed the men who *caused* her home to be burned. Her enemy wasn't the South. It was the Army of the Potomac. Colonel Allen could not have suspected then that the woman he courted, the woman who eventually agreed to become his wife, despised him. In bed her passionate hatred felt much the same as desire.

Had it really been a year since she married Richard Allen? It was such a very long time to be numb, Rose thought. She blinked, surprised to find there was the pressure of tears at the back of her eyes. Mary Catherine was watching her steadily, search-

12

ingly.

"Do you understand?" Rose asked earnestly, pushing the question past the lump in her throat. "Some of our dear old friends don't realize what we're doing, so they judge us harshly and shun us. But your Papa knows. He approves of our acting. Do you remember when we went to the theatre last month?"

Mary Catherine's head bobbed once. "*As You Like It.*"

"That's right. 'All the world's a stage,/ And all the men and women merely players.' "

Mary Catherine thought that over. It was true, she decided. She even had her own role and her own secrets. Mama had said they must remain in Washington and Mary Catherine realized then that her part was to keep the secret. Colonel Allen warned if she told even one person, that something bad would happen to Rose and Megan. He would make it happen, he warned her. Terrible, horrible changes would come to pass once Mary Catherine said anything. For the sake of her mother and sister, she had to keep her silence.

"I understand," she said. "I think I shall be an actress, too."

"Of course you will," said Rose. She hugged Mary Catherine. "And you won't tell Colonel Allen? That's important. This play has to be our secret."

Mary Catherine's attention was caught again by the toes of her red patent leather shoes. Even though she did not like Colonel Allen, she liked his last gift to her. The shoes were bright and shiny and red was her favorite color. "Don't worry, Mama," she said, sliding off the padded window seat, "I'm quite good at keeping secrets."

Rose's smile faltered at the oddly adult tone in her daughter's voice. "Mary Catherine? What do you —"

13

She kissed her mother on the corner of her mouth. "I think I'll wait in the garden with Megan. Don't worry. I won't spoil anything. Next to Megan and the dogwood blossoms, Mr. Marshall won't even notice me." The mask of premature adulthood slipped away for a moment and Mary Catherine was a child again, fly-away braids and a cheeky, dimpled smile.

Shaking her head in bemusement, Rose slipped a lace-edged handkerchief from beneath the cuff of her dove gray day dress. She coughed gently a few times, then more forcefully as pressure built in her chest. Gradually the spasm lessened. With morbid fascination she looked at the wrinkled handkerchief. The metallic taste of blood was still in her mouth, the proof of it in her hand.

She stood and looked out the window, as Mary Catherine had done earlier. The gate was being opened by a young man in a dark blue jacket with gold braid. Rose could not help thinking the curtain was drawing on her final performance.

Logan Marshall gave the white picket gate a kick with his boot heel to knock it back in place. The gate wobbled then stuck and Logan felt an absurd measure of relief that *something* was finally going his way. This morning it had been a horse that was more mule than horse. The animal had refused to jump a single fence while Logan was on reconnaissance. The obstacles had to be removed, and when they couldn't, as in the case of the stone fence surrounding most of the Fecklie property, they had to be skirted. The pack mule carrying his photographic supplies was more cooperative than the army issue Morgan. Logan was more than halfway convinced the animal had been raised somewhere south of the Mason-Dixon line and was protesting his use by the wrong army.

But the horse hadn't been his only problem. The sun disappeared almost as soon as Logan set up his tripod and camera near the right flank of the enemy camp. He had to wait for hours, cooling his heels and risking detection, until the sun cooperated with enough light for a decent exposure. Moving swiftly then, Logan took pictures and developed them in a makeshift tent which he erected in the dense scrub forest known as the Wilderness. He traveled in relative safety, scouting General Lee's army as they made camp all around Chancellorsville. He hoped his pictures would confirm the rough estimate he had made of troop strength. By Logan's reckoning, Lee had less than half as many as Major General Hooker's 134,000 recruits. With any luck, should Lee choose to fight, it could prove to be a decisive victory for Hooker, who already held the high ground. When the actual battle would take place was anyone's guess. Men were still moving into position and strategies were being planned.

At the main encampment they thanked Logan for his efforts, gave him twenty minutes to catch his breath, then sent him to Washington with secret correspondence for President Lincoln. Military intrigue had its own peculiar protocol and Logan had to go through the paces before he could get to the president. One flesh and blood obstacle was Colonel Richard Allen, a staff aide to Lafayette Baker, head of Lincoln's fledgling espionage campaign. Allen insisted that everything be checked and rechecked for veracity before reaching the president. Logan supposed it made sense, given the fact that Washington was fair to overflowing with spies, but in more cynical moments he thought Allen's dictates were the result of a small-minded man searching for a large role.

Still, Logan Marshall cooperated. He had mustered out of the army eight months earlier. Instead of going home to New York and the family newspaper business, Logan sought employment as a photographer's assistant to Mathew Brady. Brady, with a solid reputation as a portrait photographer, was using his own resources to finance the documentation of the war. Although Brady rarely left his Washington studio, his photographers were already compiling a photographic chronicle of the War between the States. Logan was one of a half-dozen men who gave up rights to his photos in exchange for the experience and challenge of field work. Logan was, to his knowledge, the only Brady photographer who doubled as a private field scout for the army. His field scout status had everything to do with his cooperation with the colonel.

Logan Marshall, though he wouldn't have admitted it, was also little more than a boy. All of twenty years old, he still had the bloom of youth on his cheeks and the soft down of early manhood on his chin. His dark brown hair was highlighted with strands of copper. Square-jawed, with sharp, rugged features, Logan was cast in much the same mold as his older brother Christian. His eyes were coolly colored, a soft pewter gray that could, on occasion, mirror everything but his own thoughts. He had a strong Roman nose which flared when he was angry, which was rarely. He was tall, a couple of inches over six feet, and carried himself with quick strides and barely contained energy. There was a light bounce in his step, a jauntiness that warned more staid men of a certain recklessness, perhaps even of irresponsibility.

These same cautious and considering men never

hesitated to use Logan Marshall. His youthful exuberance, his immature belief that he was somehow charmed, that death couldn't happen to him, made him ideal for risky missions. They planned, he performed. In general it was a happy arrangement. Easy-going and adventurous, Logan Marshall was still growing into himself.

Logan shifted the packet he carried from his right hand to his left. As he raised his fist to knock at the door to the Allen home, he heard a high-pitched giggle from the garden area at the side of the house. He grinned and lowered his hand. It couldn't hurt to allow himself to be sidetracked for a few minutes. Stepping down from the stoop, he circled to the side.

He saw Megan immediately. Her smile was coy, her eyes downcast at just the right angle to affect surprise at his entrance. Logan wasn't fooled. He supposed she had seen him sometime before he reached the house. He was more surprised to see her. The heady giggle that had drawn him like a magnet hadn't belonged to Megan.

He tipped his hat and made a small bow while his eyes darted around the garden. "Where is she? I know I heard the little witch cackle."

"Witch!" Mary Catherine's head bobbed up from behind the stone bench where her sister was sitting. "That's very mean of you, Logan Marshall! I am not a witch!"

"You are! Come here, Katy McCleary! Give me a kiss and I'll prove it to you." He hunkered down, his saber jabbing at the ground, while Mary Catherine ran into his outstretched arms.

Megan folded her parasol and tapped it impatiently as she considered the merits of strangling her sister. Logan, she decided, was making a perfect ass of himself, though she tried to pretend that he wasn't.

17

It was difficult, since at the moment Mary Catherine kissed him, he began jumping around the yard as if he were a hoptoad. His hat fell off and he dropped his packet, but neither of these things lessened his hopping frenzy.

"I must be a witch after all," Mary Catherine said, awed and thrilled by her power. Her eyes widened as Logan sighted an unsuspecting fly and hopped in for the kill. Was he really going to *eat* it? "Oh, Megan! Save him. Do something!"

"Save him? What on earth do you propose I do?" She had a good mind to hit him on the head with her parasol. Really, she thought, did he think he was *amusing?*

"Kiss him, silly," Mary Catherine said practically. "Change him back into a prince!" She blushed a little, having admitted that she thought Logan was a prince. Her eyes darted quickly from Logan to Megan and was relieved to know they didn't attach any importance to her confession. "Go on, Meg. How else is he going to—"

"Mary Catherine," Megan said quellingly. "You take the oddest notions in your head."

Mary Catherine sucked in her upper lip, biting it as Logan edged closer to the fly. "Do it, Megan! Quick! Before he—" She squeezed her eyes shut, hopped on one foot, and pulled both her braids in an alternating rhythm when she thought Logan was going to pounce.

"Oh, very well," Megan sighed. With little enthusiasm for the task, she bent and placed a kiss on Logan's forehead.

By Mary Catherine's count ten seconds passed before she ventured a peek. She was no longer hopping madly or tugging her braids. She had quieted when it seemed as though the very air had stilled.

18

The fragrance of the garden was more noticeable now. The scent of lilac and rose combined in a heady mixture. She breathed slowly, deeply, and raised her lashes the least degree necessary to view what was happening.

Logan and Megan were standing toe to tiptoe. Logan's arms circled Megan's waist; her hands clung to his shoulders. Their bodies were flush, their mouths fused. It was a kiss such as Mary Catherine had never seen before and it made her feel odd: flushed, anxious, excited, and embarrassed — all at the same time. She looked down at the ground to see if her heart was really lying there. It felt as if it had been torn from her. Her chest felt achy and queer, burning and heavy. The swell of emotion was almost painful and Mary Catherine trembled with it. She caught her lower lip between her teeth to keep from crying. She reminded herself that she was an actress, playing a role. So was Megan. Still, the next time, she thought, Megan is going to play the witch!

"When you're quite finished mauling her, Marshall, perhaps you'd come inside on the business that brought you."

Mary Catherine was almost glad for the sharp, caustic voice that broke the lovers apart. Almost. In her mind Colonel Allen's presence could never really be welcome. He was standing on the side porch, leaning heavily against the curved white railing with his arms braced stiffly in front of him. The starched points of his collar held his head immobile and furthered his stern, unforgiving demeanor.

Colonel Allen was neither handsome nor ugly. Most of his features, in fact, were quite ordinary. His hair was an unremarkable shade of brown. He wore it parted on the left side and drew it across the crown of his head to cover the beginnings of a bald spot.

19

His sideburns were long, blending into his neatly trimmed beard and mustache. He stood taller than some men, shorter than others. He was not particularly muscular, nor was he lean. Had it not been for the fact that his green eyes were flecked with gold so as to appear yellow in some light, Colonel Allen could have easily gone unnoticed in a gathering of officers. The men who served under him, in the field or in his office now that he was an aide, called him Cougar—but never to his face. It was generally believed the colonel knew about the name and was secretly proud of it, but no one dared confirm that suspicion. Richard Allen was a man who got things done, a man with powerful connections, and a man who did not suffer fools gladly. Men who crossed him were dispatched without remorse. He remembered friends and enemies. The former could count on his help, the latter, his revenge.

Upon his marriage to Rose McCleary, the colonel left his field post for a more prestigious—and secure—placement in Washington. Friends believed the move was prompted by Allen's wish not to make Rose a widow a second time. Rose alone was privy to the colonel's political aspirations.

Logan picked up his fallen hat and tapped it against his thigh a few times to get rid of bits of grass and dirt. He addressed the colonel and tried not to look guilty. He had hardly been *mauling* Megan. It was only a kiss. "Good afternoon, sir," he said, replacing his hat on his head. "Katy, be a good girl and hand me that packet, will you?"

Mary Catherine found the packet and gave it to Logan. "He's very angry," she said in a whisper that would have been more appropriate on stage.

Logan had no trouble discerning that for himself. The colonel's hard stare was nearly blinding. Logan

20

gave Mary Catherine a smile that was supposed to reassure her. It was so lacking in confidence that the little girl's anxiety increased tenfold. "Ladies," he said, "perhaps another time." He took his leave of the garden and followed Allen into the house.

"You shouldn't have kissed him like that!" Mary Catherine snapped when Logan and the colonel were out of earshot.

Megan, who had sat down heavily on the stone bench and was staring off into space, didn't even hear her sister's comment. She touched the outline of her lips with her fingertips. They were slightly swollen and still sensitive. She could feel the imprint of Logan's mouth on hers. "Hmmm? What did you say, dear?"

Mary Catherine kicked at the bench, scuffing the toe of her red shoe. "I don't think you were acting! I think you really liked that kissing!"

That brought Megan around. "Oooh, what do you know! You're just a child!" But of course she *had* liked the kissing. Very much. It could be difficult to remember that Logan Marshall was the enemy. "Go help Angel in the kitchen or something. Leave me alone."

Swallowing all the unkind things she wanted to say, Mary Catherine walked away, her chin high and her spine as stiff as a metal rod. She was a great lady, a duchess perhaps, and duchesses did not scrap like common cats—even in their own garden.

As she passed through the kitchen, she said to Angel, "I'll have tea and cucumber sandwiches in the library, I think."

Angel, who was up to her dimpled elbows in bread dough, stopped kneading long enough to issue a warning. "You go in that library and there'll be the devil to pay for it! The colonel's in there with Mr.

21

Marshall."

"Oh, very well. You may bring me tea in my room."

Sprinkling more flour on the table, Angel went back to pounding. "I'll be bringin' a switch, is more like it," she mumbled as Mary Catherine walked away. "A body never knows what notion she'll take to next. Tea and cucumber sandwiches." She snorted. "I should let her chaw on some shoe leather. That'd wake her up."

In the library, Colonel Allen was pouring himself two fingers of bourbon. He knocked the drink back quickly, poured another, and this time carried the tumbler to his roll-top desk, where he sat down. He swiveled in the cane-back chair to face Logan, crossing his feet at the ankles. Rolling the tumbler between his palms, he studied Logan consideringly. "She's quite a looker, isn't she?"

Logan felt a need to clear his throat or swallow or pull his collar loose from his Adam's apple. "Sir?" Thank God his voice didn't crack.

"Don't play the half-wit with me, Marshall. Hooker wouldn't have trusted you with that packet if you only had cotton between your ears. Tell me one thing. What are your intentions toward Megan?"

"My intentions, sir? Do you mean, do I want to marry her?"

Allen's glance became sharper and his upper lip curled sardonically. "Bravo. I mean exactly that."

"No . . . that is, I hadn't thought . . . I'm not sure I want . . ." His voice trailed off. This interview couldn't have been more uncomfortable had he been in front of his own father.

Allen leaned forward. "Listen to me carefully, Marshall. If you want her, she's yours. But if you don't intend to wed her, don't think about bedding her. Her mother and I want a good marriage for Megan. You're still green but your family's wealthy and well-connected. If you're fool enough to get yourself killed, Megan will be cared for. Do you understand what I'm saying?"

"Yes, sir." Megan was definitely a pariah as far as Logan was concerned. Marriage was not in his immediate future. Certainly not one where he had a shotgun pressed to the small of his spine. He hadn't considered taking Megan to bed either. It was only a kiss, for God's sake. If one didn't count the milk cow he lassoed for his unit last week, he hadn't kissed a female in five months.

"Good." Allen set down the tumbler. "Now let me see this packet. Make yourself a drink while I go over the material."

Logan handed over the packet, poured himself a double shot of whiskey, and sat on the edge of a delicate, spindle-legged chair covered with crossstitched roses.

Without looking up, Allen said, "You're as comfortable as a roach on a hot griddle. Take that leather chair by the hearth. This will take a while."

Feeling somewhat like a bull in a china shop, Logan moved. He sunk into the soft chair, welcomed the faint scent of cigar smoke and brandy which clung to the pores of the material, and rested his heels on the marble apron of the fireplace. He hadn't slept in thirty-six hours. In five minutes he was making up for that oversight.

Except for the muted yellow candlelight from the sconce above the mantelpiece, it was dark when Logan woke. For a moment he was disoriented. The pair of curious brown and gold eyes studying him was only vaguely familiar. When he recognized Mary Catherine, he relaxed, leaning back in his chair

23

again and smiling faintly. She was sitting on the apron of the fireplace near his feet. Her legs were curled to one side. The black-and-red-checked dress she wore was tangled and twisted around her legs and she was sucking on the end of one of her honey-colored braids. Her poise was a little unnerving. Even when he woke, when he caught her in the act of staring at him, her gaze didn't waver.

"What in God's name are you finding so fascinating?" he asked quietly. His voice was raspy and deeper than usual from sleep.

Mary Catherine removed the braid from her mouth just long enough to answer. "I was wondering if the spider on your shoulder would crawl into your ear."

"You're an outrageous liar, Katy McCleary." He wondered if he dared brush at his shoulder. Which shoulder? If there really were a spider, would it crawl in his ear? To hell with it. Logan flicked at both shoulders with his fingertips. When he heard Mary Catherine giggle, he knew he'd been had. "Just as I thought. Katy's a liar."

"You're the only one who does that," she said. Her eyes didn't waver from him, her stare was still frank. Logan Marshall was easily the most beautiful man Mary Catherine had ever seen. With some insight older than her years, she realized she would have embarrassed him, telling him that, so she made up the story about the spider. He would find it easier to believe that she was more interested in spiders than in him.

"The only one who does what?"

"Calls me Katy."

"You don't like it?"

She pitched the braid behind her shoulder and shrugged. "It's all right." She wished he would open

24

his eyes a little wider instead of watching her with his lazy, hooded stare. From the first time she had seen his eyes, their cool pewter color fascinated her. She thought she should have been afraid of eyes like that, but she wasn't.

Logan Marshall was the scout who first chanced upon the McCleary women after the battle at Stone Hollow. It was Logan who offered them protection and escorted them to Colonel Allen's camp. Rose and Megan shared a stray mount that Logan captured for them, but Mary Catherine rode with Logan. She knew she had been asleep in the beginning because the first thing she remembered was Logan's eyes, almost silver in the pale wash of moonlight, looking down at her. She was cradled against him as if she were a baby. She would have been indignant if she hadn't been so weary and sad and if she hadn't felt so safe in the arms that encircled her. She forgot to ask about the Hollow; she forgot to ask about her mother and sister. The most important thing, it seemed to her, was to know the name of her prince. "Logan," she repeated when he told her. "You're so very kind." She had fallen asleep almost immediately, his name on her lips, his beautiful face imprinted in her memory. She had been twelve then, but she knew about love.

The path of her own thoughts caused her poise to shatter. She felt a flush of hot color touch her neck and cheeks and pressed her palms to either side of her face as if she could hide her embarrassment. Logan's lazy half-smile didn't help. He couldn't possibly know what she'd been thinking, but when he looked at her that way it seemed as if he did.

"You're a singularly curious child," Logan said.

Because she didn't know what had just been said to her, and pride dictated that she keep ignorance to herself, Mary Catherine scrinched her nose and stuck out the tip of her tongue.

Logan laughed and leaned forward in the chair. Drawing his outstretched legs toward him, he rested his forearms on his knees. "What time is it?"

"Almost eight."

He swore under his breath, shot Mary Catherine a guilty glance, and raked his hair with his fingers. "Where is everyone? Why didn't somebody wake me?"

"Colonel Allen said you should sleep," she said, answering the second question first. "Mama's already aired the guest bedroom for you, as the colonel says you're to spend the night. Mama, Colonel Allen, and Megan have all gone to a ball at Mrs. Barker's to raise money for the hospital. I think Megan wanted to wake you up so you could escort her, but the colonel said absolutely not."

"I can just imagine," Logan said, thinking back to Colonel Allen's wed-then-bed policy regarding his stepdaughter. "So it's just you and me."

"Oh, Angel's here. She's keeping your dinner warm in the kitchen. We all ate hours ago and Mama wanted to wake you then but the colonel said—"

"No," Logan finished for her.

"Actually, he said that your stomach would wake you when you were more hungry than tired, but I suppose all he meant was no, we couldn't wake you."

"I think I'd like that dinner now," he said, holding out his hand to Mary Catherine. He pulled her to her feet, then she pretended to pull him to his. It was too bad, she thought, what she was going to do to him, but she supposed it couldn't be helped. For all his many kindnesses, Logan Marshall was still the enemy.

Logan almost fell asleep at the kitchen table in the

26

middle of a bite. He couldn't remember when he had ever felt more tired. If it hadn't been for Mary Catherine's help, he wouldn't have made it to the guest bedchamber. His legs were wobbly and his vision so blurry that he kept passing a hand in front of his eyes to lift an imaginary veil. He remembered Mary Catherine's wide and slightly anxious eyes staring down at him. The wet end of one of her braids brushed his cheek. It made him smile.

Mary Catherine told herself that Logan was really to blame for his own drugging. If he hadn't fallen asleep in the colonel's study, he would have attended the ball with Megan. If he had been at the ball as planned, then he wouldn't have posed a threat to Mary Catherine's mission. No threat, no drug. It *was* his fault.

Feeling somewhat relieved by the mitigating circumstances, Mary Catherine returned to the colonel's study. She used a hairpin to open the locked roll-top desk. It wasn't as difficult as Megan told her it would be. The secret drawer was hardly a secret any more. Her mother and Megan had explained exactly where it was and how to open it. Once, while fumbling for the catch, Mary Catherine heard approaching footsteps. She held her breath until Angel passed in the hallway on the way to her room, then let it out slowly. It was the trembling of her hand that finally released the spring. The panel snapped open. Mary Catherine, certain she had officially joined the Confederate ranks as their youngest — and perhaps stealthiest — spy, took out the packet Logan Marshall delivered to the colonel. The photographs, while interesting, were of less importance to her than the dispatch. Taking out the colonel's own paper and pen, Mary Catherine carefully copied the letter.

Her mind wandered as she worked. She was a

monk in a monastery, copying manuscripts for posterity in black ink and gold leaf. She wore a brown hooded robe and her back was permanently hunched because of her diligence to duty. The tip of her tongue touched the corner of her mouth as she concentrated. There was no work more important in all the world. This is my finest role, she thought.

After the ink dried, Mary Catherine folded her copy and put it in her apron pocket. She returned the dispatch and photographs to the packet exactly the way she had found them, put the packet in its drawer, secured the panel and the spring, drew down the ridged desk cover, locked it, and backed out of the colonel's study.

"I want to see you, Mary Catherine," the colonel said. His voice was chilling. He had opened the door to Mary Catherine's room just far enough to poke his head through. She was curled on the far side of her bed, her back to him. He saw her stir, relax, then become rigid as she realized she had not mistaken the intrusion for any part of a dream. She didn't turn to face him. "Now," he said. "Downstairs, in my study. Don't pretend you haven't heard me, because I know better. And don't take the time to dress."

After the door shut, Mary Catherine lay there, frozen, her knees drawn up to her chest, her hands locked into rigid, white-kuckled fists. She could feel him outside the door—waiting. The colonel *was* a cougar, a sharp-eyed, heartless predator.

"Now," he repeated stonily from the hallway.

Mary Catherine shivered. Every sense alert, she heard him walk away from the door, pause at the top of the staircase, then trip lightly down the carpeted steps. Downstairs the study door opened and closed.

She sat up and pulled on the robe lying at the foot of her bed. The hardwood floor was cold on the bare soles of her feet. Where was her mother? Megan? Her apron was hanging over the top rung of a ladder-backed chair. She checked the pocket. The dispatch was gone. Her mother had probably taken it last night when she returned from the ball. Mary Catherine wondered what time that had been. She had tried so hard to stay up but even the heady excitement of her first mission wasn't enough to keep her awake. Had her mother been pleased?

The carpeted hallway was warmer. The door to the guest room was closed. Mary Catherine was tempted to see if Logan had already left, but she didn't act on the urge. The house was very quiet. She listened for sounds that Angel was moving around in the kitchen or tidying one of the parlors. Nothing. Mary Catherine was suddenly very afraid she was alone in the house with Colonel Allen.

Her palm was slippery on the brass door handle. She had to grip it twice to twist it. The colonel was sitting at his desk when she entered. He turned in his chair, motioned to her to close the door, then crooked his index finger at her to indicate she should approach.

Mary Catherine did so cautiously. "Yes, sir? You wanted to see me?" For the first time she noticed he was holding something between his thumb and forefinger, rolling it back and forth. Her face paled. The thing that looked like a toothpick at first glance was one of her hairpins.

The colonel patted his knee. "Come here, Mary Catherine. I think we should talk."

She hesitated until his green-yellow eyes narrowed. She came to stand between his splayed knees. The movement of his thumb and forefinger was mesmerizing. When he touched her wrist she sat down on his knee without the slightest protest. One hand was at the small of her back, steadying her.

"What is this, Mary Catherine?" His fingers stopped moving. He held up the hairpin so she could see it clearly.

"It looks like one of my hairpins, sir."

Her honesty caught him off guard momentarily. "That's what I thought. Do you know where I found it?"

She shook her head. "May I have it, please?"

"In a moment. After you tell me what you were doing in my desk."

Mary Catherine imagined herself on stage. The audience was hushed as they waited for her response. She could feel their anticipation. They were with her, urging her to find a way out of the trap. "You're mistaken, Colonel. I wasn't in your desk." She heard the audience gasp. She should have thought of something better to say or given her voice more conviction. "I was in your study to wake Mr. Marshall and make sure he had some dinner. I could have dropped the hairpin then."

"I'm certain that's when it happened," he said, watching her carefully. He put the hairpin on the desktop. Now free, his hand moved to the side of Mary Catherine's face. The backs of his fingers touched her downy cheek. Her skin was velvet soft. His thumb touched the corner of her mouth.

Mary Catherine hid her revulsion. Beyond the footlights the audience held its collective breath. Here was a stunning performance. "I don't understand," she said. Her voice barely broke a whisper. She couldn't look at the colonel. His face would be flushed, his eyes dark. He wanted something from her, but he never said what it was, never told her more than that he wanted to touch her. Still, even to Mary Catherine's young eyes, he always seemed expectant.

"Tell me about the hairpin," he said. "That's what you used to pick the lock to my desk. Your mistake was to use another pin to lock it up again. You left the first one in plain view on the desktop. I saw it as soon as I lifted the cover this morning. I've straightened it already but it was slightly bent when I found it. What were you looking for, Mary Catherine?"

The neckline of her cotton nightshift was rounded. Her robe wasn't closed tightly enough to shield the smooth line of her collarbone from the colonel's gaze. She could feel his eyes on her. His fingers trailed from her cheek to her throat. She held herself very still.

"Was it money? Is that what you hoped to find?"

How foolish she had been! Of course the colonel wouldn't suspect she was a spy. Money was the obvious answer. She should have thought of it herself. Mary Catherine averted her head, feigning shame and guilt.

"I thought as much," he sighed. His large hand cupped the side of her neck. He could feel the wild flutter of her heartbeat in her throat. She was a fragile, fey child; he had thought so from the first. Her mother was handsome, her sister, lovely. But being with Mary Catherine made him feel powerful beyond all his imaginings. Her immature beauty drew him. It was his darkest, most guilty secret.

"If you wanted something, you should have told me," he said. "You know I like to buy you things. You liked the shoes, didn't you?"

She nodded.

"Come closer, Mary Catherine, whisper in my ear. Tell me what it is you want."

She didn't move. "I don't want anything. Really, I don't. You've given me quite enough. I'm not ungrateful." Even as she spoke, the colonel was pulling her closer. She strained against his grip.

"Just a little kiss for the colonel," he cajoled. "One kiss, on the lips, and I'll forgive you for breaking into my desk."

Mary Catherine wanted to cry. She hated this part of the colonel's game. She didn't want to kiss him on the lips or anywhere. The pressure on her neck increased. She gasped, a puff of air caught in the back of her throat. She felt his fingers dip just below the neckline of her shift. Her skin burned. Her ears were ringing and there was a blackness clouding the edge of her vision. She suspected she was going to faint.

"Take your goddamn hands off her." Logan spoke from the doorway. One shoulder was braced against the jamb for support. The muscles in his forearms bunched as he clenched and unclenched his fists.

"Now see here, Marshall, just what do you—"

Logan crossed the room in four long strides. Mary Catherine was terrified by the hardness in his face, the repulsion in his eyes. The colonel's hold on her was even tighter than before. There would be bruises later. But as hard as her stepfather held her, it was nothing compared to the grip that Logan placed on her. His fingers ringed her upper arm and with an ease that surprised Mary Catherine and shocked the colonel, he yanked her free. She stumbled across the floor, falling to her knees as she was flung away.

The colonel was jerked out of his chair. "How many times?" Logan demanded. "How many times have you touched her?" He didn't wait for an answer. "How long's this been going on?"

"Look here," Allen snapped. He wasn't intimidated

32

by Logan's youth, his strength, or his anger. "I don't know what you think you saw, but you've got it all wr—"

"Stuff it, you miserable bastard. I know *exactly* what I saw. I know what I heard."

"Take your hands off me." The colonel glanced beyond Logan's shoulder to Mary Catherine. "Say something," he said impatiently. The look in his eyes was meaningful. *Say the right something,* it said. *Remember our secret.*

"Please don't hurt him," she said. The tears that came to her eyes were real. "It's a mistake. You don't understand."

Logan ignored her. He pushed the colonel backward until he had Allen pressed against the wall, his head jammed in the corner made by the wall and the mantel. The gilt-edged portrait of some long-dead relative slipped off center as Logan pulled Allen forward and slammed him against the wall again. "What have you told her?" he growled. "What makes her want to protect you?"

Still icy under pressure, the colonel chose an alternate strategy. "I'm going to have you court-martialed."

"I'm not one of your men. This uniform's my own, not army issue. I work for Brady and whoever else I want to. And I damn well don't want to work for you. Now, you can take your threat and do what ever you want with it—except use it on me. When I brought Rose and her daughters to your headquarters, I thought I was putting them in good hands. When I heard you were marrying Mrs. McCleary, I was happy that I'd had a small part in it. What I just witnessed made me realize how wrong I've been. Does Rose know?"

Mary Catherine jumped to her feet. "No!" She

33

attacked Logan from behind, sending him off balance so that he released the colonel. She pounded on his back. "No! You can't say anything! You'll ruin everything! It's a secret! Our secret! Mama can't know!"

Twisting around, Logan caught Mary Catherine by the wrists and quieted her while the colonel slipped away. "Sssh, Katy. Ssshhh. Your mama wants to know this secret. Trust me."

But that was the same thing the colonel had said and he was as much the enemy as Logan Marshall. Mary Catherine didn't trust anyone. The tears that flooded her eyes dripped over her cheeks. "Don't tell," she pleaded. "Everything will change. Terrible things will happen. You can't understand about secrets like this."

Logan hugged Mary Catherine to him. The front of his shirt was damp with her tears. He watched Colonel Allen move toward the door. "Don't bother sending for someone to throw me out," he said, correctly divining Allen's intentions. "I'm leaving and I'm taking Katy with me. She's not coming back here unless Rose decides that's what she wants."

It was happening already, Mary Catherine thought. Only it wasn't Colonel Allen who was going to make her leave—it was Logan. "I'm not leaving! I can't! Please don't make me go!"

"What the hell have you said to her?" Logan snapped. His jaw was rigid with anger, his eyes steely.

"Listen to her, Marshall," Allen advised. "She's not supporting whatever crack-brained notion you've taken into your head. I suggest, for your own good, you get the hell out of my home and leave Mary Catherine here. You won't like the consequences otherwise."

"I'll take my chances." He picked up Mary

Catherine, who was struggling and squirming in his grasp, and carried her out of the study, past Allen, and into the bright morning sunshine.

Rose, Megan, and Mary Catherine left Washington later that day. Their destination was the farm homestead of Rose's second cousin just west of Richmond. There was no scandal, nor would there be. With the exception of Logan Marshall, what happened would remain a family secret. The story that circulated as a result of their hasty departure was the convenient sick relative fable. At Rose's insistence they took only a few belongings. Everything the colonel had given them seemed soiled now. Rose blamed herself for not knowing what was happening to her own child. Megan blamed her sister. Mary Catherine blamed Logan.

That very afternoon, after an uncomfortable farewell with Rose and her daughters, Logan began the journey back to his unit at Chancellorsville. Let Allen handle the dispatch, he thought. He'd done what he was supposed to do. For the first time in recent memory Logan was actually glad to be returning to the field.

He wasn't particularly surprised when he didn't make it. He had anticipated the colonel would make some kind of move against him, though the swiftness of Allen's actions caught him off guard. He estimated he was ten miles from the road junction near the farm when he was cut off by a Rebel scouting party. He looked for a way around them, couldn't find one, and spent the night writing a letter to his family in New York, preparing them for his imminent capture.

It happened the following morning, just after daybreak. Allen's betrayal became clear when the scouting party returned directly to their unit immediately after taking Logan prisoner. He did not have to be hit over the head to realize they had been sent out to assure his capture. Logan did not have time then to contemplate how the colonel had managed such timely intervention. Too many other incredible things had begun to happen.

Mary Catherine's carefully copied dispatch, delivered into Confederate hands by Rose and Megan, and sent on to the rebel troops at Chancellorsville, was no mere correspondence now, but a true godsend. General Robert E. Lee took fierce exception to Major General Hooker's boast to President Lincoln, "The rebel army is now the legitimate property of the Army of the Potomac." Since the Union general made his boast based on superior Union forces and superior tactical positioning, but did not account for the fact that no shots had yet been fired, nor any flag raised, Lee found Hooker's brash statement a trifle premature.

In a daring series of maneuvers Lee split his army into three sections, and over the next four days, from May 1 to May 4, drove Hooker and the Union forces back across the Rappahannock River. In terms of casualties it was not the decisive victory Lee could have wished for. Although the South suffered fewer losses, the percentage of deaths in relation to troop strength was far greater than the North's. Still, the victory kept the Union at bay and opened up Lee's second drive into the North, a drive that would culminate in a sleepy little Pennsylvania village called Gettysburg.

Chapter Two

November 1864 — Richmond, Virginia

"I got me twenty-four! Twenty-four! Lookee here!" John Edward held out his hand, keeping the palm flat. He had a black piece of cloth, ragged at the edges, lying over his palm. Standing out in small relief against the black background were two dozen nits that he had pulled from his beard.

"Twenty-five," said Logan, reaching into his own dark beard. He carefully extracted the lice egg with a fine-toothed comb half the length of his pinky finger. He smiled at the group of six men surrounding him. "Gentlemen. Make good your wagers."

"Dammit, Marshall!" Edward swore. "I'm thinkin' you're cultivatin' the critters! This wager weren't open to farmers!" He pointed accusingly to the lice comb that Logan was pocketing. "You never said nothin' about no equipment! Ain't fair!"

"Don't be a poor sport," one of the other men grumbled. "It was a good wager."

Logan didn't say anything as the bounty started pouring in. He got half a potato from Billy Waters, a compass from the Covington twins, Able and Joe, a watch fob made from a lock of some sweetheart's hair, courtesy of Tom Jenkins, and two carrots—a plump, bright orange stump from Davey Powell, and a scrawny, limp one from John Edward. Logan wrapped everything into a kerchief and tucked the whole of it in a black lacquered box he had won on a previous wager. Thanking the others, he turned away, keeping the box securely under his arm, and went in search of other amusement.

In Libby Prison amusement was whatever, wherever one could make or find it. Logan survived in part because he sought it out in the most unlikely places, and where it didn't exist, he created it.

Richmond's Libby Prison was nothing more than a tobacco warehouse converted for warehousing Union soldiers. On the outside it was unimposing. Redbricked and tidy, with uniform windows and well-maintained grounds, it appeared to be a satisfactory, even humane answer to the problem of what to do with Federal prisoners. But each evening, a few hours after dusk, when the dead were collected and taken to wagons waiting in the rear, Libby Prison's true nature was exposed.

It was not planned, intentional cruelty that made the prison the site of pestilence, starvation, disease, and death. It was the ravages of war. Richmond was constantly besieged by Federal forces trying to force the great city and capital to its knees. As her citizens suffered shortages of food, inadequate medical supplies, and epidemics of typhus, the prisoners, blamed as they were by their caretakers for all the ill that had befallen the South, fared far worse.

Logan Marshall knew the South was losing the war. The guards would never say it in so many words, but their actions, the negligence and apathy, the increasingly common vicious act, the retaliatory strikes against the prisoners, told the story just as

38

eloquently. Real news of the war was hard to come by. Each new prisoner had his own tale, frequently inaccurate and always self-centered. It was difficult to know the large picture when a man's world view was confined to a small section of the battlefield and his battle had been lost.

Logan had heard about Lee's defeat at Gettysburg in July of '63. Yet, seventeen months later, he still did not know that his brother David died there, nor that his brother Christian had been seriously wounded. He didn't know that by the time his letter reached Marshall House his mother was already dead of an illness she contracted while nursing the wounded. He didn't suspect that his father's grief was slowly killing him.

On the contrary, Logan spent as little time as possible thinking about family—it hurt too much. Instead he thought about surviving Libby Prison, thanked God he had narrowly missed being sent deeper into the South, planned his escape, and plotted his revenge on Colonel Richard Allen. That, and the occasional amusement, was enough to keep him busy.

The air inside Libby Prison was oppressive, stifling. In one part of the warehouse a thousand officers were confined to eight rooms. The stench was almost a visible thing, rising above bodies huddled for warmth in a cold room. Logan walked among the men, the exercise keeping him warm, and knew in his heart he probably could not survive another winter.

His copper-threaded hair was dull, shaggy, and overlong. He kept it tucked inside the frayed collar of his shirt as a kind of insulation. His skin was pale from lack of sunlight—prison gray, they called it— and he was fifteen pounds underweight. He kept himself as healthy as he could by making, and usually winning, bets for extra bits of meat or vegetables, and exercising daily to keep some muscle tone. The downy scrub that had marked his chin in more youthful days was gone now. He had a full beard and mustache that, as proved by his wager, was home for a fair-sized colony of vermin.

He felt a decade older than his twenty-two years and believed he looked it as well. The swagger was missing from his stride and his eyes, even when he smiled, were bleak. All evidence of the high-spirited, green youth that was Logan Marshall had been thoroughly snuffed out.

He was realistic now, if not completely hardened. Each day he forced himself to consider all the good fortune in his life — for a way to certain insanity in Libby Prison was to contemplate all the things one *didn't* have. Logan didn't, for instance, dwell on fresh fruit, clean water, clothing that fit, liquor, tobacco, or women. Most especially he didn't let himself think about women.

Logan thrust his hands inside his pockets and stood in a tiny patch of sunlight upwind of a gangrenous wound. Billy Waters, who had given half of his potato to Logan, joined him. He was small and angular with extraordinarily long arms. The guards called him Monkey Man.

"The twins and me," Billy said in a low voice, "we're thinkin' on goin' tonight. You with us?"

There was no hesitation on Logan's part. "No. I've decided to take my chances on my own." He was silent, wondering if Billy and the twins were disappointed or relieved. "Damn foolish of Able and Joe to lose their compass to me."

Billy looked down at the floor. He shuffled his feet in place to improve his circulation. "About that compass . . . you don't suppose . . ."

"No, I don't suppose. I won it fair and square."

"Damn you, Marshall, can't you—"

"You can have it on one condition."

"Name it," Billy said eagerly. His blue eyes brightened in anticipation.

"Are you and the Covingtons helping collect the dead tonight?"

"Sure, that's part of the plan. We're leaving—"

"I don't want to know the details," Logan interrupted. "Just tell me, can you put me on one of the wagons?"

Billy's jaw went slack. "You mean like you was dead?"

"Exactly like I was dead. Can you do it?"

"Sure, but—"

Logan didn't want to hear objections either. "Then it's settled. Put me on the wagon and you can pick my pockets. That's how the Covingtons got the compass in the first place, isn't it?" He shot a quick glance at Billy and saw by the embarrassed, guilty look that he had guessed correctly. "Well, that's how they can get it back."

Twenty-six men were removed from Libby Prison on the death wagon that night, Logan Marshall among them. Billy Waters and Abel Covington were shot and killed while trying to escape once they were outside the warehouse. Joe Covington got the compass and headed north. During the prisoners' flight the wagon was left unattended, and Logan, his mind mercifully numb to what he was doing, pushed and clawed his way free of the stiff and malodorous bodies. He chose the direction he thought least likely to be pursued, west along the James River, deeper into the heart of Virginia. He remembered Rose Allen and her second cousin's farm and prayed that if

41

he found them they would offer sanctuary.

It was only when he tasted freedom and breathed the sharp, sweet scent of pond pines and bayberry, the rich, fullsome fragrance of Virginia's fertile soil, and drank icy cold water from the James, that Logan Marshall allowed himself one luxury he could ill afford in prison.

Kneeling on the riverbank, protected by an outcropping of rocks, Logan buried his face in his hands and wept.

The first and second nights of his escape Logan slept in the woods and covered himself with humus for warmth. On the third night he took shelter in a barn after the lights in the nearby farmhouse were extinguished. The animals who occupied the barn weren't at all disturbed by his presence. Although it was difficult to know for certain in the dark, he made out his companions to be one mule, one cow, a swaybacked nag, four cats, and a collie. Logan stopped the growling in his stomach with some dried fruit and oats from the nag's feed basket and half a cup of milk straight from the cow's udder. Taking two horse blankets into the loft, Logan settled down in a stack of sweet-smelling hay. He was asleep in minutes.

"Come here, Brutus. What are you doing? Hmmm? Cornered something up in the loft, have you?"

Brutus jumped up and down, pawing at the loft ladder. He whined and whimpered, but never barked. Six months earlier, Union scavengers had come to King's Creek farm. The stock of a Yankee rifle hammered directly at the dog's throat silenced him forever.

"What is it, boy? Two-legged or four-legged?"

Brutus whimpered more energetically. He ran from the ladder and circled his mistress, licking her face when she hunkered down to scratch him behind the ears. It was ecstasy. He almost forgot about the intruder.

"Do I need a weapon?" she whispered. She wasn't really frightened. There hadn't been any fighting in the area for months. The last deserter went through King's Creek more than sixty days ago. It was far more likely Brutus had treed a raccoon or a squirrel. If she could trap the animal it would make a fine meal.

Logan heard the soft, melodious voice and the dog's anxious whining. It was apparent from the girl's conversation that she was coming up to the loft to investigate. He wanted to bury himself deeper in the hay but was afraid of any noise that would attract more attention. He reached for the black lacquered box under his head and opened it carefully. It contained a spool of blue thread, two needles, a handkerchief, a lice comb, one piece of chalk, a half-dozen marbles—including four prized aggies—a watch fob, and one spoon. It was the spoon he wanted. Honed to a fine razor edge, it was useless as an eating utensil now. But it made a superior weapon. Logan gripped the handle and waited.

"I don't see anything, boy," she called down. Brutus continued dancing, so she went over the top of the ladder and crawled into the loft on her hands and knees. Too late, just as she saw the intruder out of the corner of her eye, she realized she was in no position to protect herself.

Logan pounced. He grabbed the hem of the girl's gingham dress and began pulling her toward him. She screamed when she felt the tug and began kicking. Painful though it was, Logan withstood her blows in order to stop the real menace—her ear-piercing scream. She had opened her mouth to get a second lungful of air when Logan's hand clamped down hard, covering her nose and grinding her lips against her teeth. Her eyes were wide, dark, and terrified as she faced her assailant. Her lungs burned from lack of air. She felt something cool press against the hollow of her throat and fear paralyzed her.

He was a beast. His unkempt hair and beard made him seem more animal than man. He was breathing heavily, obviously tired from the battle for control but still much stronger than she. There were sharp edges to his face that the beard and mustache could only partially hide. The gray eyes, hard as bullets, cold as steel, were strangely familiar. Mary Catherine McCleary began to shake.

Logan studied the face below him. The eyes were brown and gold with an exotic almond shape. The brows were tawny, the lashes dark, and the hair was like honey. The last vestiges of childhood had been erased over the past nineteen months. The willowy, womanly shape pressed to his body was the least of the changes. There was something in the way she looked at him, mutinous in spite of her fear, that made him think she was old beyond her years.

"Katy? Oh, God. I prayed that I'd find . . . Is it really you?" Logan didn't lift his hand for an answer. He wasn't sure she wouldn't scream. He waited and finally was rewarded with a reluctant nod that seemed to have been dragged from her against her will. "Do you know me?" Again, the nod. He eased up on the spoon which had pressed her throat. "You won't scream, will you?"

Mary Catherine hesitated. She did not want to make promises to this man. She hated him. His betrayal, the sharing of the secret she had vowed

44

never to share, had changed her entire life. She found herself nodding again and in that moment wondered who she despised more, Logan or herself. The urge to renege on her promise was strong when Logan removed his hand slowly, as if he didn't really trust her to keep her word.

"Thank God," he said softly. Aware that Mary Catherine was watching him carefully and that the fear had not left her eyes, Logan sat up and returned his weapon to the box. He tilted the box in her direction to show her she had nothing to fear from the contents, closed it, and set it behind him. There were bits of hay on his shoulders and chest. He brushed them off, suddenly seeing himself through Mary Catherine's eyes. As an afterthought he raked his fingers through his beard and hair, plucking out strands of hay there as well. He was feeling just human enough to be embarrassed by his appearance. If she had seen him last night when he crawled into the loft, he wouldn't have given it a second thought. "Sorry," he said, shrugging his shoulders uncomfortably. "I'm not dressed to receive visitors."

How could he make a joke? She wouldn't have used his clothing for rags. His jacket and trousers were fit for burning and nothing else. Where in God's name had he come from? Everything she'd heard about the Yankees said they were well-clothed and belly full. Logan Marshall looked neither. More to the point, he looked like he was starving. It had been so easy to hate the man he had been, the man she remembered him being. She searched her heart for that emotion and discovered it had already been replaced by pity. Even as she wondered why she should spare him, Mary Catherine found herself looking away so Logan wouldn't guess what was in her heart.

45

"I didn't mean to frighten you," he told her. "I wouldn't have hurt you."

Mary Catherine shot him a disbelieving glance, but said nothing. He had seemed terribly desperate to her a short time ago.

Logan picked up one of the horse blankets and pulled it around his shoulders. Outside the sun was shining, but it was a cold winter sun. Although Mary Catherine seemed unaffected, Logan felt the chill all the way to his bones. Thin streamers of light filtered through the cracks in the wood planking. Dust motes danced in the yellow rays. A sunbeam touched Mary Catherine's hair and her face was caressed by a halo of light. "How old are you, Katy?" It wasn't what he meant to say, yet somehow the words came tripping out.

Surprised by the question, Mary Catherine heard herself answering. "I was fifteen in September."

"Fifteen," he repeated softly "It's odd, but when I thought of you these past long months, I never thought of you growing older. In my mind I always saw little Katy McCleary."

Mary Catherine sat up. She smoothed her dress and drew up her legs so the ruffled edge of her pantalettes wouldn't show. "Don't call me that."

Logan was taken aback. "Call you what? Katy, you mean?"

"Yes. No one calls me that. It's a baby name."

"I agree you're not a baby, but I like the name Katy."

"Well, I don't."

"All right," he said, making no real promise. "Where's your mother? And Megan? This farm belongs to one of your relatives, doesn't it? A cousin, I think."

Did he remember everything? Katy found Logan's

46

memory, and the memory it stirred in her, frightening. "Yes. It belongs to Aunt Peggy."

"And what will Aunt Peggy have to say about a Yankee on her Rebel property?"

"She won't say anything. Once she knows you're here, she'll show you the wrong end of her shotgun."

"Is she a good shot?"

"Very good."

"I was afraid you'd tell me that."

"I'm not lying," Mary Catherine said.

"I didn't think you were. I don't suppose it will help my cause that your mother would speak well of me?"

"That's not possible."

Logan pulled the blanket more tightly around his chest as a shiver coursed through him. "What do you mean?" he asked, puzzled. His teeth chattered, making it difficult to speak. "Rose knows I'm no threat to any of you. Why wouldn't she help me?"

"Would you like to see Mama and ask her for yourself?"

"You can bring her here?"

"No. You'll have to come with me." Mary Catherine got to her feet. "Don't worry about Aunt Peggy. She's working in the kitchen at the back of the house. She won't see us."

"I don't understand . . . what about Megan?"

"Oh, she's with Mama as well." She extended her hand and helped Logan to his feet. She had to steady him once he was standing. It was probably good that she was making him walk, she decided. He needed to move around before he was frozen through. Her brief contact with him was enough to let her know that his skin was unnaturally cold.

Mary Catherine led the way down the ladder. "This is Brutus," she said, introducing the dog to

Logan. "We would have known about you last night, but a trio of scalawags came though here a while back and one of them damaged Brutus's barking box." She didn't wait for Logan's comment. What could he say? These were dangerous times. "Come on, boy. We're taking Mr. Marshall for a little walk."

Logan expected to go in the direction of the farm-house, so when Mary Catherine set off across the pasture, he hesitated. She didn't wait for him, or even turn to acknowledge that he had fallen behind. He berated himself for his suspicions. He had no reason not to trust her. Still, she was cold toward him and he couldn't understand it. It was hard to think clearly any more. The cold seemed to numb his brain. Finally he decided to follow, loping after her with an uneven stride and keeping the horse blanket close as a shield against the icy wind.

The breeze that wafted across the pasture and followed their tree-lined trail along King's Creek was warm to Mary Catherine. Tendrils of honey-colored hair, picked up by the wind, tickled her cheeks and temples. Behind her she heard Logan tramping on fallen leaves and moving noisily through the under-brush. Sunlight dotted their path. Occasionally she raised her face to feel the kiss of its heat.

At the point where the creek widened, she stopped. The rush of water over a dam of stones was a pleasant roar in her ears. In front of her was a half-moon clearing ringed by four holly trees. It was shady here, protected from the sun by the evergreen holly leaves. The ground was dotted with bright red berries. Some fell in the creek and were carried away on the white water. She heard Logan come up behind her. She had to force herself not to cringe when he placed his hand on her shoulder for support. His breathing was heavy, rasping. Looking at the graves

48

of her mother and sister, Mary Catherine felt the familiar wash of hate and anger return. She took strength from it. Pity for Logan had made her feel helpless and she was glad that emotion was gone.

"What is this place?" asked Logan. But he knew. He *knew*. He stared at the twin mounds of stones stacked like a pyramid of cannonballs and made out the faint outline of the graves they marked. Brutus padded to the headstones and circled them several times. He sniffed at ground and finally lay down, whimpering.

"Mama's grave is the one on the left," Mary Catherine said. Her voice was calm, detached. The tone was so unemotional she could have been talking about someone she had never met. "She died last June."

"Last June? You mean a year ago?"

She nodded faintly. "Just a little over a month after we left Washington."

Logan was stunned. "Oh, God. I'm sorry."

"Why are you sorry?" It was all your fault, she accused silently.

Her question confused him. Why shouldn't he be sorry? He liked Rose. She was a fine, brave woman. "I was honored to know your mother. Why shouldn't I regret her passing?"

Just as Mary Catherine expected, he wasn't apologizing for his part in her mother's death. She shrugged off his question and reined in her accusing glance. "It was consumption," she told him. "She was ill before we left and she knew it. The traveling wasn't good for her. She caught a cold on the journey and never really recovered. It all happened very swiftly."

"If only she had said something," Logan said, more to himself than to Mary Catherine. "I could have arranged for all of you to stay in Washington. I would have seen to it that you weren't bothered." He didn't have to mention by whom.

"Oh, but you had already done so much for us," she replied, skirting the edge of sarcasm with a voice that dripped honey.

Logan's hand had been resting on Mary Catherine's shoulder. It wasn't enough to keep him upright. He moved so that his forearm lay over her. Almost immediately there was a shiver from her. "You're cold," he said. "Here, take the blanket."

"No, I'm fine." The bodice of her gingham dress was lined with canvas for extra warmth. "Really. Keep it for yourself." A Yankee firing squad couldn't have forced her to tell him the real reason she had shivered. She wouldn't let him have that much power over her.

"And Megan?" he asked. "It doesn't seem possible." Even staring at the grave he couldn't believe red-headed, green-eyed Megan was gone. He remembered the kiss in the garden and Megan's off balance, sweet response. Would things have been any different if he had taken the colonel's suggestion and married her? "What happened to her?"

"She died in childbirth."

Logan blinked, surprised again. "She was married?"

"She was raped."

He closed his eyes momentarily. "The child?"

"Buried with her." Mary Catherine brushed back a lock of hair that fluttered over her eye. She turned her head aside so the breeze wouldn't push it back. "It was a boy," she said. "I named him Richmond. It seemed fitting somehow. The armies were battling for the city back when he was born and I was afraid he couldn't go to heaven if he didn't have a name. Aunt

Peggy didn't really know, so I did it just to be safe."

"So it's only you and your aunt here now?"

"Yes. Uncle Martin was killed at Bull Run."

"First or second battle?"

"First."

Logan's lips pressed together in a grim line. "My oldest brother was killed there. Same battle. I enlisted right after the news came back of Braden's death."

"No one gets through this war without being touched," she said solemnly. Before he could reply, Mary Catherine slid out from under Logan's arm and began walking away. Brutus left Megan's graveside and dashed out in front of his mistress. "We have to go back now. Aunt Peggy will wonder about me. I have chores to do. You can stay in the barn another night or so. There's no one but me to know about it."

"Wait," Logan called after her. "I can't —" He didn't have to explain that he couldn't keep up. Her stride shortened almost imperceptibly and the pace she set slowed. "Thank you," he said when he reached her.

Mary Catherine didn't look at him and she didn't offer any assistance. "The man who raped my sister was a Yankee," she said. "Just like you. I thought you'd want to know that."

"We're not all cut from the same cloth."

Now she glanced disparagingly at the clothes he wore. The jacket was faded but still recognizable as the blue of the Army of the Potomac. The gold braid, more yellow than gold now, was torn in places but the chevron on his sleeve was intact. In spite of what he said, the Yankee bastards were indeed cut from the same cloth. "I don't remember you being an officer," she said. "Those stripes mean something. You're a sergeant major, aren't you?"

"It's borrowed," he replied tersely. "The sergeant

major who wore it died some time back."

"I see." Other than that, she expressed no interest. When they reached the barn, Mary Catherine helped Logan back into the loft. "It will be better for you if you just stay there. When I finish my chores I'll see about bringing you something to eat."

As she was turning to go, Logan grabbed her wrist. A muscle worked in his jaw while his brows drew together. "I never expected much of a welcome as long as I remained in Virginia," he said. "But I came looking for you because I thought that times being what they are and our past being what it was, you'd show me some graciousness. This isn't how I remember you, Katy. You didn't used to hate me."

So he knew. As an actress she had so much to learn, she thought dismally. "What do you know about it?" she asked. She raised her eyes and stared at Logan hard. "You were always the enemy. Mama said so. So did Megan. We knew it, even if you and Colonel Allen didn't. Do you think Mama married him because she loved him?"

"What are you saying?"

Mary Catherine yanked her wrist out of his grip. "I'll be back when I'm done with my chores. Why don't you think about it until then?"

He reached for her again but she eluded his grasp. He was too weak to chase her and the thought of Aunt Peggy's shotgun was a deterrent in itself. Logan lay back in the hay, pulled the other blanket over him, and closed his eyes. Below he could hear Mary Catherine going about her work. She talked to herself as she milked the cow and mucked out the stalls. Odd, but he thought she was reciting something. He seemed to recognize a line from *Romeo and Juliet.* " 'O! swear not by the moon the inconstant moon . . .' " He fell asleep wondering if he had imagined it.

When Mary Catherine finished her outside chores, she returned to the house. Aunt Peggy was still in the kitchen. The odor of sourdough bread set out to rise filled the air.

Mary Margaret Cook was most people's idea of the quintessential grandmother. She was petite, rounded, eminently huggable. Her skin was pale and soft, her eyes gentle and her mouth stern. She had an extra chin and a substantial bosom. It had been a long time since her corsets closed over a seventeen-inch waist. There weren't many people in the community who remembered that Peg had been a blonde before her hair turned white. Too many friends and family members were gone now, taken by old age, or more recently, the war. Peggy had been Mary Catherine's age when the British set fire to Washington in 1814, but until the Yankees had overrun Virginia, she hadn't known about hate.

"Are you feelin' all right?" she asked in her soft drawl as Mary Catherine wandered around the kitchen. "You're lookin' a little flushed, Katy. It's not that time, is it?"

Mary Catherine blushed. "Aunt Peggy," she admonished. "I don't' recollect anyone ever talking about personal things the way you do."

"Stuff and nonsense. It's just part of nature. Nothin' personal about it."

"Well, it's not my time. If I'm flushed then it's because it's hot in here."

Peggy gestured toward the door. "Then go on with you. I don't need you doggin' my steps."

"Ac-tu-al-ly," Mary Catherine said, softly drawing out the single word as she danced dreamily around the kitchen table. "I was thinking about a picnic. Just me and Brutus."

"A picnic." Peggy looked at her ward as if she'd

gone mad. "It's November!"

"It's not so cold out."

"What about Yankees? You don't want to end up like your sister, do you?" She saw her bluntness tore at Mary Catherine's heart but she wouldn't take it back or be sorry for it. Better brokenhearted than just plain broken. "It's not safe and that's a fact."

Mary Catherine worried her lower lip. "What if I just went to the barn?"

"No doubt about it, you're a strange child. Thought so from the very first. Always readin' and recitin' words from those books your mother gave you. If it makes your heart less heavy, Katy, then take what you want and go out to the barn. I'll ring the bell if I need you."

After she packed a small covered basket, Mary Catherine went to her bedroom to get a book because it was expected of her. Though her aunt had said the words with a certain amount of fondness, Mary Catherine wondered if she *was* strange. It seemed likely. No other girls of her acquaintance ever talked about making their own way in the world. The more callous belles bemoaned the war because of its disastrous effect on scores of eligible men. Yet it never occurred to them they might do something other than marry. Mary Catherine, on the other hand, never seriously considered marriage. It didn't seem to suit an actor's life.

In addition to the basket and book, Mary Catherine managed to steal away with some clothes belonging to her late uncle, a pair of scissors, a razor, and a bar of soap. There was an old copper-rimmed tub in the barn where Logan could wash. She'd find a way to dump him in it if he wouldn't go willingly.

Logan was still sleeping when she reached the loft.

She woke him by poking him in the ribs with the toe of her shoe. His reaction was swift. He grabbed her ankle, twisted, and set her off balance. She fell hard on the floor of the loft and hay scattered around her. Logan was on top of her, pinning her down with the weight of his body before she could even gather her breath to scream.

The basket had overturned. One hard-edged corner of her book had struck her shoulder. The back of her head was throbbing and clothes were scattered across the loft. Bewildered and frightened, she stared at Logan. In return he looked at her blankly. She knew the exact moment when he realized where he was. The frosty, winter gray of his eyes faded and focused with something akin to interest and warmth on her mouth. Then he realized who *she* was and the interest was replaced by embarrassment. To Mary Catherine's way of thinking, it was proof that Logan still thought of her as a child. It angered her that she felt a pang of disappointment. Not that she would have welcomed his interest anyway, she told herself. Certainly not in his present condition. Unless she missed her guess there were probably *critters* in his beard. That thought was chilling.

"You're Katy," he said slowly.

"Very good," she responded dryly. "Now that we're both certain of it, perhaps you'll let me up."

"I thought you were—"

"Please," she interrupted. "Will you let me go? You're bruising my wrists and I can barely breathe." She pushed away the thought that it wasn't only his weight causing her shortness of breath. "I would very much be obliged if you would remove your person from mine."

The request was made with such gritty dignity that Logan found himself smiling. Mary Catherine re-

55

mained unamused. "Very well," he said, rolling off her. "But in the future have a care how you wake me. I don't particularly enjoy surprises."

Sitting up, Mary Catherine began to gather the items she brought. A sideways glance at Logan reminded her how hungry he was. He was looking longingly at the heel of bread that had fallen out of the basket. Pity surfaced again as she realized it was taking all his will power not to pounce on the food. She handed him the heel.

Logan raised the bread to his mouth. He hesitated, lifting his eyes to Mary Catherine. "Will you share this with me?"

Tears sprang to her eyes without warning. She quickly averted her head and continued gathering clothes. "No. I brought it for you. I already ate breakfast. Don't worry that you have to save anything. There'll be more for supper. It's no trouble to get it out of the house." The last was a lie. Her aunt would notice missing food that couldn't be accounted for. Mary Catherine chose not to tell Logan. It was her choice, after all, to help him. Something would occur to her. She folded the clothes and placed them in a neat pile beside Logan. "These were my uncle's. The fit won't be too bad and I can always do a little alteration. Don't think about putting them on until you've bathed. There's a tub in the tack room and I'm going to fill it now. When you're done eating, call me and I'll help you down the ladder. I might as well warn you, there's no way for me to heat the water here."

Logan shrugged. Around a mouthful of bread, he said, "I'll have pneumonia, but I'll be clean. At this point it seems a fair trade."

Mary Catherine wasn't so certain he didn't already have pneumonia. His eyes were fever-bright and there were beads of sweat sparkling on his forehead. "Perhaps the bath isn't such a good idea."

"You couldn't stop me," he said.

"It's your funeral."

"Precisely my sentiment," he agreed with dark humor.

The bath *was* cold. Logan sat in the tub with his knees drawn up to his chest and clenched his jaw to keep his teeth from chattering. He started to scrub himself with the strong soap and brush Mary Catherine provided, but he tired quickly. Suddenly she was there, taking the soap from his hand and applying it to his back. He couldn't find energy for protest or indignation. Mary Catherine did not appear to be embarrassed, so why should he?

Mary Catherine would have expired from embarrassment if she allowed herself to think about what she was doing. It helped to think of herself as Kate, Petruchio's tamed shrew. She was attending to her husband's needs, that was all. It was a wifely thing to do. In her mind she recited the lines Shakespeare had written for Kate and removed herself from the present.

"What are you mumbling?" he asked.

" 'Thy husband is thy lord, thy life, thy keeper, thy head, thy sovereign; one that cares for thee,/ And for thy maintenance commits his body . . .' " She stopped as soon as she realized she was speaking aloud. "Here, take this blanket and wrap it around you when you get out of the tub. Then sit on that bale over there so I can cut your hair." She turned away to give him privacy and missed the questioning, puzzled look he shot her.

"You read Shakespeare?" he asked, hitching the blanket around his waist. He slipped on the clean undershirt and denim shirt she provided. They both carried the scents of lilac sachets and cedar chips.

"Is it so surprising?" She motioned for him to sit down. When he did, she began combing out his hair.

"I don't know. I never thought about it."

"Mama loved the theatre. It was the best thing about living in Washington, she said. There wasn't much opportunity for that sort of thing when we lived at Stone Hollow, nor once we came to King's Creek. Shakespeare was her favorite playwright. We saw *As You Like It* just weeks before we left Washington." There was a wistfulness in her voice that spoke of her youth. Logan recognized it even if Mary Catherine was deaf to it. "We're all players, you know."

"I've heard that," he said noncommittally.

Mary Catherine was astute. "But you don't agree."

"It always makes me think that I'm being manipulated. I like to believe I have choices."

"We choose the roles we play. At least I do."

"You?" he scoffed. The half-smile he gave her was patronizing. "What role have you ever—Ouch! That hurt!" He looked down at his feet. "God! How much hair are you going to cut off?"

"As much as I want to," she returned.

"Brat."

"Mr. Marshall, your hair is a haven for—"

"Don't remind me," he said feelingly. "Cut away."

When she was done she reached in her apron pocket and handed Logan part of a mirror about the size of a gold piece. "You do the beard and mustache," she said, once he approved. "Trust me, Mr. Marshall, you'll be better off clean-shaven."

Logan didn't doubt it. He eagerly accepted the razor. Twenty minutes later he hardly recognized the man who stared back at him in the mirror. It wasn't merely that he didn't look like the man he had lived with these past nineteen months. More troubling was the fact that he didn't look like the man he had been before that.

"You look old," said Mary Catherine.

Logan returned the mirror. His smile was wry. "You don't mince words, do you?"

"It's not so bad," she said. "You'll look the same way when you're really old. Even when you're thirty."

Logan nearly choked on his own breath. "My God, you're quite the flatterer."

Ignoring him, Mary Catherine picked up the things she had been using and dropped them in her apron pocket. What she hadn't said, what she *wouldn't* say, was that Logan Marshall was terribly handsome now and would be for the rest of his life. She doubted that she would be alone in thinking that. Even Aunt Peggy, before she filled his behind with buckshot, could be counted on to remark that Logan was a fine figure of a man.

"Let's go into the loft," she said. "I can make some kind of bed for you there, block it off with a few bales to give you some privacy and keep it warmer. Later, when I come back with your supper, I'll bring Uncle Martin's greatcoat."

"You're being very kind," he said in a low voice. "I'm not sure why. Earlier, when you showed me the graves, I thought you were going to send me away. You haven't even asked what I'm doing here, or where I've been. And, according to you, I'm the enemy."

"You *are* the enemy. As for where you've been — I don't care — and if you don't get up in the loft and get dressed it doesn't matter why you've come, because you're going to die here. I'd rather not have to explain that to Aunt Peg. She wouldn't understand consorting with a Yankee, even one who was — "

Logan waited, but Mary Catherine didn't finish her sentence. "Was what?" he prompted.

"Was a frog prince," she said quietly as she left the tack room. The memory, the poignant reminder of innocence lost, created an ache in Mary Catherine's heart. She glanced behind her and saw Logan slowly stand. After a brief hesitation he followed silently in her wake.

Logan was sleeping again when she returned with supper and the greatcoat. This time she did not poke him in the ribs. Laying the greatcoat over his shoulders, Mary Catherine knelt beside him. She placed the basket of food near his face where the aroma of chicken and dumplings would catch his attention. He was snoring lightly and she turned him gently on his side just as she did for her aunt. He wrinkled his nose once. Twice. The snoring stopped. Mary Catherine touched three fingers to Logan's forehead. He was warm, but not as hot as he had been before. Perhaps it wasn't pneumonia after all.

Mary Catherine unwound the plait of hair at her back while she waited for Logan to wake on his own. She combed out her hair with her fingers, examine the ends for splits and breaks, and began to rebraid it. When she finished, she was surprised to see that Logan had been watching her—probably for some time. He was staring at her hands. Self-consciously, for they were certainly not beautiful, soft, or idle hands, Mary Catherine hid them in the folds of her dress. The action seemed to shake Logan out of his reverie.

Without preamble, he asked, "What happened to the soldier who raped Megan?"

"I shot him."

"He's dead?"

"Aunt Peg only taught me one way to shoot."

"I see," he said thoughtfully. The softness was gone from her, he realized. If he had aged, then so had she; perhaps more so. He, at least, had had a childhood, an adolescence. Mary Catherine seemed to have leaped from child to adult. He wondered how many of the hard edges were Colonel Allen's responsibility.

"I think your fever's down. Are you feeling better?"

He sat up, stretched, and reached for the basket. "I'm feeling tolerably well." The greatcoat slipped off one shoulder and Mary Catherine reached across him and adjusted it. "I know it's because you don't want me dying here, but thank you just the same."

Feeling that he was trying to goad her, Mary Catherine didn't respond. "I can't stay and I can't come again until morning."

"I'm not going anywhere."

"But you do understand that you can't stay here long," she said anxiously. "My aunt will get suspicious eventually."

"I understand. What day is today?"

"Thursday."

"Then I'll be out of your hair on Monday. I promise." He stabbed a dumpling with his fork and began eating.

"Where will you go?"

"Home."

In spite of herself, she was interested. "That's New York, isn't it?"

"The city, yes."

"What will you do there?"

"Work for my father. He owns and publishes the *Chronicle*."

"Is that what you really want to do?"

"Yes. It's something I really never had to think about. I've always known I wanted to be a newspaperman. Now Christian—he's my older brother—he despises the business. Wants to be an artist." He paused to swallow his food and take a swig from the flask Mary Catherine had so generously provided. The whiskey burned the whole way down. It felt wonderful.

"I thought you were a photographer."

"I am. Christian got me interested. I want to make photography an important part of the *Chronicle*."

"Things haven't changed for you, have they?" she asked. "I mean, not really *changed*. You're going to go home and the paper's waiting for you, your family's waiting for you, you probably have a sweetheart waiting for you, and in a few months it's all going to be behind you."

Logan's eyes had narrowed as he listened to her. He could hardly believe what he was hearing. "If it'll be behind me, it's because I'll have put it there."

"It'll be as if it never happened," she said, not realizing she was treading on dangerous ground. "One morning someone will wake you by poking you in the ribs, and you won't even budge. You won't even remember why it bothered you once upon a time."

"Get out of here," he said.

"You won't even—"

"Mary Catherine." There was grit in his voice. "Leave me."

Belatedly she realized that Logan was angry. What should it matter, she asked herself. Everything she said was true. He'd return to the city and forget all about the war, forget all about her and her family. She got to her feet, brushed strands of hay from her dress, and started down the ladder.

"Katy?"

One more rung down and she would have been out

of his view. She could have ignored him then. But there was something in his manner when he called her Katy that drew her attention. She paused, poised between rungs, and raised her eyes.

"I don't have a sweetheart," he said.

She didn't know which she hated more, the fact that she blushed to the roots of her hair or the fact that he laughed and the laughter had a hint of cruelty in it.

Friday morning Mary Catherine was prepared to give Logan her coldest shoulder. She practiced expressions in her mirror that were guaranteed to cut *and* draw blood. Confident of her ability to ignore him, Mary Catherine entered the barn and did her chores before she even deigned to climb up to the loft.

Her attitude amused him. All her gestures were just a shade overdone so that it was difficult to take her seriously. He wondered if she had been reading that shrew story again.

"You're laughing at me," she accused.

"I am. You're so obvious."

"Yankee bastard."

"Yankee, true enough. My mother and father would be surprised to hear me called the second thing you named."

He was still laughing at her. Mary Catherine forgot what she had practiced. She left the loft in a huff and later that night had a serious discussion with her aunt about tolerance and forgiveness and anger. The conversation bewildered Peggy, but Mary Catherine felt better.

On Saturday she could see a difference in Logan. What color there was in his complexion was natural, not put there by the fever. He sat straighter, looked stronger. Climbing up and down the ladder didn't wind him. She brought a deck of cards from the house and they played poker with straw sticks.

"What does your aunt think you're doing in here?" Logan asked. His eyes shifted from his cards to Mary Catherine's face. She was concentrating on her hand and biting on her lower lip at the same time. Her eyes were shaded by long lashes and her cheeks were stained pink by the reflection of light on her red shawl. A red grosgrain ribbon kept her hair loosely confined at the nape of her neck. She was wearing a gray dress with a high collar and little in the way of ornamentation. She looked very demure. He thought she was cheating. "Did you hear me? I asked you a question."

"I know. I'm thinking." Her mouth pursed to one side as she caught the inside of her cheek between her teeth. "Two cards, please."

Logan gave her two. "So?"

"She thinks I'm reciting. I'll see your three straws and raise you one."

"Reciting what?" He matched her wager and showed her his cards. He had three of a kind.

"Full house," she said. "Sevens over fives. I win." She paused a beat. "Again."

"I'm glad you weren't in Libby Prison. I'd have lost my shirt to you."

Here was something she didn't want to know. Yet she heard herself asking, "You were in Libby?"

Logan nodded. He gathered the cards and began shuffling.

She told herself she didn't want to know more. "For how long?"

"Almost since the moment I left you in Washington."

"Oh, God," she said under her breath. "You just got out?"

"Yes."

"They let you out?"

"No, not exactly."

"Oh, God," she said again. "Then you're an escaped prisoner."

"From your tone of voice I take it that's worse than being a Yankee bastard."

"How can you joke about it? You shouldn't have told me this—any of it. Do you think I won't report you?" In the folds of her dress her hands were clenching and unclenching.

Logan dropped the cards and took her by the wrists, stilling her agitated hands. "Katy, what is this?"

Mary Catherine could feel Logan willing her to look at him. She raised her face, thrusting her chin forward in a defiant gesture. It was wasted on Logan. His cool pewter eyes continued to demand an answer. But it was the hint of sadness that held Mary Catherine's attention. She couldn't look away. "It's not right," she said in a low voice. "I shouldn't be hiding you at all. Until you mentioned Libby Prison I thought you were a deserter. It didn't seem so bad somehow that I was helping you. Knowing what I know now, well, it makes things different."

"Does my help in the past mean so little to you then, Katy?"

"Don't call me that."

Impatient, he gave her hands a little shake. "Does it?" he demanded.

She tore her hands away. She reached blindly for the cards and began to collect them. "I never asked for your help. Neither did my mother or Megan."

"I see." His stomach began to knot. He was glad he wasn't holding her hands any longer, because his palms were sweating. "I suppose I'm not so proud—

I'm asking for yours. I need your silence. If I'm caught, I'll be killed and if I have to go back to prison, I'll die. You agreed I could stay until Monday. Let it stand."

For some time Mary Catherine said nothing. She pulled her eyes away and began dealing the cards. "If I decide to say something before Monday, I'll tell you first. You'll have a chance to leave. That's the most I can promise." Below the loft, Brutus began to whine and the nag shuffled back and forth in her stall. The collie jiggled the ladder as he circled it. Mary Catherine reached for the ladder to steady it and called down to Brutus to be quiet.

"I can hardly believe you're serious," Logan murmured.

"We're on different sides," she said. "We always have been." She glanced up at him. "Now, do you want to play poker?"

Logan slowly picked up his cards. It was difficult to reconcile this young woman in front of him with his memory of the child she had been. The child he had saved from Colonel Allen.

"Ante up," she said.

So it went. The remainder of the afternoon passed as if nothing unpleasant had ever been discussed. Mary Catherine's winning streak continued but Logan was preoccupied with other matters. He knew that he would have to leave before Monday.

Mary Catherine was halfway down the ladder when Logan called to her in the manner of an afterthought. "When will I see you in the morning?" he asked.

She paused, dangling her foot just above Brutus's yawning mouth. The collie playfully nipped at her shoe. "Not until after church. Morning services are usually over by eleven but Aunt Peggy likes to talk to everyone. It'll be closer to twelve-thirty before I can bring you anything to eat."

"You don't take a carriage to church?"

"There is no carriage any more. We walk." Although she apologized in the next breath, her tone held no remorse. "I'm sorry that I can't manage your meals better. If you get hungry you can always milk the cow."

"I'll remember that," he said dryly. "Better yet, maybe I'll just go to the house while you're out and help myself."

Mary Catherine pulled her foot away from the dog and retraced her steps up the ladder. When Logan was in sight she glared at him. "The surest way to get yourself caught is to touch my aunt's larder. She knows precisely what she has and precisely where it is. Nothing escapes her eye."

Logan's brows drew together slightly. "But you've been feeding me these past days, surely she's missed—"

"Whose meals do you think you've been eating?" she asked flatly. She disappeared down the ladder then. Logan called to her but she refused to answer. She was angry with herself for telling him the truth. She hadn't wanted Logan to know she had sacrificed anything for him.

Lying back in the hay, Logan slipped his hands beneath his head and stared at slivers of blue sky between cracks in the barn roof. Mary Catherine might want to see him thrown to Rebel dogs, tarred and feathered, or back in Libby Prison, but Katy, his Katy, was willing to give up food from her own plate to see that he didn't starve. She was an enigma, his enemy and his friend. It seemed she could not help herself helping him. Yet sooner or later, he figured, she would despise herself for what she was doing and that's when she would betray him. All things considered, Sunday morning, while most of the King's Creek community was at services, was the perfect time to leave.

Through a series of splinterlike cracks in the planking, Logan watched Mary Catherine and her aunt leave for church. His stomach growled. He bit the inside of his cheek in an attempt to forget the empty feeling in his gut. Mary Catherine hadn't returned any time last evening with dinner for him. He noted her absence, wondering if she was being spiteful. If he'd known she wasn't coming back, he could have left under cover of night.

Moving away from the side of the barn, Logan collected his belongings. The clothes he arrived in were folded and placed in one of the horse blankets. His lacquered box of odds and ends now held a deck of playing cards and a razor, both courtesy of Mary Catherine.

Logan had one foot on the top rung of the ladder when Brutus's mad dash into the barn halted him. He didn't wait to see if the dog was in pursuit of the gray tabby or if Brutus was being followed. Dropping his things, Logan quickly retreated out of sight. He held his breath, waiting.

"Brutus, stop that! Bad dog!"

It was Mary Catherine. Logan's breath rushed out of him when he heard her laughter and scolding. He kicked at the things he had dropped, pushing them out of the way. He sat down on the floor of the loft, leaned back against a bale of hay, and tried to look relaxed instead of angry.

Mary Catherine cleared the top of the ladder and stood at the edge of the loft. She wondered if she looked as uncertain as she felt. It was important to appear confident or Logan would never go along with her.

God, Logan thought, she was exquisite. His lids lowered fractionally to hide the very real interest in his survey. Katy's honey-colored mane was tamed in a smooth chignon and dressed with tiny curls across her forehead. Drawn up and back, the style displayed the lovely curve of her ears and the slender line of her long throat. The cotton sateen material of her gown had faded from deep sapphire, which was still hinted at around the cuffs, to blue-gray. Although the dress was plain and obviously well worn, Mary Catherine's beauty was hardly diminished by it. His eyes were drawn to her as they would be to a precious stone laid against a black velvet background.

"What are you doing here?" he asked in a husky voice. "Shouldn't you be at church?"

Mary Catherine's weight shifted slightly. She nervously smoothed the skirt of her gown over her steel cage crinoline. "I wanted to see you." She walked toward him, her steps tentative, uncertain. At its base her gown was four feet across. It swayed gently as she approached. "Before you leave tomorrow."

"You promised to feed me after church," he reminded her.

"Yes, I know, but I've come about something else." She looked down at her hands which were pleating and unpleating folds in her skirt. "Last night I was thinking—actually I've been thinking about it for some time—and I was wondering . . . well, would you mind terribly—that is, do you think you could—I mean it would set my mind at ease and I wouldn't have this feeing that I was, I don't know, *missing* something. I don't plan to marry and it's got nothing to do with the fact that most of the young men are gone. I'm not so shallow as Cecily Fairburn and Jane Graves. I don't think a woman really *has* to marry any longer, do you? I think I can manage quite well on my own, only I don't want to miss the experience, you see. And I'm not too young. Pamela Courtland is my age and she's a widow."

Somewhere in the middle of her speech a shutter had lowered over Logan's eyes. "Somehow you've managed to say quite a lot and very little—all at the same time," he said dryly. He refused to encourage her. He was not so dense that he couldn't hear what she *wasn't* saying and her suggestion bordered on madness. "Take your leave, Katy. Your aunt must be wondering what's become of you."

Logan's patronizing tone rankled. Mary Catherine's spine stiffened and her jaw went rigid. "Aunt Peg isn't expecting me. I pretended to turn my ankle shortly after we left. I insisted that she go on and I hobbled until I was out of her sight."

"Not very original."

"It worked. She'll be gone for hours and we're quite alone. There's not the slightest chance that we'll be interrupted."

"Since we won't be doing anything, it's a moot point." He raised his brows slightly and pointed to the barn door with his index finger. "Take your leave," he repeated.

Far from being cowed, Mary Catherine stood her ground. "Is it because of Megan?" she asked. "Are you still in love with her? Is that why you won't do it with me?"

Logan reached behind him and plucked a piece of hay from the bale. He placed one end of it in his mouth and twisted it between his thumb and forefinger. His expression was thoughtful, cool and removed. "Your sister has no part in this. For the record, I was never in love with her. I hardly knew her and though I deeply regret the pain she suffered and her passing, I remember her with fondness rather than love. As for the reason I won't do it with you? That's simple. You don't even know what *it* is or what *it's* called."

"I do."

Logan blanched as he realized where she might have come by the experience. He sat up straighter and tore the straw from his mouth. "Did Allen ever—"

Mary Catherine's eyes widened. "No. Never. He never did *that* to me." She would never admit that she had Logan to thank for this. For she didn't thank him. She would have been willing to suffer anything if it would have kept her mother and sister with her.

Logan crossed his legs in front of him and went back to toying with his stick of straw. "Katy, I'd be lying if I said I wasn't flattered by your offer, but I'm not tempted." He hesitated, wondering if lightning would strike him for lying on the second count. "You're like a sister to me." Another lie. "I'm hardly the person you want to give you this experience."

"You're exactly the person I want. You'll be leaving on the morrow and it's unlikely that I'll ever see you again. I know you, which is better, I suppose, than not knowing you. I don't want my first experience to be like Megan's. I was lucky to have escaped being raped when it happened to her but I may not be so fortunate when the next renegade comes. And there will be another one." Her eyes didn't waver from his although it was true that she was looking through him rather than at him. "You're not unhandsome either. It's true that you're thinner than you used to be, but you're not rail-thin. I don't think I should like holding a man who was too thin. As for thinking

71

of me as your sister, well, it's too bad. I don't think of you as a brother. You'll just have to overcome your reticence."

Though Logan didn't show it, Mary Catherine's newfound poise and straightforward reasoning unnerved him. "This is a ridiculous conversation, Katy. I shouldn't even be listening to you. You shouldn't even be saying these things."

"It's called—" Her voice was solemn as she intoned the basest, crudest word for making love. "And I want to do it with you."

Logan thought he had heard most everything, but Mary Catherine's pronouncement confounded him completely. "And I want to wash your mouth out with soap. Preferably lye soap."

"Why? That's the word, isn't it?"

"It's *a* word. Hardly *the* word." He shook his head slowly from side to side. A thought occurred to him. "Have you been drinking?"

In answer, Mary Catherine approached Logan until she stood directly in front of him. There was a rustle of her skirt and petticoats as she knelt. With artless confidence she laid a hand on either of Logan's shoulders, leaned forward, and kissed him full on the mouth. It was a inexperienced kiss. She kept her mouth closed but enthusiastically pressed her lips to his. After a moment she drew back and smiled a smile much older than her years. "Well?" she asked. "Have I been drinking?"

"Don't play with me, Mary Catherine," he said tautly.

Her lightly feathered brows drew together. "I'm not playing. I'm in earnest."

"Damn you." One of his hands snaked around her neck. He held her still for a moment, waiting for her to resist the pressure of his fingers. When she did nothing except drop her gaze from his eyes to his mouth, Logan pulled her toward him and ground his lips against hers. Without pausing for instruction, he forced her mouth open with the hard, wet edge of his tongue. He swept the ridges of her teeth, pushed against the barrier until she relented, and pushed hard in the warm, sweet interior of her mouth. He engaged her tongue in a battle, probing and retreating, tasting and tormenting. They shared the same breath. When he heard her small gasp, the hungry sound of pleasure and surprise, he released her, pushing her back with enough force to cause her to fall to one side. Almost immediately Logan was on his feet.

"No," he said firmly, "you haven't been drinking. And you know what? It doesn't matter. Now get the hell out of here."

"You forget, you're the trespasser here. Not me."

"Then I'll leave."

Mary Catherine saw him pick up his box and his bundled clothes. "It's been your plan all along," she accused. "You were going to leave while I was at church!"

"What of it?"

She didn't answer. Instead, Mary Catherine rose to her feet and crossed the loft to the ladder, blocking Logan's exit. Her chignon had come loose and tendrils of hair whispered across her cheek and the tender nape of her neck. Her mouth was swollen and berry red with the proof of Logan's rough kiss. She stared at Logan defiantly and began to unfasten the row of cloth-covered buttons at the front of her gown.

Words of protest died on Logan's lips as she slipped the bodice off her white shoulders. Over her lawn shift she was wearing a corset that confined her waist to a measurement Logan could span with his

73

hands and lifted her breasts so they invited touching. When she reached behind her to attack the corset strings, the lawn shift was stretched tautly across her breasts. Logan's mouth went dry. He swallowed hard and tore his eyes away from the high curves of her bosom. "Mary Cath . . . Kate . . . Katy . . . don't take that—" The corset fell. "—off."

As far as Logan could see there was no earthly reason for Mary Catherine to wear the contraption. Her breasts were still as firm and high, her waist as small. One strap of her shift fell off her shoulder and his eyes skimmed the delicate line of her collarbone and rested on the hollow of her throat. He dropped the bundle of clothes and the box. The precious contents scattered and he didn't notice.

When he spoke his voice was taut because of the constriction in his chest. "Only one of us is thinking clearly Mary Catherine, and it's not me. I don't think you understand how long it's been . . . you're making it . . ." Hard, he wanted to say. God, she was making him hard. He could feel his rigid member pushing against his drawers. His knuckles were white from pressing his fingertips into the palm of his hands.

Mary Catherine slipped the skirt of her gown past the crinoline, then stepped over the puddle of material—toward Logan. Her hoopskirt fastened at the waist and her fingers fumbled momentarily with the ties. It collapsed on the floor when she drew it off. There were two cotton petticoats, both of them shiny with wear and mended with tiny, careful stitches near the hem. She took them off, let them fall on top of the crinoline, and stood boldly in front of Logan in her shift and pantalettes, shoes and stockings.

She waited, and when Logan still made no move toward her, Mary Catherine's composure faltered.

74

"It's because of the colonel, isn't it?" she asked plaintively. "He made me dirty."

Logan snapped. He covered the distance between them in two short strides and pulled Katy into his arms. He held her close, pressing her cheek against his chest while his fingers slipped between the soft strands of her hair. His lips touched the crown of her head, then trailed lightly toward her ear. "You're not dirty. The colonel couldn't do that to you. No one could." He held her away for a moment and looked deeply in her eyes. "Are you certain, Katy? This is what you really want? You're so young."

"You're using the wrong yardstick to measure my youth," she said softly, returning his stare. "Don't count years. Count the things I've already seen and done. Those are the markers of my age."

"Oh, God," he moaned softly under his breath. "I know I—" He didn't finish. Instead he drew Katy close again and raised her mouth to his. As the kiss deepened he lowered her to the floor, pressing her into a mound of hay. He felt her arms circle his back. She rubbed her palms along his shoulder blades. He could make out the outline of her breasts against his chest and it wasn't nearly satisfying enough.

Logan's mouth left hers. He kissed the corner of her lips, then teased her with light kisses along her cheek, her jaw, and the delicious cord of her neck. At the curve of her shoulder he paused and his teeth caught her flesh first, then the strap of her shift. With tantalizing slowness, he tugged it over her shoulder, down her arm, and lower, until the bodice of her shift slipped past the coral tips of her breasts.

Before Mary Catherine decided to approach Logan, she had given some thought to what it would be like to lie with him. What he was doing to her now

75

was beyond anything she had imagined. That he would kiss her on the lips she had anticipated; that he would want to kiss her breasts was wholly unexpected. Yet he was doing exactly that to her now. She felt his tongue flick across first one nipple, then the other. He created a peculiar ache inside her, a burning that shimmered just beneath her skin. The heat elicited a moan that she quickly bit back.

Logan heard her moan and was glad. Still stinging from her request for experience which amounted to little more than a request for stud service, he intended to give her more than she had asked for. He lifted his head and raised himself so his face was above hers. A hairsbreadth separated their lips. When Logan spoke, he could feel the brush of her mouth. Her breathing was sweetly uneven.

"I think you should undress me," he said.

The flush that stole across Mary Catherine went from her breasts to her hairline. Logan's deep, appreciative chuckle sent another frisson of heat through her. "All right," she said. Her hands trailed slowly across his back and down his arms. Logan was wearing a blue denim pullover shirt. She undid the two buttons at the front, opening the wide collar, then tugged the shirt free of his wool trousers. His hair was mussed when she pulled the shirt over his head. She smiled because he looked young for a moment, like the enchanted frog prince.

"What are you thinking?"

Mary Catherine's smile faded. She helped him remove his knit undershirt before she straightened his dark, copper-threaded hair with her fingertips. Her fingers slid lightly over the side of his face, tracing the hard line of his jaw. She touched his Adam's apple, felt the pulse beating wildly in his throat and the heat of his tautly muscled chest. Circling his back again, Mary Catherine brought Logan closer until her naked breasts were flush to his skin. "Do we do it now?" she asked.

They would have to, Logan thought, otherwise he would do *it* in his drawers. Better that he was sheathed deeply inside of her, where, God help him, he wanted to be. "Soon," he groaned against 'her lips. "Very soon."

Mary Catherine helped him with the sash that held up his trousers and they both tore at the side tapes closing his drawers. Her shift had climbed up to her hips and Logan reached under the material to lower her pantalettes. The thin cotton drawers ripped at the waist in his eagerness to have them off her. The rending sound made him realize how little hope he had of being able to stop at this point. Mary Catherine seemed to be totally unaware of what happened. She was staring at the juncture of his thighs.

Please, God, no, he thought, following the path of her gaze. Don't let her change her mind. I couldn't stand maidenly protests now. Not now. Still, raising her chin so that he could capture her eyes, he asked the question. "Have you changed your mind?"

"No," she said on a mere thread of sound. "But we'll have to, won't we? It will never fit inside me. You're as big as a—"

Logan had no idea what she compared him to. His thick, husky laughter drowned her out. He kissed her again, softly at first, then harder until his hunger leveled off at a new peak. When he raised his face he saw that her eyes were dark and vaguely unfocused. Her lips were slightly parted and tantalizingly moist. He doubted that she was aware of arching into him or spreading her legs on either side of his thigh. Logan could feel the damp heat of her against his skin. His hand slipped between their bodies and he touched the soft, sensitive bud of flesh nesting between her thighs.

Though there had been moments of almost painful embarrassment in the musky-scented arms of his first woman, moments where eagerness overruled control, Logan didn't regret the experience. This was Katy's first time, he thought, and no matter how much she believed she knew what she wanted, no matter how willing she seemed, there had to be part of her that was frightened just as he had been.

His fingers continued to stroke her, exciting her to a higher pitch, then dipping just to test her readiness. Her head moved slowly from side to side. The chignon had collapsed some time ago and hay mingled with strands of her hair. She caught her lower lip between her teeth and stifled each sound that rose in her throat.

Mary Catherine raised her hips and ground herself against Logan's hand. Whatever he was doing to her, it wasn't enough. Not quite. There was something just beyond her grasp that she continued to reach for without knowing what it was or precisely how to get it. She was certain of only one thing, and that was that Logan knew what she wanted.

She buried her face in his shoulder as she felt his finger probe more deeply between her legs. He kissed the side of her neck and sucked gently on her skin. Her fingers pressed harder into the taut muscles of his back.

Logan's hands moved to either side of her shoulders as he raised himself over her. "Now," he said parting her thighs further with his knee. "Now, Katy. Help me." He guided one of her hands to his member and let her fingers close over him. "Take me in, Katy. You'll see. We'll fit together perfectly."

The first blast of the shotgun sent Logan flying out of Mary Catherine's arms. Wood splintered somewhere near his head. "Jesus! What the—"

"Come out of that loft, bare-assed and bucknekked if you have to, but bring your Yankee hide down here."

Logan's entire face hardened. The desire that had darkened his pewter eyes faded away. The stare he leveled at Mary Catherine was cold and stony. "It was all an act, wasn't it?" he accused in a harsh whisper as he grabbed his drawers. "You planned this." He didn't give her opportunity to confirm or deny his words. Slipping into his underwear, considerably cooled in that part of him he was afraid was going to be blown off, Logan walked to the edge of the loft and held up his hands in surrender.

Standing below him near the barn door was Peggy Cook. There was nothing soft or grandmotherly about her demeanor now. In her arms she held a Confederate issue, rifle-bore, muzzle-loader musket. The steadiness with which she held the deadly weapon bespoke her experience and her accuracy. Flanking her were two men about Logan's age, each wearing gray wool uniforms that had seen better days. They were both rangy, light on their feet, and they looked like scrappers. Logan knew he hadn't the strength to take one of them down, though he was tempted. Fighting two was out of the question.

"I don't have a weapon," he said. Behind him he heard Mary Catherine scrambling for her clothes. He wanted to push her to the forefront, show her aunt and her friends just how far she had been willing to go for the beloved and glorious cause. "I'm coming down now," he told them, lowering his hands. He hunkered down, grabbed the ladder, and swung himself around. He willed Katy to look at him before he

79

disappeared from her view. When she wouldn't, he called her a bitch under his breath.

Mary Catherine heard the epithet and cringed at the venom in Logan's voice. She slipped the straps of her chemise in place and pulled on her dress. There was no time to bother with the corset or petticoats or pantalettes or crinoline. Those things were abandoned where they lay. She fastened the buttons on her bodice and smoothed the material before she stood. Logan was already being held between Hank Fairfield and Joe Littlebury by the time Mary Catherine reached the ladder. He wasn't even struggling, although that made no difference to Hank and Joe. They had him immobilized in their iron, double-fisted grips. Aunt Peg had her musket leveled at his chest.

Mary Catherine went to stand beside her aunt. "What are you going to do to him?" She was surprised to hear her voice was trembling. Out of the corner of her eye she saw Logan's lip curl in distaste and disbelief. His eyes were accusing.

It was not her aunt who answered Mary Catherine's question. Joe Littlebury stuck out his chin and aggressively demanded, "What did this Yankee trash do to you afore we got here? Answer that and we'll tell you 'xactly what to do with him."

Mary Catherine felt four pairs of eyes boring into her and the hottest and the sharpest belonged to Logan Marshall. She averted her head and stammered an unintelligible reply.

"Speak up, girl," Joe said.

No words would come and the silence began to condemn her. She looked helplessly at her aunt.

Peg intervened. "I told you at the church that Katy was afraid he was leavin' this morning. She returned to keep him here until I come back with help. Clear as the nose on your face what she had to do to make him stay. Don't look at her as if she's poor white trash now. My niece is no slattern."

Mary Catherine shuddered. It was precisely what Joe and Hank had been thinking. Logan's suspicions were confirmed. "I didn't . . . that is, he didn't . . ."

Eyes narrowing on the love bite on Mary Catherine's neck, Peg poked the barrel of her shotgun at Logan's gut with enough force to make him groan softly. "Hang him up, boys, no need for me to waste lead shot on his jewels."

Hank and Joe started to drag Logan toward a particularly sturdy-looking rafter.

"No!" Mary Catherine pulled on her aunt's sleeve. "Don't let them kill him! You don't know about him, Aunt Peg! I didn't tell you who he is!"

"Just a minute, boys," she called to them. "Hold up there. That's it, keep him steady." Peggy turned to her niece and gave her a hard look. "Now, what is it that you haven't told me?"

"His name. He's Logan Marshall. He's the one who took Mama and Megan and me from Stone Hollow."

"That doesn't speak well of him. He delivered you to that viper, Colonel Allen, didn't he?" She didn't wait for an answer, but lowered her gun slightly. "Guess he's the same one that got you away from him, too."

Mary Catherine nodded. Although she didn't thank Logan, she knew her aunt did. "It was his dispatch that I copied for Mama and Megan. Remember?"

Her revelation floored Logan. Rose and Megan and Mary Catherine? All spies?

"I know she told you all about the Yankee defeat at Chancellorsville," Mary Catherine went on. "Before

81

he could return to his unit, Logan was captured, probably because of what we did. Send him back to Libby Prison, don't—"

"No!" Logan's cry was torn from his very soul. "Damn you to hell! Let them kill me! Let them—" Hank Fairfield's fist plowed into Logan's midsection. He sank slowly to his knees, supported only by his captors. Joe's knee caught him in the jaw and he actually saw blinding splinters of light before darkness engulfed him.

Peg hefted the musket and cradled it against her ample bosom. She looked at Logan's crumpled form dispassionately, then at her niece. "He wants to die," she said. "You heard him. Prison's a terrible thing, Katy. We'd be doing him a favor by killing him now."

"No! I don't believe that!" She lowered her voice so that Hank and Joe couldn't hear her. "Please, Aunt Peg, I lied before. He had me. I could be carrying his child. It's not the same as it was with Megan."

"You sayin' he didn't rape you?"

"That's what I'm saying."

Peggy shook her head. "I can't believe that." She gave the gun to Mary Catherine and climbed into the loft. She examined her niece's undergarments, saw the torn pantalettes, and came to the only conclusion she could accept. It was easier for her to believe Katy was lying than to admit her niece had willingly taken a Yankee's seed. "I suppose I can understand that you might want to protect him," she said when she returned to Mary Catherine's side. "But I saw your drawers and I know the truth. You want to send him to prison? That's fine with me. He'll die there anyway. Probably suffer longer, too." She motioned to Hank and Joe. "Katy here wants him in prison, boys. He helped her family once upon a time so she feels beholdin'. Can you take him back to Libby?"

They shook their heads in unison. "No, ma'am," Joe drawled. "They'd kill him for certain. Not that it would matter to me, but it don't make no kind of sense to take him there just to see him kilt. Hell, we could do that here. Place to send him is Andersonville. That's where they're sendin' Yankees these days. I hear tell there's fighting down Georgia way anyhow. Sherman's got his troops headed for Atlanta. Hank and me been thinkin' of trailin' behind, gettin' us a few Yanks like they was easy pickin's at a turkey shoot. We can get rid of this 'un just as soon as we come across a prison train."

Peg turned to Mary Catherine. "That meet with your approval?"

She nodded quickly, guiltily. "They won't kill him?" she asked again, needing reassurance.

"They won't kill him," Peg promised. "But if he survives Andersonville and ever decides to look you up, you'll wish they had."

Chapter Three

May 1872 — New York City

The playbill said her name was Katy Dakota. Logan Marshall knew different. She could have changed her name to Sara Smith or Barbara Jones and he still would have known Mary Catherine McCleary. After what she had done to him, after what she had cost him, he was incapable of forgetting. Forgiving never occurred to him.

Logan tried to relax in his seat, stretching his long legs and crossing them at the ankles. The box he shared at Wallack's with his brother and sister-in-law gave him a commanding view of the stage. The play was *Manners* and it purported to show that among the New York elite, there were none. If the playwright were to be believed, then fidelity, honor, and tradition were values that were given lip service by the wealthy and left to the growing middle class to uphold. *Manners* was meant to shock theatregoers with its seduction scenes, the frankness of its dialogue on divorce, and the flouting of conventional morals by the characters. *Manners* proved to be so shocking that it played to packed houses each night since its opening two weeks earlier. Everyone seemed agreed that the play and its female lead were a scandalous success.

Jenny Marshall nudged her husband delicately and indicated with a flick of her finger that he should look at his brother. Christian turned his head slightly, just enough to see Logan's profile. He didn't know what to make of what he saw. Clearly Logan's attention was on the play, yet his eyelids were heavy and lowered, shading the cool pewter gray of his eyes. He could have been sleeping, yet there was a thread of tension running the length of him. Christian knew his younger brother well enough to know the relaxed posture was a sham. Turning back to Jenny, Christian shrugged and pretended he wasn't concerned, then his own aquamarine gaze narrowed on the stage as he tried to understand what it was his brother was seeing and thinking.

Jenny was regretting that she and Christian had talked Logan into joining them at the theatre. She had meant it to be an evening's light entertainment. Both men had been working so hard of late, holing up for hours at a time in the study discussing how the *Chronicle* should handle the latest scandal from Tammany Hall. For Christian it was a personal crusade; normally he left the running of the family-owned paper to his brother. For Logan the long hours were accepted as part of his commitment to the *Chronicle* and the competition with the *New York Times*.

Without appearing to let her attention stray from the stage, Jenny studied Logan out of the corner of her eye. The resemblance he bore to his older brother was nothing short of striking. They were of a similar height, both over six feet, with broad, tautly muscled shoulders that filled out a black tail coat so that women had actually been heard to sigh as the brothers passed in tandem. Their hair was threaded with strands of copper but Logan's was darker, more like an old penny piece. Their profiles were sharp, yet rugged.

At thirty-four, Christian was five years older than his brother, but the lines at the corners of Logan's eyes and the often serious — even grim — set of his mouth erased the difference in their ages. Jenny remembered when Christian had looked as hardened as Logan, as if he were always angry, and especially with her. The tension in the long line of Logan's body, the muscle working rhythmically in his lean cheek, and the steady rapping of his fingertips against the scrolled arm of his chair, reminded Jenny so much of Christian a few years ago that she stole a glance at her husband just to make certain he hadn't reverted.

He hadn't. Jenny was startled to discover that Christian had been watching her. When their eyes met, they smiled guiltily at having been caught with their thoughts exposed. Christian's hand slid around Jenny's slender wrist and his thumb brushed back and forth across her pulse.

Logan shifted in his chair, uncomfortable as Christian leaned toward Jenny and whispered something in her ear. He could almost feel the heat from Jenny's blush. No doubt Christian had suggested something that would have been most improper had they not just celebrated their fourth wedding anniversary a week ago. The secret, intimate exchange between Jenny and Christian struck Logan on the raw. He couldn't recall that he'd ever been bothered by their obvious happiness before. He didn't much care for his reaction right now.

There was only one explanation for it. Katy Dakota. Mary Catherine McCleary. Funny, he thought, he'd called her Katy back then, too, and she had hated it. Or perhaps she hadn't. She was quite the little actress all those years ago. Watching her on the stage, Logan realized that some things hadn't changed.

When the crowd stood, applauding wildly at the end of the play, Logan remained sitting. He clapped, but it was a rhythmic, slow, and sarcastic joining of hands. Logan Marshall was unimpressed and he didn't care who noticed.

Christian helped Jenny with her shawl. His head bent over her thick, sable hair and his lips briefly touched her temple. The sweet fragrance that was his Jenny filled his senses and his hands rested on her shoulders, holding her against him while he spoke to his brother. "We're going to Delmonico's for a late supper. You're still coming with us, aren't you?"

Logan glanced at Jenny. She was watching him carefully, her dark brown eyes curious and concerned. She was lovely, decent and kind, and Logan didn't want to worry or disappoint her. Still, there was something he had to do. "Why don't you and Jenny go ahead and I'll join you in a little while. There's someone I want to see backstage."

Jenny's beautifully modeled mouth lifted at the corners. Her smile was at once serene and sly. "Not Miss Dakota, I hope. You'll never get in to see her. I understand there's a veritable throng of admirers. Victor Donovan chief among them. She's very popular, you know."

"How do *you* know, dear sister?" asked Logan, forcing a smile.

"Yes, Jenny," added Christian, "where do you learn such social tripe?"

"Perhaps both of you should pay more attention to the society pages of your own paper," she said smugly.

"Friday's edition devoted three whole columns to Miss Dakota, her background, and her following."

Both men had the grace to look sheepish. "Point taken," Christian said, giving Jenny's shoulders a light squeeze. "Come, let's be off. They won't hold our reservations forever. Logan, we'll see you there."

Wallack's Theatre, on the northeast corner of Broadway and Thirteenth Street, was one of the largest playhouses in the city. On opening nights especially, the richly appointed lobby, draped in velvets and satins, was a place where playgoers could take refreshment and gather to be seen. Artists and authors mingled with the politically powerful and the landed gentry. Although Logan Marshall was part of the city's aristocracy, moving in circles that were both fashionable and wealthy, he avoided the public eye as much as possible. Until now Logan had never regretted missing an opening night.

Trust the presence of one Katy McCleary to change how he felt, he thought. Seven and one half years had passed since he'd last seen her and just saying her name had the power to tie his gut in a knot. The confrontation could have been over two weeks ago if only he had attended opening night.

The candle-lighted chandeliers were being lowered and snuffed by the time Logan decided to leave his box. Except for a few stagehands and ushers, the auditorium was empty and the lobby was deserted. Logan knew that he wasn't going to wait for Katy with the stagedoor johnnies. They wanted a sweet word or the favor of her company for drinks and dinner at Harbor House. Logan wanted revenge and that demanded a little more privacy — at least for the time being.

"Miss Dakota." The door to Katy's dressing room was pushed open six inches. A balding head appeared. "Miss Dakota. There's someone here to see you."

Katy's fingers paused on the laces of her corset as she looked over the top of the silk dressing screen. "I said I didn't want visitors tonight, Mr. Grant," she reminded him gently. It was difficult not to affect the cold, disparaging accents of the prima donnas she had always despised. She was anxious and weary and desired nothing so much as to be left alone. "Please tell whoever it is to leave his card and call later in the week."

Katy turned her back and continued struggling with her laces. She was beginning to regret dismissing her dresser, but then Jane's chatter had been anything but soothing this evening. Jane took particular delight in knowing who was in the audience and tonight her coup had been spying the Marshalls in their box. "Sure, and I'm thinkin' it's high time they came to see you. All those nice things that were written in their paper, well, it just didn't look right, them not seein' the play for themselves. Like they didn't believe their own press, that's what it looked like to me."

Katy had purposely not asked Jane which Marshalls were in attendance. She got through her performance by believing that only Christian Marshall and his wife had an interest in theatre. Thinking about Logan would have paralyzed her with fear.

She didn't realize her fingers were trembling until they were gently removed from her corset strings by hands that were stronger and steadier than her own. A shudder went through her and she whirled around, eyes flashing and accusing.

"Whoa!" came the soft admonishment. "You're

only supposed to be this skittish *before* the performance."

Relief shimmered down Katy's spine. "Oh, it's you. For a moment . . ."

"Yes?"

"Nothing," she said tersely, regaining control. "What are you doing here, Michael? I specifically told Mr. Grant I didn't care to entertain visitors. Can't you accept no for an answer?"

"Not where you're concerned." Michael Donovan's smile was smooth and engaging. Even when it failed to coax Katy, the smile lost none of its confidence. True, Michael's light blue eyes became fixed and frosty, but the smile never faltered. "Come here, let me finish unlacing you. I don't mind playing the lady's maid."

"*I* mind. Take a seat on the other side of the screen, Michael. Allow me some privacy."

It was definitely not the time to remind Katy he had seen a lot more of her than she was revealing now. Discretion being, in this case, the better part of common sense, Michael said nothing and took a seat on the chaise longue out of Katy's view. "I told you I would come by this evening," he called to her. "Had you forgotten?"

"I try to forget all unpleasantries," she replied. Michael Donovan was a most handsome man. An Adonis, she had heard one ingenue in the company call him. If pressed, Katy would have agreed. Michael's features were seemingly sculpted by an artist's hand with clean, strong, chiseled lines. His light blond hair was streaked with sunshine. A shade darker than his hair, Michael's mustache accentuated the line of his sensual, sulky mouth. He was tall and broad-shouldered and carried himself with pride and confidence. In all the time Katy had known him, he had only been honest about one thing—he didn't accept no for an answer.

Michael ignored her and picked up the paper lying at the foot of the chaise. It was the *Chronicle*. "Who were you expecting?" he asked casually, flipping through the paper.

"No one. That's why you startled me."

He wouldn't let the lie pass. "That's not true. You were actually relieved to see me for a moment."

"You're mistaken, Michael. I'm never relieved to see you."

"My, my. You *are* irritable this evening. Didn't the performance go well?"

"Do you mean you didn't see it?"

"I was here opening night, remember? That was enough, I assure you. You're quite wonderful in it, but, to turn a phrase, the play's *not* the thing. You are."

"I'm not flattered." She slipped into a cream satin dressing gown, stepped out from behind the screen, and sat down at the vanity. She pinned up her hair and began to remove the greasepaint that accentuated her features on stage. Beyond Katy's shoulder, Michael's reflection dominated the mirror.

"Was it my father?" he asked, refusing to drop the subject. "He left home shortly after dinner this evening. Ria remarked that he took a cab downtown. I thought he might have come here."

"I haven't seen Victor in three, no, four days. You may want to check his studio or the Union Club. Your father has a life outside the theatre and interests other than me. You would know that if you paid attention to Victor instead of his money."

"People who live in glass houses . . . well, you take my meaning. Suffice it to say you weren't expecting him."

91

"I told you, I wasn't expecting anyone. You're being particularly tiresome this evening, Michael," she drawled. "Why don't you take yourself off? Go home to your wife."

"I hate that butter-won't-melt tone." Michael sat up straighter, folded the newspaper, and tapped it against his knee. He watched her in the mirror, although she never met his gaze. "It doesn't work with me, Katy. I'm ten years your senior. Use it on one of the johnnies who sniff after your skirts, but not on me. I *buy* your skirts."

"You're vulgar. Get out of here. I mean it, Michael. I'll call someone to have you evicted. Just because you backed this play with a little money, don't mistake yourself for someone important to me."

Dropping the *Chronicle,* Michael came to stand behind Katy. He rested his hands on her slender shoulders. His thumbs stroked the sensitive nape of her neck. "You're very tense," he said, massaging lightly. His fingers itched to thread themselves in her soft honey hair. He'd make that imperious, regal expression of hers vanish once he removed the pins. The taut line of her mouth wouldn't look so inviolate after his kisses. "Do you really think you'd find anyone to throw me out? Have a care, Katy, you may be the one puffed up with your own consequence. The city's at your feet today, but that can change quickly."

"Are you threatening me?" she asked coldly.

Michael smiled. "Hmmm. I suppose I am." His hands slipped to her upper arms and without much resistance on Katy's part, he pulled her to her feet. There was a touch of cold cream on her cheek and he wiped it away with his fingertip. "Such soft skin," he said huskily, watching her closely. "You're very beautiful, Miss Dakota, but then you're probably used to hearing that. I'd wager you've heard it from my own father. He fancies himself something of a connoisseur where women are concerned. Tell me, aren't you the least bit curious about being in my bed after you've been in his?" He waited for her response. When she met his statement with silence, he probed. "What? No desire for relative comparison?"

"I don't find your attempts at humor amusing and your conclusions—"

"Shut up, Katy," he said, not unkindly. "Your mouth has better uses." Pressing one hand to the small of her back, Michael forced Katy flush to his body. His other hand cupped her head, holding it immobile as his mouth closed over hers.

Katy's lips were set in a mutinous line. She tried to twist out of Michael's grasp and when she couldn't, settled for giving him no pleasure. His mouth was hot and hard and his mustache abraded her skin.

He raised his head slightly but did not release his hold. "Come, Katy," he cajoled. "Why so reticent? Open your mouth, darling. Let me taste some of what you give others so freely."

When Katy opened her mouth it wasn't in offering. "Take your hands off me," she spit, then added venomously, "Yankee bastard."

From the doorway there was the sound of cynical applause. Katy and Michael broke apart.

"Nicely said, Miss Dakota," Logan said, pushing away from the door. "That epithet hardly seems worn when spoken with such vehemence." He looked over his shoulder at the balding little gentleman behind him. "It's all right. You can stop wringing your hands. The situation's under control." He pushed the door shut with a flick of his wrist. "Wouldn't you say that's true, Donovan?"

Michael's hands dropped to his side as Katy took

another step backward and put herself out of his easy reach. "Marshall," he said tersely in rough greeting. "What are you doing here?"

Katy nervously smoothed her dressing gown. "How do you know each other?" she asked. For all the attention either man paid her, she may as well have not spoken.

"I came back to see Miss Dakota, of course," answered Logan. "I'm a great admirer of her acting ability." He didn't spare Katy a glance but he felt her discomfort as if it were a tangible thing. It was a heady, powerful feeling. He thought he could get used to having her under his thumb. He thought he could come to like it very, very much. "If you don't want your privacy invaded, Michael, you should make certain your ladyfriend is willing. I could hear her from out in the hallway telling you to leave. That poor little man was beside himself for having let you in in the first place. I couldn't bear to see him suffer any longer."

So Logan hadn't come to her rescue, Katy thought. He had only wanted to relieve Mr. Grant's worry. His motives shouldn't have surprised her; he had every reason in the world to despise her, and yet she found herself looking over him hungrily, wishing it could be different.

Michael's weight shifted from one leg to the other. His eyes darted over Logan. They were both of the same height, similar builds. If it came to a fight Michael knew they would be evenly matched. It would be the talk of the clubs for years to come, Michael Donovan and Logan Marshall scrapping over Katy Dakota. It would also reach his wife's ears and Michael didn't want that. Ria had no choice but to accept his affairs with other women, but she asked for, and received, Michael's promise of discretion. He pulled on his mustache with his thumb and forefinger. "Odd, isn't it, that as often as you and I meet, we've never shown the slightest interest in the same woman."

"It's still true," said Logan. "As I said, I merely dropped by to tell Miss Dakota how much I enjoyed her performance. That said, I'll take my leave. Perhaps you'd join me for a drink at Georgia's?"

Michael cast a brief look in Katy's direction. She was watching him anxiously, afraid he wouldn't take Logan's offer. He hesitated, letting her worry a moment longer. "Of course I'll join you. I'd like to hear how things are over at the *Chronicle*. My father and I think you should put some stock on the market." He turned to Katy. "Another time then, Miss Dakota. I'll be sure to mention to Father that I saw you this evening." He turned on his heel and left, waiting just outside the door for Logan.

"My congratulations again," said Logan. His voice was soft, dangerously, soft, and his eyes were as frigid as arctic air. "I wouldn't be at all surprised if I decide to see *Manners* a few more times. It was an enlightening experience." His smile was chilly. He took Katy's hand in his, and raised it to his lips. "Your hand is quite cold, but then I suppose you are the exception to the rule."

Her voice sounded odd to her, forced as it was past the aching lump in her throat. "What rule?"

"Why, the one that says cold hands, warm heart." Logan Marshall dropped her hand and walked away.

Once the footsteps had faded in the hallway, Katy sank slowly onto her vanity stool. She stared sightlessly in the mirror. In her mind's eye she saw Logan, the cruelty in his gray eyes, the rigid thrust of his jaw, the taut length of him that tailored evening clothes emphasized rather than hid. The veneer of civility was thin indeed.

The lines that life experience had cut in his face were a bit deeper now but his features were remarkably the same. He would never be handsome in the mold of Michael Donovan. Logan's features were not cast for perfection. His beauty was ruggedly sculpted; his body was whipcord lean and hard-edged. Logan Marshall had grown into himself. And when he looked at her with those winter gray eyes of his, Katy knew a terrible emptiness in her soul. The only thing she had to fill it was fear.

The gentle tapping at her door interrupted Katy's reverie. Not again! She felt near to tears with frustration. "What is it, Mr. Grant?"

"Mr. Donovan's here to see you," he called through the door.

"Show him out!" What was Michael doing back already? She couldn't have been woolgathering that long. "I don't want to be disturbed." Katy sighed heavily as the door opened anyway. Obviously Michael was right, she thought unhappily. She was puffed with her own consequence, expecting people to heed her wishes just as if she mattered. "What do you wa—"

The head that poked through the door this time was neither Michael's nor Mr. Grant's. It was a graying head, thick and lustrous with no signs of thinning. Iron gray sideburns framed lean cheeks. A mustache, blackened with Mr. Church's Blacking Powder, curled stiffly above a cautious, tentative smile. The eyes were sky blue, warm and friendly. The dear face belonged to Victor Donovan, father to the man Katy had come to loathe.

"Victor!" Katy stood and held out her hands, welcoming him into her room.

"Oh, good," he said, relieved. "I was afraid I was

96

persona non grata around here. You were absolutely frigid with that little man who guards your door." He took Katy's hands and kissed each in turn.

"I'm glad it didn't stop you. You're the last person I'd want to throw out." She withdrew her hands from his light grasp and gestured toward the chaise longue. "Please, make yourself comfortable. I'm still trying to remove the last of my makeup. I let Jane go early and I've had a few interruptions this evening."

"One of them wouldn't have been my son, by any chance?"

Instead of answering directly, she asked, "What makes you think that?"

"Your reaction at the door."

"Oh." Katy leaned toward the mirror and began wiping away eyeliner. She hoped that by becoming self-absorbed, Victor would forget his question or realize that she had no intention of answering it. "What brings you here this evening? Surely you didn't see the play again."

"I wish I had. It would have been a more entertaining evening. Actually I was at the club. I had an argument with Samuel Dodson over some real estate. You can't imagine what he wants for that lot on East Fortieth."

Katy's welcoming smile faltered. "Don't you ever stop working? You're going to run yourself into the ground. Please tell me you're not really thinking of opening another store."

Her concern warmed Victor. "I haven't decided. Donovan's has done well for a long time but I think there's a need to expand as the city grows. A few stores in accessible locations would give Donovan's a boost into the next century."

"That's thirty years away."

"I like to think ahead. I'll be ninety then and I'll

97

need something to amuse me. Women won't be interested."

She laughed, put down her handkerchief, and swiveled on the stool to face Victor. "You rogue. You'll be just as attractive to women in thirty years as you are now. And you know it, so stop fishing for compliments."

Victor's cheeks took on a ruddy hue and his light blue eyes sparkled. "You're good for me, Katy Dakota." He stood, crossed the room to her wardrobe, and began going through her clothes. "And since you are so good for me, the least I can do is feed you. I've been thinking about it all evening. You haven't had supper yet, have you?"

"You know I can't eat before a performance."

"Are you hungry?"

A short time ago the mere thought of food would have sent her running to the washbasin. Now she realized she was famished. "Very. What do you have in mind?" Please don't say Georgia's, she thought.

"Delmonico's."

"I'd love it."

Victor held up a red silk and satin gown for her approval.

She hesitated, looking the gown over. The neckline was off the shoulder, dipping low in the front. It was perfectly modest, very much in fashion for evening wear, yet Katy was not entirely comfortable in the creation. Silk ribbons trimmed the bodice and the red lace shawl and overskirt. It came from Donovan's *couturiers*, a gift from Victor. Please, he had said, you'll do me such a favor by accepting it. "I don't know, Victor. It's a beautiful gown, but it's so . . . so —"

"Red?"

She nodded. "I'd rather just wear it for you . . .

98

when we're alone." Though he tried to hide it, Katy saw his disappointment and she didn't want to hurt his feelings. "It's all right. Of course I'll wear it." After tonight there would be a dozen orders for copies of the gown at the department store. This was the first occasion she minded being a living, breathing mannequin for V.I. Donovan's. She didn't think it was Victor's intention to use her that way, so she didn't accuse him. Had it been Michael, she wouldn't have hesitated. "Find my white kid gloves, will you? I think they're in that drawer over there. Oh, and the silk and ivory fan, too. It won't take me long to do my hair. I suppose I shouldn't have let Jane go."

"I'm certain you'll do fine." Victor came up behind Katy and touched the back of her neck, fingering the soft tendrils of hair that had escaped the pins. "My Annie had hair like this," he said. "Thick as thatch, but each strand as fine as silk. She complained that it wouldn't take to styling. Her maid rolled it in rags, heated it with irons, crimped it. Nothing held." His hand dropped away and he laughed self-consciously. "God, but Annie had beautiful hair." He took a step backward, avoiding Katy's eyes in the mirror. "I'll wait for you in the hall."

"You don't have to."

"No, it's better if I do."

Katy watched him go. Her heart felt heavy with a strange sensation of foreboding. Victor's touch had been—there was no other word for it—sensual. He had been talking about his wife, dead longer than Katy had been alive, and touching her as he might have touched Annie. Katy worried her lower lip between her teeth and brushed out her hair with hard, punishing strokes. Please, she thought, closing her eyes. Please God, don't let it be like that with Victor.

By the time she and Victor walked into Delmonico's, Katy had pushed all her troubling thoughts to the background of her mind. He had been attentive during the cab ride over, amusing, pleasant, and above all, avuncular. Katy's mood was relaxed, though a trifle reserved, as she let Victor escort her into the restaurant. Delmonico's was crowded but even without a reservation Victor was able to ask for, and get, his usual table. In a bastion of wealth and notoriety such as Delmonico's, there were the elite and then there were the *sacred*. Heads turned as they were led to their table. Katy assumed it was because of Victor. Victor knew better.

Jenny nudged her husband with her elbow and gestured discreetly toward the couple wending their way through the maze of tables. "There's Victor," she said. "And isn't that Miss Dakota with him?"

Christian glanced up briefly, then went back to his prime rib. "Yes, that's she."

"She's so young."

"Only a few years younger than you. Twenty-two or three, I'd say." And Victor Donovan was sixty if he was a day. The actress and the store magnate made an odd combination. Looking around Delmonico's, Christian realized he wasn't alone in his thinking.

"On stage she looks older, don't you think? Perhaps it's all the paint the actors use."

"That could account for it."

"I thought so."

"Make an effort not to stare, Jenny. One would think I don't let you out of the house often."

"You don't," she said. "You rarely let me out of the bedroom."

Christian sputtered, almost choking on his food. He shot his wife a menacing glance, put down his fork and knife, and drank some icewater.

"Are you all right?" she asked solicitously.

"No thanks to you. You do pick your moments, Jenny. Be warned, you can expect retaliation once we're alone."

"Oh, good."

One of Christian's hands crept beneath the table and found Jenny's knee. Her gown proved to be more like a suit of armor, but his caressing fingers made their point nonetheless.

Jenny's eyes widened though she managed to smile at Mrs. Abbot when that worthy matron looked in her direction. "Christian!" she admonished softly, trying to maintain her composure as his caress became more intimate. "I thought you'd wait until we're alone."

"I lied." He grinned as a blush stole across Jenny's cheeks. "You're going to give me away if you keep blushing, dearest." When Jenny's flush deepened, Christian took pity on her. He slowly brought his hand back to the tabletop and wrapped it around his glass of icewater. "Here, drink this. You look as if you could use a bit of cooling off." He held the glass to her lips and let her sip. "Better?" She nodded. "Good. You know it's hard to believe that we have a son at home. When you look at me that way I'd swear no one's ever touched you. How you can still appear the blushing innocent is beyond me."

Jenny pushed away the glass. "I have no idea what you're talking about," she said primly, refusing to look at him. Her eye caught a movement at the door. She looked up and saw Logan standing on the threshold. He saw her almost immediately and without waiting to be escorted, joined Jenny and Christian at their table.

"I'm sorry I'm so late," he said, taking his seat. He unbuttoned his black jacket and straightened his gray silk waistcoat. Without asking, he helped himself to his brother's madeira. "I met someone, shared a drink with him at Georgia's, and forgot the time." He looked over their plates as he unfolded a linen napkin on his lap. "Recommend anything?"

Victor noticed the instantaneous change in Katy's demeanor though he didn't know what prompted it. "What is it?" he asked, leaning across the table and taking her hand. "Katy? You're pale. Are you feeling ill?"

She couldn't answer for a moment but she tried to relieve him with a wan smile. "I'm fine," she assured him. "Really I am. It was just a little chill. So many people in and out of here, bringing in the night air with them."

"Perhaps I should ask for something more private than this table. Something less out in the open. Would that help?"

"No, please don't bother." The last thing she wanted to do was draw attention to herself. Logan's back was to her. With a little luck she and Victor could finish their meal and leave — all without being noticed by Logan. "Don't look now, Victor, but could you tell me who that couple is just beyond your left shoulder? I think I've seen them at the theatre before."

A moment later Victor casually turned in his chair. A glimpse was enough. "I could make introductions if you like," he said. "I've known the Marshalls for years."

So it *was* Logan's brother and sister-in-law. She should have known just by the look of the brother. He and Logan were cut from the same cloth; the resemblance was striking. "Introductions aren't necessary. I was just curious. Mrs. Marshall was looking this way a while ago. I'm certain she was asking her husband about me." She laughed lightly. "Probably wondering how she could get a gown like mine." Katy took a bit of her stuffed crepes. "How is it that you know the Marshalls?"

"I knew their father first," explained Victor. "You can see for yourself that the boys are more of an age with my son and daughter-in-law. Christian—he's the one sitting with his wife—is Michael's age. Logan—with his back to you—is just a year or so older than Ria. Sorry. I suppose I'm showing *my* age now, talking about them like that. Sometimes it's hard for me to accept how far they've come on their own . . . I wish Michael . . ." His voice trailed off and with it the dreams he had for his son. He shook off the mood quickly and went on, "They own and publish the *New York Chronicle*."

"Yes," she said as if in revelation. "I thought I'd heard the name before."

"Christian turned most of the responsibility for the paper over to Logan several years ago."

"Christian's an artist, isn't he? Like you," she added graciously.

"Thank you for that comparison." He realized he was still holding her hand and withdrew it now. "No, my dear, nothing like me. I'm a dabbler, and as you well know, I can't do justice to a beautiful subject such as yourself. Christian, on the other hand, is an exceptional talent. It's quite an honor to be singled out as the subject for one of his paintings." Victor regarded Katy's fine-boned features thoughtfully. "You know, I wouldn't be at all surprised if after seeing you here tonight, he decided to—"

"Paint her," Jenny said, stabbing a cherry tomato on Christian's plate and bringing it to her lips.

"Who?" asked Christian.

She plopped the tomato in her mouth and waved

her fork in Katy's general direction. "Miss Dakota, of course. You should paint her. Her face is really quite striking. And her hands are lovely. I noticed them on stage this evening. She uses them very well. Her gestures aren't overdone or expansive, but she manages to convey feeling with them just the same. I thought it was amazing then. I still think so. Logan, why ever are you looking at me that way? Do I have spinach between my teeth?"

"No, Jenny," said Logan. "No spinach. Tell me, are you speaking of Miss Dakota's face from memory, or is she here now?"

"Behind you," said Christian. "She came in on Victor Donovan's arm shortly before you arrived. Did you miss her backstage?"

"I never said that's who I wanted to see, did I? You both assumed that."

"Were we wrong?" Christian asked bluntly.

"Can't a man have his secrets?"

"Of course you can," said Jenny. "Don't badger him, Christian. And think about painting her, will you?"

"We're leaving for Paris in a week, or had you forgotten?"

"No, I hadn't forgotten. But if you think you're interested, send Logan round to take a few photographs of her. You could work from the stills on the voyage. It would give you something to do while I'm occupied with Holland."

"Holland's nanny will be occupied with Holland. At least she'd better be. As for me, I've given a great deal of thought as to how I want to occupy my time on the voyage."

Logan shook his head, leaned forward, poked his fork at each of them in turn, and whispered, "Try not to leer at her so, Christian. And, Jenny, if you wouldn't look so patently pleased at the idea of four weeks of complete ravishment on the high seas, people wouldn't be staring at us right now. A little decorum, please." That said, Logan went back to his dinner. "Your idea's not a bad one, Jenny, about photographing Miss Dakota. Perhaps a series of pictures while she puts on her greasepaint and becomes her character. That could be interesting."

"I like it," said Jenny.

Christian agreed with his wife. He looked past Logan to where Katy Dakota was sitting. Jenny was right. The actress was striking and Christian felt strongly that he could paint her vibrant, exotic features. "If you get some good shots, I'd like to see them. I could work up some sketches on our trip." He glanced sideways at Jenny. "Stop gloating. I have no trouble admitting when you're right, so there's no need to look so self-satisfied."

Jenny simply pretended Christian hadn't spoken. "Are you going to ask her before she leaves, Logan?"

He shook his head. "No. I'd rather wait. I can catch her some evening at Wallack's."

"After a performance? I don't think so. She's probably exhausted then. I doubt she'd be very receptive. Why don't you go to her hotel suite some afternoon? The *Chronicle* article said she has a suite of rooms at the Chesterfield."

"You're a fount of information," Christian noted dryly. "You don't happen to know the room number, do you?"

"Really, Christian, she'd never have any peace. Do you think the *Chronicle* gives out that sort of information?"

"I was beginning to wonder."

"I'm sure that Logan can inquire at the hotel."

Logan's lip curled derisively. "Perhaps I'll just ask

105

Victor Donovan. I'm certain *he* knows."

"Careful, brother. You don't want Jenny and me to think you have a real interest in Miss Dakota, do you? There are your secrets to consider."

Across the room Katy set down her fork. It was useless to continue the pretense of eating. Ever since Logan had entered the restaurant the joy had gone out of her evening. The weariness she had experienced earlier returned with a vengeance. Another night she would have enjoyed being seen with Victor, even in the red gown. Logan's presence made her feel tawdry in her finery, like the charlatan he thought she was. It was an ugly feeling and before long she began to feel ugly. "I'd like to leave, Victor. Would you mind terribly, taking me to the hotel?"

"I don't mind at all, but what is it? Should I send a doctor?"

"Oh, no. I'm a trifle tired, that's all. It came on suddenly. I guess I really haven't rested much since *Manners* opened. This success is just as tiring as rehearsals. There hasn't been a moment to rest on my laurels."

Victor was immediately apologetic. "I shouldn't have pressed you into coming here this evening." He motioned to a waiter that they were leaving, then he helped Katy to her feet. Her red dress was brilliant against his dark evening clothes.

Logan turned in his chair when he saw Jenny's and Christian's attention drift to another part of the dining room. Katy fairly shimmered as she glided between the tables, her head high, regal as a queen. Logan stared hard, willing her to look just once in his direction. Just once, he thought, and she would be reminded of the past, she would remember the foul trick she had played him. Logan intended to remind her at every turn.

"Scarlet," he said, under his breath. "The only color more appropriate would be jade."

"What's that?" Jenny asked.

"Nothing. I was just thinking aloud."

But Christian had heard and his glance darted between his brother and Katy before it finally rested on Logan. There was anger in Logan's eyes, hot, terrible anger, and there was no doubt as to the target of it. Christian actually toyed with the idea of changing his traveling plans, then thought better of it. It had been a long time since he thought of Logan as his little brother, in need of help or protection. There was no sense in thinking that way now. "Are you sure you know what you're doing?" he asked.

Logan's gaze shifted from Katy to Christian. Clearly his brother had caught his mood. "No, but I know what I'm *going* to do."

Chapter Four

The Chesterfield Hotel, frequently referred to as the Palace because of its white marble facade, was one of the finest boarding hotels in the city. Located near the Rialto, as the theatre district was known, it was especially popular with actors and actresses who had reached celebrity status with the public. The Palace would not have been particularly welcoming to bit players, the itinerant crowd, or chorines even if they could have afforded the rent. It was a respectable hotel where a man could keep his mistress in luxury and never concern himself with scandal. The Chesterfield's employees were very much aware of the men who lined their pockets and they practiced discretion above all else.

In spite of a plethora of actors and mistresses, the Chesterfield was first and foremost a place for families. The growing middle class, excluded by exorbitant real estate prices from private ownership in Manhattan, had found boarding hotels to be a satisfactory answer. The suites were generally spacious, attractively furnished, and the atmosphere, even in the enormous second floor dining room and the lobby reading room, was one of closeness, of family.

Katy's rooms were on the eighth floor. They were

alternately known as the Blue Suite by the predominance of French blue, marine blue, cobalt and cerulean blue, cadet blue, midnight blue, periwinkle, and lapis lazuli. There were warm blues and cold blues, textured, shiny, and smooth blues, and they were offset perfectly by dark walnut wainscoting and cream-colored walls. The drapes were velvet, the seatcovers satin brocade, and the fringed canopy above Katy's bed was silk.

Katy flicked at the surface of her bath water with her forefinger. Bubbles scattered. She reached over the side of the claw-footed tub, found the jar of bathing powder, and added a generous amount. Summing up enough energy to swish her hand back and forth, Katy made a thick mound of airy bubbles appear. The tops of her knees disappeared as well as the curves of her breasts. She dropped the jar on the floor, didn't even care that it tipped and spilled, and slipped a little lower in the water. The back of her neck rested against a folded towel on the tub's rim. Katy closed her eyes and a weary smile touched her lips. Wisps of hair that had fallen free of her pins lay damply against her cheeks and forehead. One tickled her throat but she let it be.

This peace was all she had wanted since finishing her performance. After the intrusion of Michael, Logan, and finally Victor, Katy felt as if she were one exposed nerve. And on lengthy reflection, which she could afford now that she was alone and safe from public eyes, it was Logan Marshall whose presence disturbed her the most. "Why shouldn't it?" she asked herself softy. "He looked angry enough to kill me."

That thought was so unsettling that Katy found herself suddenly cold in the warm water. The smile on her face changed from weary to nervous and finally faded altogether. The more she tried not to think of the way Logan had looked right through her, the sharper his image appeared in her mind. "Damn him," she swore, angry with him, angry with herself. "I should have—"

She cut herself off, sitting up and turning her head to one side as a sound came from the sitting room. Alert, she waited quietly for some repetition of the sound. Nothing. Shaking her head slowly, amused by her own imagination, Katy picked up a bar of lavender soap and trailed it across her arm and shoulder. It slipped out of her hand, dropped like a stone, and water sloshed over the edge of the tub as Katy searched for it.

"I could help you find that," Logan said matter-of-factly. He was leaning against the door to Katy's bathing room, his arms crossed casually in front of him and a smile on his lips that did not quite reach his eyes. He was still in his evening clothes and rather than appearing overdressed, he managed to make Katy feel underdressed in her own bathtub. "The soap," he said, pointing to where her hand had stilled beneath the water. "Do you require some assistance?"

"I certainly do," she snapped, angry enough to forget who her enemy was. She opened her mouth to scream.

Logan was kneeling beside the tub, his hand over her mouth, smothering her cry to a lamb's bleat.

Above his hand her eyes were wide and frightened. Logan saw it and wasn't moved to loosen his grip. When she began to struggle, he pressed tightly on the back of her neck. Her hands came up to claw at him but he averted his face, protecting it from her tapered nails. She pried unavailingly at his arms. Water splashed everywhere until Logan was kneeling in a puddle and his coat was soaked. "Have a care for your modesty," he warned her, his voice dry and calm. "You're losing all your bubbles."

His laconic, caustic observation infuriated Katy. She bit him.

Logan swore, yanked his injured hand away, and increased the pressure of his other hand on her neck. Katy was forced forward until her face hovered just above the surface of the water. She gasped for air, certain that Logan was going to push her under. She was surprised when she heard him speaking as calmly as he had a moment before.

"You have choices, Katy. You can settle down or you can scream all you want—under the water. You have five seconds."

"Bastard," she gritted.

"Two."

"Son of a—"

"Three."

"I should—"

"Four."

"What happened to one?"

"Five."

Katy sputtered as her face skimmed the water. "All right! Let me up! I won't scream again."

The words were garbled but Logan had no trouble making them out. He eased up. "I'll hold you to that promise. Break it and I'll put you under."

"Six feet?"

"What?"

She jerked her head away from him and this time Logan let her go. Glaring at him as he sat back on his haunches, Katy repeated herself. "Six feet under. As in dead and buried."

"The idea has merit."

Katy jerked in reaction to his softly spoken answer.

111

She looked at him sharply, trying to assess for herself how serious he was. He was giving nothing away. "You mean . . . you would actually . . ."

"I haven't decided."

So he *had* been considering it. Or was he still toying with her? Katy drew her knees up to her chest, conscious that all around her bubbles were evaporating. Thinking he was going to touch her, she pushed herself against one corner of the tub when Logan's fingers dipped into the water.

With a faint, cynical smile, he said, "Your bath's getting cold. You should get out of there."

"Go to hell."

Logan stood, chuckling under his breath. He stripped off his wet swallow-tailed coat, tossed it at a hook on the wall near the sink, and sat on the edge of the tub. He looked supremely confident, very relaxed. It was a pose guaranteed to raise Katy's ire and Logan was well aware of it. "Swear at me one more time," he said, "and I'll find that soap and you know where I'll use it."

Katy believed him. "Get out of here."

"In a minute." He looked around the bathing room. The floor was white and black diamond-cut tiles. The fixtures were porcelain and brass. The towels, of course, were blue. "This suite reminds me of one of Maggie Bryant's parlor rooms. She runs one of the most exclusive bordellos in the city," he explained when he saw Katy didn't realize he was insulting her. The rosy flush that covered her chest, throat, and face assured him he had hit his mark. "She has a gold parlor, a red one, blue naturally, and, if memory serves me, I think one is emerald. Her place is almost as fancy as this. It seems Victor Donovan is doing well by you . . . or is it Michael?" He paused a beat. "Or both?"

Katy wanted to kick him off the edge of the tub or drown him in her bath water or choke him with one of the midnight blue towels.

As if reading her mind he picked up one of the towels and drew it around his neck. He wiped at the dampness on his cheek and forehead. "No comment, is that it?" he asked.

"How did you get in here? I know I locked the door."

"You did. I got the extra key from the main desk."

"They wouldn't have just given it to you."

"They didn't. I stole it while the clerk was otherwise occupied."

No doubt Logan had also provided the clerk's diversion. What had he done, she wondered. Started a fire in the lobby? Paraded whores in front of the main desk? "Will you leave now? I'm cold."

"And the bubbles are gone."

"That too."

One of Logan's eyebrows inched upward. He scanned Katy's face, her hunched shoulders, the smooth tops of her knees. Below the water he could only make out the whiteness of her skin and the suggestion of her feet. "This water could be boiling and you'd still be too cool by half." He took the towel from around his neck and held it out for her. When she took it, he left, closing the door behind him.

Katy was almost as stunned by Logan's quick exist as she had been by his entrance. Shivering, she stood and stepped out of the tub. The tile floor was like ice on her bare feet. She dried hurriedly and slipped into a plain cotton nightshift and green flannel robe that had been hanging on the back of the door. Then she made straight for the parlor, intent on jamming a chair under the door handle so Logan could not possibly disturb her again.

She stopped short when she saw that he was sitting in the very chair she had planned to use. His wet trousers and shirt were making a water stain on the brocade fabric but he looked comfortable, stretched out as he was, thumbing through a stack of newspapers on the table beside him. He glanced at her when she came into the room and smiled slowly as he took in the girlish simpleness of her sleeping attire.

"Quite a change from that scarlet thing you were wearing earlier," he observed. "You look almost virginal."

"I'd like to slap that supercilious smile right off your face."

"Try it."

"You'd like that. It would give you an excuse to slap me, something you've been itching to do all evening."

"Listening to you, I have to admire my restraint."

"Why are you doing this, Mr. Marshall?"

"Logan."

"Oh, for God's sake." Katy almost stamped one foot in frustration. Instead she shoved her hands into her pockets and clenched her fists. He was not the only one who could practice restraint. "Why are you here at all? What purpose did it serve coming backstage this evening, and why follow me here from Delmonico's? I've been in New York for two years and you never bothered me. Why now?"

Logan's attention shifted to the stack of newspapers again. "I see you read the *Chronicle*."

"What does that have to do with anything?" But she knew, she *knew*. He was reminding her that she had always known he was here, while he had had no knowledge of her presence.

"You're a remarkable actress, Katy, quite remarkable, but you don't play stupid very well. There's simply too much intelligence in your eyes. Don't play stupid now, it's not your forté."

"Oh, God. There's no talking to you! You don't answer my questions, you don't even make any sense. Get out of here, Logan!"

"Sit down, Katy," he directed gently. "You're riled. Do you have a pair of dry trousers I could wear? Another shirt?"

Katy's hands came out of her pockets as she threw them up in the air. "Why would I have men's clothing here?" she demanded.

"I thought perhaps Victor or Michael might have left something behind. I think Michael's would suit me better."

The last of Katy's patience went up in flames. Uncaring of the consequences, she crossed the room to stand in front of Logan. Her adversary was expecting a slap. Katy delivered a roundhouse punch that would have blackened Logan's eye if he hadn't blocked it.

Grabbing Katy's wrist as he jerked his head out of the way, Logan pulled hard so she lost her balance and fell toward him. The chair rocked unsteadily as Katy collided with his chest and Logan had to catch his breath before he could grapple with her again. Katy's arms and legs flailed, but she was unable to make any blows count. She was so intent on hurting Logan that it didn't occur to her to scream. The sash to her robe loosened, the front of the robe opened, and Logan's hand closed over Katy's breast in the struggle. Her thin cotton nightshift was no barrier to the warmth, softness, or shape of her.

Logan's light touch stilled Katy as his strength never could. She couldn't meet his eyes, terrified of what she might see. Sitting as she was now, on Logan's lap in her nightgown, having him fondle her, was too reminiscent of another time and another man's hand. It was not acting when Katy spoke and her voice sounded much younger, strained and scared, and perfectly recognizable to Logan. "Let me go, please."

Logan released her. Katy pushed away and stood up. She was trembling and pale and she still could not look Logan in the eye. "I want you to leave," she said.

"No, that I won't do. Not yet."

Tears sprang to Katy's eyes. She turned around quickly so he wouldn't see and walked to the window. From eight floors up Katy's view of Manhattan was mostly unobstructed. There were lights in hundreds of windows and they flickered like the stars she couldn't see. Below her, all along Broadway, gas lamps illuminated passersby as they hurried to their next destination. Even from her vantage point Katy thought she saw purpose and direction in their movements. Why couldn't she divine Logan's?

Her composure gathered, she let the velvet drape fall back in place and turned away from the window. "Why did you come to Wallack's this evening?"

"Why does anyone go to Wallack's?" he asked rhetorically. "My sister-in-law enjoys the theatre and she's been after Christian to take her since she read about *Manners*. Jenny and Christian are leaving for Europe soon and tickets to the play were in the way of a farewell gift from me to them. I hadn't planned to attend but Jenny insisted I come along. I'm afraid Jenny is extremely persuasive. I have no more luck telling her no than my brother."

"Perhaps I should send someone for her and *she* can get you to leave." Katy hadn't meant or even said it seriously and Logan's reaction was unexpected.

"You will stay away from my family," he said,

116

grinding out the words. "Do you understand? I don't want you near them. Not Jenny. Not Christian. Not even their little boy. They'll be gone in a week, but they'll be back in six months. And six months or six years won't change my mind. Have I made myself clear?"

Bewildered and not a little afraid, Katy nodded slowly.

"*That's* why I came here tonight," Logan said. "That—" he got to his feet and went to her side "— and *this*." His hand snaked around Katy's neck and pulled her flush to his chest. She was too startled to fight at first and in the next second she recognized the futility of it. As Logan's mouth closed over hers Katy gave up without giving in.

His lips ground against her lips. His tongue speared her, seeking entrance that she wouldn't give. Logan changed tactics. His hold loosened, his mouth gentled. His fingertips stroked the sensitive nape of her neck and whispered through her hair. His lips moved to the corner of her mouth. He kissed her chin and trailed along her jaw until his teeth could catch her ear lobe. He tugged lightly, felt the warmth of her sigh against his skin, and returned to her mouth. He plundered, stealing the very breath from her lungs, crushing her to him so that he knew the shape of her intimately.

During it all he refused to acknowledge that she returned none of his passion and echoed none of his desire. That she was shaking and off balance when he let her go was enough for him now.

"*Now* will you leave?" she asked, wiping her mouth with the back of her hand.

Logan's eyes narrowed. For a moment he said nothing. Slowly an amused half-smile appeared on his lips. "Careful, Katy, you don't want me to think you're afraid, do you?" He reached behind her as if to tug on a braid and she gave credence to his words by flinching from his touch. His fingers only flicked at the light, loose strands of her hair before he drew his hand forward, caressing her skin. "What happened to Mary Catherine McCleary?"

"She died a long time ago. A casualty of the war, if you will."

"And Katy Dakota? How did you come by that?"

"The first actors' troupe I joined gave it to me and I liked the sound of it. It's my legal name now, not just something for the stage."

Logan's hand dropped away and he began walking around Katy's sitting room, exploring the knicknacks and personal objects that were her own. He picked up a crystal horse from the mantel and admired the workmanship. She had a collection of music boxes and Logan opened each in turn, listening a moment to the tinny melody. Had she always liked music boxes, he wondered. "But why use Katy?" he asked. "I thought you didn't like the name. Or was that a lie, too?"

"Not a lie exactly. I didn't like it when you called me Katy."

"I see. And now?"

She shrugged. "It's my name. But I suppose you can call me whatever you like. You will anyway." Katy died a little inside each time Logan picked up something in the room that was hers. He was making his mark everywhere. She wouldn't be able to be in this room without remembering his presence. Closing her eyes briefly, Katy rubbed her temples with her fingertips. The first symptoms of a raging headache were beginning just beneath her scalp. When she opened her eyes she found Logan was watching her. Katy's hands dropped slowly to her sides. "Please,

Logan, I'm so tired. I just want to go to sleep. Won't you leave now?"

Logan pointed to the bellpull, a cerulean blue striped satin sash with a large tassel on the end. It was hanging at one end of the fireplace, its tassel at the same level as the mantel. "Why didn't you pull that?" he asked. "I assume it rings somewhere in the hotel. You could have had someone come to your door."

"It doesn't work. And yes, I've complained already. Believe me, tomorrow morning it's at the top of my list of things to do."

"Tell me about Michael Donovan. What is he to you?"

Katy was ready to cry with frustration. "He's no one," she said tiredly.

"You know he's married."

"I know that very well."

"I wasn't certain. But perhaps it doesn't matter to you. After all, you were entertaining him in your dressing room."

"I was trying to throw him out. Your intervention was . . . oh, never mind." She was going to drop with exhaustion if he didn't let her go. "I can't play your game any longer, Logan. I need sleep. I'm going to bed."

"All right."

"All right? Just like that?"

"Don't get your hopes up, Katy. I'm coming with you."

She laughed nervously. "You're not serious."

"I'm afraid I am."

Looking for something to throw at him, Katy's eyes darted to objects at hand. A brass candlestick looked particularly inviting.

"I don't think you really want to do that," said

Logan, correctly divining her thoughts. "You wouldn't like the consequences."

Tears shimmered in Katy's eyes and this time she made no effort to hide them. "Damn you," she said quietly, her lower lip trembling. "Damn you to hell."

Without waiting for Logan's response, Katy went to her bedroom. She didn't bother trying to shut him out. When Logan came in behind her she ignored him. He astonished her by doing the same. He crossed her bedroom and headed for the bathing room, shutting the door behind him. Katy wasted no time trying to leave her suite. She ran back into the sitting room and pulled hard on the front door. The knob twisted but the door didn't open. She yanked harder, her palm slippery on the knob. The lock was jammed. Logan had done something to the lock! Katy collapsed against the door, sliding down it slowly until she was curled fetally at its base. She didn't know Logan had returned to the sitting room until she felt one of his arms circle her shoulders and the other slip under the backs of her knees.

"Put your arms around my neck, Katy," he said. His voice was gentle. "I'm only going to put you to bed."

"I don't want . . . I don't . . ."

"I know." He waited patiently. When Katy's arms finally eased around him, Logan stood and carried her into the bedroom. He put her down on the edge, pulled back the covers, and Katy crawled between them. "Do you always sleep in your robe?" he asked.

She shook her head. "I want to now."

"All right." He took a handkerchief from a pocket in his trousers and gave it to her. "But you don't have to use the sleeve to wipe your eyes. Go to sleep, Katy. We'll talk in the morning."

"Do you have to spend the night?"

"I think so. You see, I'm considering the merits of making you my mistress." He turned back the lamps in her bedroom. "Good night, Katy. Pleasant dreams."

Dumbfounded, Katy listened to Logan's light tread as he retreated into the bathing room. His *mistress!* That would destroy her! She'd never have the leading roles she wanted if Logan carried on a public love affair. Logan wouldn't settle for the proper, circumspect relationship she enjoyed with Victor. Katy felt helpless to act, afraid of Logan's response if she went to the police. And what if he were only bluffing? She didn't want to raise the alarm if Logan only wanted to torment her a little. That she could stand. He'd soon grow tired of his play the way a small boy grew bored with a caterpillar in a jar. By morning it could very well all be over . . . couldn't it?

Katy thought she would never sleep, but in truth she never heard Logan when he returned and stood over her, studying her face in a pale wash of moonshine. She never saw that his hands held a black lacquered box.

Logan knew there would be no music when he opened the lid. He ticked off the contents on mental fingers before looking. It was all there. She had saved everything: one kerchief, a spool of blue thread, two needles, a lice comb, chalk, six marbles, including four prized aggies, a watch fob, a deck of cards, and one spoon honed to a razor's edge.

The sweet aroma of hot chocolate teased Katy's senses. She wrinkled her nose, mouth watering as she caught the fragrances of bacon and cinnamon danish. She wished she could command this sort of dream more often, for certainly it was the most vivid dream

121

of recent memory. Stretching her legs, Katy rolled on her back, carrying her pillow with her. She hugged it and snuggled deeper under the covers.

"Wake up, Katy. I can see you licking your lips."

Katy's eyes opened abruptly. She saw Logan standing over her and she groaned softly. "It's true," she said, her voice still husky with sleep.

"Apparently."

"Oh, God."

"I've set up a table for breakfast," he said, pointing to the foot of the bed. "Unless you'd prefer eating where you are?"

"No," she said firmly. As far as Katy was concerned, the sooner she was out of bed, the better. She sat up, pushing away the pillow and throwing back the covers. "Where's my robe?" she asked, noting for the first time that she was no longer wearing it.

"I took it off you after you were sleeping. You looked uncomfortable. It was twisted all around you." He grinned, sitting down at the table and snapping open a linen napkin. "Don't worry. I won't hold my breath waiting for you to thank me." Logan pointed to the wardrobe. "I put it in there."

Katy found it, slipped it on, and stalked into the bathing room. She counted to ten, washed her face, cleaned her teeth, brushed and braided her hair, and counted to ten again. "I want you out of here this morning, Logan," she announced, standing in the doorway.

He didn't even look up from eating. "Your breakfast is getting cold."

"I mean it," she gritted.

"So do I. Your bacon is going to taste like month-old jerky if you don't eat it now." He bit off the end of one strip and chewed slowly, savoring it. "Be sensible, Katy. Don't deny yourself something to eat just because you don't like the company."

She sat down across from him. "I despise the company," she corrected.

Now he looked at her. His eyes were hard and a muscle worked in his cheek. "The feeling's mutual."

Katy was taken aback. She stared at Logan blankly for a moment, then she dropped her head and applied herself to eating. "Where did you get those clothes?" she asked when she could no longer stand the silence. Logan wasn't wearing his evening clothes any more. His brown wool frock coat was loosely cut and he wore it over a brown silk waistcoat, white shirt, and fawn trousers. They were his clothes, of that Katy had no doubt. The fit was exactly right and Logan not only looked comfortable but pleased with himself as well.

"I sent someone from the hotel round to my house this morning. I imagine it raised quite a fuss with Mrs. Brandywine—she's the housekeeper—but she's been through worse with Christian. My peccadilloes must seem mild by comparison."

"Don't apply for sainthood yet."

One half of Logan's mouth lifted in an appreciative, though mocking, grin. "By the way, I fixed the bellpull. Just in case you were wondering how I managed to order breakfast. I wouldn't suggest using it in order to evict me, however. It's quite possible the hotel staff will think we've had a tiff."

"I don't care what they think. They've seen it all before and they don't talk. That's what makes the Palace so popular with men like you and their mistresses. And since I'm not your mistress, and I pay my own way, I can have you thrown out of here on your Yankee ass if I've a mind to."

"You *used* to pay your own way. I confess, that surprised me. I'm afraid I assumed it was Victor or

123

Michael who saw to all your needs."

The slight emphasis that Logan placed on the word "all" did not go unnoticed. "You have a filthy mind," she snapped, "and it shouldn't . . . What do you mean I *used* to pay my own way. What have you done?"

Logan swallowed his bite of danish and took a sip of chocolate. He made a face. It was too sweet. He should never have refused the coffee. Setting down his cup, he said blandly, "I made a few inquiries. You were behind two weeks and I—"

"The management knows I'll pay!" she interrupted. "*Manners* is certain to have a lengthy—"

"As I was beginning to say, I wrote a draft for the two weeks you owe as well as for the next six months." He took a pocket watch out of his waistcoat, snapped it open, and glanced at the time. "Mr. Carstairs has already deposited the draft. It's quite official by this time. You're a kept woman, Katy Dakota."

Katy pushed her plate away and threw down her fork. "I don't have to stay here," she said. "You've bought yourself six months at the Chesterfield, Mr. Marshall. Alone!"

Logan didn't comment but he looked at Katy with new interest. Anger did not make Katy beautiful but it did make her arresting. The air fairly hummed with the resonance of her outrage. Splinters of gold shimmered in her dark brown eyes and the tips of her fingers were white where they were pressed to the tabletop. Her jaw was set firmly, her shoulders braced, and she looked quite capable of leaping across the table and clawing his face.

Logan wiped his mouth, then tossed the napkin on his plate. "If you'll excuse me," he said politely, pushing away from the table, "I have to be at the paper this morning. I'm already late."

He ducked in time to miss the plate Katy flung at his head. In fact, he managed to dodge all the missiles she fired in his direction on his way out of the suite. In the hallway he laughed, shaking his head as she fired another volley at the closed door. Walking away, past the wide-eyed stares of two maids polishing the hardwood floor, Logan credited himself with accomplishing everything he had set out to do. He'd warned her away from Christian and Jenny, kissed her within an inch of her life, and begun the ruination of her career. All in all, it was a satisfactory exercise.

"You did what?" Christian almost exploded where he stood and pounced across Logan's desk. He wasn't angry, just stunned. Behind him he used the heel of his shoe to shut the office door. This conversation wasn't meant for the two dozen employees milling around their desks in the large outer room, pretending to work as they attempted to get an earful. Christian pulled the shade on the window in the door.

"I really don't have to repeat myself, do I?" asked Logan. He was leaning back in his heavy oak chair, his feet propped on the edge of his desk. He was the source of calm in a room of turmoil, the eye in the center of a hurricane. Correspondence and files littered his desk. Dozens of notes of varying priority were staked on a block of wood with a spike going through it. Two floor-to-ceiling bookcases on opposite sides of Logan's desk were stuffed with books and more files. It wasn't unheard of to locate a file of important clippings inside a book. The volumes were arranged in no particular order that anyone could divine. The author's name wasn't a consideration, neither was title. Height of the book didn't matter since many of them ended up lying on their sides. Color of the binding didn't seem important. But it was an undeniable truth at the *Chronicle,* that if Logan Marshall needed to find something for himself or anyone else, he could locate it in just under ten seconds.

Christian moved aside a stack of recent newspapers from the room's only other chair, dropped them in the corner beside Logan's photography equipment, and sat down. "Perhaps a better question is why you would do such a thing. If I really wanted to paint her, Logan, I'd find a way around your scare-her-away-from-Christian strategy. I have a good idea that it's me you're protecting, not her, so the question is still why."

"I have my reasons."

"I can guess what they are. You're afraid that she's the woman who could put a wedge in my marriage."

Logan's brow rose fractionally and he raked a hand through his dark hair. "Something like that." He dropped his feet off the desktop and tilted forward in his chair. Opening the bottom left hand drawer of his desk, he pulled out a flask of bourbon, a glass, and offered his brother a drink.

"None for me." Christian frowned as Logan dropped the smudged tumbler back in the drawer and drank directly from the flask. No doubt he was overly sensitive to his brother's drinking because of his own bout with the bottle. He let the lecture pass, recalling how little good words had done for him. "You're assuming that I might be attracted to Miss Dakota," he said, returning to the subject at hand. "I have no idea what makes you think she's any different from the dozen or so women I've painted since

126

my marriage, but *I* can tell you that she's not. There's not a woman alive that could come between Jenny and me."

"You don't know Katy Mc—, excuse me, Katy *Dakota*."

"No, but it's clear that you do."

"We have a history," Logan said tersely.

"You've never mentioned her."

Logan shrugged. He had mentioned her, many times in fact, but in conversation she was always Mary Catherine McCleary. "Trust me on this one, Christian. Don't paint her. She'll make your life hell. Jenny's, too."

"That's an interesting point. If you're so certain of that, why make it appear that she's your mistress? It is *appear*, isn't it? You don't intend to make her your mistress in fact."

"God, no!"

He said it so vehemently that Christian almost believed him. It was clear at least that Logan believed himself. "You're not going to tell me about her, are you?"

Logan shook his head. He capped the flask and dropped it back in the drawer.

"You know this isn't as it was in our father's time, don't you? It used to be accepted that *actress* and *whore* were practically synonymous. The public demands a little more moral prudence these days. Surely Miss Dakota is—"

"Don't trouble yourself working up a defense for her. She doesn't deserve one."

"I'm not so sure. Last night after you sent for your clothes, Jenny got curious. She found the paper with the story about Miss Dakota in it and made me read it. It's hardly the lurid past or very public present that some of the actresses like to cultivate. Other

127

than her relationship with Victor Donovan, the nature of which is a matter of speculation, she appears to be a very private person. Prior to the leading role in *Manners* she played mostly ingenue roles and some character parts. It's only recently that she's become what the public refers to as a personality. An affair with you could stop her from getting the parts she covets or her talent deserves. Do you really want to ruin that for her?"

"Yes."

Christian was silent a moment, measuring his brother's resolve. There was no doubt that Logan was set on his path, but the direction alarmed Christian. "Your plan could come back to kick you in the head like an old mule," he said.

"You mean that her career could benefit from the notoriety."

"No, I mean that you could fall in love."

Footsteps in the hallway alerted Katy to a visitor. She abandoned the chair she was huddled in. Her wine velvet dress whispered against her petticoats as she crossed to the door and waited. Even though she was prepared for it, the pounding startled her. After a second's hesitation she opened the door and ushered in Victor.

"What is it, Katy dear? Your message said it was urgent." He dropped his hat on a nearby table, then took her hands in his and held them out at her sides. He examined her critically, taking in everything from her disheveled honey hair to her wine kid slippers. Her face was drawn and anxious. "Your hands are so cold." He squeezed them gently, then brought them together and warmed them in the cup of his palms. "Come, let's sit down. I see you have hot tea waiting for me. Sure, and you've had none yourself, I'll wager."

Katy allowed herself to be led to the settee. Victor took the white shawl that was lying over one arm and drew it around her shoulders. He was such a dear, wonderful man, she thought. Where would she be in this city if he hadn't taken her under his wing? "It always seems I'm taking advantage of you, Victor. Ever since that first night. Remember? I had my entire face pressed to Mrs. Harmer's bakery shop window."

Victor's smile was indulgent, tender. He was fond of the memory. He poured them both tea and handed Katy a cup. "I have a weakness for starving young women with their eye on Mrs. Harmer's best pastries. Even so, you never took advantage of my weakness. You never asked for anything."

"I didn't have to. You just kept giving." First it had been a meal, five courses in a restaurant that would have shown her the door if she had tried to walk in alone. Then he offered her employment behind the fabric counter at V. I. Donovan's. Victor made it possible for her to leave work for important auditions. He helped her rehearse for them in her tiny room on Jones Street in the Village, which he also helped her find. The day she won her first role at the Rialto, Victor took her to Mrs. Harmer's and bought everything behind the glass.

"I'd like to keep giving," he said, a little embarrassed by Katy's gratitude. "Tell me why you sent for me. Is it Michael? Has he been bothering you?"

"No, not Michael."

"My daughter-in-law, then. Michael's filled her head full of notions about us. She doesn't know the half of Michael's interests, but she thinks she knows all about mine."

Katy set her cup down. "No, Victor, you have it all wrong. I probably shouldn't have even bothered you. I don't know where to start."

Victor fingered his iron gray sidewhiskers absently, then smoothed the ends of his thick mustache. "Anywhere," he said. "I'm listening."

She owed him a full explanation, she knew that. Her message had drawn him away in the middle of his work. He was still wearing the wire-rimmed spectacles he used for close work and was too vain to wear in public. He'd cared enough about her welfare to forget vanity. "What can you tell me about Logan Marshall?"

The question startled and disturbed Victor but he answered because he saw it was important to Katy. "I take it you mean in addition to what I told you last night."

"Yes, please."

Victor sat back against the curved arm of the sofa and reached in his vest pocket for a cigar. He held it up, asking Katy a question with his eyes, and when she didn't object, he lit it. "I'm not certain what you want to know," he began, "but I can tell you that before the war there were four Marshall brothers. They all fought, but Christian and Logan were the only ones to survive. Their mother was also a casualty. She was struck down by a fever she contracted in one of the hospitals." Victor exhaled slowly. The pungent smoke wreathed his head. "God, but she was a fine woman. I don't think her husband ever recovered from her death. Harrison threw himself into his work with a vengeance and whatever bond existed between him and Christian was severed when Cathy died."

Trying not to appear overanxious, Katy asked, "What about Logan?"

"It's difficult to explain about that one. He wasn't around then. I believe the family had some knowledge that he had been captured by the Confederates, but when there was no news for such a long time, Christian and his father began to assume Logan was dead."

"Yes, but what about when Logan returned after the war? How did he and his father get on then?"

Victor shook his head. "Logan didn't return home until three years after the war was over. His father died almost a year before that. Who's to say how they would have got on." Through a blue-gray haze of smoke Victor studied Katy thoughtfully. "Why is it a concern?"

Katy didn't answer. It was a lifetime ago, she thought, but she clearly remembered telling Logan that nothing would change for him after the war. He would go back to New York, to his family and friends and the newspaper, and everything would be as it was. She had said it to hurt him, to show him that while he had been responsible for the suffering of others, he would manage to come through the war relatively unscathed. "Then he didn't know about his mother's death . . . or his father's," she said quietly.

"No, none of it. There was a brother who fell at Gettysburg with Christian. Logan didn't know about that either."

"But why?" she demanded. In her lap Katy's hands were clenched. "Why didn't he go home after the war? Why wait three years?" That's not my fault, she wanted to say. I didn't make him stay away.

"In a manner of speaking, Logan *was* dead," Victor went on. "At least to those who knew him."

"You're talking in riddles. I don't understand what you mean."

"I probably shouldn't be telling you this because it's

131

not common knowledge, but sometime during the war Logan lost his memory. It was not that his family had forgotten him, but the other way around."

"Lost his . . ." Her voice died and Katy closed her eyes briefly as the knot in her stomach tightened. "How could that happen?" she whispered.

"Katy, I don't think we should be talking about Logan. It's obvious that this conversation is upsetting to you. Why don't you tell me what's—"

"No." Her hand unfolded as it sliced through the air, cutting Victor off. "I need to hear, Victor. Tell me what you know about it."

Victor put down his cigar long enough to pour Katy more tea. He forced the cup into her cold hands and lifted it toward her mouth until she voluntarily took over. "I really don't know very much. I certainly don't understand anything about Logan's memory loss. I believe it happened when he was in prison. You've heard of Andersonville, haven't you?"

"I've heard of it," she said, her eyes bleak.

"He spent time there. I don't even know how much, but by all reports that filtered out about that place, it was a sentence in hell. When the prisoners were released, Logan left there not knowing who he was or where he came from. I'm afraid if you want details you'll have to talk to him or his family. I only know that after a few years he remembered something and it brought him back home. Since his return he's put all his energy into the *Chronicle*."

"He's not married, then?"

"No."

"Betrothed?"

"Not to my knowledge. I've never heard his name linked with a particular woman for very long. And he's not a, er, a—"

"A womanizer?"

132

"Precisley. He's also not one for spending a lot of time at the club or social events. Don't misunderstand, he's not a hermit, but even when he's out one gets the impression he'd rather be somewhere else."

"Where does he live?"

"In the home he grew up in, with his brother and sister-in-law and their son. It's probably truer to say that he eats and sleeps there on occasion. I understand he lives at the paper. In that he's very much like the man his father was." Victor flicked his cigar over a cobalt blue ash tray and leaned toward Katy. "Now, suppose you tell me why this sudden interest in Logan Marshall. How do you know him?"

Katy took a sip of her tea, set down the cup, and laughed a trifle nervously. Gaining composure was a hard fight, but she won. "It should be obvious from my questions that I don't know him. Last night he stopped backstage after the play to say that he enjoyed my performance."

"You didn't mention that when we saw him at Delmonico's later."

"No, I didn't."

"You also didn't mention that Michael had been to see you. I found out this morning at breakfast."

Katy could just imagine the scene that had occurred in Victor's home. Ria, not understanding Michael's real motives, would have supported her husband. The conversation would have been conducted in cool, civil tones that made even lies seem reasonable and rational. "I didn't want to upset you and I knew that it would. Your son doesn't like me, Victor. I've accepted that even if you haven't." It wasn't precisely a lie. Katy believed that Michael didn't like her and she had accepted it. He wanted her in his bed but his desire had nothing to do with liking her. Sometimes Michael threatened to tell his

133

father exactly what he wanted from Katy, but as far as she knew he never had. "Michael thinks I'm interested in your money. He wants me to stay away from you."

"Michael thinks a lot of things that aren't true. If he'd listen to anything I've ever said about you, he'd know he was wrong — about all of them."

"It's all right. Really, I don't mind. He's only trying to look out for your interests."

"I'm not senile," Victor snapped. "And he's looking out for his own interests, not mine. Sometimes I think he—" Victor stopped himself, jamming his cigar into the ash tray.

"Yes?"

"Never mind. It was a foolish thought. As you said, Michael doesn't even like you."

"That's right. Anyway, our conversation last night was brief. Mr. Marshall interrupted us and he and Michael went to Georgia's for a drink."

"Michael didn't tell me that."

"He probably didn't think it was important. Surely there's nothing remarkable about him sharing a few drinks with Mr. Marshall."

"No . . . I suppose not."

But he was thoughtful and unconvinced. Katy could see that much. "They're friends, aren't they?"

"Not friends precisely, but as you say, there's nothing remarkable about them going off together." Yet it was odd, Victor thought, because Michael had never had many kind things to say about Logan Marshall. To his son's way of thinking, Logan's character was flawed because he was too single-minded and too wholly independent. Victor had fervently wished any number of times that Michael had those same character flaws in his professional life. It occurred to him to wonder if Michael could be jealous of all that

134

Logan had accomplished at the *Chronicle*. It was something worth considering. "So, your interest in Logan Marshall stems from your meeting last evening? He must have made a deep impression on you."

"I think I made an impression on him." Katy stood up and walked to the fireplace. Turning, she leaned against the mantelpiece and wrapped her arms around her middle. "He came to my suite last night, Victor."

"You let him in?"

"I, umm, yes . . . I let him in."

"And?" He was sitting up very straight now, watching her intently over the rim of his spectacles.

"And we talked."

"And?" he prompted again.

"Mr. Marshall wants me to be his mistress."

Victor let out his breath slowly. The bottoms of his glasses fogged. He took them off, folded them carefully, and put them in his waistcoat pocket. "What did you say to that?"

Katy hugged herself more tightly. "Victor, you don't understand. He didn't ask. He demanded. He's not giving me any choice. I was a little behind on the rent for the suite and he found out and he paid it. *Paid it!* He's acting as if it's what I want! But I don't, Victor. I don't want anything to do with him. He frightens me and I don't know what I'm supposed to do. That's why I sent for you. Can you do something? Can you make him leave me alone?"

During her agitated speech Victor had come to stand in front of Katy. By the time she finished talking his arms were around her and her head was resting against his shoulder. "What would you have me do, Katy dear?"

"Something . . . anything."

135

Victor said nothing for several minutes. "Look at me, Katy," he said, lifting her chin with his forefinger. "There's something you're not telling me. This man you're describing is not the Logan Marshall I'm familiar with. I knew his father. I know how the boys were raised. Logan wouldn't do this—"

Katy pulled away from Victor. The look she gave him betrayed her hurt. "Are you calling me a liar?"

"You didn't let me finish. I was trying to say that Logan wouldn't do this without a reason. There's something you're not telling me. What is it, Katy? How can I know how to help you if you don't tell me everything?"

Feeling trapped, Katy slipped past Victor, and walked to the far side of the room. She fiddled with one of the music boxes on a walnut endtable, running her fingers around the scrolled edge of the box. "I sent him to Andersonville," she said softly.

"Pardon?" Victor cupped his ear. "I don't think I heard cor—"

She put the music box down and spun on her heel. Her skirt swayed against her legs. "I sent him to Andersonville!" Katy had never raised her voice to Victor and she was appalled to realize she had just screamed at him. "Oh, God, Victor, I'm sorry. Forgive me. Everything that's happening . . . I'm not handling it very well, am I?"

"All things considered, I'd say you're doing wonderfully." He made no move to come near her. He didn't want her to see that he was the one shaking now. The idea that was spinning in his mind had the power to make him feel lightheaded, giddy, and younger than he had felt in a score of years. If Logan Marshall had been in front of him, Victor would have thanked him, not railed at him. "Will you tell me about Andersonviille?" he asked when he could

136

trust himself to speak without giving away his excitement.

But Katy couldn't talk about it. She opened her mouth to say something and her throat simply closed in over the words. In more than seven years she had never spoken of the incident that had taken Logan from King's Creek to Andersonville. "I sent him there," was all she said.

"Katy, you were a child then. What were you, fourteen . . . fifteen years old?"

"Fifteen. And I knew what I was doing." All of it, she thought. I knew exactly what I was doing. "He wandered onto my aunt's land in Virginia," she said. "He holed up in the barn. I found him and I . . . I delayed him so he couldn't leave. Aunt Peggy captured him and I made certain he was sent to prison. He wants revenge, Victor. That's why he's doing this. He wants to hurt me for what I did to him. He's not smitten with me and he's not acting impulsively. Logan Marshall is calculating and shrewd."

Victor took a step forward. His hands were balled in fists. "Last night, when he came here, did he . . . did he . . ."

"Rape me?" she asked. "No. I don't think he really wants me like that." But she remembered the kiss and she wondered. "He hates me. He's never forgotten what I did to him and he hates me for it."

Victor relaxed, uncurling his fingers. "Logan is certain he has the right woman?" he asked.

"He's certain. I never denied it to him. He's not changed so much since I saw him last and I suspect the same is true for me." Katy's large brown eyes made a mute appeal to Victor. "Please, Victor. I need your help. I don't want Logan Marshall in my life."

"I suppose I could have him killed," said Victor.

Katy's head shot up and she blinked hard. "What did you say?"

"I know some people who know some people," he went on. "Down in the Bowery anything's possible. An accident would remove him from your life permanently."

"You're frightening me, Victor. Stop talking like that. I don't want anyone to have an accident—even Logan Marshall."

"You could leave New York."

"I've thought of that. But I have as much right to be here as he does."

"Well then, you could marry me."

"Victor!" She was ready to tell him to be serious, then she realized he was. She swallowed the words that would have belittled his proposal and horribly hurt the man. Katy found herself reaching behind her for the striped brocade chair. She sat down uneasily. "Marry you," she said softly. "Victor, I would never let you make that kind of sacrifice for me."

He smiled faintly. "I'm not a sacrificing man," he said. "I wouldn't be giving up anything."

"But you could still meet someone, someone you could really love."

Drawing up an ottoman, Victor sat near Katy. He rested his forearms on his knees. "If I may be honest, Katy, then it's you who would be sacrificing. What would you gain from marrying me except a way out of your current dilemma?"

"You mean besides access to the considerable Donovan fortune and a stepson who'd kill me before he'd let me have a penny of it?"

Victor laughed. "Besides that."

"I'd be the wife of a loving, gentle man," she said softly, solemnly. "I would be respected and treated kindly and cared for as if I were vital to his very happiness."

"Yes," he said. "You would be."

Katy began to shake her head, prepared to tell him that in spite of the honor he had brought her, marriage was not the answer. She said nothing, however, because Victor touched her wrist and held her attention with his entreating gaze. "Don't be so quick to turn me down, Katy. Give yourself some time to think. We wouldn't have to stay married forever, if that's what's bothering you. You could divorce me if you found someone you could really be happy with."

"I could be happy with you," she said.

"I meant someone you could love."

"I do love you, but not—"

"Don't say it." He couldn't bear to hear that she didn't love him as a woman could love a man, with exclusive, intimate love. "It doesn't matter to me."

"But—"

"I wouldn't press you in the marriage," he said. To make certain she understood his meaning, he added, "We would have adjoining, but separate, bedrooms and you would have the key."

"You'd do that for me?" she asked, her brows drawing together. She remembered last night and how he had stood behind her at the vanity with his fingers in her hair. The memory of that light, sensual touch was so clear that she unconsciously raised one hand to her nape. He wanted her. She couldn't deny it to herself any longer. "It wouldn't be right, Victor. That's not the sort of marriage you should have."

He grinned a little self-consciously and tugged on his blackened mustache. The look he cast in Katy's direction was endearingly sheepish. "I'm not saying that I'd give up hope. I'd probably try to seduce you several times a day. You should know that."

139

She laughed because he meant her to. "Several times a day? You flatter me."

"Most likely I'm flattering myself. At my age, who knows if I'd have the strength to follow through."

Embarrassed by his candid comment, Katy looked away. "I don't think separate bedrooms would be necessary, Victor. If I decide to marry you, then we'll be *married*. I won't have it any other way."

Victor's heart raced. Far from flat-out refusing him, she was considering his proposal now. "You wouldn't regret becoming my wife, Katy. I can promise you that. You'd never want for anything."

"That isn't what's important to me. You know that. What about my acting? Would you allow me to perform if we were married?"

Of course, he thought, she would want to do that. "On the stage?" he asked.

"Naturally. I don't want to be confined to drawing room dramas for the amusement of your friends. My singing is only passable, Victor. And you know I don't play the piano or paint. I'm afraid I have little in the way of social accomplishments. But I *can* act. That's what I want to do, what I've always wanted to do. If that can't be part of our marriage, then there can be no mar—"

"There's no reason you can't continue your career," he interrupted. There would be a scandal, he knew, but he was prepared to weather it if Katy could do the same. At his age, he simply didn't care what others thought. Not if he could have Katy. He saw she was going to raise another objection. To cut her off, he pointed out the clock on the mantel and commented on the time. "Shouldn't you be leaving for the theatre? I thought you and Mr. Easton were going to go over some blocking."

As a diversion, it was successful. Katy put everything else to the back of her mind and kept it there while she rehearsed with Anthony Easton, went over a few costume changes with her dresser, and applied her makeup for her evening performance. It was only when she stepped on stage and saw Logan Marshall occupying an orchestra seat left center of stage that everything folded in on her.

She didn't remember a thing about her performance, but the audience judged it a triumph, rising to its collective feet and offering loud, spontaneous approval.

Beyond the footlights she saw Logan. He was sitting. Smiling. And his eyes were cold enough to make her shiver.

Chapter Five

"Are you feeling quite yourself this evening?" Jane asked as she helped Katy out of her gown. "Here, let me undo these corset strings. Might be that I pulled them too tight. Heaven knows, I shouldn't. It's reed-thin you are now. I thought you were going to faint just as the last curtain came down. Remarked on it to Billy Batton, I did. He agreed with me—for once. Can't say that this is a matter where I wanted his agreement."

Katy murmured occasionally as Jane chattered on. She held a cold compress over her eyes and prayed that the throbbing in her temples would go away. The fragrances in the room were overpowering. Baskets of flowers dominated every available space. Roses were very popular—red, white, and yellow—it didn't matter. Men from the audience sent them to express everything from passionate devotion to admiration for her performance. Scattered among the bouquets were notes begging for Katy's company at dinner. Those invitations generally meant there would be a later one begging for her company in bed. Katy never responded to them any more.

Tension eased slightly when Jane plucked the

pins from her hair, brushed it out, and redid it in a braid that was soft and loose and fell over Katy's left shoulder.

"Do you want help with your greasepaint?" asked Jane. Her dimpled hands moved swiftly over the surface of Katy's vanity, organizing the bottles and tins and vials with the sure command of a general. Everything stood at attention. Without waiting for Katy's answer, Jane began applying untinted grease to Katy's face, rubbing it in gently to remove her face paint.

Katy dropped her compress on the vanity but she kept her eyes closed and her head tilted back against Jane's supporting forearm. "How do you think it went tonight?" she asked. "I was concerned about the new blocking. I missed a cue in the second act. I should have gone to the sofa when Anthony began his speech."

"No one noticed. I'm sure I didn't. Don't you listen to the audience?" Jane was watching her employer consideringly as she wiped away the paint. "They loved the play this evening and they especially loved you. Can't you feel their approval when everything goes well?"

"I don't want them to love me and I don't act for their approval."

Jane's hand stilled momentarily, caught off guard by the vehemence with which Katy spoke. "Then why?"

"I act for myself," she said, pushing Jane's hand away and sitting up. She finished removing the greasepaint herself. "For a few hours each night I get to become someone else, wear another person's

143

skin and feel and think things that are so different, and sometimes not so different, from things I think and feel. And when I do it, I want to do it well. Not for them, but for me. You can't imagine how important it is to be someone else."

Jane was thoughtful as she began putting away Katy's gowns, but she said nothing. It was a fanciful notion, she decided, that Katy Dakota acted because she wanted to escape. Escape what? As near as Jane could tell the actress had everything a woman could possibly desire. Why should she want to be someone else? "Will you want to wear the wine-colored gown home?" she asked. "I can lay it out for you."

"Yes, that will be fine." She sighed her annoyance when someone knocked at the door. "See who that is, Jane. Please, no visitors I don't want to see anyone." Katy went behind the dressing screen so she would be out of view while Jane made excuses for her.

Jane closed the door with the toe of her shoe. Her arms were full with a large bouquet of daisies. She held them up for Katy to see. "Lovely, aren't they? Don't bother yourself, I'll get a vase. I know there's one around here somewhere. There's a card. Shall I read it?"

Without hesitation Katy said, "They're from Victor." Victor would send daisies, she thought, smiling to herself. They were spring-fresh, clean and bright. Better, they had none of the cloying perfume fragrance of the roses. "He knows I like daisies."

"Maybe he does," said Jane. "But so does someone named Logan. That's who sent these daisies. That wouldn't be Mr. Logan Marshall, would it?"

"What?" There *had* to be some mistake!

Before Jane could respond, there was another knock at the door. "No peace tonight," she said, throwing up her hands.

Katy went back to dressing and paid little attention to Jane's conversation at the door. She didn't know Jane had lost the battle until she heard an unfamiliar woman's voice apologize for the intrusion. Standing on tiptoe, Katy looked over the top of the dressing screen. Her mouth went dry when she saw Jenny Marshall standing in the open threshold. "It's all right, Jane. You can leave for the night. I'd like to talk to Mrs. Marshall alone."

Jane's eyes darted between the two women. The reassuring glance she got from Katy decided her. She slipped past Jenny Marshall and left the room, shutting the door quietly behind her.

"Please," said Katy, "make yourself comfortable. There's a pot of tea on the stand over there. It's probably still warm. I'll be done in a moment."

Jenny was surprised and her eyes widened in reaction. After dealing with the dragon who guarded Katy's privacy, Jenny hadn't expected to be warmly received by the actress herself. "I admit I'm curious," said Jenny. "How is it that you know me?"

"I noticed you last evening in Delmonico's. I asked my escort who you were."

"Yes, I noticed you there also. Victor Donovan is a friend of the family." Jenny dropped her beaded bag on the chaise and poured herself a cup of tea.

145

"I promise I won't take much of your time, Miss Dakota. I came because I want to know if you would permit me to make some photographic studies of you."

There was no response from behind the screen for a few moments. When Katy finished buttoning her gown she stepped out into view. "Mr. .Marhall put you up to this, didn't he?" she asked coldly. "It's some sort of test."

"Why, no, my husband doesn't know I've come."

"I mean Logan."

"Heavens, no. Logan was against this from the beginning. That's why I'm here."

"I don't think I understand," Katy said slowly. She admitted to herself that Jenny Marshall appeared very innocent, but it was a look that Katy herself had perfected on stage. "Logan didn't send you here to see if I would throw you out?"

Jenny's soft doe eyes widened. "Why would he do that?"

"You tell me."

Jenny set her cup down and brought her chin up. She spoke quickly and evenly, proving that she wasn't intimidated by Katy's frosty accents. "I believe we're at cross purposes here, Miss Dakota. Let me explain more clearly why I've come." Jenny briefly described the conversation she had shared with Logan and Christian at Delmonico's. "I thought the matter was settled," she went on, "when we left the restaurant. Logan was going to ask you to pose for the photographs so my husband could work on some sketches and preliminary paintings during our voyage. Apparently Logan never mentioned any of this to you. I assumed that he had because he told me that you had refused to pose. I came to ask you to reconsider."

"Logan lied to you."

"Apparently. I suppose he has his reasons."

"You're quick to defend him."

"He's family," Jenny said without apology. "Whatever I think of Logan's actions I'll tell him myself—in private. I take it that he did come to see you yesterday. When he sent someone to the house to get clothes for him I assumed that he was—"

"You assume too much, perhaps." Katy sat down at the vanity and fastened pearl drop earrings on her lobes. "But yes, he was with me. All night. Does that shock you, Mrs. Marshall?"

A tiny smile played at the edges of Jenny's beautiful mouth. "I'm not Logan's keeper," she said. "If you didn't object to his presence, then why on earth would I?"

"Why do you want your husband to paint me?" Katy asked. "Aren't you afraid I'll find Logan's brother equally attractive? Aren't you afraid I might seduce him?"

"It's obvious that you're spoiling for a fight, Miss Dakota, and have been since I first made my request. Allow me to say this before I leave: I would be very surprised if you didn't find Christian attractive, and I would scratch out your eyes if you did anything to compromise him or my marriage." Jenny picked up her purse and turned to go.

"Wait!" Katy called after her, then more softly, "Please, wait. I've been unconscionably rude to you. You were right, I'm afraid. I've been spoiling for a fight. Won't you sit down? I'd like to start over."

Jenny hesitated while she took measure of the actress's sincerity. It was Katy's uncertainty, her sudden insecurity, that decided Jenny. "All right," she said.

Katy cleared the edge of the chaise longue of scripts and clothes to make room for her guest. Once she assured herself that Jenny was comfortable, Katy took some tea for herself. "Since Logan didn't ask me to sit for the photographs, it seems obvious that he doesn't want me to do them. I don't think he would approve of you being here."

"Approve? Perhaps not. But neither would he stop me. Logan doesn't have those kind of rights with me."

Why does he think he has them with me, Katy wondered unhappily. But she knew that he held everything she valued hostage. A few words from Logan and the entire city would know that she had been responsible for his imprisonment. The Yankees had forgiven much since the end of the war, but Katy doubted they would be so generous in her case. Not with Logan Marshall, her favorite son, as her victim. "Who would take the photographs?" she asked.

"I would. As you say, it's rather obvious that Logan is against the pictures, though I don't know why. I see no reason for him to even know about it, do you? My husband has a studio on the third floor of our home. There's a darkroom there that Logan and I both use for developing pictures. None of the staff would even comment on you visiting the studio with me." Jenny glanced around Katy's dressing room and paid particular attention to the vanity. "I could duplicate this setting fairly easily in the studio. You'd have to bring your pots of rouge and powder, whatever you use to paint your face. That's the type of photographs I have in mind, something of a study while you begin to grow into your character."

"My character is not particularly likeable."

"Not in the beginning, she's not. But the way you play her she has a certain vulnerability. You've fleshed out the character, made her a real person. She's wicked, yes. Wonderfully wicked, in fact. She's also very very human." Jenny laughed at herself. "Why am I telling you this? You must have realized it. After all, you practically created her."

"The playwright wouldn't want to hear that," Katy said, smiling. "But I thank you. So . . . we do these photographs in your husband's studio. He won't mind?"

"I'll present him with a *fait accompli*. He'll see the photographs after we've started our voyage. Both he and Logan will be at the paper tomorrow; there's no possibility that either will find out."

"Will I be paid for the sittings?" asked Katy.

Jenny successfully hid her surprise. She hadn't thought money would be an issue. "Of course." She named a generous figure. "That's just for the sittings. When Christian needs you for the actual painting there will be another payment. Naturally that won't be until we return from Europe. You also should know that he may not choose to paint you at all. He's been known to change his mind about models."

"I understand," she said slowly, wondering if Logan could influence his brother against doing the paintings. "You say we would do the sittings tomorrow?"

"Yes. Come round to the house at ten. We're on the northwest corner of Thirty-eighth and Fifth. It has an iron fence circling the property and—"

"I'm certain I can find it."

"You'll come, then?"

Logan be damned. "Yes," she said.

Jenny nodded. She stood, paused while she considered her question, then asked in a rush, "Do you know why Logan doesn't want my husband to paint you?"

"Yes."

Jenny waited for more information but Katy offered none. She pressed on. "Will you tell me?"

"It's well known that your husband's subjects are particularly beautiful," she said.

"So?" Jenny was bewildered.

"So? Don't you understand? Your brother-in-law knows how ugly I am."

Jenny's frown deepened. Clearly Katy believed what she said and that struck Jenny as powerfully sad. Jenny excused herself quietly as Katy turned back to her mirror. All the way home she mulled over the puzzle of Katy Dakota.

Logan was having much the same thoughts as his sister-in-law. He was lounging on the sofa in Katy's sitting room, waiting for her to return from the theatre. Occasionally his eyes would shift to the cobalt blue ash tray and the cigar butt that rested there. The faint odor of cigar smoke still permeated the room.

In his hands he held one of her delicate music boxes. He opened the lid, listened to the music for a moment, then closed it again. It played "When Johnny Comes Marching Home." A strange tune for someone who had no love for Yankees. Almost as strange as the fact that she had kept his black lacquered box all these years.

Logan put the music box down when he heard the key turn in the lock. His casual, proprietary posture was for Katy's benefit as she entered her suite. His half-smile and coolly colored eyes mocked her surprise and frustration.

"Don't you have some place you'd rather be?" she asked, tossing her coat on the back of a chair. "Some place where you're wanted?"

"I like it here," he said. "I've paid for it."

"I'll have your money tomorrow."

"Oh? Did they pay your back salary or did you pick Victor Donovan's pockets?"

Katy ignored him. She went into her bedroom and immediately became incensed when she saw his belongings on her dresser, in her wardrobe, and on her nightstand. "You're not staying here!" she yelled. She gathered up some of the clothes that he had not put away. When she turned, Logan was standing in the doorway.

She pitched the pile of clothes at him. "I mean it, Logan! I want you out of here! You have no rights where I'm concerned."

151

Amused rather than riled, Logan hunkered down and picked up his clothing. He folded each item neatly, then placed them on the seat of the rocker. "You'll have to clear me some space in the chiffonier. I couldn't decide what items you would want to take out so I left everything as it was."

"You want space?" asked Katy, her voice dangerously soft. She went to the dresser, pulled out the top drawer and upended it. Soft cotton handkerchiefs drifted to the floor. Lacy camisoles and lilac sachets scattered. The second drawer met with the same end as did the third and fourth. "Take all the space you need, Mr. Marshall."

"Thank you," he said pleasantly.

Katy stormed past him on her way to the bathing room. She slammed the door, locking it, and let the water run to drown out the sound of Logan's off-tune whistling. Staying in the tub until the water turned cold gave Katy time to map her strategy. When she emerged, dressed in a cream satin robe and plain cotton nightshift, she went directly to the spare bedroom on the opposite side of the suite. Passing him, Katy pretended not to see that Logan had made himself comfortable in her own bed. She did notice, however, that he had made no attempt to clean up her mess.

Katy turned back the bed covers and plumped the pillow. She crawled into bed and waited to see what Logan would do. She fell asleep waiting.

Early morning sunshine filtered through the sheer window curtains and made a lacy pattern of light and heat on Katy's face. She smiled faintly, stretching with the abandon and trust of a child, and turned on her side. That was when she came up short, staring into the dark, impenetrable gaze of Logan Marshall. His eyes grazed her face, studying her sleep-washed features. She knew that he had been watching her for some time and that his normally light-colored eyes were dark for one reason: he had decided he wanted her after all.

Katy started to move away and discovered that Logan was holding the end of her braid in a tight fist. Afraid now, she held herself very still. She saw his eyes skim the planes of her cheeks, her nose, and come to rest on her mouth. Breathing was difficult. She fought the urge to wet her lips.

"When you're sleeping I can almost forget what a treacherous bitch you are," he said. He closed his eyes, released her hair, and rolled away. "God, but you make me want to hurt you . . . really *hurt* you." Sitting up, Logan threw his legs over the side of the bed. He rested his elbows on his knees and his head in his hands. He raked his hair in an absent gesture.

Katy stared at his naked back. Her eyes drifted across his taut shoulders and down the ridged length of his spine. His skin was smooth, shades lighter than bronze but darker than most men who spent their days indoors. Just above the line of his drawstring drawers, near the base of his spine, there were two dimples. Angel thumbprints. She wished she hadn't noticed them. For some odd reason they made her want to cry.

Logan got up. He took some clothes from the chiffionier. "I'm going to work," he said. "It's early yet. Go back to sleep." He disappeared into the dressing room and then into the bathroom. When he returned, Katy was sitting up in bed. On the table at the foot of the bed was a pot of coffee and two covered dishes. From the aroma, Logan suspected bacon and biscuits. "Did you order this for me?" he asked. His voice was soft and gritty at the same time, like the tide over sand.

Nodding, Katy put aside the script she was reading. "I've never walked in my sleep," she said, pointing to her surroundings. "I suspect I didn't last night either."

Logan sat at the table and poured himself some coffee. It was hot and strong, just the way he liked it. "You didn't. I brought you in here after you fell asleep."

"Why?"

"In the event that one of the Donovans should come visiting, I didn't want to be caught with my pants up—so to speak. It would be rather difficult to prove you were my mistress with you there and me here."

"If you had asked me I would have told you I wasn't expecting anyone."

"That didn't stop me from coming here."

"No," she said quietly. "No, it didn't."

Logan uncovered both dishes. Steam rose from the biscuits. He cut one in half and buttered it.

"What do I have to do to get rid of you?" she asked.

Logan concentrated on his bacon. "Did you have anything in particular in mind?" he asked, infuriatingly calm. "Other than killing me, that is."

That he should hit on the first solution Victor

154

presented her caused Katy to gasp softly.

Enjoying her discomfort, Logan finished his bacon and licked his fingers slowly, giving the activity a certain erotic nuance that Katy could not fail to grasp. "So you *had* thought of it," he said, turning in his chair to face her. "Too bad. You had the opportunity to make that happen once before. Instead, you sent me to hell."

Katy felt pinned to the headboard by Logan's hard, winter-cold stare. Yet she was also relieved that at last the subject had been broached by him. "I thought you would never speak of it," she said in a rush, imploring him to listen to her. "There's something I've been wanting to tell you about that day . . . something you should know."

One of Logan's eyebrows kicked up in lazy regard. "Oh? Sorry, but it will have to wait." He examined his pocket watch, holding it up for her to see the time. "I'm going to be late for a meeting if I don't leave now. You have a performance this evening?"

Nothing of Katy's urge to scream showed on her face. The only hint of her anger was in her short, sibilant response. "Yesss," she said.

"I'll see you afterward. Thanks for breakfast."

Katy watched him shrug into his jacket and straighten his waistcoat. He glanced in the mirror once just to brush back the hair at his temples with his fingertips. Then he approached the bed. Katy felt the lift of thumb and forefinger just below her chin. She could have resisted the pressure he applied to raise her face toward him, but she didn't. He bent his head.

155

The kiss was neither gentle nor hard. But it was possessive, undeniably a mark of ownership. His mouth was warm, tasting faintly of coffee. His lips were firm and the edge of his tongue played briefly with the line of her upper lip.

When Logan stepped back he studied Katy for a moment. Her beautifully expressive eyes were wide and luminous with a faint sheen of tears. Her mouth was damp. Two coins of color appeared on her cheeks. "Now do you wish you had let your friends hang me, Katy?"

She blinked and a single tear fell. "No," she said. "I don't wish it."

"You will," he said. "You'll come to wish you had never betrayed me."

By the time Katy found her voice, Logan was long gone from the suite. "You're not the only one who was betrayed, Logan Marshall."

Katy stopped at the theatre to pick up her face paints and one of the gowns she wore in the drama. Outside the theatre she hailed a hansom cab to take her to Marshall House. She arrived just minutes before ten o'clock. The driver helped her down from the carriage and offered to carry her things to the front door, but Katy declined, wanting time alone to compose herself before entering the mansion.

Katy wondered how many times she had passed this brownstone without knowing that Logan Marshall lived in it. Dozens, at least. In the future, she thought, she would go out of her way to avoid it.

There was nothing singular about Marshall House to distinguish it from its neighbors. It bore the mark of old money, the solid, grandiose design that stated wealth but fell short of ostentatious vulgarity. The property's privacy was guarded by a spiked iron fence and an elaborate wrought-iron gate that swung soundlessly on well-oiled hinges.

There was no moat or drawbridge, just a simple stone walk that led to the imposing front entrance. In Katy's mind, a moat and drawbridge would not have been out of place. The double-door entrance was made all the more imposing by the large Corinthian columns and pilasters flanking it. There was no tower room, and probably no dungeon, Katy decided, but the heavy stone ornamentation reminded her of the great gothic gargoyles she had seen in photographs of Parisian cathedrals.

She raised her hand to use the brass knocker, but the doors swung open before she made a sound.

"I was looking for you," Jenny said, ushering Katy inside with a pleasant, welcoming smile. A young boy was clutching her skirts. "This is my son Holland. He's a little shy with strangers but it doesn't last long. You'll wish it did."

"I doubt that." Katy looked down at the boy. His eyes were light, aquamarine, and the expression in them was one of curiosity and wariness. Katy held out her hand. "I'm very pleased to make your acquaintance, Master Holland."

Holland drew part of his mother's skirt across his face and hid behind it as he slowly extended one chubby hand. A lock of dark hair fell across his forehead and Katy had the urge to brush it back. It was not the sort of gesture he would thank her for, she realized, so she did nothing.

"This is Miss Ackerman," Jenny said to Holland. She shot Katy a brief look of apology for the subterfuge. "Nothing is secret with a three-year-old."

Katy understood. Holland did not. "Four," he said, focusing on the only part of the conversation that was important to him. "I'm four."

"Almost," his mother corrected. "You'll be four when we're on the ship."

"Ship! Ship!" He lost interest in both women and went running down the hallway. He disappeared into a room at the end.

Jenny laughed. "He's so excited about our trip. Of course the only thing he really understands is that we're going to be on the water. He's been playing with his boats in the kitchen sink most of the morning. Here, let me take this gown. It's from the play, isn't it? You wore it at the end of the first act to seduce your sister's fiancé."

"Yes, I didn't know if I should bring it." She hesitated at the base of the wide staircase as Jenny began to lead the way. "What about Holland?"

"He's with our housekeeper. Mrs. Brandywine will send him to the studio when he wears her down."

Jenny continued up the stairs, chattering gaily about the gown, the play, and making every effort to put her guest at ease. From the moment Jenny had seen Katy alight from the carriage, she had been aware of the actress's hesitation and uncertainty. Katy's guardedness confounded Jenny. She couldn't help but wonder what Logan's relationship to Katy Dakota could be.

The inside of Marshall House was no less impressive than the outside. Katy's footsteps were almost soundless on the carpet and her hand slid easily along the polished banister. She tried not to stare at her surroundings, hoping to give the impression that she was, if not used to such luxury, then certainly not intimidated by it. There was no denying that her suite at the Chesterfield was elegantly appointed. Still, peeking unobtrusively when an open door presented itself, Katy began to understand why Logan likened her rooms to a brothel parlor. At the first landing on the stairs, Jenny had paused long enough to point to the left and mention carelessly that Logan occupied the south wing of the house. The south wing! He had his choice of half a dozen beds to sleep in, she thought, yet he was spending his nights in hers. Logan Marshall was mad. Absolutely mad!

The only artist's studio Katy had even been to was Victor's and by his own admission he was a mere dabbler. The truth of that was brought home to her when she saw Christian Marshall's workplace.

Jenny, seeing how the room must look through Katy's eyes, was immediately apologetic. "It's awful, isn't it? When Christian works he's rather like a man possessed. Order is not in his vocabulary." Canvases filled every conceivable space. A scarred table was littered with brushes and paints and pallets. Several easels were stacked against one wall

159

and another, this one covered by a sheet to protect a work in progress, stood in the middle of the room. There was a sitting area and two roomy alcoves with windows large enough to catch the morning or evening light.

"Over here," said Jenny, pointing to the alcove with the eastern exposure. "I've arranged this area to be similar to your dressing room at the theatre. Pretend that old brass bed isn't even there. It won't show up in the photographs."

Katy felt immediately at home in the place Jenny had made for her. The mirrored vanity was very much like the one at Wallack's. The padding on the stool was even a similar shade of green. There was a dressing screen and a chaise and Jenny had gone to the trouble of adding a few baskets of flowers. None of them were daisies.

Katy put her case on the vanity and began setting out her jars and vials and powders. "If Mr. Marshall sees this room he'll know that I've been here," she said. Her voice betrayed little of the anxiousness she felt.

"Logan won't know," Jenny reassured. "I only put this area together this morning and I'll take it apart as soon as I'm done developing the pictures. He'll never see it."

Jenny laid Katy's gown across the bed and began to work with her photographic equipment. She adjusted the height of the tripod, checked her lighting, added several gas lamps, and prepared her collodion glass plates.

"What do you want me to do?" asked Katy. It was readily apparent to her that Jenny Marshall was skilled with the unwieldy and complicated equipment. She handled everything with an economy of motion which spoke to her experience and confidence.

"I'd like to do the face studies first. I want you to sit at the vanity and do everything you normally would in preparing yourself to go on stage. I'll give you direction as needed, otherwise you can simply ignore me. You've had your photograph taken before, haven't you?"

Katy's hands stilled, betraying in the space of a moment her discomfort and something of her fear. "Yes," she said, steadying herself.

"Good." Jenny pretended not to notice that she had seen her guest's start. "Then you know that I'll need you to hold a pose for a few seconds, just long enough for the image to imprint itself on the collodion film. I'll tell you when."

Laying a linen bib over her chest and shoulders to protect her clothing, Katy watched Jenny in the mirror. She was careful when she spoke to keep her voice casual, yet the nature of her question showed her concern. "You and your husband will be the only ones to see these photographs, won't you?"

"Yes. I've already promised you that Logan won't know."

"Nor anyone else?"

"No one will see the photographs, Miss Dakota, but you realize that by posing now you are agreeing to allow Christian to paint you. That will be seen, I can assure you."

"I realize that." Her fingers toyed with a tin of face powder, turning it round and round. "When

161

we spoke of the photographs you mentioned a study of my face. Is that all you want to photograph?"

"That was my first inclination," Jenny said honestly, wondering where the conversation was going, "but you brought the dress and I think a few full photographs would be a good idea."

"But with the dress on," Katy said quickly.

Jenny stopped fiddling with the lens of her brass bound camera and gave Katy her full attention. "Of course with the dress on," she said slowly. "Oh, I see . . . you've had other photographs taken and . ."

"There's no delicate way to talk about it, is there?" Katy's eyes dropped away and she stopped playing with the face powder tin. "I posed for someone I trusted wearing a sleepy-eyed smile and little else. I've vowed since that I would never do it again. I thought for a while that being the subject of a Christian Marshall painting might be reason enough to break my promise. I find that it's not. If that's what you want, then I may as well leave now. I'm sorry. I know I should have told you earlier."

"You didn't have to tell me at all," Jenny said gently, determined to put her guest at ease again. "But I appreciate your candor and I hope you'll set your mind at rest. I really am interested in a photographic study of your face I'm sure you realize you have strong, striking features. I'd like some full-length photographs, as well, but mainly to capture the expressiveness of your hands. There will be no pictures of you wearing only a smile."

Relieved, Katy closed her eyes and sighed. A wave of embarrassment came and went. Her shoulders straightened, she raised her head, exposing the long, lovely line of her neck, and looked at Jenny with a direct, open gaze. "I'm ready," she said.

Much later, hours after Katy had departed, Jenny Marshall examined the photographs she finished developing in her darkroom. They were a remarkable piece of work and Jenny knew it. She had captured Katy's metamorphosis into her character. Using multiple exposures on the same piece of film, Jenny had found a way to show the transition in a single photograph. Katy's transformation had a ghost-like, haunting quality because of the transparency of some of the images.

Laying out the photographs on her workbench, Jenny studied each in turn. Light caressed the planes and angles of Katy's face and yet it was Katy that appeared to be the source of the light. She was radiant. Her expressions ran the gamut from serene to sly, innocent to vixen. She did it with the slant of her brows, a sidelong glance, a bewitching, sultry smile.

There was one photograph which did not belong with the others, compliments of Jenny's young son. Holland had disturbed their work only once, but his presence gave havoc a free reign. He rushed the dressing screen while Katy was changing her gown, knocking it over. Jenny was so startled that she dropped the lens cap and inadvertently exposed Katy to the film. Until now she hadn't thought about what the camera had seen.

It was obvious that Holland's disturbance had

startled Katy into stillness. If she had moved, the photograph would have been blurred and its subject probably unrecognizable. But Katy hadn't moved. She stood holding her gown clutched in front of her, her knuckles white against the dark material. One strap of her chemise had fallen over her shoulder and light shimmered across her white skin. Her eyes, as wide and wary as a cornered fawn's, held all her vulnerability. Yet there was no mistaking that the photograph held a certain eroticism. Katy was more exposed by this picture than if she had been wearing nothing at all.

Jenny studied the picture for a long time. She considered destroying it and found she couldn't. For all that it was an accident, it was still one of the finest photographs she had taken. Gathering them all together, Jenny put the most disturbing one on the bottom and carried them out of the studio under her arm. When they were halfway to Europe was soon enough to show them to her husband, she thought, particularly the one on the bottom.

The Friday night performance of *Manners* had a few unexpected hitches. The main curtain stuck at the end of act one, leaving the actors frozen on stage while stagehands scrambled to fix it. Katy was the first to respond with improvisation and eventually they got through the difficult moment. In the second act Anthony Easton forgot his blocking and bumped painfully hard into Katy as she set off in the same direction. When he reached out

164

to steady her, he grabbed so tightly that she could practically feel the bruises forming. In the third act, the actress who was playing the role of Katy's sister tripped over her partner's feet at the beginning of the ballroom scene and twisted her ankle. She hobbled through the remainder of her performance and collapsed in the wings.

By the time Katy reached the Chesterfield she was physically and mentally exhausted. The realization that she had four more performances before she could rest on Monday was not encouraging.

"That was quite some performance this evening," Logan said, looking over the top of his paper as Katy walked into her suite. "I thought you handled that business at the end of the first act admirably. I doubt anyone who hadn't seen the play before really understood that something had gone wrong."

Katy did not respond although she felt the blood drain from her face. Logan's presence in her suite was more than she could bear. She took off her cape, tossed it carelessly over the back of the rocker, and opened her beaded bag. "I have your money," she said tonelessly. "It's every bit of what you paid for the suite. Please take it and leave." She held it out to him. When he made no move to leave the sofa, Katy approached him and dropped the bills onto his lap. "It's all there."

"I have no doubt." His mouth tightened a little as he stared up at her. "But money won't get me out of your life."

Tears burned in the back of Katy's throat. "If I find another place to live, will you leave me alone?"

"I think you know the answer to that."

"You're not giving me any choice," she said, her voice just a shade above a whisper. "I hate you."

"I have no particular fondness for you either," he said evenly. "That's what makes this arrangement so interesting, don't you think?"

"I want to go to bed."

"Certainly."

"Alone."

His smile was pleasant. "I don't think so."

At her sides, Katy's hands trembled. She sucked in her lower lip to steady it. Composing herself, she walked into the bedroom, her back stiff, her head erect on its slender stem. She disappeared into the bathing room.

He did not disturb her while she bathed. Katy wondered if she was supposed to feel grateful.

Logan was standing at the bedroom window when she returned. There was enough light outside to give his hard profile substance. He was barefoot and shirtless, wearing only a pair of trousers. The suspenders were hanging below his waist and his hands were thrust in his pockets. He rocked once on the balls of his feet, then he was very still, deep in thought. He didn't give any indication that he knew Katy had slipped out of her robe and into the bed. Yet, when he turned, his eyes found hers immediately.

"I don't like you," he said flatly. "You can't really expect that I should."

"I—"

He held up his hand, cutting her off. "But something keeps happening to me when I'm with you.

166

My body responds as if I really want you. It doesn't seem to help that I tell myself you're little different from any whore I could have at Maggie Bryant's house. You're not even as pretty as some of Maggie's girls and I doubt that being Victor Donovan's mistress has made you particularly skilled in bed."

"Oh, but I had a legion of lovers before Victor."

Her sarcasm made no impact on him. "It really doesn't matter to me. I only want you long enough to get rid of this ache. Right now my body wouldn't know if I was your fifth lover or your twentieth. I only want to be inside you."

"Go to hell."

"I believe I've said it before. I've already been there."

Katy found herself paralyzed with fear as Logan sat on the edge of the bed and placed one hand on the other side of her thighs, trapping her with his body. Her mouth was very dry and there was a roar in her ears.

"I suppose I could rape you," he said quietly, "but that would bring little in the way of satisfaction to either of us."

"You're insane."

He went on as if she hadn't spoken. "Actually, I have no desire to rape you. But to make you want me? Now, there's a challenge. If I could make you want me in spite of the fact that you *don't* want me, that would be something. You could despise yourself as much as I despise the same desires in me. There would be a certain comfort in knowing that I made you feel that way."

"I think I should have let my friends kill you," she said quietly.

Logan smiled. It did not reach his eyes. "You only think it?" Raising one hand, Logan cupped Katy's chin, lifting it just enough so that her mouth was on level with his. When she tried to move away, his fingers tightened marginally. "What I have in mind will make you sure."

Logan bent his head. His mouth hovered near Katy's so that she could feel the warmth of his breath. There was the faint but unmistakable scent of brandy. A moment later she was tasting it on his lips.

"I taught you how to kiss," he murmured against her mouth. "You were so very sweet." His lips touched the corner of her mouth. He was gentle, going slowly, sipping at the sensitive line of her mouth with the delicate precision of a hummingbird. His thumb slid under her chin and began stroking the soft, vulnerable skin of her throat. He could feel the thrumming of her pulse and his laughter was low and wicked. He knew what she was feeling because he was feeling it, too.

Logan was careful to go slowly. His attention was relentless but he made only small moves that were calculated not to force her to reject him. She was frightened now. So was he. It was part of the desire building between them.

Katy swallowed and her mouth parted. She thought that Logan would pounce. He didn't. His lips grazed her jawline instead. He followed it to her ear lobe and paused, making her anticipate the moment, then his tongue flicked her ear and he

168

heard her soft gasp. "You like that?" he asked, his mouth next to her ear.

"Go away," she whispered, drawing an unsteady breath.

He didn't go away. He pressed on, nuzzling the side of her neck, burying his face in the softness of her hair. Catching the woman fragrance of her, Logan's nostrils flared and he felt a tide of heat rise just under his skin.

"I can't fight you," she said. Logan's lips were trailing across her shoulder. His teeth had caught her nightgown strap and he moved it to the curve of her arm. He placed a light kiss there.

"I know," he said against her skin.

Katy closed her eyes. She felt him straighten and knew that he was watching her. Tears pressed at her eyelids. If she opened her eyes now the dark fan of her thick lashes would become spiked with tears.

Logan kissed each eyelid and tasted the salty wetness. His voice was kind. "Go ahead. Fight me."

"It won't do any good."

"That's true. I'm stronger than you are." His mouth touched her forehead, rested briefly on her temple, then slid along the downy softness of her cheek. "Little lioness," he said. "Even so, I'm stronger than you."

"If I had a weapon . . ." She sucked in her breath as Logan's tongue speared the hollow of her throat. " . . . I'd make you . . ."

"I know." His hands cradled the back of her head and his fingers threaded in her thick honey hair. "I know," he said again. His smile was outlined against her skin, then he began sipping on her flesh.

The love bite drew a response from deep within Katy. She bit her lip to keep him from hearing the urgent little sound that rose almost instantly in her throat. Her fingers curled into the sheets. "You don't want me," she said. "Not really."

"Yes, I do," he said. "Really." He pushed the straps of her nightgown over her shoulders. The neckline held fast for a few seconds on the curve of her breasts. Logan simply waited it out. With Katy's next indrawn breath it slid past her nipples.

Katy raised her hands and tried to cover her breasts. Logan's fingers curled around her wrists, stopping her. He held her hands still and lowered his mouth, taking one erect nipple between his lips and sucking gently. Fire exploded between Katy's thighs. She pressed her legs together, ashamed.

Logan's tongue flicked at the tip of her breast. He raised his face and regarded her with eyes that, except for the cool outer ring of silver, were dark and fathomless and hot. "Yes?" he asked.

No words came. She shook her head. Strands of her hair whispered across the back of his hand.

His eyes fell on her mouth and he realized with something akin to surprise that he hadn't kissed her properly. Not once. "You have a beautiful mouth," he said. It should be kissed often and thoroughly, he thought.

This time when his mouth touched hers the contact was firmer, harder, and there was no teasing. Logan leaned forward, pressing Katy against the headboard until there was no retreat for her. His tongue darted across the line of her lips, probing. "Let me in, Katy," he said huskily. "Let me taste you."

Katy's mouth parted on a dry sob. She felt Logan's tongue sweep the ridge of her teeth, flick at the soft underside of her lip, then fill her mouth. It was no good telling herself that she wanted to reject him. She couldn't do it. This is what he meant, she thought helplessly: desire in the face of all good sense, all good reason. She hated him. *She did.* But she wanted him as much as she had wanted him all those years ago. Perhaps more. She would never tell him that, then she prayed he could not make her say it.

He kissed her for a very long time. Logan enjoyed kissing. He enjoyed kissing Katy. Her response to him was tentative at first, just as he had known it would be, but then she gave herself up to him and it wasn't in surrender, but as an equal player. "I take it back," he said, breaking the kiss. "You probably are skilled enough to work in Maggie's brothel."

A shutter closed over Katy's eyes. She would not let him see her hurt. She had that much pride left. It was the easiest thing in the world to withdraw into herself and give Logan the woman he thought he wanted. Had Jenny Marshall been present she would have recognized Katy's transitions into her character immediately. Had Logan's senses not been so drugged, he might have understood it as well.

Katy's smile was sly and sultry. Her beautiful hands rested on Logan's naked shoulders. She slid lower in the bed and he followed her, partially

171

covering her with his body. The weight and warmth of him felt good but as soon as she thought of it she dismissed it.

Logan kicked at the covers, pushing them away. Katy's nightgown followed. He caressed the flat plane of her stomach with his palm. Her skin was soft and warm. He drew ever widening circles that had her navel as their center. She sucked in her abdomen as he bent his head over her stomach and flicked at her navel with the tip of his tongue. He returned to her mouth and kissed her deeply. It was then he realized that her passion was cold, that the hands on his chest were moving but not caressing. He sat up, hands braced on either side of her head. A lock of copper-struck hair fell over his forehead. His eyes pierced hers.

"What game are you playing?" he asked, voice harsh.

"Game?"

She was as guileless as Eve tempting Adam with the apple, Logan thought cynically. "Do you want me?" he asked.

"You know I do," she answered smoothly. Too smoothly.

"Like hell," he muttered, understanding at last. "I don't want that bitch woman you play in my bed. I want Katy." He gave her a small shake. "I want Mary Catherine."

Katy abandoned the role as easily as she had taken it up, striking out at Logan with all of her strength. Her knee came up, just missing his groin as he dodged the blow. She managed to roll half a body length away before Logan hauled her back.

"Oh, Katy . . . Katy," he whispered. "You *do* want me. And you're afraid."

"I don't," she protested, shaking her head. Her eyes were wide and wounded. "I don't want you. I hate you. And I'm not afraid."

It didn't matter what she said now because Logan knew it was Katy in his bed again; Katy who was dodging his kisses and his hands until he gentled her to his touch. His fingers in her hair held her head immobile. He kissed her, drawing on her sweetness and her anger so that the passion that flowed from her into him was as real and vital as she was.

Katy made no protest when Logan left her side long enough to remove his trousers and drawers. She watched him strip because she was helpless to look away. The sight of him, taut and smooth and aroused, aroused her in turn. She didn't have to speak the words. He saw it in her eyes and there was a touch of arrogance in his smile because he had been so certain he could make her want him. Now he knew he'd been right.

"Come here, Katy," he said when he was lying in bed beside her. He was propped on his side, his head supported by an elbow. "Closer. That's it. A little more. Turn on your side and face me." One hand rested on the inward curve of her waist. His thumb caressed her skin, moving like a pendulum, back and forth from the underside of her breasts to her hip. "Put your leg across mine. Mmmm. Just like that. What's wrong, Katy? Don't you touch your lovers?"

They were so close that Katy could feel him hot

and hard against her belly. "Please, Logan. Have done with it."

"No. Not like that." His palm moved, sliding over her hip and across her thigh. There was a fractional pause when his hand reached her knee. He watched her face and saw her lips part and heard her breath catch as she waited. His hand dropped and trailed along the inside of her leg until it rested at the apex of her thighs. "Don't move," he said quietly. "Stay just as you are." His fingers dipped into the soft nest of curls. He stroked her, probed, stroked again. "That's where I want to be," he told her when one finger slipped inside her. "What do you want?"

Fire was licking at her insides. Each time he touched her she thought she would be consumed in a flash of heat and light. She wanted to touch him and she told him so.

"All right," he said simply.

Katy's arms came around him. She had thought he would stop what he was doing to her, but he didn't. Her hands caressed his shoulders and back. She touched his nipples, once with her fingers, again with her mouth. One hand slipped between their bodies. She touched him intimately and was rewarded with the sounds of his wanting and pleasure. "I still hate you," she said against his mouth.

"I know." He felt her hips grind against his hand as she tried to have her pleasure without having him. His fingers stilled. "Tell me what you want," he said again.

There was a long silence, so long that Logan thought he had lost her. Then, "You." There were tears on her cheeks, despair in her voice. "I want you."

Logan kissed her, kissed the tears. He slid between her legs, raising her buttocks. "Help me," he said.

Katy faltered for a moment before she understood. She reached for him and guided him as he lowered himself into her. Biting the inside of her cheek helped her ignore the pain his entry brought. Her hands fell to his thighs and her fingers dug into his skin.

Pain passed. Discomfort lingered. The pull of pleasure had vanished completely. Katy wondered why she had ever wanted this, wanted him. All those long years ago she had asked him to teach her what passed for intimacy between a man and a woman. How disappointed she would have been then. She was only slightly less disappointed now. Yet in an odd way she was relieved as well. She didn't even like Logan Marshall. Had he only pleasured her she would have felt even dirtier and more ashamed than she already did.

He moved in her with long, slow strokes and Katy wished he would finish quickly. She turned her head to the side and stared at the play of light and shadow on the flocked wallpaper. When Logan stopped moving and rested his weight on his forearms, Katy thought he was done using her. She tried to move out from under him.

"No," he said, his breathing harsh. Inadvertently she had tightened around him. Logan nearly came out of his skin. He nudged her face upward with his fingertips. "Look at me, Katy. Look at me. I didn't know. Dammit, how was I supposed to know you were a virgin?"

She shied away from his rough, accusatory tone and unwittingly pushed Logan's control to new limits. Her chin jutted forward defiantly but she could not quite meet his eyes. Instead, Katy's gaze centered on a tiny bead of perspiration at the corner of Logan's brow. "Would it have made any difference?" she asked.

"No . . . yes . . . I don't know. I wouldn't have . . . God! Don't move again or I won't be able to . . ." His eyes closed and self-denial tightened his mouth. "Hell . . ." He lost the battle and thrust into her deeply. There was a brief hesitation as he strained again, then his movements were involuntary, quick and shallow. Katy had always imagined that her lover would say her name and it would be as a caress. Logan spilled his seed and swore at her.

Silence yawned between them. Katy was afraid to move now. She waited for Logan. He raised himself off her and rolled away, grabbing for the top sheet. Standing at the side of the bed, he wrapped himself in it, then tossed Katy her robe. He raked his hair in a weary, futile gesture.

"Stop looking at me like that," he practically snarled. "Oh, hell. I'm getting a drink. Do you want something?" Katy shook her head but her wishes were of no account. Logan returned with a whiskey for himself and a tumbler with two fingers of brandy for her. "Drink it. Don't be tiresome, Katy. Just drink it. I'm not trying to poison you."

Katy drank it down and suppressed a cough by

176

jamming her fist against her mouth. She felt the rush of something wet and warm between her thighs. Afraid to look, she scooted to the edge of the bed.

"Where are you going?" demanded Logan.

With a credible amount of dignity, she said, "I think I'm bleeding." She brushed by him on the way to the bathing room.

Logan paced the floor of the bedroom until Katy returned. She was pale and her eyelids were puffy. There was a strained look to her mouth. "I'm all right," she said in answer to the question in his eyes. "There was only a little blood. Mostly it was . . ." Humiliated, she didn't finish.

Logan felt an unfamiliar flush of heat warm his cheeks. He couldn't remember the last time something had embarrassed him. "You could have told me you were a virgin."

"I doubt you would have believed me."

"We'll never know, will we?"

She sighed, gathering the reins of her patience. "I think we've already established that it wouldn't have made any difference. You wanted revenge. You got it—in spades."

Logan knocked back his whiskey. "What about Victor Donovan? Hell, what about Micahel?"

"It would appear you made some faulty assumptions," she said calmly.

"Don't get self-righteous with me. You wanted me."

"You made certain I did. That was your plan, after all. You proved I could want you in spite of myself. I should think you'd be very pleased with

177

yourself. It's impossible for me to loathe you—or myself—any more than I do in this moment. I would say that you've been quite successful this evening."

Logan said nothing. He had turned away and was staring out the window again.

"You'll be leaving now," prompted Katy. Then, uncertainly, "Won't you?"

He shrugged. "I don't know. I thought it would be enough. Now I'm not so sure."

She couldn't believe she had heard him correctly. His beautiful profile was in silhouette and the body that had covered hers was taut with tension. He hitched the sheet tighter around his narrow waist. His chest heaved once as a sigh shuddered through him. "You don't mean that," she said. "You can't."

"I'm afraid I do." He looked over his shoulder at her. "Go to sleep, Katy. I won't bother you again tonight."

And he didn't. It was morning before Logan slid into bed beside her, his decision made. She responded as if she had known the bent of his mind, fitting the contours of her body to his as naturally as a lover of long standing.

In Katy's mind it was a dream and in the dream she was running. At first it was difficult to know if she was running from something or running toward it. Then she became aware that it wasn't a some-*thing* but a some*one*. Logan Marshall was at her beginning; he was also at her end. She was frantic to leave him behind, yet just as frantic to find him. It was not a happy dream.

Katy's breathing was short and labored, harsh in

the back of her throat. There was a warmth blossoming inside her and she turned, seeking the source of the heat, welcoming it as a flower might turn toward the sun. There was pleasure at the core of the heat and as the heat increased so did the pleasure. Katy didn't understand it. She wanted and she didn't want. It was confusing and frightening, no longer something she welcomed, and before she knew what was happening, she was running again. This time she ran right into Logan's arms.

He held her, comforting her. He whispered in her ear, words that made no sense to her, but soothed her nonetheless. His tone and cadence was sweet and his breath tickled her. He kissed the corner of her mouth and she felt it all the way to her toes. Katy's legs tangled with Logan's. The heat and excitement, inextricably mixed, returned with a force that left Katy breathless. This time she gave herself up to it.

The intensity of Katy's pleasure rocked her awake. Sparks of heat skittered along her arms and legs just beneath her skin, tingling and tickling. A wonderful sense of well-being enfolded her. She stretched languidly, smiling, and opened her eyes — and came face to face with Logan's coolly implacable gaze.

The enormity of what had just taken place was borne home to Katy in a flash of insight. It was accompanied by searing humiliation. Logan's hand still rested between her thighs and the heat and weight of him was like a branding iron. It was too embarrassing to tell him to remove his hand. Katy jerked away instead.

"Katy?" Logan watched her sit up on the edge of the bed, her back to him. Her hair fell across her shoulders, a silky shield that his fingers itched to touch. There was a ripple in it as a shudder shimmied down Katy's spine. She looked around for her robe and Logan pushed it toward her with the toe of his foot. She put it on without looking at him or thanking him. "I didn't like it that you had no pleasure before," he said, sitting up. He leaned against the headboard and covered himself with a sheet.

Outside, the day was gray. Droplets of rain spattered the widow, pinging out a flat, one-note staccato beat. Katy thought it was fitting that nature was shedding tears for her. She had none for herself. "Don't expect that I should be grateful for what you did to me."

"Katy . . ."

"I'm only interested in one thing, Logan. Does this mean that you're finally out of my life?"

"I don't think so, Katy. I've thought of little else all night long. I want to make you my mistress."

Katy stood up. She took several steps away from the bed before she turned on him. Now that her anger had reached its zenith, Katy's eyes were more gold than brown. "I wish I had let them hang you at King's Creek," she said quietly.

Later the same day, between the Saturday matinée and the evening performance of *Manners*, Katy went to the offices of V. I. Donovan's and asked Victor if he still wanted to marry her. He did. The

180

wedding took place that night in front of a judge that Victor knew and Katy missed both Sunday performances. She didn't return to her suite at the Chesterfield.

Logan and the rest of the city read about the marriage in the Monday afternoon edition of the *Chronicle*.

Chapter Six

"It's all right, Victor. It's not your fault." Katy's head rested on her husband's shoulder as she fit her body along the length of his. In spite of what had just happened between them, it was still a comfort to be close to him. The bedroom was chilled but Victor's cotton nightshirt was warm beneath her cheek. She laid one hand on his chest and covered the spot where his heart beat heavily with her palm. "I'm not very experienced at this sort of thing. I'm certain I'll do better the next time. Please, Vic—"

"Katy dear, shut up," Victor said, not unkindly. He placed his hand over hers and squeezed gently. His eyes were focused on a watermark on the ceiling. He hadn't noticed it before. It was definitely something that would have to be repaired. "I'll speak to the groundskeeper about it," he murmured.

"The groundskeeper? What does he have to do with us?"

"Ssshh, darling," Victor said soothingly as he chuckled deeply. "I was speaking of the watermark." One finger lifted to indicate the ceiling. "I've been contemplating it these past minutes."

Katy sat up in bed, her legs curled to one side. The neckline of her nightgown gaped and she quickly fastened the top three buttons. Victor had not even glanced in her direction. "Is it because of Annie?" she asked in a low voice, uncertainly. "Is that why I can't please you?"

"Annie? What nonsense is this, Katy? My wife's been dead more than twenty years."

At least she had his attention, Katy thought. "Help me understand, Victor. I don't know what I've done."

Victor studied Katy's face. Her eyes were troubled and there was the suggestion of a frown marring the beautiful line of her mouth. Still, she was lovely. And young. Impossibly young for him. Even now she was holding the end of her braid to her mouth, sucking on it much the way she would have done as a child. The act was so unselfconscious that Victor doubted she was aware of it. "It's nothing you've done," he said finally.

"Then why . . ."

"It's *me*, Katy darling. I'm too old for you. My body's too old." He tried a smile to make light of it and failed. He could only imagine that she had compared him to Logan Marshall and found him wanting. Hell, he had found himself wanting.

"That's not true," she denied vehemently. "It's *not*. I don't believe it and you shouldn't either. Can't we try again, Victor? I know I can do better this time. Perhaps if you instructed me it would help and—"

Victor found Katy's wrist and drew her hand toward his lips. "Come, Katy. Lie beside me."

Katy abandoned her braid and slid under the covers. The soles of her feet rubbed Victor's ankles as she snuggled against him. "I don't want you to regret marrying me, Victor. I know I can be a good wife for you."

"I'll never regret it," he told her softly. He turned his head so that his mouth brushed Katy's temple. "You haven't failed me. If you weren't such an innocent, you'd understand that I've failed you."

"I'm not innocent," she objected. "I told you—"

"I know," said Victor. "Logan Marshall."

Katy simply nodded. There was nothing to be gained by discussing Logan. She told Victor everything before they were married and he said it made no difference.

"Still," Victor went on, "you're an innocent. One night of passion doesn't mean you're—"

"Please . . . don't . . ." Katy's face flamed and she squeezed her eyes shut against the humiliating images that came almost immediately to mind. "I don't want to think about it. Please don't make me."

Victor slipped an arm around Katy's shoulders and drew her close. He liked the fullness of her breasts against his chest. He could feel her nipples hardening through the material of her nightgown. Her eyes dropped away from his and he understood that she was embarrassed by her own response to him. There was so much she didn't understand; so much that he could still teach her. "I have an idea," he said. "We'll leave the city in the morning. I have a summer home north of here along the Hudson. We can stay there for a few weeks—a real honeymoon, spending time in each other's pockets. That is, if you don't mind leaving the theatre for a while."

"I told you I wasn't going back on the stage if you married me."

"You'll change your mind again. I'm not asking that of you."

"It's what *I* want to do," she reminded him. The summer home sounded wonderful to her and she told him so. Weeks away from the city and the theatre would help her adjust to the idea that she was not going to return to acting. It would help her relegate Logan Marshall to the back of her mind and she could concentrate on the person dearest to her in all the world. "I *do* love you, Victor," she said quietly. "You believe me, don't you?"

"I believe you." And he did. Victor was certain that in Katy's own way she loved him. He certainly loved her. It was a bitter irony that he hadn't been able to consummate their marriage. "I'm sorry about this evening," he said gruffly. And the two others before it, he added silently.

"Oh, God, Victor, don't apologize. It's not your fault. I'm so nervous about it. You've been so patient, so understanding. This isn't easy for me. I can't be a very good partner for you."

But that wasn't it at all, or at least not all of it. Certainly Katy was nervous but Victor had found her shyness endearing. It had excited him, made him eager to have her in his bed. That she should want to honor the vows of their marriage was

185

more than Victor had hoped for when he had first proposed. Up until the moment they were in bed together Victor thought Katy would change her mind. Yet she hadn't. She followed his lead with sweet passion, letting him touch her, explore her. There were moments when he saw the fear in her deep brown eyes and his caresses gentled. Her fear was a challenge, something that could be turned aside because he loved her so much he ached with it. When he touched her he was erasing Logan Marshall. It troubled him that he was unable to wipe away the most intimate mark Logan had made on Katy.

"We'll go to the country," he said again. "It will be wonderful there, you'll see."

"It's wonderful wherever you are."

The most amazing thing to Victor was she meant it. She *really* meant it.

"Is he here?" Christian asked the steward at the Union Club.

There was no need to ask who "he" was. The steward pointed to the wing-backed leather chair in one corner of the reading room. Logan was seated there, a leg propped negligently over one arm of the chair. His foot dangled, occasionally bumping the dark maroon leather. Even from the archway across the room the arrhythmic sound was distracting. Apparently other members had thought so too. Logan was alone.

"Jenny's worried about you," Christian said when he reached his brother's side. "I promised her I'd bring you home."

Logan smiled crookedly, scooped up the bottle of whiskey at his side, and drank directly from the open neck. He held it out to Christian when he was done. "No? Oh, well. I'd appreciate the company though. Don't feel much like going home."

"Jenny showed me the evening paper," he said patiently. "She's concerned that you might be taking Miss Dakota's marriage badly. It would seem that she's right."

"Not taking it badly, brother dear," Logan denied, lifting the bottle as if in a toast. "Celebrating a narrow escape. Almost offered the bitch marriage myself. God, what a mistake that would have been! I let myself forget, just for a moment, what she was . . . *who* she was." He laughed without any joy in the sound. The bottle slipped a little in his gasp. "You can't imagine how good I'm feeling now, Christian. I'm the luckiest man alive."

Christian relieved his brother of the bottle, grabbed Logan's wrist and pulled him to his feet. "You can tell me about it on the way home," he said, supporting Logan carefully. He motioned to the steward and between them they got Logan out of the Union Club and into the waiting carriage.

Somewhere between Seventeenth Street and Worth Square the luckiest man alive passed out.

Ria Donovan heard the connecting door between her and her husband's room open slowly.

Hidden beneath her pillow, her small, porcelain-white hands turned cold and clammy. She closed her eyes, hoping that Michael would think she was asleep and decide against bothering her. It had never stopped him before, but perhaps this time . . .

Michael stubbed his toe on a three-legged table. He swore softly but vigorously. She had done it on purpose, he suspected. Ria was always rearranging the furniture in her room so that when he came to her at night he was forever stumbling into something. It never thwarted him; it only made him angry. It made him angry now.

Lighting the oil lamp at Ria's bedside, Michael held it so a circle of yellow light fell on his wife's face. The light did unflattering things to Ria's pale skin, making it appear sallow. Michael held it there for a few moments, watching her carefully before he set the lamp down again. "I know you're awake, Ria. It's no good trying to fool me. I think you know that if I want you, I'll take you in your sleep. Hell, the way you respond to me, I probably wouldn't know the difference. It might even be more enjoyable."

Michael waited, hoping for a flash of temper, something that would spark Ria's green eyes or make her thick head of red hair suit. Nothing. In spite of her coloring, there was no fire in Ria Monroe Donovan. That knowledge further angered Michael. She was a sham, he thought. Just as their entire marriage was a sham. In the west wing his father was making love to the woman Michael wanted in his bed. He damned Ria for not being that woman.

"What do you want?" Ria asked tiredly, proud of herself for the convincing calm in her voice. "It's very late."

"It's very early," he countered, pointing to the gold leaf clock on Ria's chiffonier. "Just past five. I couldn't sleep so I went to the library to get some papers I'd been working on. Imagine my surprise when I almost bumped into Father in the hallway. He was carrying a middle-of-the-night feast for himself and his bride. I think they both worked up an appetite."

Ria sat up, moving away from Michael as he sat down on the edge of the bed. Her back was flush to the headboard and her eyes darted over him warily. "Don't be crude, Michael."

Michael gave no indication that he had even heard her soft admonition. "You'll be interested to know that he and my dear stepmama are leaving in the morning for the Willows. They'll be staying at the summer house for the rest of the month."

"How lovely for them," said Ria softly. "Your father deserves some happiness, Michael."

One of Michael's light eyebrows kicked up. The corner of his mouth lifted in a smoothly cynical smile. "What's this? A change of heart? I thought you and I were of a single mind where Father was concerned. Has Miss Dakota been able to make you see things differently so soon? Don't forget that she's an actress, Ria. I doubt that you'll ever be up to her every trick."

Ria flushed at Michael's criticism. "I haven't forgotten that she's an actress," she said, "but I find her very kind and pleasant. She's rather shy and not very certain of herself, I think. Somehow I hadn't expected that. Before I met her I assumed that she was only interested in Father's money. I'm not so sure that's true. She seems to genuinely care about Victor."

"She *has* got you fooled! My God, I can't believe what I'm hearing. What happened to the woman who harangued Father with tales about the gold-digger?"

"I didn't know her then," she said quietly. Then, in her own defense, she added, "And I've never harangued anyone. I was merely repeating things you had told me about her. I followed her career the same as you and Victor, and I read the same things you read in the paper. Without knowing Katy it's quite easy to assume that she's only interested in furthering her position in the theatre."

"Or in society."

Ria pretended she hadn't heard. "I'm merely revising my opinion, Michael, based on what I've seen since she's come to live here."

"I hadn't realized you've become such fast friends."

"Now you're deliberately mishearing me. We're not fast friends, nor is it likely that we'll ever be close. But I think I can treat her with some civility and weather the social scandal of your father's marriage. I admit it's a relief that she isn't going to return to the play."

"You really don't understand what Father's marriage means to us, do you?"

"I don't see that it should mean anything to us."

"Money, Ria. It means money." He saw her blank look and clenched his hands to keep from slapping her. "I was the heir, my darling," he said sweetly. Too sweetly. "Father's bound to leave Katy some part of the fortune whether she wants it or not."

"You know I have no head for business. Surely there will still be enough money for us."

"As you said, you have no head for business. You spend more on clothing in one month than Miss Dakota earned in a year. The upkeep of this house is enormous. The socials . . . the appearances . . ." He waved his hand dismissingly. "None of that is the point. The point is, Ria, that I've earned the right to the fortune and I'm not going to let my father's whore-wife take any part of it from me."

"Michael! Please, have a care what you say! If someone were to hear you, well, you don't want your father to know how you're feeling, do you?"

"My father's not the fool you are. He has to know I'm feeling murderous toward that bitch. I've never made any secret that I didn't want him involved with her." Michael stood, jammed his hands in the pockets of his velvet smoking jacket, and paced the floor in front of the fireplace. The bones of his face were set in harsh relief, giving his handsome features the stamp of cruelty. "They could have a child. Had you thought of that? My father could have a child to that jade and I would have a brother or sister. There would be another heir. Katy's young," he went on bitterly, "young enough to bear my father a dozen children before he dies. All of them heirs to everything I've worked for at my father's side. I won't share it, Ria. I won't."

He sounded exactly like the spoiled only child he was, Ria thought. She wisely kept her thoughts to herself. "All right, Michael," she said softly, hoping to placate him. "Perhaps if you talked to your father, discussed your concerns, he would listen to you. They seem legitimate concerns to me. After all, you've worked with your father for years now. You have a stake in the store and all the Donovan enterprises."

Michael stopped pacing abruptly. He turned and looked at his wife, his blue eyes narrowing slightly. Ria was a diminutive woman with perfectly proportioned features. Everything about her was dainty. At one time Michael thought Ria's china smooth complexion, rosebud mouth, and hourglass figure held the very essence of femininity. He had been strongly attracted to her, wooed and courted her, wed her, and discovered that he didn't love her. Sometimes lately, especially when he compared her to Katy Dakota, it seemed to Michael that he even hated his wife. During seven years of marriage he had asked only one thing of her and she had repeatedly failed him. "I want a child," he said flatly, emotionlessly. "You're going to have to bear me a child, Ria. Short of killing Father or his wife, that's the only way I see to regain an equitable share of what's rightfully mine."

Ria's mouth was as dry as cotton. Swallowing was difficult. She couldn't bear to look at her husband, knowing that he would see the fear and revulsion in her eyes and ridicule her for it. In a low voice she repeated what Michael already knew. "Dr. Turner says I shouldn't try any more to have children. Another pregnancy . . ." Her throat closed and tears glistened in her eyes. "Please, Michael, I don't think I could stand another miscarriage. Even if I survived it, I don't think I could live with it. Four babies. We've lost four babies and I couldn't carry any of them to term. I don't want to go through it again."

"Is it the thought of having a child that terrifies you or what you have to do to get one?" he asked coldly.

"Don't say things like that. I've always done my duty by you and I've never objected to your occasional mistresses. Perhaps you have a bastard child somewhere that we could raise. I swear to you, Michael, I could love your son by another woman."

"Touching as your offer is, darling, I have no bastards and don't intend that I should get any. I want a son by my wife, a legitimate heir. My father would accept nothing less and neither would I." Michael tugged at the sash of his quilted jacket. "We may as well begin," he said, shrugging out of it. "There's no telling how long it may take, though as I recall you conceive easily."

"Oh, God." Ria hugged a pillow to her breast as if it were a shield. "Don't make me, Michael. Please don't make me."

Michael approached the bed. "Don't fight me, Ria, and I promise I won't hurt you more than necessary. You suffer more because of your own cold nature than from anything I do to you."

There was no escape. Ria closed her eyes and felt her husband's weight as a depression on the mattress. The pillow was taken from her, then the blankets. He caught her wrist and drew her toward him. She felt bile rise in her throat as her palm touched his bare chest. He was so large. The thick matting of hair on his chest reminded her of an animal. With his clothes on Ria thought her husband was the most beautiful man to walk the earth. Naked, he repulsed her. Clothed or unclothed, she was afraid of him. "The light," she whispered. "Please turn down the light."

"Yes," he said. In the dark he could forget who she was. She could be Marilyn or Carole or Dawn or Richelle. In the dark she could be Katy Dakota. "Yes," he repeated huskily, reaching across Ria to turn back the wick. "Let me touch you in the dark."

The Willows was a thirty-room, white frame house with a wide, open porch that spanned two sides and a rose trellis with an eastern exposure that climbed to the second floor. It was not what Katy had imagined when Victor spoke of his summer home. An entourage of servants preceded them, opening up the house and airing the rooms and the linens. By the time Victor and Katy arrived it was as if the house had never stood vacant.

The journey to the Willows was accomplished

194

by boat. Victor was appalled to learn that Katy had never gone any distance on water before. He promised to take her to Europe. She'd rather see California, she said. That was fine with him. He stopped short of saying that he'd sail off the edge of the world with her or for her. Katy would not want to know how hopelessly in love he was.

The path from the river landing to the house was shaded by a canopy of sandbar willows. They grew in a thicket along the riverfront to almost thirty feet in height as they neared the house.

"Roses are blooming," said Victor.

"Yes," Katy sighed, slipping her arm in the crook of his. The trellis was covered with pink and white petals. "Aren't they beautiful?" She never knew he was talking about the ones in her cheeks.

Victor took Katy riding that first afternoon. He soon discovered she was no horsewoman. But she was game, he'd give her that. She would have taken the biggest stallion in his stable if he hadn't been there to stop her. He gave her a gentle bay mare named Adelphia and he almost laughed out loud when he saw her relief. They rode on trails along the Hudson, sometimes dipping near the water, sometimes rising far above it so they could see miles of the valley winding at their feet.

Katy learned that her husband was a vigorous, physical man. It was clear that he loved riding, enjoyed being out of doors, and found great pleasure in the activity. Which made it very curious, Katy thought, that Victor led such a sedentary existence in the city. Katy found herself watching him avidly, sharing his pleasure and enjoying his company. He had a handsome smile and he turned it in her direction often. The laugh lines around his light blue eyes would deepen when he was amused. Once, impulsively, as they were standing on the crest of a rocky incline overlooking the valley, Katy reached for his hand and lifted it to her heart, holding it there in the cup of her palms.

Victor's age had never been the issue to Katy that it was to her husband, but looking back on that afternoon Katy realized it was that moment on the rocks, when she took his hand, that she ceased to be aware of the years separating them altogether.

That night they crawled into bed, both a little stiff and sore from their afternoon riding. They shared a look, an understanding, and several minutes of healthy, self-mocking, yet loving laughter before they fell asleep simply holding one another.

Logan scooped his young nephew off the dock and ruffled his hair. Holland protested loudly, giggled, and gave his uncle several smacking kisses when requested.

"Are you sure you don't want me to keep him here?" asked Logan, winking at Jenny over the top of Holland's tousled head. "I would take very good care of him."

Jenny pretended to think it over while Holland looked at her with pleading eyes. "No, I'd rather have my imp with me. You'd take him to the paper one day and lose him in that office of yours. Filed under B for boy."

"If I bothered to file him at all." He gave Holland a quick kiss and handed him over to his mother.

Jenny set him on the ground and placed his hand firmly in the hand of his nanny. "Go with Miss Reade now, darling. She'll show you where we're going to stand to wave good-bye to Uncle Logan." She bit back her smile as her son tried running for the gangway, only to be held back by his nanny. "Miss Reade's going to be very good for him," she noted, turning back to Logan and her husband.

"Well," said Logan, shifting his weight from one foot to the other, "you're finally going."

Christian grinned. "So far only our son, his nanny, and a half-dozen trunks are making this voyage. Jenny seems oddly reluctant to leave."

Under cover of her long skirt, Jenny trod lightly on her husband's toe. "Pay no attention to him," she told Logan. "You know I've been planning this trip for months. Nothing could keep me here."

"You're a sweet liar, Jenny Marshall," said Logan. He bent his head and kissed his sister-in-law on the cheek. He knew too well what would keep her at Marshall House and he was having none of it. "There's nothing wrong with me that a little work won't cure. It won't be any comfort knowing that you're worrying about me — so don't do it. That's an order." He glanced at his brother. "Does she take orders?"

"Not without considerable persuasion."

"Persuade her, then."

"I'll do my best." Christian clasped his brother's hand, then abandoned the pose and hugged Logan heartily. "Don't spend all of your time at the paper," he said quickly, hoping Logan heard all the things he was leaving unsaid: don't have a bottle as your only company; don't make the *Chronicle* your lover; and don't dwell on Katy Dakota. He released Logan and took his wife's arm. "There's a transatlantic cable now, Logan," he said in his best older-brother voice. "Jenny and I expect to hear from you."

Logan thrust his hands in his pockets and nodded once. "Go on," he said, pushing his chin forward to indicate the ship. "Your son's hanging over the rail."

Minutes later Christian rescued his son, holding him up for Logan to see. Jenny stood beside her husband and waved to her brother-in-law.

"I don't know if we should be going," she said, worrying the inside of her cheek.

"Jenny," Christian said quellingly.

"I'm sorry, but he's so miserable."

"Does he look miserable?"

"That smile is for our benefit," she said.

"Then accept it graciously. Logan is a grown man. If he made a mistake by not asking Miss Dakota to marry him, then he's the one who has to live with it."

"Marry him!" Jenny's dark brows lifted in astonishment. "Do you mean he considered—"

"I'll tell you about it later," Christian said calmly. "Smile, Jenny."

Ria brushed out her hair. It crackled from the hard strokes. She could feel her husband's eyes boring into the back of her head but she never lifted her face to catch his attention in the mirror.

"Come, Ria," said Michael, patting the empty space beside him. "Have done with your hair. You're merely delaying the inevitable."

"Not tonight, please," she said in a low voice, still not looking at him. According to the information Dr. Turner had given her when she was trying to have children, today was one of her most fertile days. She wondered if Michael knew. It would explain his insistence. In the past she had been able to use illness as an excuse not to lie with him. Now he would not accept it. He had come to her room seven times since the first night and each objection she raised was summarily dismissed. On two occasions he spent the night with her, using her at his leisure until her maid came with breakfast in the morning. "I may already be pregnant," she told him. "It couldn't hurt to wait and see."

"And you may not be pregnant." Her constant refusals bored him. In the end she understood she had no choice and gave him whatever he wanted. He saw her objections as mere token protests. Like everything about Ria, there was no real heart in them. "I think we should take every opportunity to see that it happens, don't you? Put down the brush, Ria, and come here. You can turn back the lamps tonight. Do you know that

199

last time I heard you make the smallest mewling sound at the back of your throat? It seemed to me that perhaps you are coming to enjoying this after all. Do you think that's possible, darling?"

It wasn't possible. What he had mistaken for a sound of pleasure was the sound of her revulsion. When he was inside her she knew only pain and she felt only terror. Ria dropped the brush and approached her bed. She turned back the lamp and let her robe fall to the floor.

"Take off the nightgown," directed Michael.

Closing her eyes, making herself invisible in her own mind, if not in Michael's, Ria did as she was instructed. She was chilled. To her great shame she felt the tips of her breasts harden. Michael's low, wicked laughter made her wish the ground would open and swallow her whole.

"Come, m'dear," he said, trailing his hand from her nipple to her waist. "Let's see if we can't warm that cold, beautiful body of yours."

"I'm sorry we're going back tomorrow," Katy said. Her skirt was hitched up to her knees and her bare legs dangled over the dock. Occasionally there would be a splash as her toes broke the surface of the water. She held a fishing rod in her hands and, though she had had several bites, she was never energetic enough to reel them in. Consequently every fish got away.

"You don't have to, you know," Victor said. He was no longer making even a pretense of fishing. His rod lay beside him. He was leaning back on the dock, resting on his elbows. A butterfly had come to rest on Katy's shoulder. He watched that. "You could stay here at the Willows. I'd come up every Saturday and Sunday. I think there'd be times I could get away on Fridays. All things considered, it would be a very pleasant summer."

Katy stared at the water. "Why do you think I'd want to stay here without you?" she asked.

"Katy dear, it would be perfectly understandable if you weren't ready to go back to the city. We both know you married me for protection. I can offer it to you here at the Willows. There's the business at the theatre for me to straighten out as well. I'm certain no one at Wallack's is happy with you. You did drop out of sight during the middle of a run. The Rialto's probably still buzzing with the news."

"You overestimate my importance."

"I don't think so."

"It doesn't matter." She shrugged and the movement startled the butterfly. It stretched its yellow and black wings and drifted away on the back of the wind. "I'll take care of whatever trouble I've caused at Wallack's. As for staying here without you, I won't do it. I love it here, Victor, but I like being with you more. There's no need for me to hide away. I think we both know that Logan Marshall is not going to bother me now. You told me some time ago that he doesn't trifle with married women. That's what I am. A married woman. I never wanted to marry; never even imagined that I would." She glanced at her husband over her shoulder. "It's almost sinful to enjoy it so desperately."

Her smile warmed him from the inside out. He wished he could . . . he wished . . . Victor returned her smile because he did not want Katy to sense his despair. She didn't seem to care that their marriage was not complete. Not for herself, she didn't care. She minded because he wanted something more and he knew her well enough now to know that she would honor all the vows of their marriage. "Come here, Katy love," he said quietly, beckoning her with his sky blue eyes.

Katy dropped her rod beside her as Victor sat up and extended one of his hands in her direction. She went willingly into the circle of his arms, laying her cheek against his shoulder. They held each other for a long time, watching the colors of sunset wash the sky, feeling life's splendor in the moment.

Logan's head snapped up as one of the *Chronicle*'s reporters burst into his office. "It can't be so important," he said tersely, coldly, "that you can't knock."

Knocking had never been a policy, not when the door was open. Ross Hutchinson faltered a moment, unsure of himself. His Adam's apple bobbed as he swallowed hard and ducked his head to examine the papers in his hands. It was being bandied about lately by the men who had known Logan's father that working for the old man had been a pleasure compared to working for Logan of late. This was the first time Hutch had crossed the publisher's path in weeks and now he found himself on the wrong side of good judgment, just because he hadn't knocked.

"Well? What is it?" demanded Logan, spearing the hapless young man with his frigid gray glance.

"I've heard from a friend at Wallack's Theater, sir," he began diffidently.

"And. . . ?"

"Rumor has it that Miss Dakota's going to attend the play this evening."

"We don't print rumor," Logan said darkly. "Do you want to go to Wallack's yourself?"

"Yes, that was the idea. If it turns out to be true, we'll have the edge. It's the first time she's gone anywhere in public with Mr. Donovan since their marriage. And to see the play . . . well, you can see for yourself that it would make a good story. I know exactly the angle I want to play."

"It's not a front page story," Logan reminded him.

"No, sir, but that doesn't matter," he said with brash confidence. "Everyone will read it. The city's dying to know everything about Katy Dakota."

"Katy Donovan," corrected Logan.

"Right, sir. I forget sometimes."

Logan wished he could.

Michael adjusted the starched white tips of his collar, then held out his arm so Ria could fasten his cuff links. It was not a service she performed often for him and her fingers fumbled at the unfamiliarity of the task. "You can't do anything right,

203

can you?" he snapped, tearing his wrist away from Ria's light grasp.

Turning away, Ria examined her coiffure in the mirror. Her flame red hair was swept up and back, giving her the illusion of height and adding a regal touch to her bearing. There was not a strand out of place but Ria smoothed a spot near her temple anyway. "You should not have dismissed your valet," she said in cool, quiet tones.

Her assertion was not lost on her husband. Michael's lip curled. "You sound almost shrewish, Ria. Have a care that you don't display your resentment in public. I won't have it."

Ria kept her silence. She had never created a scene and in public she always demurred to Michael. They were often held up as a model couple. Michael's dalliances were invariably discreet and not many people knew that he had interests outside his marriage. Even had it been known, it would not have caused much of a stir. Ria accepted it as well. He had never humiliated her publicly. That he humiliated her in the privacy of their bedroom seemed a small price to pay for the prestige of being Mrs. Michael Donovan.

"Damn," he swore softly, fumbling with the same link that had given Ria trouble. When she came to his rescue he accepted her help without comment. "Why did she have to insist on going to the theatre tonight?" he demanded sourly. "They've only just returned from the Willows. It's in the worst possible taste."

"People will be taking their cue from us," Ria reminded him. "You mustn't show that you find

204

their decision unpalatable."

"Why do you think we're accompanying them? Our public face will be one of complete approval." Above Ria's head he stared grimly at his reflection in the mirror. Privately there was no doubt as to his opinion.

"I think Katy wants to show support of the new actress in her role. She means to attend *Manners* as a kindness. Anyway, isn't it better that they go out right away? It's bound to elicit comment. Why not put it behind them as quickly as possible? I think they're trying to be very sensible about it." She finished fastening the cuff link and returned to her own bedroom to get her shawl.

Michael put on his black cutaway jacket in the doorway between the rooms. "I can see that it does no good talking to you. You're determined to take her side."

"I'm on your side, Michael. I just happen to understand hers."

"Since when do you understand a whore's point of view?" he demanded.

It was on the tip of Ria's tongue to say, "Since I became your whore," but she swallowed the words whole. She opened her jewelry box and found an emerald and gold necklace that suited her off-the-shoulder gown. Laying it against her throat, she waited patiently for Michael to come up behind her and fasten it.

"I can't understand," Michael continued in the same vein, "what possessed Father to marry her after all this time. He's known her for two years. Why now? Why marriage? What in God's name could he have been thinking?"

"Perhaps he loves her. Had you thought of that?"

"Love her? My father love that harlot bitch? I don't think so."

"You seem willing to think the worst of her," said Ria. She was very aware of Michael's hands on the curve of her neck and shoulders. The pads of his fingers were pressing against her skin with just enough force to let her know that pain could be in the offing. She did not think he would really bruise her minutes before they were expected downstairs. Ria decided to risk his anger. "You talk as if you know she's a prostitute."

"What are you implying?" he asked, his voice dangerously soft.

"Nothing. It was merely an observation."

"She's never been a mistress of mine," he snarled.

Ria's eyes widened. "I never thought she had been. I thought . . . that is, it seemed . . ."

"For God's sake, say what's on your mind."

"I thought perhaps you had seen her somewhere before. You know, one of those houses you sometimes frequent."

"If I had that kind of proof I'd have never let Father marry her. But it doesn't matter that I don't have it. I know *her kind*. I'd have thought that Father would have known it, too." He picked up Ria's shawl and placed it over her shoulders. "They're waiting for us downstairs. God, that the Donovans should have come to this."

Ria laid her hand lightly over Michael's forearm. In the past it had never occurred her to doubt her husband's word about the actress. Now she wondered. The lady was not the only one who could protest too much.

There was a stir in the audience as word spread that Victor Donovan and his bride were being escorted to their seats. From the vantage point of his box, Logan watched heads turn and bend. Whisper fed rumor with as much subtlety as a bellows fanned fire. The hum of low voices roared in his ears like the drone of bees. The queen seemed oblivious to it.

Katy was oblivious to none of it. She was certain Victor felt her nails digging into his skin through the sleeve of his evening coat. It seemed as though they would never reach their orchestra seats. It was odd, she thought, that the people who whispered about her now were less judgmental when they thought she was merely Victor Donovan's mistress. They could accept that more easily. She had crashed through some previously inviolate social barrier when she married the man. As she listened to the audience buzzing with awe and indignation, Katy realized that perhaps she was not to be forgiven for her breech of conduct. Certainly Michael was never going to forgive her.

Michael's smile was faint but perfectly visible. He nodded occasionally in the direction of a friend or acquaintance as he and Ria were shown to their seats. There was nothing in his expression that indicated frustration, embarrassment, or rage — all of which he was feeling. How dare she, he thought. How dare Katy marry his father when she knew that he wanted her? Still wanted her. His eyes strayed away from the people in their seats and focused on the line of Katy's back. So stiff, so proud. But he'd seen her in other circumstances, when she'd been neither stiff nor proud. He'd find a way to use what he had. Marriage or no, she would come to him. He would give her no choice.

Watching the play from the perspective of the audience was an odd experience for Katy. She murmured lines until Victor's gentle nudge made her aware of what she was doing. *Manners* was a good play, she realized. Better than she had really understood when she was part of it. She had known she would miss the theatre, but she hadn't known that she would feel such an ache. Coming to Wallack's this evening to face the crowd and say a symbolic farewell to the stage had been a better idea when she and Victor discussed it at the Willows. She leaned a little closer to Victor, slipping her hand over his forearm. He seemed to understand what she was feeling because he lifted her hand and softly pressed his mouth to her knuckles. The gesture was so sweet and gentle that Katy found herself blinking back tears.

At the intermission between the first and second acts Katy felt the full censure of Victor's peers. Ostensibly in search of refreshment, Michael took Ria by the elbow and led her away from his father and Katy.

"No one knows quite what to say to us," Katy

208

whispered to her husband. Diamond and gold fili-gree earrings danced as she bent her head toward him.

"Don't let on that it bothers you. That would give them too great a pleasure."

"Acting is always harder in real life than it is on the stage. I never do very well in situations like this."

It was hard to believe that she was uncomforta-ble. The rose gown alone should have given her confidence. The bodice was tight-fitting, accentuat-ing Katy's regal carriage and the flowing lines of her slender figure. It closed with tiny mother of pearl buttons and the high collar was edged with ivory lace. The fabric of the skirt was draped up and back to form a bustle and decorated with fringing and large ribbon bows of a deeper shade of mauve. When she walked, her train swept the floor with a flourish. "You're doing just fine. Would you like some refreshment?"

Panic flared in her brown and gold eyes. "Don't leave me."

Victor was prepared to reassure her when he became aware of a stirring in the crowd. He saw that Katy's eyes were fastened at a point beyond him. Glancing over his shoulder, Victor saw Lo-gan Marshall coming toward them. He stiffened and turned to face Logan.

Logan stopped a few feet in front of Victor and held out his hand. In a voice just loud enough to be heard by others, he said, "Victor, my heartfelt congratulations on your marriage." He made a slight bow toward Katy as he dropped Victor's hand. "Mrs. Donovan, my best wishes. Your husband's dealt a terrible blow to this city by stealing you away from the Rialto. *Manners* goes on without you, of course, but I can't help but feel that it just misses the mark."

Katy was too stunned to do anything when Logan raised her hand to his lips and kissed her in just the spot that Victor had earlier. Her eyes made a silent plea to Victor to come to her rescue.

"You're kind to say so," Victor said. "I've told Katy much the same thing but she thinks I'm prejudiced in her favor."

Logan smiled pleasantly. "I'm certain you are. I'm also certain that you're correct." His gray eyes wandered to Katy. "You *are* missed in the play, Mrs. Donovan. It would be foolish for you to underestimate your own talent. As one of your earliest admirers I feel that I can speak honestly of the theatre's loss."

"As my husband says, you're very kind," Katy said stiffly.

"I mean it, Katy," he added under his breath.

She glanced up and caught his gaze. His beautiful eyes were very solemn-looking and there was something in his expression that was kind and comforting, almost as if he were willing her to believe him.

She was grateful when Victor intervened.

"How are Christian and Jenny?"

"Quite well, I suppose. They've gone to Paris."

"Oh, yes. I think I did know they were going. I had forgotten."

Logan smiled. "Under the circumstances, it's understandable. If you'll excuse me now. Again, please accept my best wishes."

Victor and Katy exchanged puzzled glances as Logan disappeared in the crowd that descended in his place. They were now greeted by people that had shunned them just minutes earlier. Logan's public acceptance had set a new standard, making it possible for others to step forward without fearing they would be shunned in turn. By the time Victor and Katy returned to their seats, Katy's facial muscles ached from the forced smiles.

The second act did not hold her attention. She kept thinking of Logan. Why had he done it?

"Perhaps it's his way of calling a truce," Victor said when Katy posed the question to him later that night. He was sitting up in bed, reading reports sent to him from the store. Papers and ledgers were scattered all over the bed. He added absently. "Or perhaps Logan's admitting that I won and he lost."

"Won? Lost? You make it sound as if there were a contest."

Victor made a few notes, then looked at Katy over the rim of his spectacles. "It was a contest of wills if nothing else." He shifted some papers, making room for Katy, and patted the space beside him. She dropped her robe at the foot of the bed and slipped in next to her husband. "Whatever his motives, Logan did us a favor tonight."

"It was unexpected, that's all," said Katy. "I hadn't thought he would be *gracious* about losing. Although I'm not so certain Logan thinks he's lost."

"How could he not?" Victor touched the tip of Katy's nose with his forefinger. When she wrinkled it, he kissed it. "I have you. He doesn't. Of course he lost."

Katy's smile vanished. "Maybe I was never the prize," she said quietly.

Victor's iron gray brows lifted.

She snuggled closer to Victor, her eyes worried.

"Why don't you sleep in your own room tonight?" asked Victor. He shuffled through the pile of papers on his lap, showing her the extent of his work. "I'll be up late going through all of this."

"I don't mind. I can sleep with the lamps on. Perhaps there's even something I could help you with."

Victor patted Katy's thigh. The gesture was unwittingly patronizing. "I don't think so, dear. Really, you'd be more comfortable in the other room. I promise I won't make this a practice."

Katy's hurt went to the very depths of her being. No, she thought, she didn't feel like a prize ought to feel. She felt neither wanted nor cherished. Her husband was turning her out of their bed. It was humilaiting beyond all her imaginings. "All right, Victor, if that's what you want."

What he wanted? Victor almost screamed with frustration. What he wanted was to take her in his arms and make love to her. He wanted to love her the way Logan Marshall had loved her. He wanted to bury his face in the curve of her neck and feel her legs wrap around his thighs while he filled her. He wanted . . . he *wanted*. "Yes," he said, not glancing up from his work. "I think it would be

212

better tonight."

Katy got out of bed. The room felt cold. She picked up her robe and went to the door which connected their rooms. "I think I'll go to the Chesterfield tomorrow," she said. "I need to collect my things. I'll pack some trunks and send one of your employees round for them later."

"Very well."

She paused in the doorway, her hand on the glass knob, and watched Victor bent over his work. She wondered if she should repeat herself. It seemed likely that he hadn't really heard her. What did it matter, she wondered. He would be at the store tomorrow and she'd be able to go to the hotel and come back by the time he returned home. Katy went into her room, closing the door quietly behind her. She found herself wishing they had never left the Willows.

The desk clerk was solicitous, asking Katy if she wanted any help with her packing. She thanked him, but assured him she could do it on her own. The steam elevator which lifted her to her room was its familiar, cranky self. Katy exchanged a few pleasantries with the operator before she alighted on her floor.

Nothing had changed in her suite. Except for a thin film of dust which covered all the furniture, everything was just as she left it. That surprised her. She had thought that Logan would have taken over the suite in some way, yet it appeared that he had not used it at all.

213

Her trunks were delivered from the storage area below the lobby, and when the bellman left, Katy set about packing her gowns. She didn't really need the clothes. Victor had given her a new wardrobe before they left for the Willows. What wasn't ready for her to take on her honeymoon would be ready for her now, and most of the things he had chosen would put her gowns in the shade. Still, these things were hers and that counted for something with Katy. She had earned these, she thought.

Katy had never thought she was prone to self-pity. The bent of her current thoughts troubled her. She pushed it all to the back of her mind and concentrated on what she was doing. There was a certain amount of pleasure to be derived from doing rote tasks such as folding and smoothing and packing.

"I see you're moving out."

Katy jumped and spun around, dropping the gown she was holding. She hated being scared and the fright fueled her anger. "Damn you, Michael! What are you doing here? Haven't you anything better to do than sneak up on people and scare them witless?" She bent and picked up her dress, folding it with quick, agitated motions. "How did you get in here?"

"So many questions," Michael chided. He stepped into the bedroom and sat on the edge of one of Katy's brassbound trunks. His fingers plucked at a piece of lint on his dark gray trousers before he leaned back and crossed his feet at the ankles. His posture was relaxed and casual as if he had every right to be where he was. "I heard you mention to

Ria at breakfast that you were coming here. It occurred to me then that perhaps this was the best time to talk to you without fear of interruption. I think you know why I'm here and what I want. Some things haven't changed at all."

"Michael, I really don't—"

"As to how I got in here, did you know there's something wrong with the lock on the door? I think it's broken. You should talk to the front desk about that, Katy. You're hardly safe here."

"Obviously," she snapped under her breath.

"And I didn't mean to frighten you," he went on. "I did knock you know, several times, but you didn't hear. The door opened on its own." He shrugged. "Here I am."

She pointed to the door. "There you go."

"Katy," he cajoled, smiling.

"I mean it, Michael. I want nothing to do with you. I never have. You're correct—some things haven't changed."

"You wound me."

"I'd take it kindly if you'd bleed out in the hallway."

Michael's smile disappeared and his eyes frosted over. He abandoned his casual pose and stood. "Enough, Katy. I'm done with you keeping me at arm's length. I don't see that your marriage to my father matters in the least. If anything, it's deuced convenient. I thought I'd have to set you up in your own house or maintain this apartment. Now I realize that's no longer necessary. You and I can arrange to see each other at home, and by practicing a little discretion, no one will be the wiser."

Katy was thoroughly appalled by Michael's suggestion. "Even if I were going to make your father a cuckold, Michael, I would not do it in his own home and I certainly would not do it with you. Frankly, I've had quite enough of this conversation. I find it incredibly distasteful. You can leave of your own accord or I can have you thrown out."

"Really?" One of his pale brows lifted. The half-smile he gave her was too knowing. "Do you think Father wouldn't hear of it? Or worse, his friends? Are you sure you want to shame him? I assure you I'd be the innocent in all this. Who'd believe your word over mine? Everyone expects the worst of you and you'd be falling into their hands. I'd accuse you of inviting me here, planning the grand seduction, and there aren't many people who'd believe otherwise."

"Have *you* no shame?" Katy demanded. "Don't you care anything for your father?" Everything that Michael said was true, she thought unhappily. She would not be believed, he would. Victor alone would stand by her side and even so Katy could imagine him watching her, wondering in some small corner of his mind if perhaps she had asked Michael to meet her. "What of your own reputation? What of Ria?"

Michael shrugged. "I don't think my reputation will suffer overmuch. You're the one with so much to lose. Have you forgotten the photographs?"

Katy flung the nightgown she was folding away from her. "You wouldn't!"

"Are you willing to take that chance?"

She didn't answer immediately. Michael had had

the photographs for months and had never used them against her. There was always the threat of using them, of course, but he never had. "All right, Michael, I won't have you thrown out, but as long as I'm your father's wife those photographs are useless to you. If you show them to anyone, your father will disown you. You know I'm telling the truth. There's only one way you could have come by those pictures and that's to have stolen them. Victor will realize it right away. You're much better off letting him think they were destroyed in his studio fire than proving to him that you're a thief. Before we were married Victor might have let you get away with it, but not now. He'll protect me even if it means cutting you out of his will. Think about that before you threaten me with those photographs again, Michael. Do you really want the city to know what a terrible woman your stepmama is? Doesn't that reflect a trifle badly on you?" Katy removed a drawer from her chiffonier and dumped the contents on the bed. "Now, get out of here, Michael, before I think better of my promise not to—"

"Bitch!" He was beside her in two easy strides. Michael grasped her elbow, pulling her away from the bed and toward him. His fingers pinched her skin. He saw her wince but made no effort to ease his punishing grip. "Where did you ever get the idea that you could speak to me that way? I won't stand for it, Katy! Don't think you can lash out at me without receiving something in return. This is my price, whore, *my* price."

Katy's head was held immobile by the hand Michael placed at the back of her neck. His fingers twisted in her hair. Some of the pins fell on the floor so that her chignon came undone. Katy pushed at Michael with her hands but his grip merely tightened in response. Tears of pain gathered in her eyes. "Michael, don't—"

Whatever she was going to say was silenced by the hard pressure of Michael's mouth. His lips ground against hers and his tongue speared her mouth. Katy was revolted. She tried to pull back and couldn't. The length of her was pressed flush to Michael and she felt herself being maneuvered back toward the bed. The thought of Michael taking her on the same bed where she had lain with Logan gave Katy a surge of strength. She bit down with her teeth and brought up her knee.

Michael reeled backward. There was blood on the corner of his mouth and murder in his eyes. Katy found herself retreating into one corner of the room as Michael slowly straightened and started toward her. Her eyes darted around the room quickly, looking for some avenue of escape. It was useless to attempt to go across the bed and to go any other way meant getting past Michael.

Katy feinted left, as if making for the bed, then sprinted past Michael as he grabbed at the air. She made it as far as the parlor when she felt Michael's hands on her skirts. He jerked her to a halt by grabbing the elaborate ruffled bustle at the back of her gown and spun her around. Off balance, Katy threw up her hands to ward him off. They were both struck down by Michael's arm. The flat of his hand connected with Katy's cheek and she fell sideways, knocking over a table and scattering the dainty porcelain figurines which rested on the top.

Pushing at the fallen table with her feet, Katy scooted backward on the floor and tried to put some distance between her and Michael. Her cheek throbbed and her hip hurt where she had hit the table. "Don't come any closer, Michael. I swear I'll kill you if you touch me again."

He laughed. "I admire your bravado almost as much as I admire your body." He bent, reaching for Katy's wrist to pull her to her feet. When she flinched away from him he merely swiped at her again. She ducked, but not enough, and his palm slammed hard against her ear.

Pain sent her reeling. Crying out, Katy protected her head with her arms and shrunk away as Michael came at her again. She never knew if his intent was to help or hit her. The blackness at the edge of her vision exploded just a moment before she fainted.

Chapter Seven

It was the sound of her own soft moan that roused Katy to consciousness. She turned on her side, hugging a pillow to her chest. Her head ached horribly, and she was aware of a dull, constant pain in her arms and legs.

It took her several moments to understand that she was no longer on the floor of the parlor and that her bedroom was unbearably hot. She unbuttoned the top three buttons on her gown with fingers that shook. Sitting up slowly, feeling as if she had been stretched on a rack, Katy rested against the headboard. Even that small movement made her nauseated. Rather than breathing deeply, Katy sipped the air in an effort to quell the unsettled feeling in her stomach. She grimaced, her reflection in the mirror across the room proving that she was as flushed and disheveled as she imagined.

The outer door to the suite opened. Katy cringed as the footsteps neared her bedroom. She was looking around for a weapon to stop Michael when Logan came into view.

"So, you're awake," he said pleasantly. "That's good. How are you feeling?"

Katy couldn't make a sound. It had never occurred to her that she could be happy to see Logan Marshall. Her eyes took in all of him in a single glance. A lock of his copper-threaded hair had fallen across his forehead and he raked it back in a familiar, even endearing, gesture. He was staring at her, but for once his gaze seemed more concerned than condemning. Katy stopped looking for a weapon. Aware that she was staring now, she shrugged in response to Logan's question.

Logan sat down in a rocker which had been pushed close to the bed. He unfastened the buttons on his jacket and the material opened over his dove gray waistcoat. "That bad?" he asked.

She nodded.

"I sent someone from the hotel to get Victor. I assume he's at the store."

"Yes," she said in a low voice.

He frowned, a thought occurring to him as he studied the swollen area on Katy's cheek. "It wasn't Victor who hit you, was it?"

"God, no," she denied.

"What happened, Katy?"

"You didn't see?"

"No." Almost immediately he knew he should have prevaricated rather than answer honestly. Since it was too late to rectify his mistake, he continued. "You were alone when I found you, lying on the floor in the other room. I put you in here and went to get someone for Victor. Perhaps I should have sent for a doctor. I have a friend who's—"

221

"No. I'll be fine."

Logan wasn't as confident. She had been out cold when he found her and she hadn't responded to his attempts to bring her around. He'd taken note of the overturned table, the bunched rug, and the discoloration on Katy's cheek. Logan realized she hadn't gotten the bruise from falling. He told her that and when she didn't deny it, he repeated his earlier request. "Are you going to tell me what happened?"

She shook her head. The movement made her lightheaded and she clutched the pillow harder. "Oh, God, Logan, I think I'm going to be—"

Logan scooped her up and carried her to the bathing room. He stroked her back while she leaned weakly against the sink and was sick. "Let me get a doctor for you, Katy. I should have done it right away instead of sending for Victor. You may have hit something when you fell."

It was the blow Michael had delivered to the side of her head that was causing the problem and Katy knew it. The ringing in her ear was incessant, annoying, and painful. "No, I don't want a doctor. I'm just dizzy, that's all." She took the glass of water Logan gave her and rinsed out her mouth. Logan picked her up and took her back to bed, ignoring her protests. "Thank you," she said primly when he finished fussing over her.

"Dammit, Katy," he said, straightening. "You're hurt. This isn't something to be kept secret."

Secret? Wasn't it just like Logan to want to tell everything? "I don't see why not. I'm an adult now, Logan, not a child. I'll thank you to let me

222

make my own decision about what secrets are meant to be kept."

Logan wasn't certain he and Katy were talking about the same thing any more. But if not, then what was she going on about?

Catching Logan's puzzlement, Katy became aware of what she was saying. She drew in a calming breath. "And if I wanted to tell anyone, it would be Victor, not you, certainly not a doctor. This is none of your business."

He sat back in the rocker. "None of my . . . no, it's not, is it?"

"That's right."

Logan said nothing for several minutes. He leaned back, resting the heels of his shoes on the bedframe, and stared at the fringed canopy on Katy's bed. "Of all the things I thought you might do, I never expected you to marry Victor Donovan."

There was something odd in his voice that Katy could not identify. It was almost as if he felt some regret. "No, I suppose you didn't. But then, you never really knew me, did you? You never took the time to learn anything important about me."

"I knew what I needed to know."

Katy heard the defensiveness in his tone. "It's easier to justify your actions if you believe the worst of me."

His glance hardened. "I have nothing to justify."

"All right," she sighed. She felt too ill to argue. "Would it do any good to ask you to leave before Victor gets here?"

"No. I want to make certain you don't tell him

223

I'm the one who put that bruise on your cheek."

Her fingers lifted automatically to her face. She gently touched the outline of the bruise, testing the tenderness. "I would never say it was you," she told him, a wounded look in her eyes. "I don't even know how you came to be here."

Logan watched Katy's hand drop away from her face. She had slender, beautifully tapered fingers. His eyes followed her movement. He remembered those hands caressing him, holding him intimately. The tips of her fingers had pressed into his back; her nails had cut half-moons in his skin. He recalled cool hands on his warm flesh and the curve of her palms on his thighs. Her wedding ring caught his eye and the memories dissolved. A frown pulled at corners of his mouth and he answered Katy stiffly. "I hoped that you'd eventually come back to the suite to get your things. I arranged to be notified when you did. Don't worry, it's all being handled carefully. Only one other person besides yourself and Victor knows I was here today."

"Why?"

"Why what?"

She raised her hands in a helpless, all-at-sea gesture. "Why to most everything. Why did you want to see me? And why help me? Why do you care if anyone knows that you're here now? I'd think you'd be happy to ruin my marriage. Why did you come to the theatre last night and why make a point of being friendly to Victor and me?"

"I don't want to ruin your marriage. I'm done with you, Katy. That's why I came today, to speak to you in private because I thought you'd never admit me in your home. I wanted to tell you that I won't be bothering you, that you're safe in your marriage, and that you needn't keep looking over your shoulder expecting me to be there." His heels slid off the bedframe and Logan leaned forward in the rocker, resting his forearms on his knees. "In spite of what you think of me, I don't want to see you hurt."

"Perhaps not physically injured," she clarified, "but you were deliberately trying to hurt me."

"Yes," he said quietly. His eyes lifted to hers. "Yes, I was."

"Victor knows that you wanted me as your mistress."

"I suspected that you told him. There's a curious streak of honesty in you that appears from time to time."

She ignored the last, too weary to fight that particular battle. What did it matter what he thought of her? "He thinks you were kind at the theatre because you've admitted that he's won and you lost."

Logan's smile was brittle, his eyes cold. "I was kind, as you call it, at Wallack's because *I* won and *you* lost. Victor's welcome to you as far as I'm concerned. I only set out to take the most important thing I could from you—your work in the theatre. I thought making you my mistress would suit my purposes. You found another way to give me what I wanted. You married Victor and gave up acting. If you told me right now that Victor was more important to you than the theatre, I wouldn't believe you. And if I did believe you, you'd live to regret your words, because I'd find a way to take him from you too."

Katy's face paled, making the bruise more livid. Hardly aware she was speaking her thoughts aloud, she said, "My God, you're a monster."

"Yes." He stood. "I'll wait for Victor in the other room. I'll tell him what I know of what happened. You can tell him anything you damn well please."

There was little talking during the carriage ride home. Victor heard everything he wanted to hear at the hotel, precious little as far as he was concerned. Katy couldn't describe her attacker and absolutely refused to involve anyone from the hotel or ask the police to intervene. It was clear to Victor that she was holding back some piece of information and equally clear that, this time at least, Logan Marshall was not the reason. Victor saw with his own eyes that Logan's concern was genuine.

Upon returning home, Katy went straight to her room. Victor poured himself a drink in the library before he joined her. Katy was just dismissing her maid when Victor reached the bedroom. He watched his wife climb gingerly into bed, turn the pillow to the cool side, and lay her uninjured cheek against it.

Victor took a swallow of whiskey, then sat down on the edge of the bed. "I think I should send Harris for Dr. Turner," he said.

"No. Really, Victor, I'm going to be fine."

"Logan said you would argue."

"As much as I hate to give Mr. Marshall the satisfaction of being right, I don't want a doctor. There's simply no need, Victor. Let's just forget this ever happened, shall we? It was an unfortunate occurrence, nothing more than that. I'm certain my attacker's intention was to rob me and when I caught him out, he panicked."

Victor stared at the tumbler he was rolling in his palms. He supposed Katy's story wasn't going to change just because they were completely alone now. He wished he could believe her. "All right," he said. "We'll forget it ever happened."

The next morning Victor hired a private detective.

Dr. Scott Turner came around to the front of his desk and rested one hip on the edge. His striking blue eyes were grave, the set of his handsome features solemn. "You're pregnant, Mrs. Donovan."

A sheen of tears gathered in Ria's eyes. She looked away, blinking rapidly. "I thought I might be," she said on a mere whisper of sound. Ria fumbled in her purse for a handkerchief.

Scott picked up a pencil and tapped it lightly against his knee, while his patient struggled for composure. "I thought I was clear when you had your last miscarriage that—"

"You were very clear, Doctor," she interrupted. Her face flushed and, after a moment, she added

227

quietly, "My husband wants this child."

Without being aware of the pressure he was applying, Scott snapped the pencil. Startled, he dropped both pieces. Would it were Michael Donovan's neck, he thought. Ria's husband deserved to be throttled for this turn of events. "When you arrive home today I want you to go straight to bed and stay there. You're not to lift anything heavier than your hairbrush. Is that understood?"

"Yes." She raised hopeful eyes to the doctor while her fingers twisted the handkerchief. "There's a possibility then that I could carry my child to term?"

"There's always a possibility," he said, wanting to hold out some hope to his patient. He knew the odds were against Ria delivering a healthy child. His first concern was that she survived whatever happened. "That possibility depends on you doing everything I say, Mrs. Donovan. I won't accept any excuses this time for not following my instructions. It would be foolish of you to suppose there isn't any danger to the baby or to yourself, but I believe we can minimize that danger. I'll come by the house every two weeks in the beginning and later at least once a week. I don't want you to hesitate to send someone for me if there's even the smallest indication that everything is not as it should be. That's very important. If you do begin to miscarry, I want to be there." Scott did not add that Ria's life depended upon it. He thought she was very much aware of that fact. "I'll speak with Michael, of course, and your father-in-law. Neither will there be any excuses accepted for either of them upsetting you."

Ria's fingers stilled. "Please, I would rather you said nothing to Michael or Victor just yet. I . . . I haven't decided what I want to do."

A ridge appeared between Dr. Turner's fair brows as he frowned. "I'm not certain I understand what you mean. What decision is there to be made?"

Agitated, frightened, and embarrassed, Ria stood up. "I've been talking to a friend," she said. She took a few steps to her right and pretended to study the framed diplomas on Dr. Turner's wall. "And she says if it turns out that I'm pregnant—which it has—then she says I should ask you about . . . that is, I should find out if . . ."

"Yes?"

"She says you could get rid of the child for me," Ria finished in a rush.

Dr. Turner's brows rose nearly to the golden fringe of his hairline. "You're talking about abortion, Mrs. Donovan. My personal beliefs aside, it happens to be illegal." Scott was amazed by the calm of his own voice. "May I know who suggested that you ask for such a procedure?"

Ria shook her head. "It wouldn't be right for me to say. My friend was trying to be helpful, that's all."

"Your friend wouldn't be Victor's actress wife, would it?"

"No!" Ria turned swiftly on her heel. "Katy doesn't know a thing about this. Why ever should you think she . . . oh, I see, it's because she was an actress. You're assuming that she's the one who would put that bit of information in my ear. Well, you're quite wrong, Dr. Turner. The woman who told me is invited to the best homes, heads three charities, and says it is not an uncommon procedure."

"Then I apologize," he said sincerely. "I should know better than to make those kind of assumptions. Nevertheless, it's a foolish idea, Mrs. Marshall, and it would be best that you forget it."

"But wouldn't it be better," she persisted, "for me to lose the baby now rather than six months from now? I'll lose my life then, won't I?" Her eyes appealed to him. "I don't want to have this baby. I don't want to die."

"Then you don't want an abortion." Scott pushed away from the desk and crossed the room. He took Ria's trembling hands in his large, capable ones. "None of us can know what will happen, Mrs. Marshall, but there's nothing to be gained by dwelling on the worst possibilities. Abortion is out of the question. The procedure could kill you."

"But you could recommend someone to me," she said. "Someone reputable."

"Recommend an abortionist? I don't think so." He dropped her hands. "I'm going to do everything in my power to see that you and your baby both remain healthy. I wish that you would do the same. You would be wise to stop listening to your friend."

Ria caught back a sob. "I thought you would help me, but you're on Michael's side. You don't care what happens to me!"

Before Scott could answer, Ria brushed passed him and hurried toward his office door. He called to her as she fumbled with the doorknob but she ignored him. Scott slumped in the chair Ria had occupied earlier and was still staring at the broken pencil pieces on his desk when his wife walked in.

"You're wanted at the hospital, Scott," Susan said. Seeing her husband's preoccupation, she frowned. The sprinkling of freckles across the fine bridge of her nose darkened slightly. "Is something wrong? That was Mrs. Donovan who just left, wasn't it?"

"Yes." He felt Susan's hand on his shoulder and he reached back to touch her. "Yes, that was Mrs. Donovan, and no, nothing's wrong."

Susan knew he was lying but she let it pass. If it was something he could share with her, he would. She bent and pressed her lips to the crown of his fair head. "The hospital," she repeated. "And don't forget that Logan's coming to dinner this evening. Try not to be too late."

"Logan?" His question gave him away. He had forgotten.

Tucking a strand of auburn hair behind her ear, Susan nodded. "Jenny and Christian asked that you look out for him remember? And you, ever the good Samaritan and friend, said you'd be happy to. Well, Dr. Turner, *I* finally managed to pull Logan away from the newspaper, *I* have a wonderful dinner planned, and *I* might even have an affair with that beautiful man if you don't show up on time."

"I'll be here."

231

She smiled serenely. "I thought you might."

A few days later, when Scott saw Victor Donovan in his office, he never mentioned his talk with Ria. He had already resolved to speak with her after one week, knowing that she needed to begin caring for herself by then or give up all but a slender thread of hope that she and her child could survive. He wondered if she would still be pregnant when he saw her next. And if she wasn't pregnant, would she still be alive? There were no reputable abortionists in the city. Scott had had little peace of mind since he had seen her.

Looking at Ria's father-in-law, for all appearances hale and hearty, Scott Turner felt as if a weight were pressing on his chest. It seemed he hadn't any good news to give out this week. Scott pushed back a lock of hair and swiveled around in his chair. His eyes caught and held Victor's.

"Well?" demanded Victor. "Tell me. Don't pretty it up, Turner. Just tell me."

"It's cancer."

Air spilled out of Victor's lungs in an abrupt sigh. There were tiny white lines at the corner of his mouth as his lips flattened in a grim line. "I see," he said finally. He felt old suddenly. Really old. He touched his mustache with his fingertips, smoothing it. "There's nothing to be done then."

"There are a few treatments which—" He stopped when he saw Victor's cynical, knowing look. "No, you're right," he conceded unhappily. There was no evidence to support the effectiveness of any current treatment. "There's nothing to be done." Scott leaned forward in his chair, resting his forearms on his desk. "The tumors appear to be localized in the prostate gland right now. That's located near—"

Victor nodded shortly. "I now where it is. You explained that before my examination. These tumors . . . they're the reason I haven't been able to make love to my wife?"

"Yes, that seems likely."

Victor rested his head against the back of the chair and stared at the ceiling. Tears pressed at the back of his eyes and he swallowed hard. "God, what a mess."

"Victor, I'm sorry. I wish it weren't so."

He grinned crookedly. "This isn't ancient times, Doctor. I'm not going to kill the messenger for the message."

Scott smiled because he knew his patient meant him to. It was not so unusual for the people he couldn't help to comfort him. "I wouldn't blame you if you decided otherwise."

"How long do I have?"

"There's no way of knowing for certain."

"Make a guess."

"Victor," Scott said, a touch beseechingly. "I can't—"

"Dammit! Make a guess! You can't cure me, at least tell me how long you think I have left!"

The anger was not unexpected and Scott didn't flinch from it. He leveled his gaze on Victor. "Based on the size of the tumors, your physical stamina, and the sheer force of your will, I'd say

233

you have a year."

"Is that a conservative guess?"

"No."

Victor felt as if he had been punched in the gut. He pressed his fingers to his temples briefly and drew in a deep, calming breath. "All right," he said finally. "I suppose that's that."

"I'll do whatever I can for you, Victor."

"Except make me well again." It was out before he could stop it. "I'm sorry. You didn't deserve that. God knows, this isn't your doing." He picked at an imaginary piece of lint on the crease of his trousers. "I'll require your help, Scott."

"Anything."

"First of all, no one is to know. I realize that eventually my illness can't be hidden, but until then I don't want my son or my daughter-in-law to know."

"What about your wife?"

The ache in Victor's middle deepened. For a moment it was impossible for him to talk. "Katy isn't to know. You probably think, along with most of New York, that I was an old fool to marry her, but the truth is, she was foolish to marry me. You'd be hard-pressed to find a more generous . . . I thought I could give her . . . but she's given me . . ." He stopped, embarrassed that he had begun to reveal so much of his feelings for his wife. He cleared his throat and continued. "I've been pressuring Katy to come and see you for weeks now. Last night I finally succeeded. Now, in light of what you know about our marriage and about my health, I think it would be wise to warn you. She's going to describe her symptoms and tell you they're directly related to a fall she took several weeks ago."

"And they're not?"

"I don't think so."

"But she had a fall?"

There was no reason to go into detail about Katy's altercation at the hotel. "Oh, yes, there was a fall, but I think Katy's nausea and lightheadedness should have passed some time back."

Puzzled, Scott's brows drew together. "What are you trying to tell me, Victor?"

"Just because you know I've never made love to my wife, don't overlook the obvious. There's a very real possibility that Katy's pregnant."

"Pregnant?" asked Katy. Color drained from her face and unconsciously one hand dropped to her abdomen. The shirred bodice of her lemon gown seemed too tight suddenly and she had trouble catching her breath. Pregnant? Her voice was barely audible when she asked Dr. Turner if he could be mistaken.

"It's very unlikely," he said, watching her carefully. Victor had been right about Katy's reaction. She was stunned by the news. Scott wondered how the actress could have been so naive about the changes in her body. He shook his head slowly from side to side. The mind's capacity for denial never failed to astonish him.

"But I can't have a baby," she said softly, more to herself than to her doctor. "How can I have a baby?"

"Women have been doing it for a long, long time," he told her.

Katy worried the inside of her lip with her teeth. "Oh, God. I can't imagine . . ."

"Victor's going to be very happy," Scott assured her, correctly divining her thoughts. That was true, though Scott himself was still trying to understand it. It didn't seem to matter to Victor that he was not the child's father; he was prepared to accept fatherhood with all its rights, privileges, and responsibilities.

Of course Dr. Turner would think that, Katy realized. He didn't know Victor wasn't the father and she certainly wasn't going to share that bit of information with him, no matter how much she wanted to unburden herself. "We never talked about children," she said instead. "I have no idea whether or not . . ."

Scott found himself wondering about the man who had really fathered her child. Had he held out some hope of marriage? Had he walked out on her or had she sent him away? "I feel certain that Victor will be pleased," he said again, stressing it as much as he could without giving himself away. He waited, expecting her to mention abortion. Victor had said that she wouldn't, but Scott thought that in the circumstances she would consider it an option. After all, Katy couldn't be certain that Victor would accept another man's child. And there was no possibility that she could make Victor believe the child was his.

"I hope you're right," she said, gathering her

scattered thoughts and presenting the bravest front she could. She stood. Her knuckles were white where she gripped her beaded bag. "Is there anything I should be doing, umm, anything special because of the baby?"

"Come see me next week and we'll talk about it. You'll be over the initial shock by then and you'll have a hundred or so questions for me. Write them down as you think of them. In the meantime don't change anything you're doing now. The nausea will pass and you'll start to notice a weight gain instead of this loss. Talk to Victor, assure yourself that I'm right about his reaction." Scott stood and came around his desk. His smile was fulsome and apparently not forced. "Congratulations, Mrs. Donovan."

That's when Katy began to cry.

Logan poked his head into Scott Turner's office. "Alone?"

"You're here again? Didn't you just have dinner with us?"

Grinning, Logan plopped himself down in the chair Katy had vacated minutes earlier. It was still warm. He caught the hint of her fragrance. In his mind he had a fleeting vision of Katy's slender hand resting on his chest, her mouth pressing against his shoulder. He turned in his chair and threw one leg over the arm, trying to pretend a casualness he didn't feel. "Your wife feels sorry for me, Scott," he said. "So it's dinner again. I can't help that she's made me the object of her good works."

"She's happily married, Logan."

"So *you* say."

"I'll start worrying when you show up at the breakfast table ahead of me." Scott closed the file on his desk and placed it on a corner stack. "If I thought you were a real threat, I wouldn't let you through the front door." He stretched, leaned back, and cradled his head in the palms of his hands. "Unless there's an emergency, I'm done for the day. Can I get you anything to drink?"

"No, nothing for me. Was that your last patient I just saw leaving? She almost knocked me down out there. I don't think she even saw me." Logan knew for a fact that Katy hadn't realized how close she had come to barrelling into him. He had managed to sidestep her at the last possible moment and she had never looked up. Dumbstruck, Logan had found himself staring in her direction long after she had disappeared into a waiting carriage. "I thought she looked a little like Victor Donovan's wife."

"You should know," Scott said. "The *Chronicle*'s printed her picture enough times."

"That's not precisely the confirmation I was hoping for."

"If you're looking for a story, Logan, then that's all you're going to get from me. My patients are entitled to their privacy. You're one of them, remember?"

Logan held up his hands in a gesture of innocence. "No story. Just personal curiosity. She appeared to be upset."

238

"That would be an understatement." Scott got up and poured himself a cup of tea. He added a generous dollop of honey and stirred the brew idly, wondering about Logan's interest.

"She's not ill, is she? I mean, not *really* ill? I realize she wouldn't have come to see you if she weren't sick." Logan wondered if he sounded unconcerned. He didn't feel that way. "I've known Victor Donovan since I was a boy. In fact, he introduced me to his bride when I saw them at the theatre a while back. Whatever you tell me is not for publication."

Scott put down the spoon and sipped his tea. "No, Logan, she's not even a little bit ill. And for future reference, I wouldn't tell you if she were."

"You certainly have a knack for making yourself unclear."

"Good. I'll take that as a compliment."

They bantered several minutes longer until Scott was called away by his wife. He never gave a thought to the files on his desk. Logan had never stopped thinking about them.

"I'll understand if you want to divorce me," Katy told Victor. She was sitting across a candlelit table from her husband. Two glasses of wine had brought a flush to her cheeks and given her a measure of courage. Ria was eating in her own room this evening and Michael had gone to the club. Katy could not think of a better time to broach the subject of her pregnancy. It was fated, she decided.

"Divorce you?" Victor asked after he had waved away the hovering servants. "What nonsense is this?"

Katy realized she was putting the cart before the horse. The wine was more potent than she thought. "I'm saying this rather badly, Victor. I just want you to know before I go on that you can divorce me. It's a perfectly reasonable expectation for me to have."

"All right," he said gently, "now that it's been said, perhaps you'll explain why I would want to do that." He wished he could ease her fears ahead of time, tell her that he already knew what she was trying to say. Her honesty touched him. "Katy?" he prompted. "Why would I want to divorce you?"

Katy took another long swallow of wine. "Because I'm pregnant." She said it so quickly that even to her own ears it sounded like one word.

"I see."

Silence yawned between them. "That's all? You don't have anything else to say?"

Searching Katy's exquisite face, Victor said, "I wish with all my being that it were my child."

"Oh, God." Katy's features crumpled and she hid her face in her hands. Her shoulders shook with the force of her sobs. She heard the door to the dining room open and then Victor dismissing the servant in a rough tone he rarely used at home. She wished he would yell at her, say out loud all the horrible names she was calling herself. Slut. Whore. Victor did not deserve such shabby treatment at her hands. She did not deserve Vic-

240

tor.

"Katy darling," Victor said softly. He left his chair and came around the table. Taking her wrists, he gently pulled Katy to her feet and cradled her in his arms as unhappiness shuddered through her. He murmured her name repeatedly in a gentle, soothing voice while she apologized for being all the terrible things she thought she was.

"Your shirt's soaked," she said shakily when Victor handed her a handkerchief.

He dismissed her concern. "Blow."

She did, giving him a watery smile when she was finished. "Thank you."

"Let's go upstairs," he suggested. "It's obvious we need to talk about this and just as obvious that we'll have little privacy here. Go on, I'll talk to Duncan about sending up a tray with our meal."

Katy left Victor reluctantly and went to the rooms they shared. She was sitting on the edge of the settee, uncomfortable and uncertain, when Victor walked in. Her hands were folded in her lap but her agitation was evident each time she plucked at her wedding ring.

Victor's eyes dropped to the betraying nervous movements of her beautiful hands. His faint smile held a hint of sadness. "I'm never going to ask you to take that ring off," he said. "There's no divorce unless it's what you want."

Katy's head shot up and her eyes widened. "I don't want it," she whispered, her throat aching. "But you . . . are you certain?"

He sat beside her. In the late evening light his

241

hair was more silver than iron gray and the lines about his mouth and eyes seemed to be cut a little deeper. "I'm certain," he said gravely. "I shall be quite happy to provide for you and your child. *Our* child. Do you understand, Katy? When I married you I knew this was a possibility, even if you didn't fully comprehend it. I had hoped, I suppose, that if there were a child early on, then there would be no way of knowing whose it was. Now I find that it doesn't matter that I know I'm not the father. I'm willing to accept the baby as mine. Oh, no. Don't start crying again. I can't believe you could possibly have any tears left." He chuckled to himself as Katy launched herself into his arms. His smile rested against her honey hair and occasionally he kissed the crown of her head.

"Why are you being so good to me?" she asked.

There was only one answer for that. "I love you."

"Oh, Victor," she said sadly. She knew then that she would never be able to return his love with the depth of emotion he shared with her. Admiration, respect, great affection, and gratitude were paltry substitutes when compared to the love he bore her. She loved Victor, yes. But even if she said the words, they would both know her love was not the equal of his. Katy was filled with emptiness. Until this moment she had not thought such a contradiction possible.

"You want this baby, don't you?" asked Victor.

Katy raised her face. "I . . . yes. Yes, I want my baby."

"And what about Logan?"

"Logan? What does he have to do with anything?"

Victor laughed, hugging her, then set her away from him. "Oh, darling, I'm certain you'd like to believe you did it all alone, but your child does have a flesh and blood father. What are your intentions regarding Logan?"

"I have none."

"Then you're not going to tell him that he's the father?"

"No! Even if you sent me away, I wouldn't tell Logan about the baby. He has no rights to my child!"

"I won't hold you to that," Victor said. He got to his feet and walked to the window. On the corner a vendor was trying to sell the last few bunches of flowers from his cart. A beat cop sauntered along, swinging his stick in time with his jaunty stride. Victor loosened the sashes, closing the drapes. The room darkened. "There may come a time when you feel differently."

"I can't imagine that."

Victor shrugged. "Perhaps not. I just want you to understand that if, let's say, circumstances change, and you want to acknowledge Logan as the father, then you have my permission."

"I would never embarrass you that way," she protested.

I can't be embarrassed after I'm dead. Victor let the thought echo inside his head and said nothing out loud.

"You're not angry with me?" she asked into the silence.

243

"Angry? Because I'm gong to be a father? I don't think so."

Katy's heart lightened. Trust Victor to know exactly the right thing to say.

Ria Donovan did not look up from the book she was reading when Katy walked into the library. The morning sun was behind Ria, throwing her face into shadow, and she knew it protected her from Katy's searching gaze. Ria had caught her reflection in the mirror earlier and in spite of the cold compresses, her eyes were still puffy and her complexion blotchy from long bouts of crying. She found herself resenting Katy's breezy entry, the happiness inherent in her step, then despised herself for her uncharitable thoughts.

"Here you are," Katy said brightly, pretending she wasn't being ignored. "I've been looking everywhere for you."

"I've been here."

"Yes, well, I'm going shopping and I thought you might like to join me. It's such a beautiful day, there's no reason to spend it indoors. We could take a turn in the Park if you like. We haven't spent much time alone of late. I'd like to remedy that."

Ria shut her book but continued to look down, pretending interest in her buffed nails. "Yes, I'd like that, too," she said. Perhaps she could confide in Katy, she thought. Ria remembered that Dr. Turner had even assumed that Katy had been the one to suggest abortion. Until then Ria had not considered sharing her dilemma with Katy, but now it seemed perfectly reasonable that an actress would know where she could go for one. "I'll need a few minutes to get ready. I want to change my dress."

"Of course." Katy hesitated a moment, uncertain of Ria's mood. She felt ungainly in Ria's presence. Michael's wife was delicate and diminutive, soft-spoken and unfailingly correct in her gestures and manner. Self-consciously she straightened the sleeves of her pink-and-white-striped gown, tucking a bit of lace edging back in place. Katy could only imagine that anyone drawing a comparison between the two Donovan women would find it was Victor's wife who was lacking. "I'll get my bonnet and wait in the foyer," she said.

Sunshine washed over the open carriage as it rolled sedately down Fifth Avenue. Katy's elaborately plumed bonnet protected her complexion while Ria was shielded by an apricot silk parasol. Their driver was impeccably turned out in a black top hat and livery. People on the crowded sidewalks glanced in their direction as they passed.

"I'm glad you came with me," Katy confided. "I can't get used to the kind of stares I receive since I became Victor's wife."

"One would never know it," observed Ria. "You always look supremely confident. I admit I'm envious of your grace under pressure. I should like to be just a quarter as comfortable as you."

That made Katy laugh. "Oh, Ria, if you only knew how I churn inside when I walk into a room of strangers."

245

"But you're an actress."

"When I'm in front of an audience I have a script," she said, sighing. "Would that I had someone writing for me in real life. Sometimes I grow weary of all the improvising. It's rare that I know what I'm supposed to do in any situation."

"I know what you mean."

"Do you?"

Ria thought she would never have a better opportunity. She plunged in, her voice dropping to a whisper. "Can you recommend an abortionist?"

Katy was shocked. "Ria! This isn't the place."

"There is no other place. At home someone might overhear and Michael will find out."

Katy glanced at the driver's back, asking Ria a question with her eyes.

"Harris is practically deaf," said Ria. "That's why I specifically asked for him. Please, Katy. You must help. I can't have this baby."

"This is something you should talk over with Michael. I can't advise you."

"I don't want your advice. I've already made up my mind. Tell me where I can go. You must know."

She did know. It would have been hard to avoid conversations related to pregnancy and abortion while working at the Rialto. Katy had found herself learning things she would rather not have known. "Is this why you came with me this morning? Because you wanted information?"

Ria nodded. "Please, don't take offense, Katy. I don't dare ask anyone else where I can go. No one else even knows that I'm pregnant. Just you

246

and Dr. Turner. There's no one else I trust . . . no one at all."

"I'm sorry, Ria." Katy shook her head. "I can't help you." It didn't matter that the sky was still cloudless; the sunshine had vanished from Katy's day. "I also had an ulterior motive for inviting you to come with me. You're not the only one who's seen Dr. Turner recently. I was in his office yesterday and he, well, he didn't confirm my suspicions because frankly I had none, but he gave me the same news as you. I'm going to have a baby, Ria."

Blinking rapidly, Ria managed to halt the tears that welled in her eyes. "Then you've sentenced me to die," she said quietly, and turned away.

Stricken, Katy asked for an explanation and received nothing in return. Her entreaties made no impact on Ria and finally Katy had no choice but to tell the driver to return home. Once inside, Ria took to her room, locking the door behind her and barring Katy's way.

"You did the right thing to send for me," Scott assured Katy, dropping his bag on a dark oak end table. His eyes wandered to the rows of leather bound books filling the walls before he took a seat in one of the deep armchairs. "I've given her a powder to help her rest. She'll probably sleep until dinner. What about Michael?"

Katy shook her head and passed Dr. Turner a cup of tea. She sat down opposite him. "I wanted to hear what you had to say first," she said. "Ria told me this morning that you and I are the only ones who know she's pregnant. I wasn't comfortable being the one to tell Michael, especially when she's so desperate to rid herself of the child."

"I can appreciate that. It would be better if Ria did herself, of course, but quite frankly, I'm not sure we can trust her to do that. Don't worry, I'll talk to Michael myself. I owe him a piece of my mind. This pregnancy was completely avoidable. He had no right to use his wife as if she were a breeding—" He stopped abruptly and looked away. "Forgive me. I've said more than I should."

"It's all right. On reflection I suspected it was something like that. The pregnancy's going to be very hard on her, isn't it?"

"Yes. Ria's had four miscarriages. The last one was . . . well, suffice it to say that I told her then she shouldn't think about another child."

"Is she going to die? Is that what she meant when she said I had sentenced her to death?"

"God, she said that to you? No wonder you look pale as ash." He set down his cup. "I won't lie to you, Mrs. Donovan. Ria's pregnancy is dangerous, but if she follows my instructions and takes care of herself, there's certainly a chance that she *and* her child will come out of this healthy."

"What can I do to help?"

"Don't tell her about Madame Restell," he said, naming the most expensive abortionist in the city. He saw that Katy knew the name.

"I was surprised she didn't know," admitted Katy. "The woman is notorious."

Scott sighed, pushing back a lock of yellow hair that had fallen across his forehead. "Thank God she's too naive to know such things. Ria's a gentle soul."

And Michael Donovan was a beast, Katy thought. She thought of several things she would like to do to Victor's son, all of them excruciatingly painful.

"And what about you?" asked Scott, changing the subject. "Does Victor know?"

Katy found she couldn't help smiling. "You were right. He's very happy."

"You?"

"Oh, yes." She remembered all the tears in the doctor's office. Had that really only been yesterday? "Happy hardly describes it."

Scott stood, picking up his bag. "Good. That's what one hopes for."

Standing in the doorway, framed by white marble pilasters, Katy watched Dr. Turner drive off in his carriage. She shut the door slowly and leaned against it. Closing her eyes momentarily, she wondered how Victor would react to the news of impending grandfatherhood.

Chapter Eight

"Holland! Come back here with that!" Jenny lurched forward in her chair to make a grab at her young son. Holland laughed gleefully as his mother caught the waistband of his short pants. "Give me that photograph."

Still giggling and holding the picture away, Holland glanced at his father. Christian wasn't smiling. Holland's dimples disappeared along with his laughter. "Here, Mama," he said, solemnly passing the photograph to Jenny.

"Thank you," she said politely, letting him go. "Now play over there. I'll be with you when your father and I are done." She added the photograph to the others spread out on the table in front of Christian. It was torn and crumbled at the edges, thanks to Holland's deathlike grip on it. "What do you think?" she asked her husband.

"I think we should have asked the nanny if seasickness was going to be a problem," he said, flicking the abused picture with his ring finger. He looked at Holland, who was now playing quietly with his toy soldiers on Christian's and Jenny's bed. Last night one of those lead soldiers had caught Christian in the small of his back at a most inopportune moment. It hadn't seemed very amusing then. Now Christian found himself chuckling at the memory. He turned his attention back to Jenny. "Remind me to check the bed thoroughly tonight."

Only a hint of a smile altered her beautifully serene expression. "I'll do that," she said. "Now, tell me what you think of these pictures."

"They're amazing," he said honestly. "It's as if you've captured the essence of the actress and her character. The multiple exposures were very effective. When did you do them?"

"A few days after we first came up with the idea," she admitted. "Remember? At Delmonico's."

"I remember. I also remember that Logan told us later that Miss Dakota didn't want any part of posing for the camera or for me."

"Yes, well, Logan was lying. He never even asked Miss Dakota if she would do it." Jenny's dark brown eyes held Christian's. He looked away first. "What's more, I think you knew that."

"Actually, I did. He had his reasons."

"Perhaps if he had been honest with me I wouldn't have gone to Katy and asked her to reconsider her position."

"I see." It was easy to understand what had transpired then. The photographs were proof of that. "I can't say that I'm sorry you went around Logan. They're remarkable, Jenny. Really remarkable. I want to paint her."

"I thought you might."

"She's willing?"

"She said she was. She's really rather shy, Christian. Your sketches will be very important to her. I don't think she'll enjoy posing." Jenny sifted through the photographs. "Damn," she swore softly. "I wonder what happened to it."

Christian began looking too, even though he didn't know what he was looking for. "Happened to what?"

"Did you see one where Katy is standing with her dress held up in front of her?"

"I think I'd remember that," Christian said dryly.

She went through the pictures again, then looked under the table to see if it had fallen there. Jenny stood up, glanced behind her on the chair, shifted her skirts in the hope that the photograph would somehow miraculously appear. It didn't. She looked suspiciously at her son, who paid absolutely no attention. His cherub face was intent on leading a force of troops over the rough terrain of a mound of pillows. There was no use asking him. "Oh, Christian," she said unhappily, "it was a superb picture. The dressing screen dropped, you see, and Katy was caught off guard. She looked so —"

—vulnerable. Logan couldn't think of any other way to describe her. He held the photograph carefully, scarcely believing that he held it at all. In the wake of finding the photograph, Logan didn't remember what had sent him to the third floor studio in the first place. He sat on the narrow steps, one shoulder leaning heavily against the faded floral-patterned wallpaper, and stared at Katy's image staring back at him.

It was Jenny's work, of course. Christian rarely

did photography any more. Logan's professional eye acknowledged that it was an excellent picture. The lighting was exactly right, emphasizing the smooth ivory contours of Katy's naked shoulder and the slender stem of her neck. Katy's eyes were enormous, her lips parted fractionally. A shadow deepened the cleavage between her breasts. She stood there expectantly, waiting. Logan wondered what she had been thinking in that moment, what she had been waiting for.

He couldn't find it in himself to be angry. After all, he had lied to Jenny. But Katy? Katy knew he didn't want her anywhere near his family and yet she had defied him. Yet he couldn't be angry.

She was achingly beautiful, perhaps more so in the photograph than she was in reality. The stillness surrounding her, the watchfulness of her expression, made him aware of every graceful line of her body. His finger lightly traced her arm from shoulder to wrist. Her eyes beckoned him.

Logan slowly got to his feet. He considered dropping the photograph on the stairs where he had found it, leaving it there for Jenny to discover when she returned from her trip. But someone else, a servant perhaps, might look at it as something other than what it was.

He decided to keep it.

Katy was sitting in the dining room, finishing her breakfast while reading the newspaper, when Michael walked in. She didn't look up from the *Chronicle*. Using a variety of tactics, Katy had avoided

253

being alone with him since the incident at her hotel. By her calculations, Michael should have left for the store an hour ago with Victor. Katy would have eaten in her room if she had known he was still in the house.

Michael served himself from the sideboard, taking a liberal helping of eggs and steak from the silver warming trays. He split a muffin, added it to his plate, then poured himself a hot, dark cup of coffee.

Katy rose to leave as he placed his breakfast on the cherrywood table. Michael grabbed Katy's wrist.

"Let me go, Michael," she said between clenched teeth. "So help me, I'll scream if you don't release me."

"Don't make idle threats, Katy dear. We both know you're not going to scream to bring the servants running. It would get back to Victor and you don't want that." His fingers uncurled slowly. He held her eyes for a moment, then he sat down and snapped a linen napkin open on his lap. "Sit down, Katy. I think we need to talk. God knows, it hasn't been easy to be alone with you. You've thwarted me any number of times here at the house. Outside I have that damn detective my father hired to contend with. You can't imagine—"

"Detective?" She sat down, holding onto the edge of the table to keep her hands still. She searched Michael's handsome face for some clue, but he was giving away nothing. He had actually nudged the newspaper away from her place and was pretending calm interest in the headline article. "What detective?" she asked.

Michael finally looked up. "You're looking quite lovely this morning," he noted. "You should wear that shade of rose more often. It puts color in your cheeks." His blue eyes dropped to the bodice of her gown. Katy's dress buttoned at the front, from her waist to the hollow of her throat. He thought the fit was more snug than it had been several weeks ago and told her so. "Pregnancy becomes your figure."

"I won't sit here and permit you to bait me, Michael," she said, feeling the embarrassed flush steal over her throat and face. "I'll ask Victor about the detective myself." She began to rise.

"His name is O'Shea. Liam O'Shea. Father hired him the day after you and I had our . . . er . . . our misunderstanding at the Chesterfield."

"Why would he do that?"

"Isn't it obvious? Father was suspicious of your story. He wants this O'Shea fellow to protect you and he wants to find the man who accosted you. Quite the noble knight, my father."

"Don't belittle him," she said quietly. "He's doing what he thinks is best for me. Frankly, if it's kept you away, then I'm grateful to him."

"Are you really?" he asked, raising a cynical brow. He forked some eggs and a small piece of steak. "I find that a little hard to believe. You could have removed me from your life—if my father had swallowed your story—yet you didn't say a word about me being in your hotel suite that day. Why not, Katy? Why didn't you tell him who was with you before Logan Marshall got there?"

She wondered how Michael had found out about Logan. She certainly hadn't mentioned it. It was just the sort of thing he would twist to suit his own purposes. "My reasons aren't important," she said.

"I beg to differ."

"All right, Michael," she said wearily. "I had some foolish notion of not setting father and son against one another."

Michael shook his head slowly from side to side. "I think you were afraid that Father would think the worst of you and you didn't want to lose your position in this family."

"That's absurd!"

"Is it? I don't think so. Did you know you were pregnant then?"

"No! How could I? Your father and I had been married just a little over a month."

Michael's fair brows rose a notch. "Are you seriously trying to tell me that you and my father never . . . my God! . . . it's true, isn't it? He never had you until you were married. That's how you got him! You held out for marriage! Madam, I applaud your enterprise."

"I've heard enough."

"Sit down, Katy," he said sharply. "That's better. You'll leave when I've decided you will and not a moment before. Don't call my bluff because I can make things quite uncomfortable for you. There's no detective in here, remember." He got up and locked the door. "Now we won't be disturbed."

"What do you want, Michael?" Her eyes glittered with gold and her fingers pressed whitely against the tabletop.

"Your question bores me," he said, returning to

his place and picking up his knife. He buttered a muffin. "I've answered it often enough. I want you."

"I'm your father's wife!" she protested.

"So? You're not my mother." He took a bite of muffin and studied Katy consideringly. "It brings up an interesting point, though. Your child will be my child's uncle or aunt."

"I suppose so. I hadn't thought about it."

"Your child will be my half brother or sister."

"Yes." There was no other answer, not without admitting that Logan was the father of her baby. As long as Victor was willing to accept her child, then *he* was the father. "What is your point, Michael?"

His eyes narrowed, his mouth hardened. "My point is that your child will have the right to share in part of the Donovan fortune, Katy. And I don't think I like that."

"What are you talking about, sharing the fortune? You make it sound as if Victor already has one foot in the grave. I don't want to hear that kind of talk again."

"Katy . . . Katy . . . be realistic. My father won't live forever and he's going to want to provide for you and the baby."

She put her hands over her ears and closed her eyes. "Stop it, Michael. I don't want to hear any more."

Michael moved quickly. He grabbed her wrists, pulled them away from Katy's ears, and yanked her to her feet. "You damn well better listen to me," he grated out harshly, shaking her. "You'd be wise to do everything in your power to make certain Ria carries my child to term. No more talk about abor-

257

tion with my wife." He saw Katy's shock. "Ria doesn't have any secrets from me. None that I can't eventually find out."

Katy's mind wandered back to her conversation with Ria in the carriage. Perhaps their driver was not as deaf as he wanted Ria to believe.

"I'm not going to let you and your baby take away what's rightfully mine," Michael continued. "I'll do anything, *anything*, Katy, to keep what belongs to me."

"What do you mean?" she asked shakily, her face pale now.

He glanced at her abdomen. "Use your imagination."

"Let me go, Michael." She paused. "Please."

He dropped her hands but his arms circled her before she could back away. "I like it when you say 'please' in just that way. It's very intimate, did you know that? As if we were in bed together; as if we were making love."

"Michael . . . don't."

She turned her head to one side just as his lips lowered. They brushed her temple instead and Katy closed her eyes in distaste. She pushed at Michael's chest. His breath was hot and moist against her cheek. He said her name in a low tone and she hated the sound of it on his lips; hated the way he made it seem dirty and ugly. Then she surrendered.

"Oh, Katy," he said as her mouth opened up beneath his. He kissed her deeply, tasting her lips and soft inside of her mouth with his tongue. They turned together and Katy was backed against the table.

"Michael," she murmured. "Oh yes, please." One of his hands cupped the fullness of her breast, making the nipple rise. The other hand slid behind Katy and pressed her close. It was that hand she stabbed with the sharp tines of her fork.

Michael jumped away from her, swearing and nursing his wounded hand in the palm of the other. Droplets of blood beaded at four distinct points. "Damn you, bitch! You'll be sorry you did that!"

Holding up the fork threateningly, Katy cautioned him as he stepped toward her. "I swear I'll really hurt you with this if you come any closer." He hesitated. "I mean it, Michael. I'm not bluffing. I don't want you to touch me."

"You wanted me! I felt it."

"I'm an actress, remember? I wouldn't count myself much of a thespian if I couldn't fake passion—even for someone I despise." She skirted the table, putting it between them, then went to the door without turning her back on Michael. "Don't ever threaten to harm my baby again. If you do, I'll go to Victor. Don't think I won't. He won't tolerate your threats and neither will I." She opened the door behind her and backed out of the room, leaving Michael stunned and speechless. She didn't realize she was still holding the fork until a servant passed her in the hallway and gave her an odd look. She handed it over. "Please tell Cook the steak was a little raw for my tastes," she said calmly.

The door to the library opened a crack but Katy didn't notice. She was standing on the ladder that

259

was used to reach the upper volumes of Victor's extensive collection of books. Her position appeared a little precarious to the intruder. Only one of Katy's feet rested on a rung of the ladder; the other dangled below the hem of her pale blue day dress. She swung the foot back and forth lazily, just catching her kid slipper with her toes before it fell off. There was a large gold leaf and leather bound book open in front of her, lying on the ladder rung at eye level. She marked her place with one hand while the other held on loosely to the ladder.

It was clear she wasn't expecting visitors. She hadn't taken any time to dress her hair. It was plaited in a simple, girlish braid and even now Katy was chewing on one end of it, deep in thought. Unaware that she was being watched, she suddenly spit out the end, turned slightly on the ladder and began reciting lines from the balcony scene in *Romeo and Juliet*.

Logan watched, fascinated by the lilting, youthful quality in her voice and the longing in her expression as she called out for her love. Unable to take his eyes from her or disturb her in any way, he moved quietly into the room. He was struck again by the enormity of her talent. She breathed life into the words and made him feel a mixture of despair and desire. For Juliet, he reminded himself. Not for Katy.

She saw something move out of the corner of her eyes. Startled, she lost her balance. The book landed with a solid thud and Katy realized she was meant for a similar fate. She grabbed at the ladder, missed, and squeezed her eyes shut.

The impact she anticipated never happened. Logan caught her.

"I'm sorry," he said, letting her slip down his body until her feet rested safely on the floor. "Katy? You can open your eyes now."

She didn't, not right away. She waited for him to release her and step back. When he did, she drew in a shaky breath, let it out slowly, then stared at him, anger tempered with relief that the intruder wasn't Michael. It had been a week since he had last bothered her, but Katy found herself still jumping at shadows.

Bending down, she picked up the book and held it in front of her like a shield. A moment later Logan hunkered down and picked up something as well. Katy gave the folder he carried a cursory glance, then raised her eyes to Logan's. It annoyed her further that he was not winded while her heart was still pumping like a captured bird's.

"Someone should have announced you," she said coolly. "Does Duncan know you're here?"

"If he's that formidable fellow with eyes like a dead fish, he does."

Katy refused to be amused. "Victor's at the store. He'll be there the rest of the afternoon."

"I didn't come to see Victor. I came to see you. I didn't know you'd be rehearsing when I told Duncan I'd show myself in."

"I wasn't rehearsing," she said. "I was reciting. There's a difference, you know. Rehearsing's what you do when you're going to be appearing on stage. That's behind me now." Katy lowered the book fractionally, some of her anger ebbing. "I can't imagine why you've come unless it's to cause problems between Victor and me. He'll know you've been here. Even if I wasn't going to tell him, the detective would."

"The detective? Oh, you mean O'Shea. So Victor hired him."

"How do you know?"

"After that business at the hotel, Victor decided he wanted someone to watch you. He knew my brother had hired someone a few years back when Jenny was in trouble and he asked me about it. I gave him O'Shea's name."

"Then Mr. O'Shea probably won't tell Victor you've been here."

"Liam's working for your husband, not me. I may have a word with him though and convince him to keep silent. I think that's probably him in the carriage across the street."

Katy went to the window and cautiously drew back the curtain. There was indeed a closed carriage on the opposite side of the avenue. She let the curtain fall back and turned to Logan. "There's no sense in speaking to him," she said. "I'll tell Victor you've been here myself. I don't like to keep things from my husband."

"As you wish."

Katy set the book down. Uncomfortable with her hands at her sides, she crossed them in front of her. It suddenly occurred to her what she was trying to do. Logan couldn't know about her pregnancy, she thought. It was unnecessary to try to hide anything from him, especially when Victor had only told her that morning that except for the slight fullness in her breasts, she wasn't showing any signs of the baby. Birth was still six months away. Katy's hands dropped slowly back to her side. "Can I get you something to drink?" she asked politely. "A brandy?"

"Tea would be fine," he said, noticing the silver service on the table near the fireplace.

"All right. I'll ring for a second cup and some cakes."

A few minutes later they were seated opposite one another in deep leather armchairs. Logan's folder was lying beside the silver tea tray. He had served both of them and was now watching Katy over the rim of his teacup. "Before I came here today I considered it very likely that you'd have me thrown out. Yet you haven't. Why not?"

"Hasn't anyone ever told you not to look a gift horse in the mouth?" she asked. An honest answer to Logan's question meant that she would have to tell him how lonely she was. Ria's pregnancy confined her to her room. Victor was at the store all day and Michael had to be avoided. That left the servants and she wasn't even certain they liked her. Certainly none of them struck up a conversation with her. She wasn't invited to join the same exclusive circles to which Ria belonged, and her friends from the theatre were uncomfortable coming around to her home. It was a solitary existence in too many ways. She hadn't realized how solitary until she found herself playing hostess to Logan Marshall. "I may still have you thrown out," she said. "What brings you here, Logan? I can't imagine what could tear you away from the paper in the middle of the afternoon."

"My hours are my own. That's a publisher's pre-rogative. Today, anyway." He set down his cup. "You're looking very well, Katy. It seems that this marriage agrees with you."

She looked away briefly, uncertain of herself beneath Logan's thorough study. "You're not going to ruin it for me, are you?" she asked quietly.

"No. No, I swear I'm not. Look at me, Katy. I'm telling you the truth."

Looking at Logan was a mistake. His gray eyes were gentle now, faintly imploring. He made her believe him. Quite against her will she found herself wondering about the child they had made together. Would their baby have Logan's dark, copper-struck hair, his handsome patrician features? She could imagine holding a little boy to her breast with slumberous, heavy-lidded eyes or teasing a little girl who had a wonderfully warm smile when she wanted to be charming. It would be better if the baby resembled her. No one would ever think to question the parentage then.

"All right," she said. "I believe you. But you still haven't answered my question. Why are you here?"

Picking up the folder, Logan leaned forward in his chair and handed it to her. "Here's your answer."

Katy took the folder and opened it up. She stared at the photograph, her face paling alarmingly. "How did you get this?" Her throat was constricted, making it difficult to speak. Were all the Marshalls liars, she wondered. Jenny had promised her that Logan wouldn't know about the photographs so soon, yet here he was. Logan promised he wasn't trying to ruin her marriage, yet he had something

264

like this to use against her. "What will this cost me?"

Logan took the folder from Katy's shaking fingers, closed it, and set it aside. "I found it on the stairway to the studio," he told her. "It was obviously dropped there by accident. As to your second question, it's clear you don't believe me after all. I have no intention of asking for anything. The photograph is yours. I want you to have it."

When he gave it to her she shredded the photograph into small unrecognizable pieces, missing Logan's wince as she did so. Katy dropped the folder and the shredded photograph into the fireplace, took a match from the mantel, and lighted the paper. The evidence disappeared in a flash of fire and some black curling smoke. She dusted off her hands, returned to her seat, and picked up her teacup. "What's wrong?" she asked, seeing Logan's odd expression for the first time. "You said it was mine, didn't you? That photograph was an accident anyway. I didn't pose for it."

"I wouldn't have known that," he said. "I've seen a lot of Jenny's work. That photograph was one of her best. Everything about it was exactly as it should have been: the lighting, the mood, the depth of shadow It wasn't under- or overdeveloped. It was a stunning piece of work, Katy."

If he had wanted to make her feel guilty about what she had done, then he'd succeeded. "Perhaps you should have saved it for Jenny. You obviously think it was more her work than mine."

"It was," he agreed. "I found it over a week ago. I didn't decide until today who I wanted to give it to.

265

I think I made the right choice. It was Jenny's work, your privacy."

"Thank you," she said after a moment when their eyes caught and held.

It was Logan who broke the silence. "Tell me how Jenny came to photograph you."

Katy passed Logan a tea cake and related how the photographs had come about.

Logan loved listening to her. Sometimes her southern origins softened the edges of her speech. It was as if she tasted her words, melting them in her mouth in the moment before she spoke them aloud. "You said the one I showed you was an accident," he prompted when Katy's explanation trailed off. "What sort of accident?"

"Holland tipped the screen while I was changing. I think Jenny dropped that piece that goes over the glass."

"The lens cap, you mean."

"Yes, I suppose so. I remember she picked something up and complained about the ruined plate. I righted the dressing screen and Holland was banished to the downstairs. I felt a little sorry for him. He hadn't meant to do it."

Logan could imagine his nephew slinking off, affecting an injured air. He'd probably forgotten all about it by the time he reached the second floor landing. "Then you weren't waiting for anyone?" he asked. He saw her puzzled look. "In the picture you seemed expectant, as if you were thinking of someone, waiting for him."

"Is that what you saw? How odd," she said quietly, more to herself than to Logan. "I was afraid in

266

that moment. Nothing more."

"Afraid?"

Old wounds, she thought. Without meaning to, Logan was scratching at old wounds. "If I was expecting anyone," she said, her voice without inflection now, "it was Colonel Allen. Sometimes he used to . . . used to surprise me when I was dressing. I suppose I may have been thinking of him. I only remember being afraid."

"I'm sorry, Katy. I didn't mean—"

Forcing a smile, Katy sat up a little straighter. "I know. It's just as well I destroyed the photograph. It was too provocative. I understand why you thought what you did."

"Do you ever wonder what happened to Colonel Allen?" he asked.

Her smile faltered. "No. No, I don't." She didn't say anything for a moment, then, "Do you know?"

"He's a member of Congress. Has been since just after the war. He represents a district in Pennsylvania."

"Married?" she asked.

"No." He heard the question she wasn't asking. "No children in his life, no little girls."

The conversation was much too uncomfortable for Katy. She didn't know where to look or what to do with her hands. The teacup rattled in its saucer, further betraying her nervousness.

"That was stupid of me," Logan said. "I shouldn't have brought it up. Forgive me."

"No, it's all right. After all this time it shouldn't bother me."

"I don't know why you should be so different

from the rest of us mortals. There are matters I still find difficult to talk about. I imagine it's true for most people."

"Do you really think so?"

"You've never heard me talk about Andersonville, have you?"

She shook her head. "I'd like to hear about it. I'd like to understand why you hate me so."

He'd almost forgotten he hated her. He should have been grateful that she reminded him. It had begun to feel too good sitting near her, exchanging pleasantries among the memories.

"Your friends and I traveled a hundred miles together," he began, "before stumbling upon one of the few remaining train lines in the South. That's where they abandoned me. Stuffed me in a boxcar with forty others just like me and let me take my chances in Andersonville."

Logan saw Katy's shiver and he ignored it. "You'll recall I was never in any real condition to travel in the first place. By the time I reached the train I was out of my head with fever. At least that's what the other prisoners told me later. I don't remember much about the journey except that it was impossible to move, cramped as we were. Somehow I survived the trip, but by the time the prison car reached Andersonville I recalled almost nothing of what had come before it. When I finally saw the light of day in Georgia, I didn't know my own name, my family, or where I came from. For lack of a better name, they called me Red. My hair, I suppose."

Katy was very still and watchful. Logan was not

looking at her. Rather his cool gray eyes were lifted up and to the right a bit, recalling the past by focusing on some point beyond Katy's shoulder. His long, lean fingers absently tapped the brass tacks in the curved arm of his chair. She didn't want to hear what he was telling her—and yet she did. It seemed that Logan could always make her think and feel contradictory thoughts and emotions.

"How to describe Andersonville?" he asked rhetorically. "The conditions at the camp were so deplorable that our enemies felt compassion for us. Sometimes women met the trains with baskets of biscuits. They tossed them at us as we jumped out of the cars." A glimmer of a smile touched Logan's mouth. "We ducked at first, thinking they were going to pelt us with rocks. When we realized they were biscuits . . ." His smile vanished. ". . . We cried."

He looked at Katy then to gauge her reaction. Her eyes were wounded, as if she was feeling his pain. He went on with brutal frankness. "Imagine living in an area the size of this room with a dozen other people. That will give you an idea of how much space each soldier had. Now imagine there's no roof over your head. When it rains you can feel the wet down to your bones. When the sun comes out it's so hot you imagine they're bleaching right through your skin.

"Think about the tall pine forest just beyond the fifteen-foot-high stockade, a place that could supply shelter if camp commanders had had either axes or nails. As it was, straying too near the stockade could get you a bullet in your back. Guards set up

269

a railing nineteen feet inside the pine walls. Go close,"—Logan shrugged—"and you died. There were men who found suicide at the deadline preferable to dying slowly of hunger.

"Some of the latrines emptied into the drinking water. Disease was part of life there. We had sweetgum for malaria, pokeweed plaster for pneumonia, and pine resin for dysentery. I arrived long after the prisoner exchange system had broken down. The only real hope for release was in waiting out the war. Some tried tunneling. They exploded canteens on a campfire and used shrapnel as digging tools. The hard red Georgian clay consumed their energies and offered little in return. There were two dozen tunnels while I was there, and I only ever heard of one escape. Like most of the other prisoners, I prayed for the gates of hell to open from the outside.

"Everyone knew the South was losing, but no one talked about it within earshot of a guard. Those poor bastards were almost as hungry as we were, twice as mean, and they carried guns."

Logan shook his head slowly from side to side, smiling faintly and humorlessly "No, we never talked about the South losing the war."

Katy's mouth was dry and her eyes were wet. After a moment she managed to ask, "What did you talk about?"

His voice softened. "The usual things. Family. Friends. Sweethearts. I was a curiosity. They used to make things up for me just to give me a past. We made it a contest once, to see who could compose the best life story. Monroe Needlemeyer won an extra ration of corn bread."

"Was it a good story?"

"I thought so at the time."

Katy thought he might elaborate, but he didn't. She watched unhappy memories cloud his eyes.

"Of the forty men I traveled to Andersonville with, only twenty-eight walked out. Libby Prison was a sinkhole but Andersonville was something else again. Blankets were scarce; food scarcer. Robust men were reduced to skin over bone. The government seemed to have abandoned us and our captors were murdering us by slow degrees. The camp commander hanged later for war crimes. A lot of men cheered his passing but I was too weary by that time. God, I just wanted to put it behind me."

Katy was the first to speak after a long silence held their most private thoughts. "You didn't come north after the war was over, though. Why not?"

He looked at her sharply. "How do you know that?"

"I asked Victor some time ago."

Logan shifted in his chair, stretching his legs. He pretended interest in the toes of his shoes rather than stare at Katy. He damn well didn't want her pity. That was the last emotion he meant to elicit from her. "I had no reasons to go north, no expectations of being able to find family. There were no assurances I even had family. It seemed impossible to me that of the tens of thousands of men at Andersonville, I never met anyone who knew me. I moved all around the camp, hoping that I'd be able to change that fact. I never did."

Katy would have taken some tea if she could have

raised her cup with steadier fingers. "You stayed in the South, then?"

He nodded. "In Georgia. Savannah, to be exact. Oddly enough, I gravitated toward a job on a newspaper."

"Really."

"Really. The *Savannah Press*. I started out doing odds and ends, sweeping up, inking the press, setting type, anything anyone wanted. Gradually I began to do some stories."

"They accepted a Yankee?"

"I made up my own past for the paper. No one knew anything about me except what I wanted them to know."

"You still didn't remember anything?"

"Nothing. I had given up ever knowing. The life I had seemed reasonable and satisfying enough. I was doing some photography and making woodcuts for the paper. The publisher liked me and I thought I had a good future with the *Press*."

"Was there anyone special?" she asked. "Someone . . . someone —"

"Female?"

"Yes."

"No. No one special." Because he didn't want Katy to arrive at the wrong conclusion, he added, "There were women, but in the back of my mind I thought I might already be married. It kept me from pursuing any kind of permanent attachment."

That was her fault as well, she realized. Somehow she was to blame for his loneliness and if Logan had denied he was ever lonely she wouldn't have believed him.

"I stayed with the *Press* for about two years. One day we picked up a story out of New York about an heiress in hiding who exposed a bank fraud. She used a simple device called a pin-hole camera. It was the pin-hole camera that struck some lost memory chord. It vibrated for days inside my head. Gradually I began to remember things: odd, silly things that could have only given me pleasure. A week later I was in New York, disrupting everything at Marshall House, including my brother's wedding day. The heiress in the story was Jenny and the man who helped her with the pin-hole camera was my brother Christian."

"That's astonishing. I had no idea."

"Not many people know what brought me back."

"Victor doesn't know. He did tell me about your family though."

"Then you know that because of you, I never again saw my father alive."

"Because of me, you're still alive," she said.

Logan's eyes turned frigid. "You think I should be grateful to you for not letting me hang? After you returned from your trip to church and blocked my escape with that calculated seduction scene of yours? That's what caused my capture. You delayed me long enough for your aunt to bring help. I hold you as much responsible for that as for anything you ever did to me."

Katy's eyes glittered and she raised her chin. "You think you know so much about what happened that day! You can't possibly attribute my actions to anything but—" She broke off, horrified by what she had nearly revealed to Logan.

273

Katy stood abruptly. "I think it would be for the best if you left now, Mr. Marshall."

"Mr. Marshall? Katy, sometimes you're ridiculous."

She flushed, embarrassed and angry. "All right. *Logan*. I'd like you to leave."

"Of course." He saw that she was surprised by his easy acquiescence. "I didn't come here to harass you," he said, his voice gentle.

Logan stood, and let Katy precede him to the door. As she passed him he caught her fragrance. Her fragrance. It elicited a flood of memories that were almost overwhelming in their power. Logan had to stop himself from reaching for the braid that had fallen over her shoulder.

"Is something wrong?" she asked, turning to Logan as she opened the door. The expression on his face was one she could not identify. His eyes had narrowed slightly and his head was tilted to one side.

He blinked. "Nothing's wrong," he said. His mouth hinted at a smile; mostly it was sad. "Good day, Katy."

Victor looked up from the work that surrounded him on the bed. He slipped off his spectacles, put them on the night table, and rubbed his eyes with his thumb and forefinger.

Katy stopped brushing her hair and regarded him with curiosity and worry.

"I wish you wouldn't work so hard," she said softly, sitting down on the edge of the bed. Papers slid from their neat stacks and she made no attempt to make the piles right again. Her thumb passed back and forth over the brush bristles as she spoke. "Ever since we returned from the Willows you've been obsessed with your work. There's no room for me in your bed any more." She waved her hand over the papers and ledgers and bonds and certificates. "Is it me? Is it the baby?"

Victor closed the ledger in his lap and pushed it aside. "It's not you and it's not the baby."

"Then it's you." Her large, almond-shaped eyes appealed to him. "Please, Victor, tell me what it is. I miss being with you, being held by you. I miss talking to you and laughing with you. I don't want to sleep in that other room any more. I want to be with you."

He leaned across the bed and took the brush from her nervous fingers. His hand circled her wrist and he needed only to tug lightly to bring Katy to his side. Leaning against the headboard, a pillow at the small of his back, Victor held Katy so that her cheek rested against his shoulder. Her nightshift had ridden up to her thighs so that her beautiful long legs were pale and smooth as cream against the deep blue of his robe. She was curled in the crook of his body, one of her arms across his chest. She laid a finger against the side of his neck. He caressed her knee with his palm.

"I could hold you for a lifetime, Katy," he said softly. "Believe that."

She frowned, her brows drawing together slightly.

"It's just what you said, it's me. I'm afraid I've been rather a poor excuse for a husband."

"That's not true!"

He chuckled. It was laugh or cry and he was not going to cry in front of Katy. "It most certainly is. If you had more experience you'd know that. I want to make love—"

"I don't care about that, Victor! I don't!"

Victor said nothing for a moment. "But I do," he said finally, quietly.

"Oh, Victor," she said sadly, tears pricking the back of her eyes.

"I've come to despise my body for not being able to meet the desires of my heart and mind. Some days I despise my heart for loving you with the passion of a youth. And my mind . . . can you possibly understand what I'm talking about, Katy?"

She nodded slowly, adding in a broken whisper, "I've been so selfish, thinking only of me, thinking only of what I wanted. I'm sorry, Victor."

He stroked her hair, holding her to him when she would have broken their embrace. "No," he said. "Stay here. I shouldn't turn you out of my arms and my bed just because I can't be all that I want."

"But your work."

Victor rarely swore. Now he told her in very explicit terms what he thought about his work.

"The papers are wrinkled," she said.

In response he began pitching everything over the side of the bed. What he couldn't reach he kicked off. "There," he said, satisfied. Trust me, V.I. Donovan's records aren't any worse now than when you and I came back from the Willows."

"But Michael handled everything for you then."

"Precisely," he said dryly.

Katy laughed lightly and snuggled closer. "Victor, you're certain everything's all right, aren't you? With you, I mean. You looked a little tired at dinner this evening."

Victor was determined to skirt the issue of his health. "If I'm tired of anything it's the way Michael seems so bent on creating trouble between us."

"You mean his comment about Logan being here today."

"Exactly that. He brought it up without giving you any opportunity to mention it yourself."

"You handled it quite well anyway," she said. "Thank you for that."

"I trust you absolutely."

"Michael thinks you're foolish for that."

"My son and I have disagreed on any number of things over the years. Now we can add you to the list. I wish it had been I who saw Logan leaving the house instead of Michael, but there's no changing it. He can think what he likes." He turned his head and kissed Katy's brow. She couldn't see his eyes; couldn't see the faraway look in them. "I know how you feel about Logan Marshall."

Katy sat alone at one of the dark oak booths in Crestmore's Ice Cream Parlor. She ordered a cherry phosphate from a young waiter wearing a starched white shirt and baby blue sleeve garters. He looked at her oddly, as if he was struggling to recognize her face but couldn't quite make out how he knew her. She had gotten used to the look when she was on the stage. It was a novelty now. Katy smiled and

277

kept the secret to herself.

When her phosphate arrived, she sipped it slowly through a paper straw. Her eyes were lifted, focused beyond the large plate window at the front of the parlor. Victor's store, situated diagonally from the parlor, was in her line of vision. There was a steady stream of people in and out of the store. It seemed to Katy that most of them went in empty-handed and came out with at least one small parcel. In the case of Mrs. Easton-Brooks, it was seven large boxes and they were carried for her by three obsequious clerks.

Katy looked down at her side where her purchases lay. She had bought a book for Ria and fabric for herself. Ria was lonely and bored in the prison of her bed and Katy had taken it upon herself to keep Michael's wife entertained and her spirits lifted. Today nothing had helped. Ria cried until she made herself sick and Katy lost patience with her. Leaving Ria to her maid, Katy realized she needed to get out of the house before she began to equate it with a prison herself.

With no particular destination in mind Katy had eventually found herself in V.I. Donovan's. She purchased the book for Ria in the way of a peace offering and the fabric as an afterthought, then went to Victor's office and invited him to lunch at Crestmore's.

He'd seemed amused and pleased by the idea, but Katy had the sense that his enthusiasm was mostly for her benefit. When she first entered his office, he'd been sitting with his back to the door, staring out the window and deep in thoughts that seemed intensely personal. There were lines at the corner of his mouth she had never seen before and they worried her.

Katy frowned as someone moved into her field of vision, throwing her face in shadow. She glanced up and her frown deepened. "What are you doing here?"

Michael sat down in the booth opposite her. "Father sent me over to say he'd be later than he first thought."

"That's all right. I'll wait for him." She expected him to go then, but he didn't. He stared at her, his blue eyes sliding over her face until they rested on her mouth. "Your lips are cherry bright," he said in a low voice. "Very kissable."

"Don't do this here, Michael. I don't want a scene."

"There won't be one unless you cause it. I'm quite content to just sit here and imagine how things might be if you'd ever lower your guard around me. I could make you happy, Katy."

"Stop it," she hissed, pushing her half-finished drink to the middle of the table. "I don't want anything from you. And you can stop trying to make trouble for me and your father. Your remark last night at dinner was uncalled for. You tried to insinuate there was something between me and Logan Marshall and you couldn't be more wrong. Your father knows that, even if you don't."

"Then why was Logan at the house yesterday?"

"That's none of your business."

Michael persisted. "And why was he the one who found you in the hotel room?"

279

"Who told you that?"

"No one. I saw him. I was still in the hallway when he came up the stairs. I ducked out of sight until he disappeared into one of the suites. It was your suite he went into, Katy. I stayed around long enough to confirm that much. What is Logan Marshall to you?"

"He's no one to me."

"I don't believe that."

"I'm not listening to you any longer." She slid across the bench, gathered her packages, and stood. "Tell your father I decided to leave. I'll see him at home this evening." With her purchases in the crook of one arm and her beaded bag dangling from her wrist, Katy used her free hand to pick up the cherry phosphate. She lifted it to her lips, smiled frostily, then poured the drink in Michael's lap. "Waiter! There's been a bit of an accident here." Setting the glass down, Katy left the parlor.

Michael caught up to her on the sidewalk when they were directly across from Victor's store. His finely drawn features were pinched and flushed with anger. He grabbed her elbow, jerking her toward him so that she was forced to halt in her tracks. A few passersby slowed in their steps, glancing in Katy's direction. Michael's hard glare sent them hurrying off again.

"Let me go," she said under her breath.

"You need to attend to your manners."

"Not with you, I don't. I suggest you be careful, Michael. That detective Victor hired is bound to see you with me and begin to wonder."

Michael's grip eased. Finally he dropped his hand

280

altogether. "You're not always going to have the upper hand, Katy. Remember that."

Victor had just come out of the store. Ignoring Michael completely, Katy raised her hand to wave to her husband. Broadway was crowded with traffic and a hansom cab blocked Victor from her view. She caught a glimpse of him as he turned to go down the walk so that he could cross closer to the ice cream parlor. She tried to attract his attention again but it was a hopeless task in the midst of the traffic and the pedestrians. Carriages and carts and cabs filled the wide boulevard and people dodged the horse-drawn vehicles and impatient drivers in order to negotiate the crossing.

All except Victor Donovan. Looking in neither direction, he stepped onto Broadway and into the path of a coach and four.

Chapter Nine

Katy was a lone figure at the grave, a stark black silhouette against the evening sky. Occasionally a breeze would sweep across the knoll, suggesting movement when there was none. The hem of Katy's black gown fluttered; her bonnet was nudged further back on her head and her veil pressed lightly at the contours of her face. She remained immobile, her head bowed and her hands folded around a prayer book.

She wished it would rain. Rain would have seemed appropriate today, she thought. All nature should weep for Victor.

People had been parading in and out of the house for two days to offer condolences to Michael and pay their respects to Victor. Katy had never suspected how fondly Victor was regarded until she saw the swell of people gathered earlier for the funeral. Employees from the store, business acquaintances, his club friends, peers in his social stratum, all turned out to bid Victor farewell. She found little comfort in their appearance. Most often they spoke to Michael and regarded her suspiciously when they regarded her at all. Even at the end there were whispers about Victor's foolish marriage.

"Ma'am?" Liam O'Shea took off his bowler and held it in front of him. He cleared his throat to attract Katy's attention. "Mrs. Marshall? You should come away now. It's getting dark. You don't want to stay out here alone."

Katy's head turned slowly. She looked at O'Shea without really seeing him. "Pardon me?"

"I said you should come away now. Sure, and it's not a good thing for you to be out here alone."

Kay pushed her veil back and her eyes focused on the man at her side. He was a few inches shorter than she with dark, wind-ruffled hair and a stiffly waxed handlebar mustache. She remembered the mustache. "You're Mr. O'Shea, aren't you? The detective."

He nodded. "I wasn't sure you would know me. We met under less than pleasant—"

"I remember," she said quickly. "You were very kind."

O'Shea wanted to apologize for mentioning the circumstances of their meeting. He didn't because it would have only made things worse. It should have been clear to the meanest intelligence that Katy Donovan was grieving from her heart, yet O'Shea had been watching most of the day and had seen only a few people offer her comfort. He recognized them as theatre people, Katy's friends before she married Victor Donovan. None of Victor's friends gave Katy more than a brief word.

O'Shea was not generally at a loss for words. His glib tongue and easy manner made him a comfortable companion. He felt anything but comfortable now. Standing beside the grave, he was recalling everything associated with Victor's horrible accident. He couldn't imagine that it was any different for Victor's widow.

Liam had been following Katy that day, just as he did every time she left the house. He knew what purchases she had made, knew that she had been to see Victor, and knew that she had gone to Crestmore's for refreshment. He had watched her leave alone and seen Michael Donovan give chase. He had been on the point of interfering when Michael released her. Moments later Katy's attention was focused across the street and Liam glanced that way once to see what she saw.

There was nothing he could have done to save Victor. His warning shout could not be heard above all the other noises on Broadway that afternoon. Victor was knocked down by the lead horse and trampled by the pair behind. He was dead before the driver was able to pull up his team some fifty feet down the boulevard.

Katy's first instinct had been to run into the street but it was Liam, sprinting through the suddenly immobile crowd of onlookers, who held her back. Michael stood beside them, unable or unwilling to help, until Katy collapsed in Liam's arms, whimpering Victor's name over and over in a grief-stricken litany of loss.

"Mr. Marshall's carriage is waiting over there to take you home," Liam told her, pointing to the gravel drive which circled its way up the knoll. "He saw you refuse to go with young Mr. Donovan earlier and thought you'd need some

284

help getting home."

"I can walk."

O'Shea's mustache lifted at one end as he gave her a lopsided smile. "He told me you'd say that." Liam offered Katy his arm. "Please, Mrs. Donovan, Victor asked me to look after you. He'd want me to do this, and even if he didn't, *I'd* still want to. Won't you come with me?" When she still didn't move, Liam played his last card. "I can't leave until I've put you in that carriage. Not that I mind stayin' for myself, you understand, but my wife, well, she's not always so agreeable when I come home late."

"Very well, Mr. O'Shea," Katy said, taking his arm. She cast a last look over her shoulder at her husband's grave before allowing the detective to lead her away. At least Victor wasn't alone, she thought, still seeing the twin stone markers in her mind's eye. He was with his beloved Annie now and Katy was able to find some small comfort in that.

Liam knew the exact moment when Katy realized the carriage was already occupied. He felt her stiffen and hesitate before she finally made her decision to join Logan in the carriage. He realized that Logan had been right to do it this way, that Katy would not have gone with Logan if he had approached her first. Feeling the full force of Katy's cold stare, O'Shea ducked his head in an embarrassed apology, shut the carriage door, and told the driver he could leave. He waited until the carriage was out of sight before he left the cemetery on his own mount.

Katy was so furious that she couldn't even look at Logan for fear of striking him. She clutched the prayer book and stared out the window.

"I'm sor—"

Logan got no farther than that. The sound of his voice tipped Katy's emotional scales. She rounded on him, her eyes burning with gold fire and her voice shaking with the force of her anger. "How dare you do this to me! Won't you ever leave me alone? My God, Logan, Victor's not cold in his grave and you're sniffing after my skirts again! I've just spent three days ignoring snickers and innuendoes of people who think I married my husband for his wealth and position. They think Victor's death is what I've been waiting for! They think I'm mourning for show, that widow's weeds and weeping are for effect! I'm sick to death of all of them! All of them! And none more than you! You're the only person save myself who knows why I married Victor Donovan and *God damn* you for making me hurt like this now! I came to love my husband! I l-loved him! H-He was w-wonderful and gentle and k-kind and—"

Katy didn't know when it had happened, but sometime during her heartfelt speech Logan had moved from his side of the carriage to hers. He'd taken the prayer book from her gloved hands and encircled her with his arms. He gave up his shoulder to her and she leaned against him, clinging even while she cursed him. She hated him for witnessing her pain; hated him for opening his arms to her.

286

"Th-they're all wrong about me," she whispered. "Everyone. I cared for Victor. I wanted to b-be his wife for a long, long time."

"I know," Logan returned softly. He was crushing her bonnet so he loosened the ribbons and tossed it on the opposite bench seat. He gave Katy a handkerchief. She didn't use it and he didn't care. He let her cry until she was spent and even then made no move to release her. Through the carriage window he recognized landmarks that signaled the near end of their journey. "We're getting close to your home, Katy. What do you want to do?" When she didn't answer immediately, he repeated her name, thinking she had fallen asleep.

"I don't want to go home," she said at last, her voice barely audible. "They're reading Victor's will tonight and I don't want to be there."

Logan understood that he had won her company be default, not because she was choosing him. "Is there somewhere I can take you?"

Sitting up, Katy impatiently brushed away tear stains with her fingertips. She was surprised to find she held a handkerchief. She blew her nose. "I suppose you could take me to Wallack's," she said. "Jane was at the funeral today. She said if I needed anything I should—"

Logan held up his hand, interrupting her. "I have a better idea," he said. "Will you let me decide?"

He was asking her to trust him and Katy couldn't think of one reason why she should. In spite of all good common sense she felt her head bob once in assent.

"Good," he said. He opened a panel in the carriage and told his driver to take them to Marshall House. He saw the objection rising in Katy's throat before he heard it. "You said I could decide," he reminded her. "You were very clear earlier about what you thought of me being here, but you were also very wrong. I purposely only spoke briefly with you when I came to pay my respects and I avoided you today at the funeral. I thought it's what you would want."

"It was. So why did you stay after everyone else had gone?"

"Precisely because everyone else *had* gone. I didn't want to leave you alone. In spite of what you think, Katy it's clear to me that you're grieving. I'm not — what did you call it? — sniffing after your skirts?"

Her face colored as he repeated her words. "I should have found another way to say what I meant."

"I've heard worse." He raised his hand and briefly touched her cheek. "The color is good for you. You were as pale as salt before." The carriage stopped and Logan didn't wait for the driver to open the door for them. He leaned across Katy and flicked the handle with his fingertips. "This is where I'm getting out, Katy. You don't have to. Say the word and I'll have Joe drive you home."

In answer, Katy gave Logan her hand and let him help her down from the carriage.

The front parlor was crowded with furniture, figurines, and photographs. It was a homey room, filled with family treasures, and Katy would have liked to explore. Instead she sat on the edge of one of the settees and tried not to show how tired she was.

"You can relax, you know," Logan said, turning from the doorway with the tray the housekeeper had just handed him. He blocked Katy from Mrs. Brandywine's curious glance, tempering his rudeness with an-over-the-shoulder smile. Mrs. Brandywine backed away quietly. "You look like a fledgling bird, perched that way."

"One can't really relax in a dress like this," Katy said, indicating the bustle behind her. Her black train was made of yards of satin which she had swept to one side. The wire crinoline which kept the bustle in place remained exactly where it was meant to. "It's deuced uncomfortable."

"So take it off."

Katy blinked, her mouth parting slightly. "You're not serious."

Logan set down the tray and began pouring tea. "I am," he said, adding a generous finger of whiskey to Katy's glass. "Not the dress. Just that contraption attached to your backside. It fastens around your waist, doesn't it?"

"You know very well how it fastens," she said, bristling. "I'm sure you've released a fair number of women from them."

"Now don't try to flatter me," he said, not at all put out by her observation. "I'll turn my back and you can untie it and it will be our secret. Then you can sit back and curl up in the corner of that couch. Who knows, you may even be able to sleep for a few hours. I'm guessing you haven't slept

289

more than an hour here and there since Victor's accident."

"Well, I certainly can't fall asleep here."

He ignored her objection. "I'm turning my back."

Katy hesitated for all of five seconds. She wondered what it was about Logan Marshall that made her fall in with his most outrageous suggestions. Maybe he understood her too well, she thought unhappily. Perhaps he only suggested things she was halfway to thinking herself. The idea didn't bear scrutiny.

The furtive rustling of all that fabric made Logan smile. He stirred Katy's tea and waited for her all-clear signal. "Much better," he told her when she finally let him turn around. She'd drawn up her legs to one side and her head and shoulder rested against the back of the settee. "Would you like a blanket?"

"No. I told you I'm not going to fall asleep here. How would I explain that to Michael?"

Logan gave Katy her tea. "Drink this." He sat down at the other end of the settee, turning slightly in her direction. "Why do you have to explain anything to Michael?"

"Because he's going to want to know why I wasn't there for the will reading."

"So tell him you were with—what was her name?"

"Jane. She was my dresser at the theatre."

"So tell him you were with Jane."

"Lies usually have a way of getting found out," she said. "Never mind. It's my problem, not

290

yours. I don't know why I care about lying to Michael anyway. He's a—"

"Yes?"

"Nothing." Her weariness was going to make her say something she would regret. Katy vowed to be more cautious. She sipped her tea. "What did you put in this?" she demanded, jerking herself upright.

Logan reached across the couch to steady Katy's saucer before she spilled her tea. His hand brushed hers. The contact was brief and light and powerful enough for Logan to feel the wanting as a burning just under the surface of his skin. He withdrew his hand more quickly than he meant to. "What does it taste like?" he asked, striving for lightness.

"Whiskey."

"That's what it is."

Katy set her saucer down and wrapped her hands around the dainty, gold-rimmed cup. The warmth of the cup did nothing to lessen the tingling in her fingers. She told herself it was the whiskey. Any other explanation was unacceptable. "Are you trying to get me drunk?" she asked, eyeing Logan suspiciously.

"No." He raked his dark hair and loosened a few buttons on his black swallow-tailed coat. It parted, revealing a black sateen vest and pristine white shirt front. "I was hoping it would help you relax," he said, picking up a snifter of brandy. "I'm not trying to seduce you, Katy. I respect your loss. Victor was a friend of this family, remember?"

She nodded, raising her cup. "I'm sorry. I hardly know what I'm doing or saying these days. The accident was such a shock and then Dr. Turner told me . . ." Not realizing she had Logan's absolute attention, she let her voice drift off and drank more of her tea.

He waited as long as he could to hear the rest of her sentence. "You were saying?" he asked casually.

"Oh . . . I don't know if I should . . ." Katy shrugged, her eyes filled with misery. "I don't suppose it matters any more. Dr. Turner was Victor's doctor, you see, and he came to see me after he heard about Victor's accident . . . well, actually he came to see Michael and me together and told us,"—she took a steadying breath—"told us that Victor was dying of cancer."

"Oh, Katy." Logan didn't know what else to say. Her pain was very real to him.

"He says Victor would have been fortunate to live a full year. I think Victor was in some pain but he would never talk to me about it. He never said a word that there was anything seriously wrong with him; never hinted at it. I can't help think but that I failed him, that I should have somehow known. He gave me so much, Logan. I never gave enough back."

Tears dripped silently from her dark, luminous eyes. Logan didn't dare touch her for fear of betraying some emotion other than sympathy. "Your handkerchief," he said, pointing to where she had tucked it in the tight sleeve of her black mourning gown.

Katy looked away, withdrew the scrap of linen, and pressed one corner to her eyes to stem the flow. "I don't know why I'm telling you any of this," she said brokenly. "Victor should be here listening to me. He's the one I want here now, not you."

Logan's slumberous, heavy-lidded eyes hid what he felt in that moment. He remained immobile at his end of the settee, still as stone.

Finishing her tea, Katy set down her cup. "I should go," she said, staring at her hands. The handkerchief was a knotted, useless ball now. She stood and wavered slightly on her feet. Logan was at her side immediately. He helped her sit down, ignoring her objections when he put her feet on the settee and took off her shoes.

"There," he said, placing a cream wool blanket over her. He gave her a decorative throw pillow. "For your head."

"This really isn't necessary," she said.

Logan stared at her, waiting. He didn't change his stance until she was lying down, then he tucked the blanket around her. "When's the last time you ate? And if you have to think about it, it was too long ago."

"It was too long ago then," she murmured. Her eyelids fluttered. She fought to keep them open. "I don't want anything to eat."

"You didn't want to go to sleep earlier either."

"I'm not going to sleep," she denied. "Just resting."

"Of course." Logan stood over Katy, watching her. He looked at the delicate whorl of her ear and the feathered arc of her brow. Her skin was pale, still marked in places with tears, and her lashes were spiked. His cool gray eyes followed the line of her nose and rested briefly on her beautifully modeled mouth. He looked away then and after a few minutes he walked quietly out of the room.

"Where the hell was she?" Michael paced the floor at the foot of his wife's bed. Once he grabbed one of the corner posts and rattled it so the entire bed shook. "Where the hell *is* she? Did she say something to you before she went to the funeral?"

"Nothing," Ria whispered. Realizing that Michael hadn't heard her, she repeated herself more loudly. "We didn't talk at all today. She came to see me last night, but she never mentioned any plans for this evening."

"Did she talk about the will?"

"No! She talked about Victor. She's taking his death hard, Michael. She really loved your father."

"My father left her half of everything! Half!" He spun on his heel, his face taut with rage. His eyes were like splinters of glass. "At the worst I expected he would leave her a third. A quarter seemed likely. But half! He was out of his mind. My father was absolutely out of his mind!"

Ria brushed a wisp of flame red hair away from her mouth. Her dark emerald eyes appealed to her husband. "Have some pity, Michael. Can't you feel for what was happening to your father? Dr.

Turner told you Victor knew he was going to die. I know what he must have thought, what he must have felt."

"Stop it, Ria. You're not going to die. You're going to have a baby. Stop comparing your situation to Father's. It's not the same thing at all."

She wanted to scream. She wanted to throw things. What she did was swallow all the hurt and pressed the pillow more tightly against her swollen breasts.

Michael wasn't watching his wife. He was staring at the floor, his hands jammed in the pockets of his bed jacket, and tasting the flavor of something Ria had said in his mind. "The cancer," he said softly. "It stands to reason he was scared, that he wouldn't be thinking clearly when he made the will . . ."

"What are you saying, Michael?"

But Michael didn't hear Ria. He walked to his own bedroom and began dressing. He'd wait for Katy, he decided. If she returned tonight or tomorrow, he'd be waiting. The sooner she understood that he held the upper hand, the better.

Reaching across the bed for Victor, Katy's hand found nothing but a pillow. She sat up with a start, pressing the heels of her hands to her eyes. It was a horrible, chilling realization to know that Victor would never be within her reach again.

Slowly Katy's hands dropped away from her face. She lifted her head and looked around, the unfamiliarity of the setting making her uneasy.

295

Still groggy with sleep, it took her several moments to recall that she had been with Logan after the funeral and that she had never left Marshall House. She had a dim recollection of sitting in the parlor with him and an even dimmer memory of protesting while he was carrying her out of the room. Obviously he hadn't cared about her objections, because she was in one of the Marshall House bedrooms now, sitting in one of the Marshall House beds, and wearing something that belonged to a Marshall House woman. She sighed, plucking at the sleeves of her voluminous nightshift. Logan was a force to be reckoned with.

As her eyes became accustomed to the darkness, Katy could make out the room's sparse appointments. There was a corner brick fireplace, a large cherry wood wardrobe with brass handles, a ladder-backed chair on the left side of the bed, and an oval table on the right. The table held a washing basin, a pitcher, and several towels.

Katy put her legs over the side of the bed, resting her heels on the frame. Her hands cradled her head and her fingertips pressed against her temples. The raging headache she had had earlier had diminished to a dull ache. Feeling stronger, Katy stood up and went immediately to the wardrobe. She was relieved to find her clothes. She left them there and returned to the bedside, where she poured water into the basin and washed her face. Her eyelids were tender and faintly swollen from crying. She drenched one of the cloths with cold water, folded it, and held it over her eyes for a few minutes. Somewhere in the house a clock chimed out the hour. Katy counted three.

She swore softly. It seemed impossible that she could have slept so long or so deeply. If she hadn't reached for Victor, she might well have spent the entire night in Logan's home. It didn't bear thinking what Michael would do if he ever found out.

Katy dropped the washcloth and patted her face dry. Still holding the towel, she moved to the bedroom's sole window and parted the heavy velvet drapes. Fifth Avenue was quiet. A cat strayed into the circle of lamplight on the corner and leaped away again. A closed carriage moved slowly down the street. The driver's chin rested on his chest and his head bobbed with the motion of the carriage. Katy smiled to herself, realizing the man was sleeping. She hoped the horse knew the way.

Dropping the drape, Katy turned away, still smiling.

Logan was standing just inside the bedroom, one hand still on the doorknob. His hair was tousled and though his eyelids seemed heavy with sleep, there was a certain watchfulness about him. He was wearing a quilted robe tied loosely at his waist. The satin looked cool against his skin and the color was the same pewter gray as his eyes.

"I heard you moving around," he said. "My room's just next door."

"I'm sorry I disturbed you."

Logan's hand dropped away from the doorknob and he took a step further into the room, thrusting his hands into the pockets of his robe. His eyes slid over her quickly, assuring himself that she was all right. The nightgown he had pilfered

297

for her from one of the maids was yards too big everywhere but in the length. The hem just reached the top of her ankles. Her bare toes played with the fringed border of the large area rug. The gown's scooped neckline was too generous for Katy's shoulders and the soft cotton fabric rested precariously at the edge of her left shoulder.

"Is there something I can get for you?" he asked, his voice husky from sleep.

A carriage, she should have said. But instead she looked at Logan helplessly, willing him to understand what she could not put into words. Loneliness was a powerful ache inside her. "I woke up looking for Victor," she said.

Invisible pressure squeezed Logan's chest. The heaviness inside of him made it difficult to breathe. "That will probably happen for a long time to come. It's natural that you're going to miss him, especially in bed."

Katy looked away, hugging herself. The room wasn't the least cold and yet she was chilled to the marrow of her bones. "Is that why I want . . ."

Logan waited. The air was very still. The question she could not finish hung between them.

"I loved him," she said finally, softly. "So why do I want . . . why . . ."

Crossing the room, Logan stood in front of her. He applied just enough pressure against her chin with his fingertips to get her to look at him. "What is it you want, Katy?" he asked.

She stared at him. His hand was warm against the side of her face. Her eyes dropped to his mouth and stayed there. "I want to feel alive again."

"You will," he said. His fingertips trailed down her cheek and throat. His thumb rested in the delicate hollow of her throat. He remembered when his mouth had touched her there. He remembered the salty-sweet taste of her skin, the fragrance that was uniquely her own. "This isn't the right . . ."

"Take me to bed, Logan." Her arms circled his neck as he lifted her.

"You'll hate yourself for this," he told her.

"Probably."

He bent his head and caught her lips with his. The contact was brief, a mere promise. As he lowered her to the bed, the edge of her shift finally fell over her shoulder. "I've been waiting for that since I walked in here." His mouth skimmed the line of her collarbone as he stretched out beside Katy. Her skin was cool. He heard her indrawn breath when his tongue touched her. "Is this what you wanted?"

"Yes," she whispered. "Touch me again."

He did. Raising himself slightly, Logan touched the downy soft skin of her temple with his mouth. Her pulse beat lightly against his lips. It made him smile. "Undo your hair," he said.

Katy took the pins from her hair, never once looking away from Logan. It seemed that he could hold her immobile with those eyes of his. They were like hot liquid silver in the dimly lit room. She dropped the pins over the side of the bed and closed her eyes as Logan's hands slid under her head. He cradled her briefly in the palm of his hands. "Look at me, Katy. I want to see your eyes when I touch you."

Her eyes fluttered opened. Logan combed out her hair with his fingertips so that it spilled over her bare shoulder. "Milk and honey," he said, looking at her hair against the pale cream of her complexion. The silky strands slid off the curve of her shoulder and lay against the pillow. Logan's forefinger trailed from her ear to her neck, paused, then went lower until it met the neckline of her nightshift. He traced the edge slowly, dipping just below it on his second pass. "I think we should get you out of this," he said. "But first . . ." His mouth lowered over hers, finally delivering on the earlier promise.

Katy's lips parted as she matched Logan's hunger. Her mouth was warm and inviting and accepting. The kiss he slanted across her mouth made her rise up to meet his body. She felt herself straining against him, trying to touch him with her breasts and stomach and thighs. Her hands circled him and her nails made a little rasping sound as they scraped across the slippery satin of his robe. She knew he wasn't wearing anything beneath it, had known it when he first stepped into her room. It hadn't occurred to her to tell him to leave. Perhaps even then she had known what she wanted from him.

One of her feet nudged aside the hem of his robe. Hiking up the length of her gown, Katy was able to feel his bare calf against hers. Their knees bumped. Logan's legs parted, trapping one of Katy's between them. She whimpered with frustration.

The tiny sound made Logan's heart race. He murmured Katy's name as he tugged on her lower lip. His tongue slipped inside her mouth and rubbed the soft underside of her lip. It swept the ridge of her teeth and clashed intimately with her tongue. She broke the kiss, breathing shallowly, and pressed quick, tasting kisses along his jaw and at the corners of his mouth. A moment later she was deepening the kiss, pressing into his mouth, repeating his earlier motions. Her fingers traced the velvet lapels of his robe, making him want the feel of her against his skin. He held his breath when her hands slipped between them and found the sash of his robe.

She pulled at it, untying it. Her hands slid up his smooth, warm skin and eased the robe off his shoulders. He sat up long enough to shrug out of the robe, then lay beside her, partially covering her with his body. She could feel the hardness of him pressing against her belly. She moved, adjusting her position so that he was cradled by her thighs. This time it was Logan who moaned, frustrated by the barrier of Katy's nightgown. His hips ground against hers. He was somewhere between feeling relieved and feeling tortured. Turnabout was fair play.

Logan's hand smoothed Katy's shift over her breast. His thumb passed back and forth across the tip, feeling the nipple harden. When he heard her tiny sound of pleasure, he shifted his attention to her other breast, then he bent his head and circled her nipple with his mouth. His tongue laved the fabric, wetting it, and he suckled her between his lips.

It was maddening. The feel of his mouth, the wet cloth against her breast, the ridge of his teeth, all of it was maddening. Katy had not meant for Logan to take time with her. She had wanted him close, quick, and fierce. She wouldn't have cared if he'd hurt her. It may even have been preferable to what he was doing to her now, a fitting punishment for betraying Victor. Surely she would be damned for letting this man have her now, for wanting this man to have her, and for finding pleasure in the touch of his hands and the caress of his mouth.

"Please, Logan," she said on a thread of sound, her fingers tugging on the dark hair at the nape of his neck. "Hurry. Don't make me—" She bit her lip and swallowed her words and the urgent, throaty murmurings that he was creating in her.

But Logan would not be hurried. He never said it in so many words; he showed her in the lengthy exploration he made of her ear, tracing the whorl with his tongue and whispering her name so reverently that it could have been a prayer. He kissed her closed eyes, her cheeks, and found the hollow of her throat with his mouth. Her shift was removed in precise increments as Logan built excitement and savored anticipation. In the end she was the one who pulled it over her head. His deep chuckle sent a frisson of heat down her spine.

Katy did not want to want him. Not like this. She did not want the emptiness inside her filled with something this fine, this beautiful. *I should* have had this with Victor, she thought, miserably aware that she responded wherever Logan touched her. *Victor is the one I loved.*

Darkness protected her from Logan's eyes, but not from his hands. Katy found herself holding her breath, sipping the air in tiny measures, while Logan's palms learned the shape of her body. She felt tension pulling her limbs taut and Logan's fingers dipped between her thighs.

"Logan?"

"Hmmm?" He began stroking her intimately.

Katy didn't answer, *couldn't* answer. Heat blossomed at the core of her, coaxed to life by Logan's insistent, implacable touch. When his mouth replaced his hand, Katy tried to push him away. Later her heels pressed into the bedding as she lifted to meet him and Katy sucked in her lower lip to keep from crying out. He made her liquid inside, so hot she was melting. Her legs curved around him and she felt his hands slide under her buttocks. She hovered on the edge of a precipice, frightened and uncertain, then gave herself up completely as Logan made her come alive in his arms. Strings of tension dissolved and her skin tingled with pinpricks of heat. She said his name over and over and when she turned her head to the side she felt a tear slide along her temple and into her hair. Until then she hadn't known she was crying.

"Ssshh," he said, raising himself up on his elbows and sliding over Katy. He kissed her wet face. "No tears, Katy."

She nodded, afraid to look at him, afraid he

could see what was in her heart. "You made me feel . . . it was beautiful."

"*It's* not over."

"It isn't?" Then he was inside her, sheathed by her body. She rested her hands on his shoulders and felt him begin to withdraw, then thrust forward again. Her smile spoke of pleasure. "No, it's not, is it?"

Logan adjusted his position. Even the smallest movement bought an agony of pleasure. She seemed to close around him, holding him hotly and tightly. He kissed her on the mouth, the neck, and shoulders and finally his lips closed over the peak of one breast. Drawing her nipple into his mouth, Logan's hips ground against hers. He felt her knees draw up on either side of him as she accepted the fullness of his entry. Her heels caressed the back of his thighs and the hollow of his buttocks. Her hands stroked his arms and shoulders. He raised his head once, only to bury it in the curve of her neck. She could feel his warm breath against her throat, and the damp kisses he placed on her skin made heat unfold in the center of their joining.

He moved hard against her and Katy's fingers tangled in his hair, unconsciously tugging on it in a rhythm that matched his. Logan felt the familiar coil of tension as he moved deeply in her. The excitement he had nurtured in her was part of him now.

"Katy," he said.

That was all. Just her name. And Katy felt as if she had been given something precious. She felt the muscles bunch in his shoulders and neck. The entire length of him was taut and hard and his breathing changed to the quick and shallow rhythms of his body. When release shuddered through him, Katy felt it in her. She held him tightly, liking the weight of his body flush to hers. She hid her disappointment when he finally moved away.

Logan didn't move far. He turned on his side, propped his head on one elbow, and kept Katy close by placing one leg over both of hers. His fingers trailed slowly over her chest so that the back of his hand brushed one breast. "Cold?" he asked when she shivered slightly.

Katy shook her head. Her breasts were incredibly sensitive to touch. Logan's caress made her want to come out of her skin. She raised one hand and placed it over his, stilling his movements. "It's too much," she said. "Almost painful."

He nodded, withdrawing his hand. It fell in the curve of her waist and his thumb stroked her abdomen, passing back and forth across her navel. "Better?"

"If you have to touch me, then, yes, that's better." She had not meant for her words to come out quite so stilted or cool. It was just that she felt too vulnerable when Logan touched her belly or her breasts. The changes pregnancy brought to her body were obvious to her and she feared they might be obvious to Logan as well.

"I see," he said, matching her tone. "You're done with me, is that it?" He purposely kept his hand right where it was.

305

"No," she said quickly. "No, I didn't mean it like that. You make it sound as if . . ."

"Hmmm?"

"As if I was using you," she finished quietly.

"Weren't you?"

"Please, Logan, don't be horrid. I thought you understood."

Logan thought he had understood, too. In the beginning, perhaps he had, but making love to Katy altered his perspective. On reflection he saw that he had refused to take her quickly because he wanted her to know that he was the man in her bed, not Victor. Loving her thoroughly, making her want him, was his way of punishing her for marrying Victor in the first place. He hadn't realized that until now. No matter what she needed from him, he couldn't play understudy for her husband. And all the while he was touching her he knew it was the last time he would hold her. She would never come to him again. "I'm sorry," he said finally, his hand dropping away. "We do better when we're not talking."

Katy sat up and searched the foot of the bed for her nightshift. She found it, but when she started to put it on, Logan stopped her. He took it from her and dropped it on the floor, then pulled the sheet over them, bringing Katy to lie along the length of him at the same time. She turned in his arms and her mouth brushed his shoulder. His skin was warm and still faintly damp. "I should be going," she said.

"There are no 'shoulds' right now," he told her. "What is it you want to do?"

"Stay here, with you, just like this."

"Then that's what we'll do."

"But—"

He placed his finger across her lips, silencing her. "There's enough time for shoulds in the morning." Logan felt the outline of her sleepy smile against his skin. "Tired?"

"Mmmmm."

Logan's fingers whispered through Katy's hair. "Get some rest, Katy. I'm not going anywhere."

He was as good as his word. Long after Katy's even breathing signaled sleep, Logan remained awake, holding her, adjusting his position when she turned in her sleep. His hand strayed to her abdomen and he palmed the unfamiliar tautness of her belly, knowing the cause and haunted by it. He often wished he'd had enough will power not to look at Scott Turner's patient records. Knowing Katy was pregnant with Victor's child aroused a myriad of conflicting emotions. "It should have been my child," he said softly to himself. "Then there'd be no question of giving you up."

In the darkness, Katy stared straight ahead.

"You'll be all right?" Logan asked as Katy sat back in the hansom cab he had summoned for her. She fussed with the stiff folds of her mourning gown, trying to smooth the material over her lap. It did not command any special intuition on Logan's part to know that she was nervous.

"I'll be fine," she said tersely.

Logan leaned into the cab a little more. "You

307

don't have to go back to Victor's home if you don't want to, Katy. I'm certain some other arrangements can be made."

Katy had a pretty good idea of what those arrangements were and she wasn't having any. "Of course I'm going back. Don't forget, it's *my* home, too. I can't keep avoiding the place just because it reminds me of Victor at every turn."

She had her back up this morning, Logan thought, and he recognized his powerlessness to make things any different. "Already hating yourself for last night?" he asked.

She refused to look at him. "You predicted it."

"You could have proved me wrong," he said, trying to raise a smile.

"Would you please let me go now? You're holding up the driver. He may have other fares this morning."

"For God's sake, Katy, it's just barely daylight. Don't worry about the driver and his damn fares." His sharp tone brought a quick, surprised glance from her. "We didn't do anything wrong last night! You've nothing to be ashamed of!"

"Lower your voice!" she snapped. "Do you want all of Fifth Avenue to know what happened here?"

"I wouldn't care."

"Well, I would. You should have never put that whiskey in my tea."

Logan's voice dropped to a harsh whisper. "Are you trying to tell me that everything you did last night was because of a little alcohol in your tea? You're embarrassed, so it's *my* fault now? One of us needs to accept a little responsibility here,

308

madam, and it's *not* me. I was perfectly satisfied with last night's outcome and if you're honest, so were you."

Katy retied the ribbons of her bonnet, trying to block out what Logan was saying. "Stop it," she said. "I don't want to listen to this and I don't have to." The gentle, husky sound of her own voice was a roar in her ears. She could hear herself saying Logan's name over and over as he made her respond to him. It should have been Victor's name on her lips. "Tell the driver I want to leave now. And give him Jane's address in the Bowery. I'll find another cab there to take me home."

"You're *not* going to the Bowery. It's not safe."

"I'm not going home from here either. The newspapers would have that story by afternoon. The *Chronicle* included. As soon as the driver stops this cab in front of the house, he'll know who I am. I'm not going to shame Victor's memory that way." She turned to him then, her face pale as ash and her brown and gold eyes anxious. "Tell him, Logan."

He hesitated a moment, studying her resolve. Tapping the side of the carriage, Logan got the driver's attention and gave him a location in the Bowery. "Good-bye, Katy."

She nodded faintly. When she spoke she could only mouth the words. "Good-bye, Logan."

He shut the door, tapped the side of the carriage again, and stepped back onto the sidewalk. He stood there alone, stoic and still, long after Katy's cab had vanished from sight.

Katy gave her bonnet, gloves, and cloak to the servant who met her in the foyer. His expression was nothing so much as indifferent. If he had an opinion of Katy's early-morning arrival after an all-night absence, he managed to conceal it from her. Katy had one foot on the first step of the grand staircase when he called to her.

"Mr. Donovan's waiting for you in the library, ma'am," Duncan said. "He was most insistent that you join him the moment you returned."

"Was he?" Katy asked coolly. "I'm certain he didn't mean I should forego the niceties of dressing for the occasion. Tell him I'll join him when I'm quite refreshed." Without giving Duncan an opportunity to assert Michael's wishes again, Katy ascended the stairs and went to her room.

The bath drawn for her was hot and soothing but Katy couldn't relax. There was a dull, almost pleasurable ache in the lower part of her body that made it impossible for her to forget what she had done with Logan. It was too easy for her to imagine Logan inside of her again, moving against her, making her all too aware of how she wanted to be pleasured.

"Forgive me, Victor," she said, drawing her knees to her chest and hugging them. "It should have been you."

Katy stayed in the tub until the water turned cool, then she scrubbed herself pink. There were marks on her body, tiny bruises made by Logan's mouth that no amount of washing could erase.

chose one of the oversized leather armchairs near the fireplace, turning it so that it faced Katy. He was close enough so that when he stretched out his legs, his heels rested on the marble apron. Had he wanted to, his toes could have nudged the hem of her gown. Raising his face, he stared at Katy thoughtfully. "Black becomes you, Katy. I wouldn't have thought you could look so lovely in mourning, but you do. That bodes well for me, I think, since you'll be wearing that color for at least a year."

"Why did you want to see me, Michael?" She hated the way his pale blue eyes traveled over her. Even the slack set of his mouth was a cold, calculating leer.

"Straight to the heart of the matter, eh?" He raised his glass to his lips and sipped from it gingerly. "You should have come in when you first returned, if you were so anxious. Where did you go last evening?"

"You remember Jane? My dresser at the theatre? I took a cab from the cemetery to her home in the Bowery. I just couldn't face coming back here and listen to the will reading. Perhaps I should have told someone, but I didn't know that's what I was going to do till it was done. I'm sorry if you and Ria were worried."

Michael listened to her story without comment and merely grunted at her apology. "I'm sorry I didn't keep that detective on," he said finally.

"You don't believe me?" she asked, affronted.

"It doesn't matter, since something of this sort won't happen again. In the future you'll answer to me. I'll want to know where you're going and what you're doing."

"Don't be absurd, Michael. I don't have to answer to you. And I won't."

"As my mistress you will."

Katy shook her head. "How often do you have to hear me say no before you understand that I mean it? I'll leave this house before I'll let you lay a finger on me."

"Just so," he said smugly.

She was taken back by his smile. Her brows lifted in a question. "What do you mean?"

Michael set his glass aside. "In point of fact, if you don't want to be my mistress, then you'll not only have to leave this house, you'll have to leave the city as well. Aren't you just the least curious about my father's will, Katy?"

She was perfectly bewildered. "What does one have to do with the other?"

"He left you and your child half of everything," he said calmly, examining his nails.

"Half? But that's—"

"Absurd. Patently absurd. And that's what I'm going to prove, Katy." He looked up at her now, his eyes darkening with anger. "My father made out his new will soon after he found out he had cancer. I've spoken with his lawyer. Mr. Lockwood freely admits that my father was greatly troubled at the time of the rewriting. Of sound mind? I don't think so. Victor Donovan wasn't thinking clearly when he had Lockwood draw up the new papers, and if there was the slightest doubt, my father's suicide ended it."

For a moment Katy couldn't speak. "Suicide? What are you talking about? Victor's death was an accident. You were there. You saw it the same as I."

Michael cocked his head to one side and raised a cynical brow. "I saw my father deliberately step in the path of a speeding coach."

"That isn't what happened," she gasped. At her sides her hands clenched into fists. "You can't want to make people think Victor killed himself!"

"Can't I?" he asked. "I've had a long time to think about it, Katy. Most of the night, in fact. Shall I tell you what I've come up with?" He didn't expect an answer to his question. "I plan to contest Father's will. I think I'll find it very easy to prove he was so despondent that he can't be held accountable for the terms of the will. I feel certain Lockwood will come around to my way of thinking and Dr. Turner can be brought in to verify my father's illness. There were plenty of witnesses who saw my father trampled by the horses. How many do you suppose saw what I saw?"

"How many are you going to pay?"

"I don't think I'll have to do that, but it's an alternative worth considering." He stood up and advanced on Katy, pinning her where she stood with the force of his gaze. "I'm not letting you take what's rightfully mine, Katy. You're not entitled to a penny from my father's estate."

"I don't want anything. I told you, I never cared about Victor's money."

"You don't really expect me to believe that, do

you? What about your baby?"

Katy's hands folded protectively in front of her abdomen. "Victor wanted to provide for our child," she said with quiet dignity. But it was not a position she could maintain and Katy knew it. Had her baby really been Victor's she would have fought relentlessly for the child's birthright. It was a gallant gesture on Victor's part to want to provide for her and the baby, but it was also unnecessary. She had been on her own before and could manage this time as well. "You should consider honoring his wishes."

"I've considered all I want to." His hand came up and cupped her chin, holding her face steady. "Now consider what I have to say. You have a decision to make, Katy dear, and I'm going to outline your choices." His hand dropped to her neck when she jerked her head away from him. His grip was tight enough now that she couldn't move. "You can remain here as my mistress. You will quietly renounce your right to any part of my father's fortune. Except for Lockwood, who will draw up the papers, no one will ever know the true nature of our relationship or that you have given up your part of the estate. When your child is born I will settle a small portion on him or her, an eighth, perhaps, of the total Donovan holdings. That's a handsome sum under any circumstances."

"Go to hell, Michael."

His smile was feral. "I would not be so quick to send me to perdition or to dismiss one of your alternatives. You've yet to hear the others."

"I'm not interested in being your mistress. I

316

never have been. All the money in the world isn't going to change that."

Michael ignored her dismissal. "Another option is to accept a small gift from me." He named a figure that was generous if one did not take into account the worth of the entire estate. "Note the gift is from me. It's yours for not accepting the will. In this case you will leave the city and endeavor to live with some degree of anonymity in another part of the country. If you can plan wisely, you should be able to manage on the money I'll settle on you. You're resourceful as well. I shouldn't think it would be long before you've found some other man to see to your needs. If you're lucky, perhaps he'll die and leave you a fortune — without the complication of children from another marriage."

Katy slapped him.

Michael's features became rigid and his eyes bored into hers. His hand dropped away from her neck. Before she could take a step back he raised it again. Katy flinched but it wasn't enough. He hit her with enough force to drop her to her knees. Michael simply stood there, looking down on her while he regained his balance.

"Your last choice," he began emotionlessly, as if there had been no altercation, "is to fight me when I contest the will. You'll lose."

She was afraid to get up, afraid of what he could do to her and her child. Still, she could not cower in front of him. Raising defiant eyes to him, she said, "God, but I despise you. That you could be Victor's son is one of nature's nastier

317

surprises. Perhaps you'd be wiser not to challenge me, Michael. I could relish fighting you in court. I've played the bitch on stage. There can't be much to taking the role in real life."

"If it were only your reputation at stake, I really believe you'd do it," he said, brushing the side of her face with his fingertips. He could feel the heat from the slap he'd delivered. "But it's not just your reputation. It's my father we're talking about here. And Ria and your child and . . . and Logan Marshall."

"Logan Marshall?" she asked, carefully making her features a blank. "What does he have to do with anything?"

"I'm not certain. But it would be easy enough to discover, wouldn't it? He was at your hotel room at least one time that I know of. On reflection, I think he might have known you when he came backstage to your dressing room. And he was here not long before my father committed suicide."

"Stop saying that! It was an accident!"

"Perhaps my father was despondent over more than his impending death. After all, we're all of us mortal beings. What if Father was moved to kill himself because he knew his wife was straying from the nest?"

"You're vile."

Michael shrugged. "I may not be able to prove it, but I can raise the question often. And the public being what it is, well, you understand that they'll come to their own conclusions. I can't be responsible for what they might believe." He took a step backward, turned, and picked up his drink. He carried it to the door. "With the exception of reminding you of the photographs I still retain, I think I've said everything I wanted to say. I'll expect an answer tomorrow morning. That gives you twenty-four hours to make a decision, Katy. If you make up your mind more quickly than that, I'll be at the Union Club. Duncan can reach me there." He raised his glass again and this time a little bourbon spilled over the edge and spattered the carpet. He grinned crookedly; a boyishly handsome expression adorned his Adonis face. "Good day, m'dear."

When he was gone, Katy sat back on her heels. He thought he had given her three choices and yet there was only one worth considering, one which he hadn't offered at all. She could leave the city without accepting any of Michael's money or renouncing Victor's will. It sounded like what she should do, she thought, fingering the cameo at her throat. She would be independent again, out of reach of Michael's threats and without reminders at every turn of her brief marriage to Victor. It would be a challenge to start again somewhere else, she maintained silently. She didn't have to stay in New York.

Her hands folded over her abdomen and she pressed them there in expectation that the baby would provide some answer. "If I'm doing the right thing," she asked, "then why do I feel as if I'm running away?"

Chapter Ten

February 13, 1873 — Washington, D.C.

It was just as the curtain was closing on the matinée's second act that Katy's water broke. There had been twinges and aches since last night, but she had resolutely ignored them. This was a little more difficult to ignore. Her undergarments were wet but nothing showed on the gown she was wearing. Thank God for small favors, she thought. If she ruined the gown, she'd have the wardrobe mistress to contend with. She didn't think she was up to facing that dragon now.

Off stage she sat on one of the prop chairs and tried to catch her breath. All around her stagehands and actors moved with purpose and the grace of long practice as they set up the next scene and costume change. The activity was a well-choreographed blur and Katy, excused from lifting a finger this late in her pregnancy, had nothing to do. Usually she stood out of everyone's way in the stairwell. This evening she couldn't walk that far. Still, no one noticed her until John Burja needed the chair she was sitting on.

"Sorry, Miss Dakota. You'll have to move. This

320

chair belongs in the next—" He broke off and his large furry brows joined in a single line above deep-set eyes. "Hey, are you feeling all right? You're not going to whelp right here, are you?"

The contraction had passed. Katy smiled without pain and stood up. She touched John on the shoulder and shook her head. "No, John, I'm not going to—"

A small screech interrupted Katy. Donna Mae Polk pushed John at the small of his back moving him along. "Whelping is what a bitch does," she said matter-of-factly. "And Katy here isn't a bitch. Now take the chair and stop standing around asking foolish questions. Anyone can see that our Katy's going to have a baby, not a litter." She turned her back on Katy and presented an unlaced corset and the open back of her gown. "Do me up, would you, dear? I can't find that no-account dresser of mine. Not that I care. Thanks to her I couldn't breathe through the first two acts. God, I wish intermission was longer. You're lucky you don't have to be bound up in one of these blessed contraptions. What a piece of good fortune it was to cast you for the part of Alice. 'Course, I'm sure most of the audience thinks it's pillows you've got under your gown."

"I do have one," Katy admitted.

Donna looked back over her shoulder, her baby blue eyes wide. "Go on with you," she said in disbelief. Donna Mae had deep dimples on either side of her mouth. They disappeared as her lips curved in a small O of astonishment. "Really?"

"Really. I never got very big. I suppose because

I'm so tall, I just—" She broke off as another contraction gripped her.

"Oooh, not so tight with the laces, dear." When Katy's grip didn't ease Donna Mae glanced back again. "Hey! You're really going to have this baby right now, aren't you?"

Katy managed a small laugh, her face pale. "Not right now. Everyone in the company who's had children tells me the first one takes awhile. I'll be able to finish the third act."

Donna threw up her hands, raising her eyes to the rafters. "Just don't drop that baby while I'm on stage, dearie. I'm not going to have you stealing my best scenes."

Considering the circumstances, the third act of *Hampstead Heath* was carried off with hardly a hitch. On two occasions, pain made Katy mute and each time Donna Mae covered for her. The other cast members, in whispered asides, soon realized what was happening and made allowances for Katy's condition. The last act wasn't *Hampsted Heath* as the playwright intended it to be, but only the actors were aware of the changes.

Katy participated in two of the three curtain calls. By the last one she was being led off-stage and into Donna Mae's dressing room.

"Well," Donna Mae sighed as she entered the room. "That was much, much too close." She plucked at the fingers of her elbow-length gloves and surveyed the people crowded around Katy. Two stagehands were holding her up, another was pacing the floor. Donna Mae's dresser was wringing her hands while yet another cast member

322

searched through Donna's wardrobe, looking for something that might be of use. Behind her, players were already filling the doorway. Donna Mae dropped her gloves in her dresser's lap and immediately took charge. "Please, someone put her on the divan over there. John, there's some bed linen we use in the first act. Bring it down here."

"But—" The objection came from Katy as she was escorted to the low couch. She was ignored. John rushed out to do Donna Mae's bidding. The diminutive lead actress was a force to be reckoned with. She gave orders with authority of a general and tolerated no excuses from her legion of followers. Mutiny was unthinkable.

"Now, Henry, you fetch Katy's doctor. Ramsey, isn't it?"

Katy nodded. "But—"

"He's over on Connecticut Avenue. Ask someone if you can't find it. Tell him it's the baby and that her labor's not going to be a long one from the looks of it. Florence, get some nightgowns out of my wardrobe and help Katy into one of them. The ones in the second drawer will be fine. Jacob, see about some hot water. And will someone *please* undo the back of my gown? I swear I can't breathe again. As for everyone not engaged in a meaningful task, take yourself off. This is one time an actress doesn't want an audience. Isn't that right, Katy? Honestly you'd think babies were never birthed backstage before."

"But I want to have my baby at home," Katy finally got out, her mouth set tightly against the pain.

"Of course you do," Donna Mae offered soothingly. "But I don't think that's what your baby wants." She sighed with relief as her dress and corset were loosened. "So much better. Thank you, Flo. As soon as you help Katy with her nightgown you can wait outside. Bring the sheets in when John returns, the water when Jake brings it back, and show the doctor in. I'll see to anything else that our Katy needs."

Katy realized that as long as she remained an actress she would never be without family. Everyone took care of everyone else. She wasn't even afraid that the doctor might not come. He was a thespian from his Hasty Pudding days at Harvard and some ties were stronger than blood.

"Are you crying?" Donna Mae demanded suspiciously, peeking through the yards of petticoats she had raised above her head.

Blinking back tears, Katy shook her head.

"Good." Donna finished removing her undergarments, letting them fall to the floor with a flourish. "There's no sense getting yourself worked up now. You're going to need your strength for when it *really* starts to hurt."

"You mean it hasn't?"

"No, it hasn't." She opened her wardrobe and passed her hand back and forth across her clothes. "Are you anticipating a girl or a boy?" she asked.

"I think I'd like—" Another contraction came and Katy curled fetally on the divan, her nails digging into the plush velvet upholstery. "—a girl."

Nodding, Donna's fingers curled around a shell pink wrapper and plucked it out. "I'll wear this then. No sense tempting fate by wearing blue." She shut the wardrobe door and saw that Katy was in some distress. "Try to relax, darling. And be careful not to fall off the sofa."

"Relax?" Katy gasped. Her expressive brown-gold eyes were suspicious. "Donna Mae, do you have any children of your own?"

The actress sat at her vanity and began removing her greasepaint. Katy was reflected in her mirror. "I've been married to the theatre for thirty-five years, dear. I like to think of all of you as my children."

"I was afraid it might be something like that," Katy commented to herself. More loudly, she said, "Then you've never actually given birth."

Donna Mae paused in wiping rouge off her cheeks. "I've presided over half a dozen, so don't think I don't know what's to be done. I'm much more experienced than you are."

The sheets arrived then and Donna Mae stopped what she was doing to help make up the divan with a double set. Katy lay back down on her side, drawing up her knees. "I think I could have made it home," she said, thinking about the freshly painted nursery waiting for her baby. She really hadn't thought she was so close to birthing when she left for the theatre. Ever since coming to Washington, Katy had been making plans to have the baby in her little red brick house on E Street not far from the theatre. That seemed a more fitting setting for Logan's child and Victor's heir than Donna Mae's dressing room.

Katy sighed, touching the tip of her tongue to a

bead of perspiration on her upper lip. It just wasn't meant to be. Donna Mae Polk, she of the generous curves and heart, was kneeling at her side now, wiping greasepaint from her face and chattering on about names for the baby.

When she left New York, Katy had some idea of what obstacles she might encounter. She was young, widowed, pregnant, and traveling alone. It was unfortunate that in combination these things worked against her, inspiring strangers to whisper after her rather than offer any sort of assistance. Still grieving for Victor, Katy bore their censure without indicating that she knew it existed. It was a blessedly short train ride to Washington.

The capital was the logical place to set down new roots. She was passingly familiar with the city even though there were many changes since she'd lived there as a young girl. There were enough theatre productions to support an actress who didn't want to travel with tours and the quality of those productions compared favorably with what the Rialto offered. Katy was confident she could find work. That Washington was also the home of Richard Allen when Congress was in session was something Katy had learned to live with. She was no longer a frightened little girl — something her stepfather would discover if he ever dared approach her.

Although Katy had accepted nothing from Michael, she had gowns and jewelry from Victor which she was able to sell. The jewelry turned out to be especially valuable. She parted with everything but her wedding band in order to buy the house.

Taking back the name Dakota, Katy found work in brief productions of *Romeo and Juliet*, *Twelfth Night*, and *Much Ado about Nothing*. Even before her pregnancy would have been evident to an audience, Katy did not aspire to command the lead roles. She preferred small character parts, playing shrews and peasants with equal fervor. With the proper padding she took on several minor male roles, and performed a feat of acting that remained unknown to her audiences.

Katy played older women—grande dames and smothering society mothers—in several melodramas that were popular with the public, though not critical successes. In January, just when she thought she would have to excuse herself from work, the part of Alice in *Hampstead Heath* was offered to her. It was a daring character to play because Alice Hampstead was supposed to be a free-spirited thinker, one of the Bohemians of pre-Civil War Manhattan. She was unmarried, pregnant, and flaunting both those facts in front of her very staid, very circumspect family. The irony, as Donna Mae had discovered earlier, was that Katy wasn't large enough to flaunt anything without extra padding.

It seemed to Katy that she drifted in and out of reality as the contractions came harder and faster. There was scarcely time to breathe between them, let alone collect her thoughts. Donna Mae kept up a steady stream of encouragement and wiped Katy's damp face with a cool cloth. Henry brought the doctor just after six o'clock, and a few minutes

327

before nine Katy delivered her baby.

"Oh, darlin'," Donna Mae murmured, placing the child against Katy's breast. "You never told me what you're going to call your little girl."

"It's a girl?"

"I'm wearing pink, aren't I?"

Katy's eyes caressed the red-faced infant in her arms. The baby's hair was so light she appeared bald. Her skin was wrinkled and her mouth was opened so wide that her eyes were mere creases. Her dimpled knees were folded against her chest and her tiny fists flailed at the air. Red-faced, wrinkled, and bleating like a lamb—she was simply the most beautiful baby in all the world. Katy touched the back of her forefinger to her daughter's soft, downy cheek. "I'm going to name her Victoria," she said quietly. "After my late husband."

"Victoria," Donna Mae repeated, raising puzzled eyes to the doctor. If Victor was her late husband, she wondered, then who was this Logan person Katy called for during her labor?

New York City

Michael paced the hallway outside his wife's bedroom. He would have liked to have gone downstairs and sought refuge in his study. The disapproval he imagined Dr. Turner would level at his head kept him precisely where he was. Dr. Turner had already expressed some concerns that Michael wouldn't let him move Ria to Jennings Memorial. A hospital! It was out of the question.

328

It was a place for the infirm and the dying. His wife wasn't sick and she wasn't going to die. She was too afraid of him to do that. Ria was having a baby, for God's sake. Women did it all the time and they damn well didn't have to do it in a hospital.

He stopped his wife's maid as she stepped out of Ria's room. "How is she doing, Emily?"

Emily shook her head, her expression bleak. "The baby just doesn't want to come, sir. Miss Ria's strength is nearly sapped." She bobbed a quick curtsy and hurried on her way.

Michael swore softly and kicked at the dark oak wainscoting once Emily was out of earshot. Just once, he thought angrily, couldn't Ria do something right? He let his mind wander to Katy for a moment. She would be nearing her time; possibly she had already given birth. And she'd probably done it with a lot less caterwauling than Ria. Michael vowed that if he heard his wife cry out one more time he'd go in and give her something to really scream about. Did she think she was the only one suffering?

To hell with what Scott Turner wanted, Michael decided. If he was expected to endure his wife's labor, then he'd endure it with bourbon.

When Dr. Turner found Michael in the study a few hours later, the master of the house was drunk. Scott ordered Duncan to bring a pot of hot coffee and do what he could to sober Michael up.

"Your wife's sleeping now, Mr. Donovan," Scott said, trying to keep disgust out of his tone. He was less than successful. "When she wakes up, she's going to need you. I suggest you heed Duncan's instructions and do what's necessary to make yourself presentable."

"I won't stand for being talked to in that manner anywhere — certainly not in my own home." Michael took a belligerent step forward and did not seem to realize he was wavering. "S'what about the baby?" he asked, thrusting his chin out.

So he did remember. Scott was beginning to wonder. "A little girl," he said. He added bluntly, "She lived only a few minutes."

"Damn that Ria," Michael muttered under his breath.

"Pardon?"

"I said . . . never mind. It doesn't matter. Dead, you say? That's that, then. Nothing to be done but try again when Ria's well."

Scott sucked in his breath. His knuckles were white on the handle of his black leather bag. "Your wife shouldn't have been pregnant this time, Donovan. Another pregnancy will kill her."

"That's what you said before — and you were wrong."

"Well, I'm not wrong now. She's still not out of danger and her state of mind is fragile. I don't want to learn that you've tormented or upbraided her for what happened. She did what she could to keep her child and —"

Michael grunted, raising his glass to his lips. "She wanted an abortion when she found out she was pregnant. You call that doing what she could to keep her baby? She's done this to spite me. She

330

and Katy have conspired against me." He tipped back his wrist and drained his glass, vaguely realizing that he had said more than he meant to. "Go ahead, Turner, take your leave. I'll take care of my wife without any help from you. Send a bill, but don't bother coming back to see her again. It won't be hard to find another doctor who knows a damned sight more about women and babies than you do."

Scott's jaw clamped together as he bit back half a dozen things he wanted to say to Michael Donovan. He made a slight bow, his striking blue eyes frozen with contempt. "As you wish. Only see that she gets medical treatment first thing in the morning. I cannot stress enough how fragile she is now."

"Yes, yes," Michael said impatiently, waving Scott away.

"You would do well to understand that Ria's in mourning."

"Persistent bastard, aren't you?" The door to the study opened and Duncan walked in, wheeling a tea cart. Michael pointed to the doctor and addressed his butler. "Show him out, Duncan."

"I can find my own way." Scott brushed by the butler. At the door he paused. "Mrs. Donovan named the baby. You may want to know that for when you have the stone cut for her grave. Your daughter's name was Victoria Anne—after your parents."

"That came for you today," Mrs. Brandywine

told Logan, taking his coat and hat. She pointed to the slim crate leaning against one wall of the foyer. "I was going to send someone 'round to the paper to tell you—I thought it might be important—but then I realized you'd be home any time. That was six hours ago." She clucked her tongue twice in a disapproving sound that Logan was deaf to after all these years.

"I had to work late, Mrs. B.," he said, flashing her a quick, apologetic smile.

She sighed. "You're just like your father, drowning in your work. Come up for air from time to time."

Logan was investigating the crate. He hunkered down, running his hands along the top of the wooden slats. He whistled softly. "This is from Christian in Paris. Was there a letter to go with it?"

"Nothing. Only the crate." She hung up Logan's coat and hat. "If you ask me, it's just as well. Sure, and every time we hear from·them they're announcing it will be a few more months before they return. Holland's going to be out of short pants the next time I see him."

He glanced up at the housekeeper, his eyes grave. "I miss them, too." Logan ventured a faint smile. "Come on, Mrs. B., ask Reilly to get a crowbar for me and we'll see what Christian's sent us. From the size of it I suspect it's a painting. What do you think? One of his own or something he wrangled from a private art collector?"

Twenty minutes later they had wrested Christian's gift from the crate. It was indeed a paint-

332

ing, a portrait to be exact, and Logan knew the subject intimately. He simply stared at it and wondered what he could possibly say that wouldn't lay bare his soul.

Mrs. Brandywine, however, had no trouble filling the void. "Why, it's that woman—that actress," she declared, a frown creasing her well-lined brow. "Whatever is Christian thinking of, painting that woman? And how could he from memory? You don't suppose that she's in Europe, do you?"

"I believe Miss Dakota has begun a career for herself in Washington," said Logan. "And it's likely that Christian's working from photographs that Jenny took." He pointed to Katy's luminous eyes in the portrait. "See? He's got the color of her eyes wrong. They're not green at all, but brown with splinters of gold. And her hair's a darker shade of honey, more amber than this gold that Christian's mixed."

"No, I don't see. And how do you know what color her eyes are?" She set her hands on her hips. "Used to be that I knew most everything happening in this house. Now there are more secrets than I've got gray hairs, which is saying something since you and your brother are responsible for most of them."

Logan let Mrs. B. fume, murmuring occasionally so she thought she was being heard while he studied the portrait. Actually he felt helpless to look away from it. Katy's profile was presented at three angles, as if she were turning toward him. The pose suggested motion and when Logan's gaze drifted, Katy's seemed to follow. Her eyes may have been the wrong color, her hair a shade too light, but Christian had caught the radiance that made Katy's features so striking. Christian had used subtle shadings of light to follow the transition of the actress to her character. She was soft, even vulnerable, in the first pose. There was a shift in the second, a tilt to her head that suggested haughtiness. In the third, the lines of her face were hard, the set of her mouth brittle and bitter, her eyes cynical. The study was a tribute to Christian's skill as an artist, Jenny's talent as a photographer, but most of all to Katy's work as an actress.

Logan stood, lifting the painting by the gilt-edged frame. He held it in front of him for a moment, then hefted it under one arm.

"What are you going to do with it?" asked the housekeeper.

"I'm going to hang it in my room until I hear from Christian. I don't know what his plans are for it, but if he wants to sell it I have a buyer already in mind." Although Mrs. Brandywine was silent, Logan suspected she knew he wanted the portrait for himself.

He set the painting on the mantel of his fireplace and prepared for bed. Occasionally he glanced at the portrait, only to find Katy's eyes watching him no matter where he was in the room. It could have been an unsettling feeling but Logan was used to visions of Katy clouding his thoughts.

Long hours at the paper didn't help erase Katy from his mind. At odd moments, for no apparent reason, she insinuated herself into his thoughts. He'd remember her standing on the ladder in Victor's library, reciting Juliet's lines, or pacing the floor of her aunt's barn, playing at being Kate the shrew. He saw her in her bath trying to be both modest and defiant while being undermined by disappearing bubbles. There were moments when her smile would hit him with the force of a blow and he would actually have to stop what he was doing to catch his breath. He'd hear her laughter, the giggle of young Mary Catherine, and it made him wonder what her adult laughter sounded like. He had never heard her laugh and he realized that he was a poorer person because of it.

Sometimes the vision that caught him off guard was an erotic one. He'd imagine her lying beside him as she had the last time he'd seen her, her long legs flush to his. He could almost feel the milk-white smoothness of her flesh. Her mouth would be touching his shoulder, his chest. She would draw his fingers into her mouth and suck gently, watching him all the while with darkening eyes.

Lying back in bed, his head propped on an elbow, Logan stared at the painting. He wondered about her baby, if she had had it yet and if it was a boy or a girl. He wondered if he was responsible for her abrupt departure from the city. Most of all he wondered if she ever thought of him.

Logan reached across the bed and turned back the lamp. That night he dreamed of Katy only indirectly. His nightmare was Andersonville.

July 7, 1873 — Washington, D.C.

"'I just don't understand why you won't take a larger part," Donna Mae said. She blew a raspberry against Victoria's bare tummy and the baby chortled gleefully. Donna Mae's dimples appeared. She bent her head over Victoria again and nuzzled the baby's soft skin with her nose.

Katy intervened, scooping Victoria from Donna's lap. "Being my daughter's godmother doesn't give you the right to smear greasepaint all over her tummy." She held out her hand for a cloth which Donna Mae obligingly dropped in. "I'm quite happy with the roles I've been getting," she said, returning to Donna Mae's original query. "The only time I was out of work was when I was recovering from having this little muffin. I've been busy since the middle of March."

"There's busy and there's famous," Donna Mae countered. She turned around on her stool and finished removing her face paint. "You've talent enough to be playing in New York or London or Paris. The *lead* roles, Katy, not just these character parts you put your heart and soul into."

"You're supposing I want to be famous. I don't. I had a brief taste of that before and it turned my life upside down. Victoria and I are just fine with the way things are, thank you very much. We lead a very private life."

"You live like a hermit. I'd venture you don't know three people in this city who aren't part of the theatre."

Michael had suggested that she live in anonym-

336

ity and Katy had taken his words to heart. For a few hours, five days a week, Katy stepped into the limelight. When the curtain dropped she all but disappeared from public view. "I really am happy with my life," she said.

Donna Mae snorted indelicately. "Pull the other one, it's got bells on."

"I *am* happy."

The older actress swiveled around in her seat again and leveled Katy with a hard, knowing look. "You need a man," she said with authority.

Katy blinked at Donna Mae's tone. "I'm in mourning."

"It's been almost a year. Anyway, I'm not suggesting you take up with the first man who offers. But you could look occasionally. You never seem to notice any of the men who come around here and, by God, Katy, they do notice *you*." I've walked down E Street with you and seen men actually stumble in their steps while they're looking after you."

Katy hid her warming cheeks against Victoria's downy cap of dark hair. "You're exaggerating—and you're wrong. I do look. Not so long ago I thought I saw someone I knew at the market."

"A man?"

"Yes, a man. That's what we're talking about, isn't it?" Katy could have sworn she'd seen Liam O'Shea—not once, but several times since she'd moved to Washington. It was an unsettling feeling to think that Michael might be having her watched. Each time she'd tried to approach the man she thought was Liam, he'd disappeared. "So, you see, I do notice, and I'm just not interested. End of subject."

Donna Mae never ended a discussion simply because the other party was bored with it. Now was no exception. She set her auburn wig on its stand and ruffled her frizzy blond curls, prepared to do battle. A knock at the door interrupted her. "We'll save this for later," she told Katy meaningfully as she went to the door.

Katy played with Victoria, giving no thought to Donna Mae's guest. The actress had several gentlemen this month who were courting her favor. Katy was more amused by Donna Mae's continuous juggling of male callers than envious. Katy thought her own life was filled quite full with her daughter.

Victoria Rose was an endless source of pleasure and, less frequently, vexation. At almost five months, she was fourteen pounds and twenty-five inches and possessed an independent streak to match her strength and length. She babbled to herself and lifted her head, gray eyes solemn, when she heard her name. Right now she was fascinated by her mother's drop earrings and reached out with her tiny hands to grab at one of them.

"There's a caller for you, Katy," Donna Mae said, turning away from the door. She closed it slightly so her conversation could not be heard. "John told him you'd be here if you hadn't left the theatre already. Do you want to speak with him?"

Katy set Victoria on her lap so the baby was sitting up, her back supported by Katy's arm. "I don't think so," she said. "Take his card and fob him off with one of those excuses you're so good at."

Shrugging, Donna Mae stepped into the hallway. A few seconds later, she ducked her head back in the room. A frown pulled the corners of her mouth down and she was looking at Katy oddly. "Mary Catherine?"

Katy's head jerked upward and she stopped playing with Victoria's bare toes. "Who is it at the door?" she asked, a tightness compressing her throat.

"He says he's your stepfather." Donna Mae watched every vestige of color drain from Katy's face. "I'll tell him to leave," she said.

Katy stood up. "No." She was surprised that she could speak, more surprised by what she had said. "No, I want to see him. Will you take Victoria and give me ten minutes alone here with him?"

Donna Mae's frown deepened. She thought it over. "Ten minutes. Not one second more—and I'm only going to be waiting in the hallway."

"That's not—" Katy didn't bother to finish her sentence. Donna Mae was plucking Victoria out of her arms and the militant look on her face said she could not be swayed.

The first thing that struck Katy when Colonel Richard Allen stepped in was how young he looked. Ten years ago when she had last seen him he seemed a very old man to her. Time had changed her a great deal while the colonel was remarkably much the same.

His features were still quite ordinary, neither

339

particularly blunt nor sharp. Allen displayed a few threads of gray in his side whiskers and neatly trimmed beard and mustache, but he still parted his hair on the left and his bald spot was only marginally more noticeable than it had been a decade earlier. He carried himself rather stiffly, with his shoulders thrown slightly back, giving the impression of authority and command. His eyes, more gold than green, reminded Katy that he had been called Cougar.

Allen shifted his silk top hat from under one arm to the other. Even before he cleared his throat to speak, Katy realized he was uncharacteristically nervous.

"Thank you for seeing me," he said.

Katy's chin raised a notch. "I'm not certain why I did," she said honestly. "Perhaps I'm just a little surprised that you'd dare come here at all. I had to see you to believe it."

"I saw this play for the first time two weeks ago and I've seen it three times since. I was never completely sure that it was you behind the footlights. It's hard to believe." His voice dropped to a whisper and he shook his head slowly from side to side in the manner of a man drawing on memories. "Mary Catherine McCleary—an actress. You always were something of an odd child."

Allen's faint smile chilled Katy to the bone. She spoke sharply, "I'm not a child any longer, Colonel Allen."

"No, you're not, are you?" He'd seen that for himself during each performance. She was as tall as he now, slender and gracefully curved as a

340

saber.

"What do you want?" she asked.

"I came to inquire after Rose and your sister."

"They're dead."

He drew in a breath and let it out slowly. "I'm sorry. I never heard . . ."

"It's been a long time. They died before the end of the war."

After a moment, the colonel said, "You were on your own then."

"I managed." She paused. "I understand you're a congressman now."

"Yes. I'm going to run for the Senate. After that . . . who knows?"

"I see."

Allen cleared his throat again and his eyes could not quite meet Katy's. "Do you plan to make trouble for me?" he asked.

So that was why he came, Katy thought. "I've lived here for almost a year and I've made no attempt to sully your reputation during that time. I'm really not a threat to you, Colonel. I've always kept our dirty little secret, haven't I? Logan Marshall is the one who betrayed—" Katy stopped, her expression very still with thought. She'd been about to say that Logan Marshall had betrayed them both and now it was borne home to her that she was wrong, horribly wrong. The guilty light in Allen's eyes, his suspicion that she would cause trouble for him, reached Katy as nothing else ever could. For years she had lived with the thought that she was responsible for the things her stepfather did to her. And for all those long years she'd blamed Logan for revealing it. "I think you should go—"

"No!" Allen held up his hand, cutting her off. "No, you said something about Logan Marshall. You implied that he was a threat."

"As long as you don't amuse yourself with little girls, you don't have to worry about Logan," she said coldly.

"But Marshall's dead," Allen objected, bewildered. "I saw the records myself. He died in Libby Prison. He was picked up by a rebel patrol and taken to Libby after the battle at Chancellorsville. It was all arranged; everything was arranged."

"Pardon me?" Katy's arms crossed in front of her chest. She hugged herself. "Do you mean Logan was picked up by rebel scouts—*at your request?*" It wasn't necessary for the colonel to answer because Katy saw it in his eyes. A moment before the cold shutter was drawn over them, she had seen his answer. "My God, you did, didn't you? You betrayed him because he knew what you were doing to me. All this time I thought that somehow I'd been responsible for his capture."

"You?" scoffed Allen. "How could you have—"

Katy took a pin from her hair and dangled it between her thumb and forefinger. "Remember this? I used one just like it to unlock your desk. I copied all the plans Logan brought to the house that day and Mama and Megan made certain the right people got them."

He was stunned. "You mean General Lee's men."

342

"Of course I mean his men. Unlike you, I never betrayed one of my own kind. You were the enemy, Colonel Allen. So was Logan. I can live with what I did for my country, but how do you live with what you did to Logan? He was one of yours."

"Apparently I didn't do anything to him," he countered. "It seems he's alive."

"He survived Libby *and* Andersonville."

"Where is he now? In New York?"

She nodded. "Publishing the *Chronicle.*"

"You've talked to him?"

"He's the one who told me you had a seat in Congress. I think he takes note of what you do. That's why you shouldn't have troubled yourself with me. If I were you, I'd be very careful not to upset Logan Marshall. You have no idea how devastating *his* revenge can be." Katy brushed past the colonel, careful to keep anything but her skirts from touching him. She opened the door. In the hallway Donna Mae was cooing to Victoria. "I can't say that it's been a pleasure, but it has been interesting. I think you'll agree there's no reason for us to see each other again."

Donna Mae came into the room slowly, looking over her shoulder all the while at Richard Allen's stiff exit. "My," she said on a puff of air. "What was that all about?"

Katy took her daughter from Donna and hugged Victoria, raining tiny kisses on the baby's head and brow. "None of it's worth repeating," she said softly.

* * *

"Ria! Open up this door! I only want to talk to you!" Michael kicked the bottom of the door again. It was a useless gesture, because the lock held.

Ria flinched when the door shuddered but she didn't move from her place in the corner of her bedroom. She huddled deeper into the blanket she had dragged from the bed when Michael first started pounding. "Go to your whores," she whispered, pressing her knuckles to her mouth. She ground them so hard against her lips that she tasted blood. Her eyes were wild with fear.

"This can't go on, Ria," Michael said. Trying another tact he softened his voice. "I was patient in the beginning. You know I was."

"You didn't talk to me for three weeks," she said under her breath.

"It's been almost five months. How long do you think you can remain here at the house without going out or inviting anyone to see you? People are asking about you, Ria. Your friends want to know when you'll join them again. They miss you, darling . . . I miss you."

Ria leaned her head against the wall and shut her eyes. He'd tire of standing there in a little while. He'd tire of talking with no one talking back. In a few more minutes he'd go back to his own bed and forget about wanting to get into hers. It was a pattern that was repeated several times each month when Michael stayed too long at the Union Club. His whores wouldn't have him then and he'd come after her.

344

Ria pushed the blanket away when she heard Michael move from the connecting door. At her feet was a photograph. She picked it up and placed it in the cradle of her arms, staring blankly at the stark image of her tiny baby lying in a white pine casket. Victoria's eyes were closed. She could have been sleeping. Ria spoke softly to the photograph. "I'll find you, darling. Mama will find you. Everything will be fine then, you'll see. Once you're with me he'll have his heir. He'll never want to touch me again and I'll make certain nothing happens to you. We'll protect each other." Ria smiled faintly. "Yes, Victoria, we'll protect each other. You'll see how much Mama loves you." Then she crooned a lullabye and fell asleep still cradling the photograph as if it were her child.

"Make a wish," Susan Turner directed, touching Logan on the shoulder to stop him from blowing out the thirty-one candles prematurely. "And don't tell anyone what it is."

Logan wickedly raised one eyebrow. "Even you? You figure largely in this wish."

Scott tapped his fork against the edge of the table. "I wish you'd get married and stop flirting with my wife."

"You have absolutely no sense of humor," said Susan.

Logan blew out the candles quickly and Scott humbly waited for his piece of cake until Susan and Logan were served.

"Make sure you leave something for your

daughter," Susan said when Scott kept widening the angle of his slice. "Amy likes my chocolate cake as much as you do."

"Where is she?" asked Logan.

Susan pointed to the grandfather clock in the corner of the dining room.

"You keep her in the clock?"

"I wanted you to take note of the time," she said. "Amy goes to bed at eight. You were supposed to be here at six. It is now ten. Two more hours and you'd have missed your birthday altogether. Do you really have to spend every waking hour at the *Chronicle?* Haven't you ever heard of delegating work?"

Logan's mouth quirked to one side. "So much for that birthday wish coming true. You're not supposed to nag me for twenty-four hours."

"I promised Jenny and Christian I'd make your life miserable," she said primly.

"Oh, good. They'll be so pleased to hear you're making such a fine job of it."

"Truce," Scott interjected. "Please?" Just to make certain the subject stayed away from Logan's endless hours at the paper, Scott asked him what he'd heard lately from his brother.

"They promise me they're getting on a ship in September. That should put them in New York some time late in October or early November. They're even talking about building a home farther uptown when they get back."

"Goodness," said Susan. "What will you do in that big house all by yourself?"

"I'm going to open a brothel," Logan replied

without missing a beat.

Susan rapped his knuckles with her fork and tried unsuccessfully to be severe. "Beast," she said, her green eyes bright with amusement. She raised the coffeepot and offered some to her husband and guest. "Perhaps you'd be better off making Marshall House a museum. In the last letter I received, Jenny wrote that Christian's sent you a number of paintings."

"Eight."

"Really?" asked Scott. "What's inspired him?"

"A Parisian market. Fishermen on the Seine. Paris at night. I've sold everything he's sent."

"You have?" Susan asked. "But I thought he wanted to have a show when he returned."

Logan spoke around a mouthful of cake. "He does. But word got out about the paintings — Mrs. B., I think — and there were a lot of inquiries. Christian's show is going to be sold out before it opens. I wouldn't let anyone take any of the pieces. Everything's still at the house."

Susan saw her husband was casting a greedy eye on the cake. "Here, Scott, you can finish mine." She pushed her plate in his direction. "Jenny wrote that there was a very fine portrait of that actress — what was her name? — you know, the one who married Victor Donovan."

Logan and Scott both spoke at once. "Katy Dakota."

Susan's eyes darted from her husband to her guest. "Yes," she said slowly. "That's it. Who bought that piece, Logan?"

"I can't remember," he lied without remorse. "Is

it important?"

"No, I was just curious. She was a patient of Scott's, wasn't she, Scott?"

He nodded. "That was some time ago. Before Victor died. I tried to find out what happened to her, but Victor's son, swore he didn't know. Ria Donovan couldn't tell me anything either."

"She lives in Washington," Logan told them. "From time to time something about her comes across my desk at the paper." Which was true, he thought, but not the way Scott and Susan would think it was. "She's still involved in theatre." He hesitated a moment and asked casually, "Is it true that Victor was dying of cancer?"

Scott's fair eyebrows rose a notch. "How could you possibly know that?"

Logan shrugged. "I don't remember where I heard it," he said, not wanting to reveal that Katy was his source. "It's not for publication, Scott. Victor's been dead almost a year. It's very old news."

"I suppose. It's not the sort of thing that deserves a public hearing—even if it were new news. There was a lot of speculation about Victor's marriage to Miss Dakota anyway and his cancer would only fan the flames."

"How do you mean?"

"Aside from the fact that people might think she married him because she knew he was dying—which is absolutely untrue—and would stand to inherit a great deal of money, there would be lots of questions about Victor's particular cancer."

"His particular cancer?" asked Logan.

"Tumors can appear in different parts of the body. How or why, I don't know. In Victor's case the tumors were in his prostate, making him impotent."

Logan set down his fork slowly. "Impotent? But surely . . . Katy's pregnancy . . ."

"Victor's wife was pregnant?" asked Susan. "You never told me that, Scott."

"I never told anyone but Mrs. Donovan," he said, looking sharply at Logan. "Victor knew, of course. And I imagine Michael and Ria were told as well. How the hell did you know?"

The lies were mounting, but Logan didn't want to tell his friend he'd looked at private files. "Victor told me himself," he said. "I told you once before that the Donovans and Marshalls go back a few years. I didn't know there was anything secretive about it."

Scott pursed his lips consideringly. "Well, that makes sense, I suppose. Victor was very happy about the baby. I've wondered off and on if his wife delivered safely. Since you seem to know so much, you wouldn't know about that, would you?"

Logan shook his head. "No," he lied again, "I don't know anything about the baby. But tell me more about Victor being impotent."

"Really," Susan interjected. "Do we have to discuss this here?"

"I think Susan's right," said Scott. "This really isn't —"

"All I want to know," Logan interrupted, "is how Victor's wife could be pregnant if Victor was impotent."

"And I want to know," Scott shot back, "why it's so important to you. Your friendship with the Donovans doesn't give you special rights to their private affairs."

"Dammit," Logan swore, his anger rising. "I don't care about the Donovans' private affairs. I care about Katy's!"

Scott glanced meaningfully at his wife. Susan instantly began gathering plates and silverware and made her excuses with perfect ease.

"That wasn't necessary," Logan said.

"I thought you might speak more frankly if she wasn't here. More frankly . . . and more truthfully. Now, exactly how well do you know Miss Dakota?"

"That hardly—"

"Logan, don't make this so hard for me. I can't share confidences with you. But perhaps if you tell me what's going on, you'll get the information you seem to need."

Pushing back from the table, Logan stretched his legs. His elbows rested on the arms of his chair and his hands were folded in front of him. He stared down at his tapping thumbs. "There was a time not so far back that I considered making Katy Dakota my mistress," he said at last. "I . . . I pressed her too hard and she . . . well, she ran straight to Victor Donovan. They were friends, you see, though I think he loved her and she . . . that is, Katy came to love him."

"When you say you pressed her . . . what exactly does that mean?"

Logan returned Scott's direct gaze. "I decided

she was going to be my mistress whether she wanted it or not."

"Marriage—"

"Was out of the question. I hated her."

Clearly there was much more to the story than Logan was willing to share with him. Scott did not press for the past. "But you made love to her," said Scott.

Logan nodded. "I wouldn't have called it that. She hated me as well. It happened only one time. The next day she went to Victor." Logan's eyes drifted toward the bay window as a carriage rattled past the house. Even when it was quiet again he continued to stare out. "She told him everything about her relationship with me, what I wanted from her, why I despised her. Victor didn't hesitate to marry her."

"Victor did love her," Scott said. "And he was very protective of her. If he knew that you and Katy had a past he wouldn't have told you about her pregnancy. That was a lie you told earlier. How did you know she was pregnant?"

This time Logan told his friend the truth.

"I see." It was all Scott could think to say. With some effort he reined in his anger. "You saw her file only?"

"Only Katy's. I didn't glance at the others." Logan leaned forward in his chair. "I can't explain everything that's between Katy and me, Scott. Sometimes I don't understand it myself. I was trying to punish her for something she did to me a long time ago. Years later, when I saw her in Wallack's, it never occurred to me she wasn't as

351

worldly as the character she played. I thought she was Victor's mistress then. Or Michael's."

"And she wasn't?"

"No." Logan squeezed the corded muscles at the back of his neck. "God, no. I was the first man she knew."

"And she married Victor the next day?"

"Yes. I told you that before."

Scott mulled that over. With seeming indifference he asked, "By any chance did you buy the portrait of Katy that Christian sent?"

Logan's head jerked up. His hand fell away from his neck. "I don't see what—"

"Humor me."

"Yes," he admitted reluctantly. "But I don't see—"

Scott reached across the table and touched his friend's forearm. His eyes and his voice were grave. "I think you should go to Washington, Logan, and have a talk with Katy Dakota."

Chapter Eleven

Katy pressed her forehead against her bedroom window and peered down the length of her nose into the garden below. Donna Mae was sitting on a blanket, her legs splayed as wide as her skirt would permit. The unladylike pose was to accommodate Victoria, who was content to lie on the soft fabric of Donna Mae's gown and have her toes tickled.

Tapping the window lightly, Katy got her friend's attention. Donna Mae dutifully raised Victoria and lifted the baby's hand to wave at her mother. Smiling, Katy waved back. After a moment she left the window and reluctantly returned to the script that was lying on her bed. There was just no avoiding learning her lines, she thought, picking up the first page. She was envious that Donna had played her role once before and could recall most of her lines. *Seven Deadly Sins* was new to Katy but she thought the little morality drama was likely to be popular in Washington. President Grant's administration seemed to be passingly familiar with most of the sins. Katy herself was playing Pride. Donna Mae was Lust. Everyone was going to have a fine time pointing fingers at everyone else.

Amused by the thought, Katy began reading her lines.

In the garden, Donna Mae opened her parasol and set it on the blanket so it protected Victoria from the early morning sun. "I know, sweetings, you want to play with your mother," she cooed, "but you'll just have to settle for Donna Mae. What would you like to do? Have the ball?" She held up a cloth ball just out of Victoria's reach. The baby's arms worked like windmills to reach it. "Oh, here it is. Don't make that face with me, young lady. I'm a godmother and I just *don't* have to put up with it."

Victoria blabbered happily and passed her ball from one hand to the other. She found this trick very impressive.

"You like that, don't you? I'll wager you think you're just wonderful." Donna Mae smoothed the baby's hair at the nape of her neck. "Everyone says you're—" She stopped because a shadow had fallen across the blanket that was not made by the parasol. The shape of the shadow was definitely a man. Donna Mae leaned back on her hands and looked up, lifting her face with a saucy tilt. Her smile faltered a little when she saw the hard cast of the man's features.

His cool gray eyes were on Victoria and he was studying her with an intensity that made Donna Mae nervous. When he dropped to his haunches beside the blanket, she sat up quickly and started to reach for the baby. He stopped her, placing one of his hands on her wrist.

"I'm not going to hurt her," he said quietly. "I only want to see her."

Donna Mae heard something in his voice that

stopped her from calling for Katy. Tenderness, she thought. Gentleness. How odd it was to hear those things when his expression suggested pain that went right to his soul. "She's a lovely little thing, isn't she?" asked Donna.

He nodded. "What color would you call her eyes?"

"Gray. Blue as blue when she was born but they soon changed."

"I thought they looked gray. And her hair?" Very gently he touched the baby's cap of dark hair. His arm bumped the parasol and it rolled just enough to allow sunshine to highlight the threads of copper in Victoria's hair.

Donna adjusted the parasol again. "Auburn." Her eyes drifted to the stranger's hair. "Perhaps I should get the baby's—"

"No. Not yet. May I hold her?"

Before Donna could answer he was picking Victoria up. The cloth ball dropped in Donna Mae's lap but the baby didn't seem to notice. She was used to being handled by people. At the theatre she was constantly coddled by anyone who wasn't on stage. Still, Donna Mae couldn't recall Victoria ever taking to a stranger the way she took to this man.

She babbled happily and loudly, showing off a bottom tooth that had only made its appearance two days earlier. Her hands flailed the air in front of her and sometimes connected, making a small clapping sound that delighted her. Her wide gray eyes darted over the stranger's face, and when he smiled Victoria responded with a short burst of laughter. After that the stranger seemed helpless to do anything but smile.

Katy stood protectively behind the kitchen door screen. The script page she held in her hand soon slipped to the floor. She made no attempt to pick it up. She stared mutely at the man holding her daughter in his large, beautifully shaped hands. Hunkered down as he was, accepting what passed for a kiss from Victoria, Katy was reminded of another time, another garden, and the frog prince she had loved with all the desperate, innocent passion of youth.

Her hand trembled slightly as she pushed open the screen door and stepped out onto the porch. The door swung closed behind her and the jarring noise made three heads turn in her direction.

"Logan," she said. Could he tell her heart was in her mouth?

"Katy." He shifted the baby in his arms and stood slowly. "She's a beautiful little girl." His eyes wandered over Katy, taking in the slender, fluid line of her body as she walked to the edge of the porch. A breeze ruffled her honey-colored hair. She raised a hand to smooth a strand behind her ear. The gesture was self-conscious and Logan realized she was as nervous as he.

"Why have you come?" she asked.

Logan took a step forward, paused, and glanced back at Donna Mae, a question in his eyes. That look was not one the actress was about to ignore. She got to her feet, gathered the parasol, blanket, and ball, and gave them to Katy.

Raising her parasol over her shoulder, she whispered conspiratorially, "You can tell me everything later." Donna Mae turned then, gave Logan a thorough raking with her eyes, and sighed a trace longingly. "God, but you make me wish I could see twenty-five again." Twirling her parasol, she sashayed through the garden to the street.

"That was a very pretty compliment Donna Mae gave you," Katy told him. "As a rule she doesn't flatter gentlemen. She likes them to flatter her." Katy was unable to stop her nervous chatter. "Would you like to come in? Victoria's had quite enough sun."

Logan tried not to seem overly curious as Katy led him through the house to the front parlor. The rooms were small, well-kept, and furnished with items that could have only come from the theatre. Nothing quite matched, much of it was dated without being antique, and many of the scarred pieces showed several coats of paint. He realized she had spent whatever money she had on the house itself.

Katy noticed his interest. "I've inherited the prop room's overflow," she explained. "It's rather like living on stage round the clock." She pointed to a settee and Logan sat down. Victoria's small head rested comfortably in the crook of his arm. Katy gave the baby her ball and folded the blanket, dropping it over the back of a chair. "Can I get you something? Tea? Lemonade? I think there's some coffee that Donna—"

"Nothing for me, Katy. Won't you sit down?"

"Oh." She dropped like a lead weight into the chair behind her and sat perched on the edge. "Shall I take Victoria?"

357

"She's fine where she is."

"This is Mrs. Castle's day off. Usually she's here to help, but I don't have a performance tonight so I told her to—"

"No need to explain. I know about Mrs. Castle. I know you don't have to go to the theatre today. That's why I chose today to visit. And in answer to your next question, I owe my knowledge to the services of Liam O'Shea."

All this time she'd been blaming Michael and it had been Logan. Almost imperceptibly her back straightened and her chin thrust forward. "That was a horrible thing to do," she said. "I thought he was hired by—" Katy stopped herself and her hands tightened in her lap. "If your purpose was to scare me, then you succeeded very well indeed."

Logan wondered who Katy was afraid of. "The purpose was simply to assure myself that you were safe. You left New York so suddenly—"

"You told me once before that you were done interfering in my life. Haven't you had your fill of revenge yet? Do you find some perverse pleasure in spying on me?"

She didn't let him answer. Victoria had fallen asleep in Logan's arms. Katy got up and took her baby from him. Victoria stirred but didn't wake. "Let me put her to bed. She'll sleep for an hour or so."

"I'll go with you."

Katy decided against arguing with him. The staircase was narrow, bare of a runner, and so frequently used during the house's long history that each step sloped gently toward the middle. Passing

Katy's room, Logan saw an ancient tester bed littered with script pages. The cream-colored walls were freshly painted, but the room was sparsely furnished and the hardwood floor would have been better served with a rug to hide its deep scratches.

In contrast, Victoria's room was bright and cheerful. The wallpaper was patterned with tiny periwinkle blue flowers and the woodwork was painted white. There were several braided area rugs and the polished floor was littered with a variety of toys, most of them too big for a five-month-old baby. Katy's friends at the theatre again, Logan thought. Liam had told him that Katy and her daughter had been adopted by the other actors. Logan picked up one of the toys, a sturdy puppet hand-carved from balsa wood. The puppet had painted yellow hair and wore a red and white gingham dress, a pinafore, and oversized red patent leather shoes.

"This looks a little like you did at twelve," he told Katy.

Katy covered Victoria with a light blanket and turned to see what Logan was talking about. In spite of herself, she smiled. "Yes, I thought it did, too. The red shoes . . ." Her smile faltered. Colonel Allen had given her the shoes for keeping the secret. "I was very proud of my red shoes then," she said with a trace of sadness.

Logan set the puppet down. "Katy . . ."

Her eyes shone with false brightness. "Let's go back downstairs. Victoria needs to—" Just as she reached the doorway, he stopped her, touching her elbow with infinite gentleness. She raised her face to him, a question in her large, exotically slanted eyes.

"Is Victoria my daughter, Katy?"

She had often imagined Logan asking that very question. Sometimes, in the middle of the night, she would wake up, damp with perspiration because he had posed that question to her. In the waking part of her mind, Katy truly believed she would never see Logan again, yet in her dreams she heard his voice as clearly as she heard it now. "Please, Logan, can we go down—"

"Is she my daughter?"

"Yes." She tore herself away from his light touch and hurried downstairs.

Logan stood over Victoria's sleeping basket for several minutes. A bubble of saliva formed at the corner of her tiny pink mouth. He watched it break on her next breath, making her lips soft and dewy. She was a miracle to him.

He found Katy in the kitchen, sitting at the small square table, holding a cup of coffee as if to warm her hands. She was staring beyond the screen door and into the garden. He pulled out a chair and sat down, taking care not to block her view.

"How long have you suspected?" she asked dully.

"Not as long as you might think. A week only."

Logan told her everything: how he had looked at her patient file in Scott's office, how he had learned more about Victor's illness than she had told him, and how finally he had turned everything at the paper over to others so he could leave New York and learn the truth firsthand. "Even when I first learned you were pregnant it just didn't occur to me that your child might be mine. I assumed it was Victor's." He leaned forward and rested his elbows on the tabletop. "Did Victor know?"

"Yes."

Logan sighed heavily. "Is that why there was nothing in his will for you? Is that why you left New York? Katy, you could have come to me. I would have—"

Katy set down her coffee cup so hard the table shook. "Victor was not so small-minded as you seem to think," she said angrily. "He was a kind, decent man. Generous to a fault. He knew about the baby and he was willing to accept it as his own. He loved me *that* much. My husband provided for me and my baby."

Logan glanced pointedly around the kitchen. "You've made a decent home for yourself here, but it's obvious that you haven't money to spare."

"Are you calling me a liar, Logan? Victor willed half of his estate to me and my child—and I refused it. *Refused*, Logan. Turned it down. I left New York with the things Victor gave me during his life. I didn't want anything from him beyond that. As for coming to you—why would I want to do that? I've managed quite well without any help from you. My home may not be as grand as yours, but it is more than adequate for my needs. More importantly, Victoria has everything she could want here. If Mr. O'Shea had been doing his job properly, he would have told you that."

"He did," Logan sad. "There was never any doubt that you were managing on your own. More

361

than managing, really. You started another career for yourself, surrounded yourself with a family of friends, and made certain that Victoria wanted for nothing. If it weren't for Victoria—I don't know—perhaps . . . perhaps I would never have come."

It was a brutally honest confession and nothing Katy hadn't already suspected. What shocked her was that hearing it hurt so badly.

"I'm perfectly aware that you're here because of Victoria."

"I made a promise to you that I wouldn't inter-fere—and I meant to keep it. You obviously wanted nothing more to do with me. You kept your pregnancy a secret even . . ."—Logan held Katy's gaze—". . . even when you stayed with me after Victor's funeral."

Memories washed over Katy and brought a transparent flush of color to her cheeks. *It should have been my child,* he had said while he thought she slept. *Then there'd be no question of giving you up.* Katy stared at her hands. "I don't want to talk about that night."

He shook his head. "You could have told me then, and you didn't. You could have told me any time after, and you didn't. What were you afraid I might do, Katy?"

"The same thing I'm afraid of now," she said, facing him squarely. "That when you leave here today, you'll try to take Victoria with you. I couldn't let you do that, Logan. I won't let you take my baby."

Her brown eyes glittered with splinters of gold and he could feel the strength of her conviction.

She would be as fierce as a lioness protecting her cub, he thought. No, she wouldn't let him take Victoria. "I want my child, Katy," he said softly. "I also want her mother."

The air between them was still, thick with silence. "I'm not going to be your mistress," she said finally, slowly.

"I'm asking you to be my wife."

"Your *wife*? You'd marry me to get Victoria?"

"No, I'd marry you to get you. I'd fight you in court to get Victoria."

"Is that what you'll do if I say no?"

"I'm hoping I won't have to make that decision." Reaching across the scarred kitchen table, Logan pushed aside Katy's cup and saucer. He took her hand in his. "Will you marry me, Katy?"

She slipped her hand out of his. Her chair scraped the floor, making a grating sound as she pushed away from the table. Katy stood and walked to the other side of the kitchen and leaned back against the china cupboard, hugging herself. She was unaware of how wary she appeared to Logan, how her eyes regarded him like a cornered fawn's. "Do I have to give you an answer right now?"

His chest felt very tight. Patience was not a virtue to which he aspired. "No," he said. "Not right now."

"How long do I have?"

"I'll tell you when the time comes."

"But—"

"I'll tell you," he repeated. "Until then, perhaps you'd better show me where I can put my things. I

363

noticed there are only the two bedrooms upstairs. I suppose I can sleep on that settee in the parlor. It might be a trifle short but I think I can manage. You might want to think about giving Mrs. Castle more time off. I'm more than willing to take up her responsibilities while you're working."

As if it were the most important consideration, Katy heard herself say, "Mrs. Castle needs this position. I can't ask her to take time off."

Logan waved her concern aside. "I'll pay her salary. But I'd rather not have her underfoot while I'm getting to know my daughter."

"That won't be a problem," Katy said sweetly, "because you won't be staying here."

"Yes, I will be."

"Oh no. This is my home and I can have you thrown out on your backside if I want."

Logan stood up. His mouth flattened momentarily and his eyes were the cool color of nickel, revealing little. "You can," he agreed. "But I hope you'll think twice before doing it." His glance was meaningful now. "I've said I would give you time. Give me some time as well."

She heard the implied threat. If she made him leave, she could expect to see him in court right away. What chance did she have there? An actress against a powerful newspaper publisher. "All right," she said ungraciously. "You can stay."

"And Mrs. Castle?"

"She won't be back until tomorrow afternoon when I have to go to the theatre. If you still want her to go, I'll talk to her—provided you really will pay her wage."

"I will."

"You're not doing this so you can take Victoria way, are you?"

Logan swore softly under his breath. He crossed the kitchen in three long strides, slipped his arm around the small of Katy's back, and slanted a hard, hungry kiss across her mouth. He broke the kiss as suddenly as he began it. Katy's lips were parted, moist. Her eyes were wide and startled. "I told you what I wanted, Katy," he said. "Now, where do you want me to put my bags?"

Somehow she managed to show him without tripping over her feet or her tongue. There was a wardrobe in Victoria's room he could use and she pointed out the linen closet for pillows, sheets, blankets, and towels. When he brought in his valises from where he'd left them on the front stoop, Katy shut herself in her room and worked on her lines, letting Logan unpack.

Victoria began to cry an hour later and Katy quelled her first instinct to go immediately to her daughter's bedside. Let Logan cope with his daughter, she thought. He'd soon realize that the baby made incredible demands on time and personal freedom. He might not be so anxious to let Mrs. Castle go. He might even change his mind about wanting Victoria altogether.

She wasn't surprised when he knocked on her bedroom door. She went to the doorway rather than let Logan in her room. "Yes?" she asked, her voice dripping with honey. Victoria was squalling loudly, but Logan looked completely unperturbed by the noise. The baby had on a fresh diaper and a clean cotton gown.

"She's hungry," he said. His eyes dropped briefly to Katy's breasts.

"I've started to wean her," she said. "I give her a bottle for the noon feeding. Everything you need is in the kitchen." She started to shut the door. "Call me if you need help." She thought she heard him muttering something like "over my dead body" as he walked away, but she wasn't sure. She went back to her reading and the small ache in her breasts eventually passed.

The next time there was a knock at her door it was Logan announcing lunch. Surprised, Katy interrupted her work with the intention of joining him downstairs. Instead there was a tray outside her room and Logan and Victoria had already retreated to the parlor. Standing at the top of the stairs, her ears straining, Katy could hear Logan talking to his daughter in a language only a baby could appreciate or hope to understand. Bemused, Katy picked up the tray and slowly returned to her room.

Dinner did not come on a tray. Katy was escorted to the dining room and served up the delicious stew that had been tantalizing her sense of smell for hours. "You didn't have to go to this trouble, Logan. I would have cooked. I meant to actually, I just got lost in what I was doing and forgot the time."

"I saw the script on your bed. I know you're busy. That's why I didn't bother you." He passed her the bread basket after taking a slice himself. "Is it a new play?"

366

"Hmmm. *Seven Deadly Sins*. Do you know it?"

"No, but it sounds lurid enough to enjoy a long run. What part do you have?"

"I'm one of the sins." She paused in buttering her bread and smiled a smile that was at once cool, reserved, and haughty. "Pride."

He noted her expression. "I see you've been practicing."

She nodded. "Donna Mae came to help me with Victoria and my lines. Rehearsals start in earnest tomorrow." Katy speared a carrot with her fork. "I'm supposing my daughter's asleep again."

"*Our* daughter," Logan corrected. "Yes, she's sleeping." He hesitated, dipping one corner of his bread in his stew. "I could help you with your lines."

"You don't have—"

"I know I don't. I want to. Unless you don't think it would do any good. I could only read things. I have no pretensions of being an actor."

"All right," she said quietly. "I'd like that. Perhaps after Victoria is down for the night."

"When is that?"

"Usually just after ten."

"Ten? So late?"

"It has to be or she won't sleep past six. After a late night at the theatre I appreciate sleeping in a little in the morning."

"You work too hard," he said bluntly. "O'Shea says you've taken one role after another with only a short break after Victoria's birth. You shouldn't have to—"

"Very dangerous ground you're traveling," she warned him. "I was really enjoying this meal, too."

367

Katy watched Logan mentally swallow whatever he had been about to say. Relieved, she smiled, thanked him, and changed the subject. "Where did you learn to cook like this? You may not aspire to acting, but you have some talent in the kitchen."

"I can make four dishes and they all taste like stew," he said. "I learned to cook during the war—before my capture. It doesn't seem to matter what I put into the pot. It comes out tasting like this."

"You could do much, much worse," she said, amused by his modesty. After a moment she put down her fork. The laughter that had touched her mouth and eyes was gone now. "Logan, there's something I want to tell you, something I think you should know about the first time you were captured. Not so very long ago Colonel Allen—no, he's not a colonel any more, is he?—Congressman Allen came to see me backstage at the theatre. It doesn't really matter why he was there," Katy said, cutting off Logan's interruption. "What's important is that he thought you'd been killed in Libby Prison. He didn't realize you've been running the *Chronicle* all these years. I imagine he thought it was one of your brothers in charge. He was *so* certain you'd died a prisoner."

"Really?" Katy had his full attention. "And why did he think that?"

"Because he was behind your capture. I have no idea how he managed it, but he admitted as much to me." She frowned. "You don't seem surprised."

"I'm not. He was the fist person I thought of when the patrols found me so easily. I expected Cougar would want some kind of revenge; I miscalculated how swiftly he could act."

"But I thought you blamed me."

He shook his head. "You and your mother and sister may have had a great deal to do with what happened at Chancellorsville that day, but nothing that was in that dispatch you copied was responsible for my capture. That could have only been the colonel."

"Why have you never done anything?" she demanded, her eyes flashing. "Or is it just that I was an easy target for your revenge?"

Logan remained calm in the face of her anger. He finished chewing slowly. "As to your first question, who says I've never done anything? As to your second, a lot of years went by before I found you. That hardly made you an easy target."

She looked at him suspiciously, ignoring half of what he said. "Whatever you did to Richard Allen couldn't have been very effective. He didn't even know you were alive."

"When the scandal involving Congressman Allen breaks, it's going to make the crimes the *Times* uncovered at Tammany Hall seem petty. This isn't state government now. This is national government—Grant's administration. Allen's been lining his pockets with bribes and kickbacks. He's knee-deep in graft. When this all comes to light in the *Chronicle,* the Cougar's going to know that Logan Marshall didn't die in Libby Prison." He stabbed at a potato and a chunk of meat, darting a glance at Katy. "My revenge may not be swift, but it's sure."

"Yes," she said. "It is that."

They finished their meal in silence.

369

It was almost eleven before Victoria went to sleep for the night. Katy sat back and watched, waiting to see who would tire first — Logan or his daughter. Finally it was Victoria, but only just.

"You don't have to help me with my lines, Logan," she said as he stifled a yawn. "Really, I'll finish studying in my bedroom and you can go to sleep here on the settee." She started to get up but Logan waved her back down. He picked up the script from her lap, thumbed through it, and sat on the floor at Katy's feet. She lifted her legs and curled them to one side so Logan could lean back comfortably. The back of his head rested against her knees. Katy resisted the urge to straighten the strands of dark hair that Victoria had ruffled. "Start with the second scene. That's the first time I'm on stage. Just read a few lines before my part."

Logan did and then he let Katy's voice wash over him like a cleansing rain. He closed his eyes, relaxing, and missed his cue.

"Logan, you're too tired to do this. I'll—"

"No." He blinked hugely and worked his jaw back and forth a few times. "I want to do this. I like listening to you. You're very soothing."

"I'm not supposed to put the audience to sleep, you know."

"I'm ready now," he said. He gave her the next line.

At some point during their rehearsing, Katy slipped to the floor beside Logan. A little later they were leaning against each other, shoulder to shoulder. Then Logan took off his jacket, rolled up the sleeves of his shirt, and stretched out. It seemed

370

the most natural thing in the world that his head should lie in Katy's lap.

"I don't understand you at all," she said quietly when it was clear he had fallen asleep. Now she did not resist touching him and her fingers smoothed the crown of his hair. "Not at all."

Katy took the script from his hands and put it down. She leaned back, resting her head against the settee, and closed her eyes. She was asleep in minutes.

It was nearly eight when Logan woke. He groaned as he moved slowly and took inventory of stiff and aching muscles. It took a moment for Logan to orient himself. The last time he had slept this close to the ground he'd been a prisoner. He sat up, pushing at the blanket that was tangled around his hips and thighs. His clothes were hopelessly wrinkled and he was still wearing one shoe. Logan found the other one under the settee. He put it on and rose cautiously to his feet, rubbing the back of his neck while he rotated his head. He winced as vertebrae cracked.

Logan wanted to soak his head in a pot of coffee. He'd never survive another night on the floor. He thought about the bed in Katy's room, big enough for sharing, and he swore softly. The floor was likely to be his bed for some time to come. Folding the blanket, Logan dropped it on the settee and went in search of his daughter.

Victoria wasn't in her basket or anywhere else in her room. For a moment Logan knew complete and overwhelming panic. When reason asserted itself, Logan went to Katy's bedroom and opened the door without knocking. The sight that greeted him made his mouth go dry. He couldn't have looked away if someone had leveled a gun at his head.

Katy was lying on her side in the bed. Sunshine poured through the lace curtains in the window, dappling her reclining figure with white light. The first four buttons of her cotton nightshift had been loosened to bare one breast. Victoria lay protectively in Katy's shadow, nestled in the curve of her mother's body. Her tiny fist pressed the smooth, taut skin of Katy's breast while she suckled.

Katy looked up and saw Logan standing in the doorway. He looked the way she imagined she had looked yesterday, when she had first seen him with Victoria in the garden. The light in his eyes spoke of wonder, of magic. It may have even spoken of love.

"Come in," she said, gesturing toward the bed. "I've weaned her away from the afternoon feeding and sometimes we don't do one before bedtime, but this one is still very special to us. This is our morning cuddle. We make plans and giggle and sometimes she lets me sleep a little longer."

Logan sat down gingerly, careful not to disturb mother or daughter. "She's very dainty, isn't she? She just sips."

Katy nodded, smiling. "Mmm. In the beginning I thought she wasn't getting enough milk, but apparently this is just her way. It's the only thing she does in a ladylike manner."

"I'm beginning to appreciate that," he said, thinking back to all the demands Victoria had made on him yesterday. She was particularly vocal about her displeasure. It was difficult to equate this baby, snuggled so contentedly at her mother's side, with the one who *howled* when he put her to bed last night. He brushed his daughter's cheek with the back of his forefinger. "Mrs. Castle will be here this afternoon, you said?"

"Hmm-mmm. If you'll pardon me for saying so, Logan, you look like hell."

"The floor was a trifle . . . floorlike."

"Washington has a number of hotels and boarding houses. You'd be more comfortable in any one of them."

Logan knew where he'd be most comfortable but that invitation wasn't likely to be offered any time soon. "Thank you for the blanket."

"You should thank Victoria. It was hers and it was handy."

"I wasn't very helpful last night. I'm sorry about falling asleep on you."

"That's all right."

Victoria moved a little restlessly and broke contact with Katy's nipple. A pearl drop of milk glistened on the tip. Before he considered the wisdom of his action, Logan's finger moved from Victoria's cheek to Katy's breast. A shudder went through Katy, a deep, abiding ache that had nothing to do with the sensitivity of her skin. It was a reaction of sight, seeing Logan's beautiful hand, with its long, lean fingers touching her breast with the same gentleness he had just used with his daughter. Katy watched, entranced, as the droplet of milk bubbled on Logan's fingertip and he lifted it to his mouth.

He tasted it with the tip of his tongue.

Victoria was still hungry and she let both her parents know it, breaking the spell that misted around them. Katy was the first to tear her eyes away. "Excuse me," she said, barely able to hear her own voice. "I have to turn over. Victoria wants—"

Logan nodded, picking up Victoria and cradling her in his arms until Katy had turned on her other side. Leaning over her, he put his daughter beside Katy when she uncovered her other breast. He sat there a little longer, looking at the sunshine caress Katy's shoulder and listening to the dainty wet suckling of his daughter; then without a word he left.

Mrs. Castle appeared at two, just as Katy was readying to leave for the theatre. She tried to explain everything to the woman, but finally gave up when Mrs. Castle simply emitted a series of disapproving clucks and clicks and shook her head repeatedly. Logan came up behind Katy, rested his hands on her shoulders, smiled the smile that had kept him in his housekeeper's good graces for years, and promised he would explain everything to Mrs. Castle's satisfaction. Just a trifle uneasy about what he might say, Katy nevertheless allowed herself to be gently pushed out the door.

Rehearsal did not go well. Katy couldn't seem to get her lines right. Once she had the director's attention, he kept singling her out all afternoon for even the most trifling of mistakes. Donna Mae was all sympathy, but her knowing, sideways glances and secretive, self-satisfied smiles didn't ease Katy's mind. The older actress was looking so pleased, Katy expected her to say that Logan's arrival in Washington was her idea in the first place.

The evening performance of *Frisco Gold*, a slightly ribald and comic tale about miners, bawds, and claim jumping in the early days of the California strike, went much better. The theatre was filled to near capacity and Donna Mae's entrance as the owner of a boarding house—as it was euphemistically called—brought a long round of approval from the mostly male audience. Katy played one of the female "boarders." It wasn't a demanding role and Katy had a lot of time backstage to mull over her poor work at rehearsal. When she returned home, she was discouraged and tired.

Logan met her at the door, holding Victoria, and ushered her inside. He helped her off with her cloak. "Did you walk or take a cab home?"

"I walked," she said, untying the ribbon of her bonnet. She laid her hat on the newell post and went into the parlor. "I always walk. It's a perfectly reasonable way to go from one place to another."

Logan looked down at his daughter and raised both eyebrows, silently asking her what he'd done wrong. "Do you want something to eat or drink? I could get—"

"How long are you going to be here, Logan?" she said, cutting him off. "What gives you the right to come here and turn my life upside down again?"

"You can ask me that when I'm holding my daughter?" he asked softly.

"She's *my* daughter." Katy's hands slipped under Victoria and took her away from Logan. "You may have fathered her, but you're not her father. I named her after her father! It's only because you were so hellbent on revenge that Victoria's here at all. You never gave a thought to the consequences of your act; you admitted as much to me yesterday morning. She doesn't belong to you; she belongs to me. Do you think *wanting* is enough for either of us?"

Katy turned her back on Logan as Victoria began to fuss and cry. "Hush, baby. Hush . . . Mama's not angry with you."

"Katy . . ." Logan took a few steps toward her.

She could feel him close to her, too close. Katy spun around and glared at him. "I wish I had never *wanted* you. I'm talking about the first time we were together—the time *I* came to *you*. I know what it seemed like afterwards, but that doesn't make it so. Until Aunt Peg called for you to come out of that hayloft, I had no idea she knew you were there! I didn't leave her on the way to church because I planned to keep you from escaping. I didn't even know you were planning to go. I came back because I lay awake the night before, thinking about you and wondering what it would be like to kiss you and touch you and . . ."

She fell silent as heat rose from her neckline to the crown of her head. Victoria had stopped crying but her eyes were still dewy with tears. She regarded her mother solemnly. "I thought you were my one chance to learn what happened between a man and a woman. *That's* why I came to the loft. It wasn't to detain you or trap you or send you off to Andersonville. I came for reasons that had nothing to do with the war."

Logan felt Victoria's eyes shift to him, as if she were waiting for him to defend himself. "Your aunt told a different story, remember?" he reminded her. "She said you did what you had to do to keep me there."

Katy's jaw stiffened and a muscle jumped in her cheek. "What was she supposed to say? 'Oh, excuse my niece — she's a slut'? Aunt Peg was trying to protect my reputation! She didn't want anyone to think I had *willingly* consorted with the enemy. Perhaps I should have spoken up and told the truth then, but it wouldn't have helped your case. I did what I thought was the best thing: I told Aunt Peg she arrived too late and that you could have fathered a child. I begged her not to let the others hang you.

"I can't change what happened to you in Andersonville. I can't make it right or make it up. But I'm damned if I'm going to suffer any more at your hands because I didn't let you die!" She brushed past him and walked quickly out of the room.

After giving Victoria her night feeding and putting her to bed, Katy got her own bedclothes and took them to the kitchen, where she prepared a bath for herself. Dragging in the copper tub from the back porch, Katy filled it with hot water and bathsalts and had a long soak.

When Katy stood on the threshold of her bedroom Logan was half-sitting, half-leaning on the windowsill, his back supported by the window. His long legs were stretched out in front of him, crossed at the ankles, and in his hands he held a black lacquered box.

"Why have you kept this?" he asked.

Katy dropped her clothes on the bed and tightened the sash of her dressing gown. "How dare you? You had no right to go snooping through my things! What were you looking—"

"This," he finished for her. "I was looking for this. I wondered if you still had it. I noticed it before in your hotel suite. You didn't have it hidden away then."

"Kindly remove yourself from my room."

Logan pushed away from the sill and took a step toward the bed. He opened up the box and dropped the contents on the coverlet. Out fell a kerchief, a spool of blue thread, two needles, a lice comb, chalk, six marbles, a watch fob, a razor-sharp spoon, and a deck of cards. "Except for the cards, which you gave me, this represents the sum total of my existence in Libby Prison," he told her. "This box was the most important thing I owned. I think I would have murdered any man there who tried to take it away from me." He dropped the box and picked up the marbles, rolling them back and forth in his palm. "Six marbles. I would have killed to keep two glassies and four aggies. Can you imagine any man's life being worth only six marbles? Why did you keep the box all these years, Katy?"

Stricken by the gentle appeal in his voice, Katy looked away. "If you won't leave my bedroom, then

I will." She turned on her heel and went to the hallway linen cupboard. After taking out a pillow and two blankets, she went to the stairway and started down the steps.

Logan stopped her when she was almost at the bottom, pinning her to the wall. Her hair was still damp from her bath and she hadn't yet braided it for bed. It was seldom that he ever saw her with her hair unbound. Honey-colored tendrils brushed her cheeks and fell softly against her neck. Just looking at Katy, her beautiful eyes searching his face, her lips, pink and parted, Logan felt the return of an all-too-familiar ache.

The narrow stairway was dimly lit and the bowed steps made their balance precarious at best, but these were secondary considerations to Logan now. He tore the pillow and blankets from her arms and pressed his body to hers, holding Katy's wrists at her sides. "Why must you make everything so difficult?" he asked, his voice husky.

Katy ducked her head to one side, trying to avert Logan's mouth. She felt his lips on her cheek, her ear. He accepted the long line of her neck as though she had offered it to him. The touch of his mouth on her throat made her whimper weakly and close her eyes. She tried to push him away and found that his hold was secure. "No, Logan," she whispered. "Please don't do this to me."

"What am I doing to you?" His mouth slid to the hollow of her throat. His tongue made a damp line from there to the neckline of her gown.

There was a trace of despair in her voice. "You're making me want you again." She tried to shake him off.

Logan held her firmly but carefully pulled her with him as he sat on the steps. "Is that so horrible?" His teeth tugged at the shoulder of her robe and nightgown.

"No . . . yes . . ." Her breath came in a short sob. "What are you doing?" She felt his warm breath on her bare shoulder, then his mouth. The rough pad of his tongue scraped her skin with its delicious heat.

"Tasting you," he said. Her skin was smooth and pale as cream Her hair brushed his cheek and the fragrance excited his senses. Logan groaned softly. "Do you hate it?"

"I *want* to hate it." Which was not the same thing at all, she thought miserably. She bent her head and found the tip of his ear with her mouth. Her tongue traced the curve.

Logan raised his head. He searched out her eyes, held them. "Oh, God, Katy," he murmured. Then his mouth found hers and he kissed her with bruising passion. She opened her lips to him and gave him the deep, hungry kiss he sought. His hands eased up on her wrists and he felt her fingers slowly climb the length of his arms, until they circled his neck and threaded at the back of his head. She pressed him closer, and, when the feverish kiss broke, it was Katy who pulled him back.

Logan's heartbeat thundered in his chest. He pressed his hands at the small of Katy's back and tried to bring her body flush to his. He heard her wince and let her go. The huskiness in his voice didn't mask his concern. "Did I hurt you?"

Katy was equally breathless. "The step . . . my hip . . ."

"Up?" he asked, thinking of bed.

"Down," she said. "We're closer."

Logan stood, grabbing a blanket in one hand and Katy in the other. He pulled her down the last few steps and into the parlor. There was a lamp burning on one end of the table. Its light was sufficient for Logan to see the proof of his kisses on Katy's mouth. He folded her in the circle of his arms and pressed another to her lips.

She helped him out of his clothes, eager to feel the smoothly sculpted muscles of his back and chest with her fingertips, with her mouth. Her nightshift and robe were discarded as well.

He simply stared at her, taut with need. Her cool beauty and the passionate promise of her eyes blended into a single vision. He could not imagine wanting her more. His hands cupped her face and when her mouth parted and her lower lip trembled he bent his head until he was touching her. He strove for gentleness and quickly realized he could not deliver. He lowered her to the floor and rolled so that he was supporting her. Pulling her close, his hands gliding over her skin, Logan encouraged her to take the same license.

Katy did so willingly, aching with her own needs. He whispered in raw, husky tones that he wanted her, had always wanted her. The pleasure of listening to him was enough for her for a time. He guided her hands to his waist, then lower, between his legs. She cupped him and slowly

381

moved down his body, making a trail with the moist edge of her tongue. She pleasured him with her mouth the way he had once plasured her and only stopped because of his rough command that she do so.

Startled, afraid she had done something wrong, she warily searched Logan's face when he turned and hovered over her. The planes of his face were hard with self-denial and she understood then that far from being displeased with her, he was balancing anticipation and frustration.

Katy's hands rested lightly on his shoulders. Her thighs parted at the first nudging of his knee. "Come in me now," she urged him.

"You're not—"

"Yes, I am."

She was ready for him. Logan buried his face against the curve of her neck as he thrust into her. She took all of him and the heat generated by his caresses seemed to scorch her. Her sensitive breasts created heat and tension in her whenever he touched them. His body rocked against hers and Katy's hips rose and fell in response to the rhythm of his thrusts. Her nails dug into his shoulders and the tiny sounds of pleasure and need that came to her lips drove him harder and faster.

Their bodies glistened in the lamplight and his dark hair mingled with the honey of hers. She climaxed first, as he had intended, and cried out her satisfaction when she cried out his name. Katy arched, pushing herself against Logan, meeting his thrusts until the tension in every line of his body collapsed under the impact of his shuddering pleasure.

Katy thought their breathing sounded too loud in the stillness of the room. Beneath her the floor was incredibly hard and Logan's leg felt very heavy where it lay across hers. "Oh, God," she said mournfully, staring at the ceiling.

Logan slipped an arm under her head, cradling her. His bare toes nudged the blanket he had carried into the room. He slid it toward him until he could reach it with his hand, then he opened it up and placed it over Katy's flushed, perspiring body. She accepted the covering without comment. Logan saw a sheen of tears in her eyes. As he watched she tried to blink them away, and failing that, one slid past the corner of her eye, past her temple, and disappeared in her hair.

"I don't know if it will help," Logan said quietly. "But wanting's not enough for me either. I love you, Katy."

Chapter Twelve

"You don't have to pretty it up," Katy said in a low voice. Her throat felt thick with tears. She swallowed hard and wiped impatiently at her eyes with the heel of her hands. "I'm not crying rape."

"God!" The single word exploded from him with soft menace. "You make me want to crawl under a rock when you talk like that. Am I really so vile? Will I have to forego touching you the rest of our lives because you're ashamed of what you feel?"

"Why shouldn't I be ashamed? The first time you came to me, you made no bones about despising me—and I still responded to you. Later, on the day of my husband's funeral, I went to your home and betrayed his memory by giving myself to you. And yesterday—it was only *yesterday*, Logan—you stepped in here with your demands, your threats, and your questions, and I stood up to everything except your touch. How is that supposed to make me feel?"

Logan's fingers twisted in the soft, curling tendrils of her hair. "Doesn't it make any difference that I love you?" he asked.

She looked at him with sad, rebellious eyes. "Why should it if I don't love you?"

Breath whooshed out of Logan's lungs. He was silent for a long time. Finally he said, "You just aren't satisfied with plunging the knife in, are you? You make certain you twist it." He eased his arm out from under Katy and sat up, pushing the blanket toward her. He grabbed his trousers, stood, and jammed his legs into them. Out of the corner of his eye he saw Katy sit up slowly, draw the blanket around her like a cocoon, and press her forehead against her folded knees. She was trembling, alone suddenly and afraid. Frowning, Logan turned and stared down at the crown of her bent head. Then he staked his soul on the hope that she'd just lied to him.

"Katy . . . why did you keep the box all these years?" he probed gently, hunkering down beside her.

She didn't look at him. She couldn't. The fight had drained out of her and she heard herself answering his question honestly. "It was all I . . . all I had left of you."

Her eyes were closed, her lashes spiky with tears. "I've loved you for such a long, long time." She swiped at her tears and darted a glance at him. Her smile was self-mocking. "You carried me away from Stone Hollow on your horse. That wasn't . . . wasn't fair of you, Logan. I was only twelve years old. How was I *not* supposed to fall in love?"

"Oh, Katy." His smile was infinitely tender. He remembered a young girl with flyaway braids, a frank, open stare, and a giggle that invariably made him smile.

"Did you know then?" she asked.

"No," he said. "I didn't know."

She sighed, relieved. "I was so afraid you would guess the truth," she said quietly., "When you were around, I followed you everywhere . . . I couldn't seem to help myself."

"I didn't mind. I liked you, Katy."

"Not quite the same thing. I *loved* you."

"Have your feelings changed?" he asked.

The admission came as if torn from her. There was pain in her voice. "A dozen times since then."

"And?" Logan held his breath.

"And I always come back to loving you."

Logan dropped to his knees and pulled Katy into the circle of his arms. His mouth rested against her hair. "Oh, Katy . . . Katy. Why did you lie to me before? Why didn't you want me to know?"

She drew back stiffly, moving out of his embrace. Her eyes were unhappy. "Because I don't want to love you." Keeping the blanket protectively about her, Katy stood. "Victoria and I were making our own way without you," she said. "It's been almost a year since I last saw you, Logan. Don't you see? We were doing all right." Then she left the room and quietly mounted the stairs.

Love was all that Logan thought he'd wanted from her. Now, as he picked up her robe and nightshift and slowly followed in Katy's footsteps, he realized he wanted and needed her trust.

When Logan walked into her room, Katy was putting the items he'd dumped on her bed back into the lacquered box. She replaced the box in the bottom of her wardrobe precisely where he had found it.

"May I have my shift?" she asked.

Logan gave her the robe and the shift. She hung up the robe and turned her back on him to put on the nightgown. The blanket lay at her feet. She stepped over it to get to the bed and turned down the covers. She adjusted the wick on the oil lamp at her bedside, turning it back so that it provided only a thin finger of yellow light.

Logan's thumbs were hitched in the waistband of his trousers. "Do you want me to leave?" he asked.

Katy didn't answer because she didn't know the answer. In her mind's eye she tried to capture Victor's image and found she couldn't do it.

Logan sat down on the edge of the bed and drew up one leg. "Is loving me so terrible?" he asked.

One of Katy's arms rested under her pillow, elevating her head a few degrees. A strand of hair had fallen across her cheek when she turned on her side and she flicked it back. She was aware of Logan's steady regard. "It isn't fair," she said softly. "I should have loved Victor this way and I couldn't. I wanted to, Logan."

"You *did* love him."

"But not like he loved me. I never gave him enough . . . never. I didn't understand it then, but I do now." She returned Logan's gaze. "It was you," she said miserably. "All the time it was you holding my heart. And I think Victor knew that."

"Then he knew more than either you or I did," Logan said gently. "I was not so wise about my feelings back then. Were you?"

She shook her head. "I was afraid of you."

387

"I gave you reason to be." His hand rested on Katy's shoulder. "You never betrayed Victor. You were honest about your reasons for marrying him and he accepted them. You always paint such a noble, unselfish picture of Victor, but the marriage wasn't one-sided at all. I think you made him very, very happy and I don't believe he would begrudge your happiness now." He saw her eyes cloud, her thoughts turn inward. "You never betrayed him, Katy," repeated Logan. "In fact, I don't think you've ever betrayed anyone."

Katy understood then that he believed her about that day in the barn so long ago when they had first held each other.

Something Victor had said to her when she told him about the baby came back to her now. "Victor once asked me if I was going to tell you about the baby, and I said no. But then he said that if I ever changed my mind, I had his permission to tell you. The way he said it sounded like he was giving more than his permission. It sounded like a blessing."

"It may have been," Logan said quietly.

A whimper from the other room caught their attention. They were both silent, waiting for the sound to come again.

"I'll go to her," Katy said when Victoria began to cry heartily. She started to rise but Logan held up his hand and stopped her. He was out of the room before she could protest.

Logan scooped his daughter out of her basket and cradled her against his chest. Her tiny body was warm and her cheeks were damp with tears.

He cooed softly in her ear and wiped her cheeks with one corner of her blanket. The sound of his voice had an almost immediate effect. Victoria snuggled against Logan, a beatific smile on her face.

Watching from the doorway, Katy thought: like mother, like daughter. She turned around and went back to bed.

At first Logan thought she was asleep. The covers on the other side of the bed had been turned down. It was not an invitation he intended to ignore. Logan took off his trousers and slipped in beside Katy. After a moment's hesitation he turned on his side and conformed his body to the contour of Katy's. He grinned in the darkness. Katy had taken off her nightgown.

"Witch," he whispered, sliding an arm around her waist.

To Katy's ears it sounded like an endearment. She fell asleep smiling.

She woke up the same way. Logan was placing small, tasting kisses along the line of her neck. One hand was stroking her hip while the other was smoothing her hair against the pillow. Katy stretched languidly and turned toward him. "Mmmm."

Logan's chuckle was deep in his throat. He kissed her eyelids. She hummed her pleasure again and adjusted her position, stretching sinuously so her entire body rubbed against his. "Are you awake?" he asked softly.

"Only just," she said.

"Just enough?"

"Mmmm."

He took that as a yes. In contrast to the previous night, it was a gentle sort of loving they shared now. Caresses were maddeningly slow, part of an exploration, part of the learning. Touching was discovery.

She liked to have his fingers just brush the nape of her neck. He could actually feel pleasure shimmer through her when he did. She made a tiny sound of enjoyment when he placed his mouth on the curve of her shoulder and later traced the line of her collarbone with his damp edge of his tongue. His lips pressed hotly to the side of her arching throat and the love words he whispered against her flesh were like tiny brands.

He liked it when her leg insinuated itself between his. Her mouth traveling down his chest made his breath catch in anticipation of a more intimate touch. He hadn't known about the twin dimples at the base of his spine until she found them with her tongue. He hadn't realized his skin could be so sensitive, yet he responded wherever she touched.

They both liked kissing. They teased each other with soft, sweet, light kisses that kindled their senses by promising more than they delivered. They sipped delight. Kissing was a prelude.

Logan pulled Katy on top of him so that she straddled his hips. Sliding his hands under her buttocks and lifting her slightly, he communicated his desire. Katy's eyes widened momentarily. Then she smiled a siren's smile and guided Logan into her, sheathing him with the warm velvet walls of her body. His hands slid up her ribcage until his palms cupped the underside of her breasts. The tip of her tongue touched the center of her upper lip and she drew in a sharp quick breath as his thumbs brushed her nipples.

Katy's ivory skin was a canvas for the pale colors of dawn. Morning dappled her body with light. She moved slowly over Logan, lifting, falling, lifting again, all the while watching his gray eyes mirror the pleasure of her darkening ones. She leaned forward, bending her head to kiss him, and her hair parted at the back, and fell across her shoulders. The silky curtain on either side of her face threw her features into shadow.

Logan filled her and yet the sharing was more than physical. She touched his soul. He was her heart.

Katy cried out his name as sensation rippled through her. A moment later she was on her back and her legs were curled around him as he directed the last seconds of his pleasure. She cradled him with her body and murmured loving words in his ear. Her fingertips ran the length of his spine and paused just as his taut muscles shuddered with the force of his release. Her hands resumed their movement, keeping him close to her when he would have lifted himself away.

"God, Katy," he said softly. "I love you."

She nodded. "I think you really might."

"I wish . . . I wish I had never . . ."

Katy placed a finger over his lips, stopping him from completing his sentence. "There are so many things I wish were otherwise," she said. "Let's not dwell on them."

He kissed her fingertip and turned on his side. He stroked Katy's soft cheek. "Victoria will be awake soon."

"If she's not already." Katy made an abrupt little yawn that brought a smile to Logan's face. "I should go to her."

"No, stay here. I'll bring her in when she wakes. I want to watch you feed her. You can't imagine how beautiful the two of you look together."

Katy's eyes dropped away shyly. "I should have told you about the baby after Victor died. When I left New York I felt that I was running away, but I thought then that I was running from—" She stopped, catching herself before she said Michael's name. Shrugging carelessly, as though what she had been about to say was unimportant, Katy continued. "I realize now I was running from you . . . running from myself."

Logan's comment was forestalled by Victoria's babbling in the next room. He grinned, sitting up and swinging his legs over the side of the bed. "She's asking for you." His toes found his trousers on the floor and he flipped them in the air. He caught them with his hand. When he glanced back at Katy, her gaze was directed heavenward and she was shaking her head. He planted a quick kiss on her mouth, then slipped into his trousers.

Logan returned to Katy's bedroom a few minutes later. Victoria was in a new diaper but decidedly cranky about the delay with her morning meal. He gave Katy the baby and asked if he could get her anything. She asked for a glass of water.

After he brought it to her, he stood leaning against the bedposts, watching her.

"Liam O'Shea told me she was born at the theatre," he said suddenly.

Katy smiled, smoothing a lock of Victoria's dark hair behind her tiny ear. "Yes, she was born there. Not much escaped Mr. O'Shea, did it? I hope he got a great deal of money from you."

"He did," Logan said, not a bit regretful. O'Shea had been worth every cent. "I asked him to tell me everything he could."

She nodded. Days ago that would have infuriated her. Today it made Katy feel very warm. In Logan's voice she heard the longing he'd had to know about her. She'd been important to him then. Her baby had been important. He had wanted to know all about Victoria even when he hadn't realized he was the father. "I hadn't planned to have her there," she said. "But Donna Mae took over and it didn't seem to matter what I wanted."

"I'm glad you weren't alone."

Katy's eyes lifted to Logan's. "Donna Mae says I called for you."

Logan could not find the words to tell her how much her simple confession touched him. She could have kept that secret and he would have been none the wiser. That she had asked for him at Victoria's birth made his heart swell. He left the room quickly before he made a complete ass of himself.

"He loves us very much," Katy whispered to her daughter when Logan was gone. "More than I ever thought we might be loved."

393

Mrs. Castle arrived at ten o'clock, minutes before Katy was due to leave the house for rehearsal. "Didn't you straighten this out with Mr. Marshall yesterday?" Katy asked as she fastened her bonnet. Behind her she heard Logan coming down the hallway from the kitchen. "Logan? I thought you said that Mrs. Castle wouldn't be—"

The housekeeper interrupted Katy. "Mr. Marshall and I have a satisfactory arrangement," she said sternly. "He talks nonsense to Victoria all day long and I do everything else." She marched down the hallway, past Katy, past Logan, and disappeared into the kitchen.

Katy raised an eyebrow at Logan and leveled him with a suspicious stare. She remembered how clean the house was yesterday when she arrived home. When she put Victoria to bed there had been a neat stack of laundered diapers on her dresser top. And when she'd taken her bath last night there'd been the lingering smell of fresh-baked bread. "You were going to let me think you'd done it all, weren't you?"

Logan lifted Victoria so that her tiny body partially hid his sheepish expression from Katy's view. "I told you Mrs. Castle couldn't be counted on to keep the secret," he said to his daughter. "Let's go see what the old harridan's up to now." Victoria giggled as he spun on his heel and hurried back to the kitchen.

Katy glanced back in the mirror and fixed the ribbon at the side of her bonnet. Even to her own eyes her smile was hopelessly giddy. "I'm going to marry that man," she told her reflection.

She told Logan a week later when she realized that nothing was going to change how she felt this time. He'd left Victoria with Mrs. Castle and gone to walk her home after the play. It was such a lovely evening that they took an open carriage to Stohlman's Confectionary Shop in Georgetown for ice cream. Right there in Stohlman's, at their little marble-topped table, amid potted palms and rows of candy jars, Katy said she'd marry him.

Logan swallowed his ice cream so quickly that he got an ache behind his right eye. He pressed the heel of his hand to the spot. "You will?" he asked.

She nodded. Then she laughed because he looked so odd sitting on the edge of his cane chair and staring at her with one wide, astonished eye.

It had been far too long since Logan had heard that sweet sound. The giddy grin he gave her was one Katy recognized. It was the mirror image of her own earlier that week.

"What made you decide to tell me then and there?" he asked her much later. They were sitting up in bed, Logan at the foot, Katy at the head. Her feet were in his lap and he was massaging her arches.

She wiggled her toes and sighed with pleasure as his thumbs pressed her sole. "I don't know. You were just asking me this and that about the play and frankly I couldn't remember much of what I'd done or said because all day long I'd been thinking of how to tell you. I didn't mean to blurt it out in quite that manner." She smiled. "How's your eye?"

"Fine, since you kissed it and made it better."

"In that case, all of you should be feeling very,

very good."

He raised her foot, tugged on her big toe with his teeth, then kissed the mark away.

"You haven't asked me about my plans concerning the theatre. What will you want me to do?" she asked.

"What I want you to do is make your own decision."

Katy regarded Logan suspiciously. "Next you'll be telling me women should have the vote."

"Oh, no. I have very strong opinions about *that*."

She gave him a look that said they could argue women's suffrage later.

"Do you think I'm a good actress?"

There was no hesitation on Logan's part. "I think that you could easily be the premiere actress on the New York stage. You're already a good actress, Katy I believe you could be great." He cupped her heels and his thumbs passed back and forth across her ankle bones. His pewter eyes were warm now, and earnest. "If you leave the stage because of our marriage, only a handful of people will ever know what might have been. Could that be enough for you, or will there always be regrets?"

Katy did not think there would be regrets. "If it were not enough," she said, "then I could be your mistress. I would have the stage and I would have part of you. But that wouldn't be enough. I would rather have all of you and none of the stage."

Logan searched her face. "Are you certain, Katy? I wouldn't ask you—"

"I know." Her smile was faint. "But you'd rather

I didn't go back after we're married."

"Was I so obvious?" he asked. "I didn't want to influence you. God, Katy, I swear to you that if you want to go back to the stage, I won't try to stop you."

"It's all right, Logan," she said softly, sincerely. "I understand what society accepts and what it rejects. Marriage to Victor gave me a taste of that—and I wasn't acting then. You'd be held up to a great deal of ridicule if I stayed on stage. Victor was, and he never offended a soul in his life. You offend people all the time with that paper of yours. Wouldn't they just love to get some of their own back by going after you through me."

"I could stand it," he said. "For myself I could take it. But for—"

"Victoria," she said. "Yes, Victoria would eventually suffer for it. I'd thought of that as well." She sighed. "Some day things may be different."

"And some day women will have the vote." His tone said, *And pigs will fly.*

Katy smiled and withdrew her feet from his lap. She edged down the bed until she was close enough to kiss him on the cheek. "You cynical man. I had no idea you felt that way."

"And I had no idea you were a secret suffragette."

"Hmmm. It was a character I played in *Hampstead Heath* that started me thinking." She cuddled against him. "Do you want to take back your proposal?"

"I think I can accept a wife with her own opinions."

"As long as she can't vote on them."

"Something like that."

She punched him lightly in the stomach. "This discussion is *not* over."

He gave her a meaningful glance. "It is for now."

"Whatever you say . . . master."

Logan attacked her then, pinning Katy's wrists to the mattress. He followed with his body and attempted a wicked, leering look when his face was close to hers that only made her laugh. He made short work of his blanket and her sheet. Her laughter changed to a girlish giggle when he began teasing her with light kisses.

After that, they abandoned playfulness and their pleasure took on a sense of urgency.

Michael Donovan tilted on the back legs of his chair. His feet rested on the corner of his desk. He was oblivious to the precariousness of his position; his concentration was on the photographs in his hand. He thumbed through them quickly at first, shuffling them from top to bottom as he went. When he had seen all eight, he started again, studying each one carefully this time.

It had been quite awhile since he'd looked at them and he'd almost forgotten the impact they made. The twisting in his gut was a familiar reaction. So was the tightening in his loins.

It was impossible to catch Katy's eye in any of the photographs. She always appeared to be looking slightly askance. It made her expression sly and knowing. Michael wanted Katy to look at him in just that manner, beckon him to her bed as she did in each photograph.

He damned his father for having had the pleasure of Katy Dakota, yet it wasn't just Victor he despised. Michael knew he'd damn any man for having what Katy repeatedly denied him.

Michael ran his finger along the naked curve of Katy's body. She was reclining on the divan in Victor's studio, one knee drawn up modestly in a classic pose that was both demure and provocative. Her fingertips were lightly touching the upper curve of her left breast. Her hand drew the eye and Michael had no difficulty imagining himself stroking her skin there. She wanted to be touched, he thought. She wanted men to react to her in exactly the manner he was reacting now.

Sifting through the rest of the photographs only convinced Michael that Katy had played him for a fool all along. It was inconceivable to him that she had chosen the father when she could have had the son. Marriage had to have been the key. Victor was willing to offer what Michael could not.

Michael opened a desk drawer and angrily tossed the photographs inside. Pushing the drawer shut with the heel of his hand, his thoughts turned to Ria. As a bed partner she was useless to him now. He couldn't remember the last time he had even attempted to seek his husbandly rights. He let her come and go as she pleased, uncaring and uninterested in what kept her busy outside his home. It was enough that she no longer confined herself to her room and the glazed, frightened look had vanished from her eyes. Recently she had spoken of hosting a dinner party for some friends as soon as the anniversary of Victor's death passed. Michael had been pleasantly surprised by her suggestion, finally admitting that he'd given Dr. Turner's diagnosis more credence than it deserved. Ria's state of mind was no more fragile than it had ever been. It seemed as long as he did not press his rights in her bed, Ria could fulfill all other wifely duties.

There was no longer any talk of children. With Katy gone there was no reason to trouble Ria with the necessity of bearing him a child. Since procreation was the primary reason for wanting intimacy with Ria, Michael was mostly satisfied with the current arrangement. Complete satisfaction would have required Katy as his mistress instead of the succession of whores he enjoyed now.

Michael sighed, pushing away from the desk. It was an imperfect world.

The marriage of Katy Dakota and Logan Garret Marshall took place in a small white frame church in Georgetown. Donna Mae wept throughout the ceremony, while Victoria was uncharacteristically quiet. Friends of the bride filled the church pews, many still in greasepaint and costume, since the wedding fell between the Saturday matinee and evening performances of *Seven Deadly Sins*. If the minister found the assortment of well-wishers odd, he kept his own counsel and presided over the exchange of sacred vows with solemn authority.

A few hours after the wedding, Katy was on stage again, giving her last performance as Pride.

Logan was in the audience. Once more he was struck by the breadth of Katy's talent as she subtly commanded each scene merely with her presence. Her fluid grace on stage, the artfulness of her gestures, drew his eyes and his admiration. Katy's voice, cool and haughty for this role, brought a smile to his lips. How often he had heard those practiced tones when she was feeling most vulnerable and how little he had heard them of late. It was a good omen, he thought, and flooded her dressing room with violets and daisies and orange blossoms after the performance.

They took a suite of rooms at the Arborfield Hotel in Washington for their wedding night, while Mrs. Castle and Donna Mae took responsibility for Victoria. The parting was more difficult for Katy and Logan than it was for their daughter.

Stepping behind her, Logan joined Katy on the balcony outside their bedchamber. The evening was cool and except for the steady rustling of a row of black locust trees, the street below them was quiet. Logan's arms circled Katy just below her breasts and he drew her back so that she leaned against him. His chin brushed her unbound hair and his touch seemed to release the fragrance that Logan found so powerfully compelling. He breathed deeply.

"What are you thinking?" he asked in a low voice, reluctant to break the silence.

Katy's arms covered Logan's, keeping them just where they were. She didn't answer right away, absorbing his closeness, his strength. "I didn't become an actress because I wanted to be on stage. I

401

did it because I wanted to be someone else. To-night, in the middle of my performance, I realized that wasn't true any more." She turned slightly in his arms, tilting her face toward him. "Here, with you, I'm finally who I want to be."

They had the luxury of time, the heady thought of a shared future. For once the urgency they felt was solely their creation, unhindered by pressures beyond their control. Logan raised Katy's hand to his mouth and placed a kiss over her wedding band, reaffirming the ancient rite of ownership. It made him smile, the thought of owning Katy. It simply wasn't possible. More likely she owned him. Her mouth was reclaiming territory along his collarbone, his throat, and the underside of his jaw. Her hands ran up and down the length of his arms. Her breasts sheltered his heartbeat.

He kissed her on the mouth. Paused. Kissed her again. Katy turned her head sideways and he caught the corner of her mouth. The tip of her tongue peeped out to touch her upper lip and he caught that, too, drawing her tongue into his mouth and giving her the intimate taste of him. Between kisses there was the sound of Katy trying to catch her breath and Logan's murmurs of approval at her growing excitement.

Logan's thumb passed back and forth across her nipple, raising the sensitive tip to a pearl-like hardness. She arched beneath him, offering her breast to the hand that cupped its smooth underside. His mouth slipped to her chin, along her jaw, then moved carefully down her slender neck. His final destination was never in doubt but Katy had little appreciation for the detours he took. Her frustration mounted steadily until Logan's mouth closed over her aching and swollen breast. He suckled her gently, rolling the tip between his lips, wetting the nipple with his tongue. When he moved to her other breast, his hand slid down her ribcage and between their bodies to rest at Katy's thighs. He stroked her skin, teasing her with touching that came ever closer to the very core of her pleasure.

Katy raised one knee. She pressed Logan's hip and felt the taut, warm skin of his buttocks. One hand cupped the back of his head and her fingers threaded in his hair. Her other hand moved restlessly across his shoulder and arm. Without conscious thought she arched toward Logan as his fingers probed her readiness to take him. There was no denying that she wanted him. She felt herself being lifted and then his rough command to watch their joining. Her eyes lowered and, helpless to look away now, she watched him enter her, surging upward to take him fully when his control proved greater than her own. She was unashamed by her eagerness, even when Logan's low, husky laughter confirmed he was aware of it, too.

They moved together then, sharing the sensation of pleasure rising. They were of a single mind, giving and taking excitement in a touch, in a word, in a movement. Katy's throat arched and there was the whisper of Logan's name on her lips. He watched, fascinated by the rising tide of sweet desire that brought her body so close to his. Her legs tangled with his, rubbing. Her hands were a constant caress.

The release of tension, pleasure, and love caused them each to cry out in turn. Caught up in the moment, they were hardly aware they had spoken aloud. Replete, heavy of limb and light of spirit, they lay side by side with Katy's head resting in the crook of Logan's arm. Beneath the sheet her toes nudged his ankle. Her knee bumped his. They made slight adjustments, and, still holding each other, slept.

The bedchamber was dark when Katy woke. She realized that Logan must have roused himself enough to turn back all the gas lamps. She blinked sleepily, her eyes adjusting with the help of street light filtering through the balcony doors. After a moment she turned on her side and faced Logan. His eyes were closed, weighted down by the heavy fringe of his dark lashes. His breathing was even and light.

Katy stretched, moving nearer but not touching. There was a lock of hair slanting across his forehead. She looked at it for a long time before lifting her hand to brush it back. His hair was thick and soft and she liked the texture of it between her fingers. Her nails flicked lightly across his temple. She could feel the steady beating of his pulse.

Her forefinger traced the curve of Logan's ear, then followed the line of his jaw. There was a trace of stubble on his face and her gentle caress made a rasping sound. It seemed very loud to her in the stillness of the room. She paused, waiting to see if it would wake Logan. When it didn't, Katy continued her loving exploration, running her thumb across Logan's lower lip. His breath was warm. She knew his mouth was hot.

Katy's palm slid down his throat. She leaned over and kissed him at the base of his neck. Her tongue darted out to taste his smooth and faintly salty skin. The musky male scent of him was an erotic fragrance. Katy laid her cheek against his flesh. Her hair fell forward and brushed his chest. She picked up a lock of it and used it to caress his nipple. Moving lower, she kissed him on the spot and felt the involuntary arousal her touch had caused. Pressing a wicked, sultry smile against his flesh, Katy pushed the sheet down to Logan's hips and followed with her hands and mouth.

The backs of her fingers slid carefully and lightly across his abdomen. A knuckle found his navel. She circled it with her thumb, then kissed him there. One palm moved back and forth along his thigh. Katy didn't even notice that his breathing had changed.

"Touch me there," he said, his voice thick with sleep and desire.

"There?"

"Hmmm . . . with your mouth."

She did.

"God, Katy," he said much later. "Will you always surprise me?"

She smiled. "Perhaps."

"I have so much to learn about you." He felt her stiffen. Teasing, he asked, "Secrets, Katy?"

She thought about Michael, his ugly threats, her fears of returning to New York, and spoke of none of it. "You know me better than anyone," she said. "What secrets could I possibly have from you?"

Chapter Thirteen

September 1873 — New York City

It seemed all it had done since returning to the city was rain. Anticipating another day of the same made Katy pull a pillow over her head when Logan nudged her awake.

"What are your plans for today?" he asked, straightening the cuffs and collar of his shirt. "More nanny interviews?"

It was no use, she thought, trying to sleep a little longer when Logan wanted conversation. She turned on her back and threw her pillow at him. It missed him by a yard. "I'm seeing three applicants this morning," she said, stifling a yawn with the back of her hand. "Then I'm going to answer invitations. A dozen more must have arrived yesterday."

Logan caught the hint of surprise in her voice. Katy still hadn't been able to accept that she was going to be accepted. Their marriage caused a stir, of course, just as Logan had known it would, but there was never any question in his mind of being a pariah in society — unless he chose to make himself one. He reasoned the invitations for dining and dancing were more often extended out of curiosity than courtesy, but that was no reason not to accept them. People would see for themselves that the fabric of high society was not completely rent by the inclusion of one former actress.

"It's because of the *Chronicle*, isn't it?" asked Katy.

Logan paused in buttoning his vest. "In part."

She sighed. "I never appreciated what a powerful man you are in this city." For all of Victor's money, she realized, he had still been only a merchant in most people's eyes. Logan commanded another position entirely, where wealth and influence were irrevocably intertwined.

"Don't think about it," he said. "I know I don't. Power is a highly overrated acquisition. The paper is an enormous responsibility—one that I don't take lightly. If people really think I'd use the *Chronicle* to make certain my wife isn't snubbed, let them think it. They're fools anyway." He finished fastening his vest, shrugged into his jacket, and kissed Katy lightly on the forehead. "I'll be home for dinner if you tell Mrs. Morrisey to serve at six."

Katy automatically added ninety minutes. She was beginning to understand Logan's hours at the paper. The *Chronicle* might be put to bed on time, but Logan Marshall rarely was. "All right," she said, giving an abrupt little yawn that made Logan smile. Her eyes followed him out of the room.

Interviewing prospective nannies took most of the morning. None of them satisfied Katy, although all of them were satisfactory. At the end of the third interview she realized the problem was that she wanted Mrs. Castle back. She suspected that Victoria felt the same way, although Logan's housekeeper was making herself very important in the little girl's life.

Katy responded to invitations until luncheon was served. Afterward, aware that the sky was clearing and the sun was actually threatening to shine, Katy dressed Victoria in her most becoming bonnet and gown, put her in the white wicker carriage that Logan had recently purchased, and took her daughter for a leisurely walk along the avenue.

It seemed a great many of her neighbors were coaxed out of doors by the promise of sunshine. Katy made it a point to look even the most disapproving, stern-faced society matrons in the eye and bid them good day. Victoria, without even exerting herself, seemed to win them over. If anyone noticed the baby bore a strong resemblance to Logan Marshall and virtually none at all to Victor Donovan, there were no raised eyebrows in Katy's presence.

Enjoying herself, her daughter, and the unexpected loveliness of the day, Katy was unaware of how far she walked until she stood on the southeast corner of Fifty-second Street, directly across from the large brownstone residence of Madame Restell. Katy was struck again by the irony of the city's most expensive abortionist enjoying such a choice location along Fifth Avenue. Reportedly Madame Restell had received a number of generous offers for her property—all of which she turned down. No one dared push too hard, for fear she would reveal the skeletons everyone was so eager to keep closeted.

Katy began to turn Victoria's carriage around. She stopped. A side gate entrance to Madame Restell's home opened and a familiar figure stepped onto the sidewalk. For a moment Katy thought she must be mistaken. It was broad daylight. That fact alone made Katy doubt her eyes. Women of wealth and status came and went from Madame Restell's all the time, but always at night. It was easier for Katy to believe she was seeing things than to admit it was Ria Donovan leaving the brownstone.

To her credit, Ria kept her eyes lowered and her face averted from passers-by. No one seemed to pay much attention to her. She was dressed plainly in a simple black day gown and her striking red hair was mostly covered by a black straw bonnet. She could have been in mourning, or she could have been a servant.

"Ria?" Katy said her name gently.

Ria's head jerked up. She blinked, not quite believing the evidence of her eyes any more than Katy had earlier. "Katy! It's you?!" She held out both hands which Katy took immediately and squeezed gently. "Oh, Katy," she said softly. "How good it is to see you." Then, as if suddenly aware of where they were, she pulled free of Katy's light grasp and turned. "Please," she said. "Walk with me."

Katy wheeled the carriage around and began walking south along the avenue again. "What were you doing there?" she asked.

Ria didn't answer immediately. Instead she placed one hand on the carriage handle and cast a pleading look at Katy. "May I?"

"Certainly," said Katy, stepping aside to let Ria push.

"You know about my baby?" asked Ria.

Katy nodded. "Logan told me. I'm so sorry, Ria."

"Don't be sorry." She reached into the carriage and traced the lace edging of Victoria's bonnet. "I often wondered if you fared better than I. She's beautiful. I understand you named her after Victor."

"I wanted to write," said Katy. "So many times I started a letter to you and each time I put it away again."

"Why? Why did you leave without a word? Michael was frantic with worry. He said I must have done something to offend you." She glanced at Katy again. "Is that true, Katy? Did I offend you in some way?"

"No! Don't even think that. Michael's wrong! Quite wrong." Katy had to rein in her anger. How dare Michael lay the blame for her disappearance at Ria's feet. He was perfectly aware that his ultimatums were the catalyst for her departure. "I left because everything I saw was a painful reminder of Victor. I just couldn't stay at the house any longer. I should have talked to you first, told you what I was going to do, but I wasn't thinking clearly then."

"And later?" asked Ria. "You said you wanted

411

to write. What stopped you?"

"I can't explain it," Katy said lowly. "I wish I could, but I can't."

"And neither can I," Ria echoed.

"What?"

"About Madame Restell's. I can't explain. Can you accept that?"

What choice did she have, Katy wondered. "Yes. I can accept it."

Ria nodded, satisfied with Katy's answer. "I named my little girl Victoria," she said softly.

Katy's heart went out to her friend. "Logan didn't tell me that," she said after a moment. "I don't think he knew."

Ria was very careful not to jostle Victoria as she tilted the carriage over the curb. "He may not have," Ria agreed. "I confess I was surprised to read that you married him. I hadn't realized you were acquainted."

"We knew each other many years ago."

"I told Michael it would be something like that."

"Michael spoke of my marriage?"

"Several times since it first appeared in the papers." She cast Katy a sidelong look. "You and Michael never really got on, did you?"

"No, we never did."

"He was so jealous of your place in Victor's life."

That was true, Katy almost said, but not in quite the manner Ria thought. "He should be pleased that I've remarried. I have no claim to Victor's will now."

"Is that what you think?"

"Of course. It's true, isn't it?"

Ria shook her head. "Victor's will provided for you regardless of whether you remarried. And there is still the matter of Victoria's claim."

"Oh dear. I thought all of that was in the past. Believe me, Ria, I don't want anything from Victor."

"I believe you. It's Michael who's so unreasonable about the entire matter. He really does believe he's entitled to every part of Victor's fortune."

Katy didn't want to hear about Michael or even think of him. She changed the subject. "Tell me about you, Ria. You're looking well." It was not idle flattery that prompted Katy to speak. Ria's mourning clothes did not detract from her appearance. Her green eyes were bright, her complexion smooth and fair, and her hair, even tucked and coiled as it was, had a thick, lustrous sheen to it. Her petite figure had returned to its previous hourglass shape, so envied by society mavens. "Are you happy?"

"Happy?" Ria smiled faintly. "Trust you to ask that. Do you know, I've never even thought about it." Ria nodded politely to the mother and daughter who strolled past them on the walk. "Good day, Mrs. McKitrick. Lynne." When they were out of earshot she confided, "Yes, I think I'm happy." She smiled as Victoria laughed for no apparent reason. "Really happy. Children are good for one's spirits, aren't they?"

Katy nodded. "Oh, yes. Victoria lifts mine."

They walked on in companionable silence. At the corner of Forty-third and Fifth, Ria stopped

413

and gave the carriage over to Katy. "You'll come to afternoon tea sometime, won't you?"

"I'd like that, but—"

Ria read Katy's mind and stopped her objection. "Don't worry about Michael. I shall plan it for a day when he's not home until late. There's no reason you have to see him at all."

"Then I'd like to come."

"Good. It's settled. I'll send around a note for you." She raised two fingers to her lips, kissed them, then laid them lightly on Victoria's cheek. "You're a darling," she said softly. "So much like my—" She stopped herself and looked at Katy. "You've really been blessed. I wish—" Ria turned then, her emerald eyes feverishly bright, and before Katy could reply, she hurried off in the direction of the Donovan mansion.

Katy stood on the corner for several long seconds, watching Ria's retreating back, wondering at what she had only glimpsed in Ria's expression. Just below the level of her awareness some of the joy of her encounter with Ria faded, leaving Katy with an oddly chilled feeling that she couldn't put her finger on.

The invitation to afternoon tea came several days later. Katy, still without a nanny, left Victoria with Mrs. Brandywine and had Joe Means drive her to the Donovan's. "You needn't wait, Joe," she told him as she alighted from the carriage. "Come back in an hour or so. I can't imagine I'll stay much beyond that."

"Very good, ma'am." He tipped his hat and climbed back into the carriage, but didn't move from curbside until he saw that Katy was welcomed into the home.

"Thank you, Duncan," Katy said as the butler showed her into the front parlor. He held her light summer cape and feathered bonnet in the crook of his arm. The train of her rose silk gown brushed the side of the door as Duncan closed it behind her.

She saw him too late. There was an ominous click from the other side as Duncan turned a key in the door from the hallway. Katy stood perfectly still in the threshold of the room and willed herself to keep a level head. It wasn't as if no one knew where she was. Joe Means was coming back for her, Mrs. Brandywine was expecting her for dinner, and she told Logan only this morning that she planned to visit Ria in the afternoon. Reminding herself of these things calmed Katy. She met Michael Donovan's probing gaze with cool disinterest.

She was every bit as beautiful as he remembered. Her lion's mane of hair was swept up and back and coiled loosely at the back of her head. The honey color was a gilt frame for her face. Her dark brown eyes were defiant; the splinters of gold clearly evident. She held her head stiffly, chin raised slightly, and his gaze was drawn to the slenderness of her neck and the cameo which was pinned to her high collar and nestled at the base of her throat. Katy's shoulders were set back militantly, but her posture merely pulled Michael's

415

eyes to her breasts. At his side his hands folded into loose fists.

Aware of what he wanted to do with his hands, Michael pointed to the forest green settee, touching the polished wood trimmed arm with his fingertip. "Please, Katy, won't you sit down?"

Just as if nothing were wrong, she thought. He could never fail to astonish her with his incredible gall. "I prefer things as they are—more or less."

"Very well," he said. "A drink then?" When she merely glared at him, Michael shrugged. He made no move to fix himself anything. "I imagine you're wondering about Ria. Most every afternoon for the past six weeks she's had a meeting with her friends. Something to do with planning a charity ball, I think. She spares me the details, thank God."

Katy continued to stare at him stonily.

"I realized it was only a matter of time before Ria would invite you here herself, so I took the initiative. You obviously didn't suspect a thing."

Not by so much as a flicker of an eyelash did Katy betray her surprise. He didn't know that she'd already seen Ria or that she'd been expecting Ria's invitation. The realization lightened Katy's heart. Ever since she'd walked into the room she'd had the niggling doubt that Ria had somehow been involved in setting this trap. Now she criticized herself for even thinking it.

"I applaud your patience. You've yet to ask what it is I want."

"I knew you'd arrive at the point eventually." He hadn't changed. Clever, spoiled Michael Donovan.

As far as she knew, he had ever had only one thing on his mind where she was concerned.

"You should never have come back to New York," he said bluntly.

Letting her breath out slowly, Katy said, "I've told you before, Michael, I don't want anything from Victor's estate. Nothing for me, nothing for Victoria. I'll sign anything you want to that effect."

Michael's upper lip curled derisively. "Feeling differently, are you, now that you have all of Logan Marshall's money at your fingertips." He didn't wait for Katy to deny it. "Hell, yes, I want your signature. I had the papers prepared the moment I read about your marriage to Marshall." Now Michael left his place by the settee and went to the walnut escritoire. To take advantage of the sunlight, it was placed at an angle by the room's large, arched windows. He nudged the paper lying on top toward Katy. "You'll have to sign this over here."

Katy hesitated. Her reluctance to be within an arm's length of Michael was evident in every tense line of her body. She took a step forward, then stopped. "I'd like my husband to read it over before I sign."

Michael shook his head. "Believe me," he said flatly, as if his credibility had never been questioned, "it's not necessary. The language is simple enough. You'll be able to understand it. There's nothing complicated about refusing my father's bequest. Come on," he cajoled. "You should have done this before you disappeared. I've had a hell of a time with the estate. Half of it was tied up, waiting for you to claim it. I considered having you declared dead."

"That would have proved awkward for you," she said. "Since I'm very much alive."

"Where did you go?" he asked. "Washington? That's where the *Chronicle* said you were married."

"That's where I was."

"Logan knew?"

"He found me," she said tersely, not wanting to talk about Logan. She didn't like the way Michael seemed to smirk each time he mentioned Logan's name. She approached the escritoire and picked up the contract. "Give me a moment to read this." Katy found it difficult to read, not because of the language, but because she could feel Michael's eyes wandering over her again. Without even touching her, he had the ability to make her feel dirty. She fought the feeling and forced herself to concentrate. "It says here that I acknowledge that Victor's will was written when he was under duress and that his suicide invalidates the terms he set down."

"So?"

"But that's not true. Not completely. Victor didn't commit suicide and I won't sign anything that says he did. Victor was troubled before he died, but he was not incompetent—and I won't say he was."

"Katy, don't make this difficult. That passage is necessary in order to invalidate his last will. You can either sign it privately or I make the matter public. You can't refuse my father's bequest otherwise."

"I don't like it."

"Dammit! Do you think I do? He was my father far longer than he was your husband! I have no desire to drag the Donovan name through the courts, but, by God, I'll do what I have to to keep what's rightfully mine. Don't underestimate me, Katy. I'm damned if a Marshall is going to have access to Donovan money."

Katy put down the paper and didn't pick up the pen. "I don't know, Michael. Let me think about it, talk to Logan, and then meet with you again. Perhaps there's something you haven't thought of, a way for me to refuse my share without making it seem that Victor wasn't of sound mind."

The lines of Michael's beautifully chiseled face became sharp and angular with anger. His lips thinned and his nostrils flared. He grabbed Katy's right wrist, picked up the pen, and thrust it into her hand. "There *are* no alternatives," he said tightly. He quelled Katy's inadequate resistance and forced her hand toward the desktop.

The pressure of Michael's fingers on her wrist was so great that Katy lost her grip on the pen. She winced, tears of pain gathering in her eyes. "You're going to break my wrist," she said tautly, hating the note of pleading she heard in her voice.

"Sign it," he repeated. He released her wrist and handed her the pen. "Now."

"No one will know what this says?" she asked.

"No one."

"Very well. If it's the only way." Katy put her

419

name to the document.

Michael slid the paper from beneath her nerve-less fingers and examined it. "Katy Dakota Marshall? Is that your legal name?"

"Yes."

He put the contract in a desk drawer. "Couldn't wait to rid yourself of the Donovan name, could you?"

Katy didn't think his comment was worth a reply. "Will you please open the door now? I'd like to leave."

"You heard Duncan lock it."

"Yes, I know. I presume you have a key."

He shook his head.

Katy believed he was lying but she didn't press the issue. "I'd like to leave," she repeated.

Michael moved away from the escritoire, but instead of reaching for the bellpull to summon Duncan, he approached the fireplace. Resting his shoulder blades against the high mantel, he faced Katy. His arms were crossed in front of his chest; his chin was lifted and cocked to one side. He watched Katy eye the green brocade sash and he knew what she was thinking. "It requires a special ring to bring Duncan in this case," he said. "I doubt you could stumble on it easily. Just put it out of your mind, Katy, and talk to me. The difficult part is over now. We only have to finalize arrangements between you and me."

Katy looked past Michael's shoulder to the clock on the mantel. She only had to keep him at bay for forty minutes or so. Joe Means would be coming to collect her at the end of that time. Michael could hardly keep her against her will after he arrived. "What arrangements?" she asked.

Michael's eyes studied Katy with insolent familiarity. "The last time you were here I believe I outlined your alternatives. Your signature on that document was only part of what I wanted and you knew it. I was quite clear before, that if you chose to live in the city it would be as my mistress."

"You're insane. We've been over this ground before, Michael, and my feelings haven't changed. I'm also married now. I know you haven't forgotten that fact, which makes your proposal even more insulting."

"I should think you'd be flattered," he said with a half-grin. "I can't recall that I've ever pursued a woman with such single-mindedness. There's never been anyone quite like you, Katy."

"You don't want me," she said. "Not really. For some reason that I can't fathom, you enjoy the pursuit. If I said yes you'd throw me over in a week."

"An interesting theory. Shall we test it?"

Katy's voice was stiff as she ground out the words. "I don't think so. Being alone with you now is more than I can stand."

"I still have the photographs, Katy. There's nothing to keep me from using them now. No one will ever believe that my father took them because he wanted to paint you. They'll expose you for the slut you are." He pushed away from the mantel, thrusting his hands in his pockets. His posture was casual, thoughtful, and meant to provoke his

421

guest. "I can't help but wonder what Logan would have to say about them."

Katy's mouth was dry as sand. Her mind was a blank. She could only stare at Michael's handsomely cut features with loathing. The ugliness that was at his core seemed to reach out to her from across the room. Involuntarily she found herself taking a step back.

"But then perhaps Logan understands the kind of woman you are. You were seeing him while still married to my father. Can he really expect that you'd be any more faithful to him? He might be convinced those photographs were taken after your marriage to him. I doubt that would set well."

"I'll tell him all about the photographs myself, Michael. He'll believe me. There's a portrait of me in our home." In the bedroom I share with Logan she nearly added, thinking back to her surprise when she had first seen it. Nothing she said could persuade Logan to move it to another location. She gave up when she realized that he treasured the portrait in a way she never could. "Christian Marshall painted it, working from a photograph his wife took. Logan once returned such a photograph to me. You're wrong if you think he'd believe you over me."

"Really? Then we'll just have to see about that, won't we? I'll send one photograph to Logan and one to the city editor of the *Chronicle*. That should be an interesting dilemma for Logan. And if he can't rise to the challenge, I'll send a photograph—anonymously, of course—to the *Times* and another to the *Herald*. We'll see what his competitors do with the information. If the news doesn't circulate in the morning editions, it's certain to circulate the city by word of mouth. You'll make Logan a laughingstock."

Katy felt the blood draining from her face. "Why are you doing this, Michael? I can't believe it's all in aid of getting me. There's something you're not telling me."

"No, Katy, I've told you everything. You underestimate your own attraction. You always have. I doubt a day goes by when I don't think of you, think of touching you. You owe me peace of mind, Katy, if nothing else. Allow me to get you out of my blood, out of my thoughts, and perhaps I *will* be able to let you go." His smile held a trace of self-mockery "Though I doubt a week will be long enough. Come, Katy, sit down. You don't look as if your legs will support you much longer."

This time Katy obeyed Michael, accepting a seat on the settee. Had her mind been clearer, she would have taken a chair so that there would be no chance of him sitting beside her.

"Your alternative is to leave the city again. Leave Logan Marshall."

Katy suddenly understood something she had been blind to in the past. "This isn't just about me," she said, conviction in her voice. This is about hurting Logan. It *was* about hurting your father. You'll take what belongs to another man just to prove you can do it."

"I can hardly believe you'd admit to belonging to any man." He slipped over the arm of the settee, folding one leg under him as he sat down. Leaning toward Katy he took her hand and brought it toward his lap. "Besides, you're quite wrong. I'm willing to share you with Logan."

Katy tried to pull her hand back and found it caught securely. "I can't, Michael. Please . . . I can't. You don't know what you're really asking of me. Logan will kill you when I tell him."

"You won't tell him."

She hated the confidence in his voice, yet she knew he was right. She'd do anything to spare Logan the public humiliation of those photographs. "If I become your mistress, I'll want the pictures."

"Of course—after an agreed upon period of time. Shall we say one year?"

"You're perfectly insane," she said in a shocked whisper. "I'd never agree to those terms."

"Not so long ago you said you'd never agree to be my mistress," he reminded her. "Things have a way of changing upon a little reflection."

"Three months," she said.

"One year. The only way it will be less is if I decide to end the relationship." Katy was silent so long Michael thought he had pushed her too far. He meant what he'd said about using the photographs, but he hoped she wouldn't push him. They had value only once. Made public, they could never be used against Katy again. He was giving up all hope of having her if he showed those pictures to anyone.

"All right," she said finally. She closed her eyes briefly against the pain of her decision. "Whatever you want."

He was immediately suspicious of her surrender. "You'll regret it if you're playing me for a fool."

Katy shook her head. "I'm the only fool here," she said softly. "I believed I deserved all the happiness I'd found."

Michael raised her hand to his lips, kissing the back of her fingers. "You won't regret this."

Regret was too paltry a word to describe what Katy felt in the moment. Her heart was bruised, her soul offended by this devil's agreement. "I'll need time," she said. "Time to get used to the idea. My routine . . . I just can't change everything in order to meet you. It would rouse suspicion."

"Of course," he said. "I understand. I've waited this long. I can wait a little longer while we explore the best arrangements. We'll correspond as though Ria were writing."

"Just as you did to get me here."

"Yes. It worked well."

Too well, she thought. She said nothing.

"I'll want something now. A token of good faith that you intend to keep your side of the bargain."

Katy had been staring at her hands. Now her head jerked in Michael's direction. "A token?" she asked.

"Mmmm." His forefinger stroked his mustache in an absent gesture while his light blue eyes settled on Katy's mouth. "A kiss."

"One?" she asked, her voice barely audible.

"I'd rather not be held to that."

What choice did she have? Still, she would not

give in without something for herself in return. "I'll want a token from you as well," she said. "One photograph."

Michael chuckled. "You have a trader's heart, Katy. I think I like that." He excused himself from the settee and returned to the desk. "I put them in here this morning in the event you wanted to see them." He lifted them out of a drawer and fanned them like he was holding cards. "Any particular one you want?" he asked.

"You choose."

Without examining them, Michael drew out one and put the others away, this time locking the drawer. He dropped the key in his pocket and returned to Katy's side. "Here."

Taking it from his outstretched fingers, Katy barely glanced at it. It was enough that she saw the flash of her naked leg. She tore it in quarters and thrust the pieces back at Michael. "The fireplace," she said.

"Very well." He took them to the hearth and dropped them on the cold ashes. "It's too warm for a fire."

Katy could have argued the point. She was frozen inside. She started to get up, intent on retrieving the pieces to dispose of them more completely, when Michael stopped her by blocking her path.

"I'll take care of it," he said, taking hold of her just above the elbows. He drew her toward him. "Now, the proof of your promise, please."

She didn't know how she was going to let him touch her without being sick. The feel of his hands sliding along her arms to her shoulders caused her stomach to churn. She would never be able to make him believe she wanted him. She wasn't that good an actress. His fingers were fumbling with the cameo at her throat, unpinning it. He had three buttons unfastened before she found her voice. "You said a kiss."

Michael bent his head. "I didn't say what I was going to kiss."

Katy moaned softly, tears coming to her eyes as Michael's mouth touched the bare skin of her neck. She felt the tug of his lips, the suck of his mouth, and knew he was leaving a mark on her skin. "Oh, God," she whispered. "Please stop, Michael. Don't do this to me."

He ignored the softy spoken words of protest. His fingers moved swiftly over the front of her gown until he had it open to her waist. His hand moved under the material of her gown to cup Katy's breast through her chemise. Michael's thumb moved back and forth across her nipple.

Katy bit the inside of her lip as her breast responded to Michael's stimulation. How was it possible, when she was dead inside? Her throat clogged with unshed tears and her eyes closed as Michael's mouth moved across her chest. His fingers pulled the neckline of her chemise lower until most of her breast was bared. His lips hovered at the level of her nipple and then she felt the quick, snakelike flicking of his tongue across the sensitive and swollen tip.

"No!" With all her strength she shoved Michael away. Turning aside, Katy righted her chemise and began to close the front of her gown, all the while stepping backward, putting distance between herself and Michael. "You said a kiss!" she said accusingly. "That's all you said." Her fingers were trembling so badly that she could barely work the buttons.

"Are you reneging on our arrangement already?" he asked, his blue eyes icy.

"No," she said quickly. "No, but I told you I need time. I can't . . . I'm not ready to . . ."

"Damn you, Katy," he said, crossing the room. "You'd better give me something to show you mean to keep your promise!" He backed her against the door, his arms on either side of her shoulders. She averted her face as Michael lowered his head. Undaunted by Katy's attempt to get away, he placed his hand under her chin and forced her head around. His lips ground against hers. Katy stopped fighting him, hoping the terrible pressure would ease. It didn't. She sobbed once, helpless, as his tongue speared her mouth.

Abruptly it was over. Katy raised the back of her hand to her mouth and stared at Michael with wounded, wary eyes.

"Don't you dare wipe my kiss away," he said, his voice soft with menace. For a moment the only sound in the room was Michael's labored breathing. His face was flushed. Passion, equal parts anger and arousal, had darkened his eyes. "You won't like the consequences." The unspecified threat hung in the air between them.

Lowering her hand, Katy denied she had been about to do just that. "I want to leave," she said.

Sensing that he had been the victor in this brief encounter, Michael nodded. "I think you've honored your promise, if not quite with the spirit I'll expect in the future." He moved away from the door and yanked twice on the sash, paused, then pulled it again. A quick assessment of Katy brought the sharp, humiliating comment, "You've misbuttoned your gown."

Katy wanted to sink her nails into his face. Instead, she clenched her fists and sank them into her palms. Duncan opened the door and it was Michael who left. Katy collected herself in private, and when she felt she could face Michael's manservant, she asked for her cape and bonnet in the hallway.

"Is Mr. O'Shea still following me around," she asked abruptly. The question, and the demanding tone in which she posed it, startled her almost as much as it startled Logan. She saw him pause in lifting his fork to his mouth, look at her oddly, then take a bite of rare roast beef.

Logan swallowed. "Have you seen him?" he asked politely.

"No."

"Then why would you think he was following you?"

Katy had been pushing her dinner around on her plate since Mr. Reilly served the meal. She'd hardly been aware of Logan's attempts to engage her in conversation. Since leaving Michael, she'd only been able to think of him, think of the promise she had made in exchange for the photographs. She tried to shed Michael's touch by taking a hot bath the moment she returned home. It didn't help. Thinking about him brought back the memory of his touch. She couldn't put it behind her.

"I didn't think Mr. O'Shea was following me," she said impatiently. "I simply asked if he was. Can you never give me an answer without interrogating me first?"

Logan held up his hands, palms outward, in a gesture of innocence. His eyes widened slightly at her tone. "Liam O'Shea stopped working for me when I went to Washington."

"Thank you," she said ungraciously. "That's all I wanted to know." Relief swept through her briefly. If O'Shea hadn't followed her, then there was no one to suspect she met with Michael today and not Ria. Her future meetings with Michael would be just as secret. Katy nearly moaned aloud; the thought of seeing Michael again made her feel nauseated. She put down her fork and folded her hands in her lap. Without quite meeting Logan's eyes, she excused herself from the table.

Logan made no attempt to call her back. He watched her go in silence, taking note of the tense set of her features and the vague, unhappy expression in her dark eyes. He was glad he hadn't been strictly honest with her. Liam O'Shea *had* stopped working for him when he went to Washington. But they were in New York now and Logan had never felt the incident at the Chesterfield Hotel had been settled. Seeing Katy now, Logan didn't think he was being overly cautious. She had left New York for a reason and he didn't believe he was that reason. Whatever haunted her now, Katy was determined to exorcise it alone. Logan was equally determined that she shouldn't.

Logan was sitting up in bed, reading, when Katy entered their bedroom. She wasn't completely successful in hiding her disappointment that he was still awake. Logan pretended not to notice. He continued making notes on the editorial he was preparing, until Katy finished readying for bed. When she slipped between the sheets, he put his papers on the nightstand and started to turn back the lamp.

"You don't have to stop what you're doing," she said. "I can sleep with the light."

"I'm done for the night anyway." He extinguished the lamplight. After a few moments his eyes adjusted to the dark and he could make out Katy's profile. She was lying on her back, staring straight up at the ceiling. Logan moved toward the middle of their bed and lay on his side, propping his head on an elbow. "Were you with Victoria?" he asked.

She nodded. "Mrs. B. told me she was fussing, so I went to see what I could do."

"She's all right?"

"It's the beginning of a cold, I think. She'll be fine. I'll send someone for Dr. Turner in the morning just to be safe."

"Good idea." Logan's fingertips sifted gently

through the hair at Katy's temple. "Did you enjoy your tea with Ria? You haven't said a word about your visit."

"Haven't I?" she prevaricated. After a moment she added casually, "It wasn't particularly eventful. We brought each other up to date and made plans to meet again soon. You won't mind, will you, if I see Ria? I think she's so lonely, Logan, in spite of all her social interests. I just knew she really didn't want me to leave." Katy thought she would choke on her lies.

"I don't mind," he said. "Not if it's what you want to do."

"I do. I'm worried about her. I didn't tell you, but when I bumped into her the other day she was leaving Madame Restell's."

He waited, hoping she would tell him more. She didn't. Finally he asked, "Are you certain you want to spend time with her? You don't seem particularly happy about the prospect."

"Of course I am," she said quickly. "What a foolish idea." Katy turned on her side away from Logan. She thought he might move closer, take her in his arms. She didn't know what she would do if he did. As much as she wanted to be held, she didn't want to be touched. If it made absolutely no sense to her, how could she explain it to Logan?

"Katy, have I done something to make you unhappy?"

Guilt washed over Katy. She turned toward him this time and found his arms open and waiting for her. Despair sent her into the sanctuary of his embrace. Her arms circled his neck as she pressed her body against him. Katy's mouth touched the underside of Logan's jaw. Her breath was warm and sweet as she whispered against his skin. "It's nothing you've done, darling. Nothing. It's me. Forgive me. You can't possibly know how much I love you." Hardly realizing what she was about, Katy began an assault on Logan's senses. She raised her mouth to his, touching him with the tip of her tongue. Her fingers trailed along his neck, then her palms caressed his shoulders. The sheet that covered his chest was pushed lower. She urged a response from him with kisses that tempted and teased.

Uncertain of the desperation that propelled her into his arms, Logan held Katy close, sheltering her, and returned the sweet kisses that made heat ripple along his spine. Her legs tangled with his. He felt one of her hands drift to the small of his back and then she stroked his buttocks and the backs of his thighs. It seemed she couldn't get close enough to him.

"Katy," he said softly, running his hand along the sensitive underside of her arm. "Talk to me, Katy. Tell me what you're thinking." Loving her now was akin to gentling a frightened filly. She was skittish and restless, torn and troubled.

"Love me, Logan. Just love me."

He did. He felt very nearly helpless to do anything else. It hurt that she didn't trust him enough to share her troubles, but it eased the pain when she still turned to him with her need.

Logan loved her slowly and tenderly, raising the

pitch of desire between them until neither of them was thinking clearly. They touched, retreated, touched again, exploring this time, waiting for the response that was no less exciting because it was familiar. He caressed her belly and thighs, liking the murmur of his name on her lips as she welcomed his touch. He cupped her breasts and kissed each in turn, arousing her with the rough, damp edge of his tongue. Her breasts were smooth, faintly swollen from his attention. The skin was silky and a musky fragrance arose from the valley between her breasts. Logan pressed his mouth to her heartbeat. He made her feel adored.

She made him feel desired. She opened herself to him, took him inside, and held him there, commanding his stillness until she began to rock her body against him. She kissed him, running her fingers through his dark copper-threaded hair. She cradled his narrow hips against her thighs. Her need was deep and only he could fulfill it. She told him this, speaking her love in a language that had few words but found eloquence in the shared pleasure.

When it was over and their breathing calmed, Katy did not move from the circle of his arms. "I would never do anything to shame you," she said when she thought he had fallen asleep. "Never."

Logan said nothing about Katy's forlornly whispered words or the hot tears that scalded his chest. He felt her pain as keenly as if it had been his own.

Chapter Fourteen

Michael's invitation arrived on Wednesday. Katy stared at Michael's bold, decisive scrawl and wondered how she had ever mistaken a similar invitation as one of Ria's. He wanted to meet her in the afternoon on the following day. Katy understood now that Ria would be gone and that she could expect no interference from any of Michael's staff. She wanted to scream her frustration, wanted to throw things. What she did was slip the invitation under the sleeve of her gown and go to the nursery to be with Victoria. Her daughter seemed the only anchor in a world of shifting, dangerous tides.

At Printing House Square where the *Chronicle* was published, someone else's world was shifting. Logan sat back in his swivel chair, his feet resting on an open desk drawer, and stared at the quartered sections of a photograph he had arranged on his knee. The photograph had arrived innocuously enough in a plain envelope addressed to him in care of the paper. It sat on his cluttered desk most of the morning with a dozen other pieces of mail he didn't have time to go through. Just before lunch he organized the pile, slicing through the envelopes one at a time with a sterling silver letter

435

opener. He stopped, and the remainder of the pile was forgotten, when he reached number three. Neatly torn pieces of the photograph fell onto his lap and a note, penned in a neat, spare style, had only one word: *Whore.*

Logan made a fist around the note, crumbling it. Disgusted, he pitched it across the room, where it bounced off a window before it fell to the floor. The photograph was Katy. There was no mistaking that in spite of how the picture was torn across her lower face. It was not an especially good photograph. The composition was grainy, the lighting poor. The length of her naked legs was underexposed. Logan knew this wasn't his sister-in-law's work. He remembered very well the photograph he found on the studio stairs and he also remembered Katy's reaction to it. She had torn it up, tossed it in the fireplace, and torched it.

Logan picked up one of the pieces, rubbed it between his thumb and forefinger, then examined his hand. The pads of his fingers were gray with the residue of ash. He thought about that a moment, putting a similar chain of events together in his head. Katy had been given the photograph, quartered it, and very deliberately pitched it in a hearth. At some point, however, before the picture was burned, it had been retrieved. By whom?

Logan dropped the four parts of the photograph in his pocket and stood. Crossing the room he found the wrinkled wad of paper he had thrown earlier. He smoothed it out on the surface of his desk and examined it again. *Whore.* The handwriting was simple and spare, lacking flourish or embellishment. It was also unfamiliar.

He had many more questions than answers. The only thing the photograph possibly explained was Katy's distracted, secretive manner of late. Logan examined the postmark on the envelope and saw the letter was mailed from within the city. Masterful detective work, he mocked himself. He had just eliminated all but the city's nearly one million population and tens of thousands of its visitors.

But Katy would know. It was to that end that Logan picked up his coat from the back of his chair and shrugged into it. A few minutes later he was hailing a hack on Broadway.

Katy would not let Duncan take her bonnet or her cape after he let her in the foyer. She did allow him to assist her with Victoria's carriage but she took her daughter out immediately, refusing him the opportunity to bill and coo over the little girl. He showed her quickly to the parlor where Ria was waiting for her. This time the door was not locked behind Katy.

"Thank you for seeing me, Ria," she said. In her arms Victoria began to fuss. "When I sent Joe over here with the message, I didn't know if it would be possible. I appreciate you making time for me."

"Making time? Really, Katy, you make it sound as if my calendar is overflowing with commitments. I'll always have time for you." Ria watched Victoria's small face redden as she twisted in her mother's arms. "May I?" she asked, extending her hands, palms up.

437

"Of course." Katy handed Victoria over and her daughter quieted instantly. Katy understood what Ria didn't, that Victoria's fussing was due mainly to her own nervousness.

Ria tickled Victoria's chin and spoke nonsense to her until the child began to laugh. Satisfied, Ria pointed to the settee and invited Katy to sit down. "I thought your request to see me today was a matter of some urgency," she said. "Or was I reading into it?"

Katy sat down while Ria slowly paced the area in front of the fireplace. Victoria's dimpled fingers reached for the lustrous pearl buttons at the front of Ria's gown. "No," said Katy, "you're right. It is urgent that I talk with you."

"I wish I had been able to keep my promise to invite you earlier," she said, sighing gently. "It just wasn't possible."

"I understand. Actually, it's on the matter of your invitation that I've come. You see, I did receive something from you . . . or at least I thought it was from you." Katy's discomfort was evident in the way she fidgeted with the folds of her pale lilac gown. "This is difficult for me, Ria . . . I'm not certain how to—"

Ria's attention turned from Victoria to Katy. The expression in her dark green eyes was frank and knowing. "It's Michael, isn't it? That's what you want to tell me."

"Yes," she whispered, embarrassed for herself and for Ria. "It was Michael who sent for me. He wanted to talk to me about Victor's will."

"And what else? You see, I'm well aware that

438

there's always something else with Michael. Usually it's a woman. Plainly speaking, I'm happy that he has other women because it keeps him out of my bed."

"Ria! I'm not one of your husband's women!"

"It had occurred to me that your dislike of one another might merely be a facade for deeper feelings."

"For my part, the only deeper feeling is one of disgust. I'm sorry, Ria, I realize he's your husband, but I have no liking for Michael. I never have."

"What can I do for you?" asked. Ria. "Understand that I have little influence on my husband. I only ever asked that he not conduct his affairs openly. Thus far, I've been satisfied with the arrangement."

Katy stood, hesitated, then crossed the room to the escritoire. "Michael wants me as his mistress, Ria. He has for a long time."

In spite of her earlier words to the contrary, a brief look of pain shadowed Ria's beautifully gentle features. "I see," she said. Now she sat down, holding Victoria on her lap. Her play with the baby was distracted. "I'm still not certain what it is you want from me."

"The key to this desk."

Ria blinked, frowning. "But I don't have a key."

Katy removed her bonnet and took a pin from the smooth coil of her honey hair. She held it up for Ria to see. "May I?"

There was a moment of uncertainty on Ria's part, then she nodded. "Very well." She turned away so that she didn't have to see what Katy was doing and entertained Victoria with a game of peek-a-boo and pat-a-cake.

Katy worked for five frustrating minutes before she managed to slip the lock. Relief was short-lived. The drawer that had contained the photographs was empty. Swearing under her breath, Katy examined all three drawers. None held the damaging pictures. She sat down heavily on the chair and stared out the window.

"What is it?" asked Ria. "Haven't you found what you're looking for?"

Katy could only shake her head in reply. Her throat ached with suppressed tears of anger.

"Perhaps if you told me," said Ria. She carried Victoria to Katy's side, patting the baby's back.

Turning in her chair, Katy lifted her pale and troubled face to Ria. "Is Michael at the store?"

"Yes. He'll be there until late this evening."

"Ria, I need to talk to him. It's important. He expects me to meet him here tomorrow and I can't do it. I don't know why I ever thought I could. Even his threats don't matter any more."

"What has Michael threatened? Katy, what are you talking about?"

Katy stood and pushed her chair under the escritoire. "I have to go while I still have my nerve."

"You can't mean to take Victoria with you!"

Katy picked up her bonnet and smoothed the ribbons between her fingers. No, it wouldn't be right to take Victoria with her. And it might be infuriating for Michael to meet his presumed half-sister. "I'll take her home first."

"Nonsense. Leave her with me. I'd be happy to

sit with her until you return. I'll enjoy it."

And she would. Katy could see that. She held Victoria with the ease of someone used to holding a child. Ria wasn't bothered by Victoria's flailing arms or her constant babbling. She responded naturally to all of Victoria's movements, instinctively seeming to know what it was the little girl wanted. "All right," she said. "Her carriage is in the foyer. There are a few toys in there that she likes and she'll want a little milk and—"

Ria laughed. "I'm sure we'll manage just fine. You can't imagine how I've been looking forward to a day just like this." Her smile softened, growing faintly sad as she looked at Victoria. "It will almost be like—" She broke off. "Go on, Katy. I admit I don't understand why you need to talk to Michael, but I can see that it's very important to you."

Katy kissed her daughter on the forehead, then carefully slipped on her bonnet. "I won't be long. What I have to say to Michael won't take above a minute."

Ria thought about that after Katy left. She tapped Victoria's button nose with the tip of her finger. "Then we'll have to hurry, won't we, darling? Mama's not going to let you out of her sight again." With that she left the parlor and mounted the staircase to her room.

Mrs. Brandywine's smile widened when she saw Logan coming in the front door. "This is a surprise," she said, glancing at the tall pendulum clock standing in one corner of the entrance hall. She wiped her hands on her apron and reached to take Logan's hat. Belatedly she realized he wasn't wearing one. "Should I have Mrs. Morrisey prepare luncheon for you?"

"That'll be fine. I'll have it with Katy."

"Mrs. Marshall isn't here. She took the baby out for a walk, oh, over an hour ago, I'd say. She should be back any time."

Logan was not very good at masking his disappointment. The quartered pieces of photograph in his pocket seemed to weigh him down. "I'll wait for her in the dining room. Make certain she knows I'm here."

"Of course." Mrs. Brandywine's smile faded as Logan brushed past her. She sensed his anxiety.

Logan sat at the head of the dining table with his heels propped on the table's edge. That only lasted the first few minutes. He told himself there was no urgency in seeing Katy; he could easily wait until this evening to show her the photograph. And yet he couldn't. He pushed away from the table and paced off the area in front of the windows.

Words that Katy had whispered in the stillness of their bedroom came back to Logan now. *I would never do anything to shame you.* Had she been referring to this photograph? Did she really believe that it would change the way he felt about her? Oh, Katy, he thought, come home right now so I can tell you how little this matters to me. He couldn't stand the thought that she had been frightened by the threat of exposure.

He sat down again and tapped out a rhythm on

the table's edge with his fingertips. He promised himself he would not keep checking his pocket watch and failed to keep the promise. The door to the dining room opened once and Logan looked up hopefully, but it was only Mrs. Morrisey, checking to see if Logan still wanted to wait for his wife. He did.

After nearly an hour, Logan's patience came to an end. He went in search of the housekeeper and found her in the front parlor. "Is it usual for Katy to be gone so long?" he asked Mrs. B.

Mrs. B. excused the young maid she had been talking to before she spoke to Logan. "Not precisely usual," she said, "but no reason to be alarmed. Was she expecting you?"

"No. She thinks I'm at the paper."

"Then it's reasonable to assume she's not in any particular hurry to be back."

Logan was not in a mood to be reasonable any longer. "Do you know which way she walks, where she might go?"

"She usually just walks the avenue, although judging by the lateness of the hour, she may well have accepted an invitation to lunch. I do recall her saying something about Mrs. Donovan. Perhaps she's gone there."

Logan wished he had had that information an hour ago. "If my wife comes home, please tell her I was here."

"You're going back to the paper?"

"Yes," he lied. "Good day, Mrs. B.," he said. He bent and bussed her on the cheek and then he was gone.

From the parlor window, Mrs. Brandywine watched Logan mount his horse and head north along the avenue. Printing House Square was south. Just who did he think he was fooling?

As a courtesy, Logan asked to see Ria Donovan when he arrived at her home. Duncan ushered him inside, but told Logan that Mrs. Donovan had gone out a short time earlier. "I'll check to be sure, of course," Duncan said, "but Mrs. Donovan is generally out of the house every Wednesday afternoon."

"Don't trouble yourself." Inside his pocket, Logan's fingers played with the torn photograph. "Has Mrs. Marshall been here today?"

Duncan was nervous. At the corner of his right eye a muscle twitched. He wondered what Logan Marshall knew about Katy's meeting with Michael a week ago. He regretted following Michael's directions then. Facing Logan now, he more than regretted locking Katy in the front parlor. "Yes, but Mrs. Marshall left some time ago."

"Do you happen to know where my wife went after she left here?"

The butler's long face was nearly colorless with the strength of his anxiety. How much allegiance did he owe Michael Donovan? "As a matter of fact," he said, "I hailed a cab for Mrs. Marshall. I believe she intended to go to Donovan's."

"Shopping?" asked Logan, surprised. He'd never known Katy to express the least interest in shopping at Donovan's, certainly not with Victoria in tow.

"I couldn't say, sir." Duncan's fear of Logan Marshall was once again tempered by his fear of Michael Donovan.

"Very well." He paused while the butler opened the door for him. "Thank you for your help." Logan's long stride carried him quickly down the walk.

Michael Donovan occupied a large office on the fourth and highest floor of the store. Secluded from the smaller offices of the clerks and accountants, he had always thought of it as his father's lair. It had taken some getting used to, this position of authority and power, but Michael knew he was equal to the task—had always known it—even when he thought Victor hadn't.

Donovan's was flourishing. True, it did not serve the general populace as well as it had when Victor had been in charge, but it did count many of New York's best families among its clientele. Michael imported the finest crystal and china, gowns from Paris, rugs from the Orient. If it was rare, if it had something unique to recommend it, it generally could be found at Donovan's. All prices were a touch above the common man's reach, but Donovan's had become dear to the hearts of those who wanted expensive and exclusive items for their homes or for themselves.

Michael had succeeded in making the store something associated with him, not his father. The same was true of the office. No longer the sparsely furnished, utilitarian workspace that Victor had enjoyed, Michael's office was elegantly appointed, crowded with the luxuries that were now a hall-mark of the store itself. The divan, the tables, and vases all bore a Chinese influence. The chairs in front of the desk were Chippendales. Between the two chairs was a butler's table. A gold and blue enamel card case rested beside the crystal liquor decanters. The crystal was from Italy, the bourbon from Kentucky. Only Victor's enormous cherrywood desk and leather chair remained as symbols of inherited authority.

When Katy entered the office, she half-expected it would be Victor who swiveled in his chair to face her. It wasn't. At the quiet click of the door, Michael turned from the window.

He was quiet for a few moments, studying Katy as she stood with her back to the door. There was a nervousness about her as her hands fidgeted behind her. As if sensing this put her at a disadvantage, she removed her bonnet and held it in both hands in front of her. The defiance inherent in the gesture made Michael smile. Her honey-colored hair was a perfect frame for her face, warm and full and soft. The line of her mouth was damp, as if she had run her tongue across it before coming in the room. It was a heady thought.

The gown she wore was lilac, a pale, cool color that flowed like a waterfall around her. She swept the train of her dress to one side and approached his desk. He marveled at the way she moved, fluid and graceful. It was not calculated to catch his eye, yet he could not look away.

Dropping the papers he held in his hands, Michael pushed away from his desk and leaned back in his chair. Light from the window behind him placed his features in shadow and made his expression difficult to read.

"I believe you're early," he said. "The invitation I sent you was for tomorrow."

Katy placed her bonnet on top of Michael's desk. Her fingertips absently smoothed one of the ribbons. She watched Michael's eyes drop to her hand and she quickly stilled the movement.

With some difficulty Michael lifted his eyes back to Katy's face. "So why are you here?"

"I've changed my mind."

Michael sat forward, ready to come out of his chair. His eyes flashed with anger but his voice was quiet and low, carefully controlled. "Think again, Katy I still have these." He reached into the middle drawer of his desk and pulled out the photographs. He fanned them open in front of her, watched her blanch, then shoved them back into the drawer.

"I don't think you understand, Michael. I haven't changed my mind about the bargain we struck. I've changed my mind about wanting you."

One of Michael's brows arched skeptically. "Oh, really?"

"Really."

"I'd like to believe you, Katy, but it's been less than a week since we talked, and at that time you swore you couldn't tolerate my touch. Are you telling me that after six days you've had a change of heart?"

"Something like that."

"Don't play me for a fool, Katy. I've warned you, you won't like the consequences."

447

Katy skirted Michael's desk and came to stand in front of him "I see I'll have to work very hard to convince you." She paused. "Shall I lock the door or shall you?"

Michael stood slowly. He crossed the office and turned the key, leaving it dangle in the lock. "All right," he said, returning to her side. "Show me this change of heart."

Placing her hands on his shoulders, Katy raised herself on tiptoe just enough to reach Michael's mouth with her own. Closing her eyes, she kissed him. He didn't respond at first, forcing Katy to take all the initiative. She teased Michael's lower lip with the tip of her tongue, then drew it into her mouth. She nibbled on his mouth while her hands slipped beneath his jacket and stroked his chest. Her fingers played with the buttons of his vest and shirt. She tugged on the material so it came out of the waistband of his trousers. Katy's fingers curled around one strap of Michael's suspenders, snapping it lightly against his chest.

The kiss deepened as she engaged Michael's response. She pressed herself against him, forcing him to feel the shape of her body in contrast to his.

Michael's hands lifted from his sides and traveled slowly across Katy's arms. They rested lightly on her shoulders, then moved along her collarbones until they circled her neck. He pressed the hollow of her throat with his thumbs until she whimpered and broke the kiss. Even as she raised darkening eyes to his he did not lessen his grip.

"I haven't forgotten you're an actress," he said,

his voice soft with menace.

"I'm not acting."

"So help me—"

Katy raised one hand, placing a finger to Michael's lips. "Don't misunderstand, Michael, I still want the photographs. But I couldn't let you name all the terms. It isn't my way to wait at home for your summons. You can't have everything your way. I wanted to name the place and the time." She could feel the tip of his tongue against her finger. His hands on her throat were making it difficult to breathe.

It was Katy's honest admission that she still wanted the pictures that encouraged Michael to lower his guard. That, and the fact he had always found it hard to believe Katy didn't want him. He lightened the pressure on her throat. "I'll only give you one photograph today," he said. "You can't expect more than that."

"I don't."

"I, on the other hand, expect a great deal." Michael pulled Katy toward him. This time it was his mouth that descended hungrily on hers. He kissed her hard, making her taste him. His tongue swept along the ridge of her teeth, sought entrance, and found it. He cupped her breasts. Through the cool silk of Katy's gown he could feel the heat of her skin. Her sensitive breasts swelled faintly at the steady insistence of his caress. The tips of her nipples pressed like small pearls at the center of his palms. She made a sound at the back of her throat that made Michael's heart race. He leaned back against the edge of the desk. Half-sitting, he

449

opened his legs and drew her between them, holding her so closely she couldn't fail to know the effect she had on him.

He murmured something under his breath.

"What is it?" asked Katy.

Michael reached beneath him and pulled out the letter opener he accidentally sat on. "This." He dropped it on a pile of papers behind him, then circled Katy's wrists with his hands and brought them back to his chest. "Keep touching me, darling. I want to know precisely where your hands are."

But it wasn't Katy's hand that he needed to fear. It was her knee. She brought it up hard against Michael's groin when he pressed himself against her. His scream of pain was muffled as Katy pulled his jacket up over his head and pushed him away. She grabbed the letter opener in one hand and yanked open Michael's desk drawer with the other. Scooping up the photographs, Katy ran for the door.

She was proud of her foresight. When she first came into the office, knowing Michael's preference for locked doors, her fingers had brushed the skeleton key. She turned it then, locking herself in the room with him. When she encouraged Michael to see to their privacy she knew what would happen. Instead of locking the door, he had unlocked it.

Now Katy twisted the handle, fumbling with the letter opener and the photographs. Behind her she heard Michael swear, his voice close. He knocked something over in his frantic attempt to reach her. Katy had the door opened three inches before it was roughly slammed back into place. She felt Michael's hot breath on the back of her neck. Turning, her eyes wild with fear now that all of Michael's earlier suspicions had been confirmed, Katy thrust the pointed end of the letter opener at his abdomen.

Michael dodged, catching only the blunt edge of the opener. The graze was not enough to hurt Michael, but it made Katy recoil. Michael wrested the weapon from her without difficulty and shoved her away from the door. This time, when he turned the key, he made certain the door was locked. It only took a few seconds. At his back he heard the sound of the photographs being ripped.

When Michael turned on Katy, his face was taut with rage. She backed away even as she realized there was no place for her to go; her fingers were frozen on the halved pieces of the photographs.

"Give them to me," demanded Michael. He held up the letter opener when she hesitated. "So help me God, Katy, I'll use this on your face and no man will ever want you."

The backs of Katy's knees collided with a chair. Her legs buckled momentarily and Michael stepped closer. Before she could think better of it, she tore the photographs again and threw the pieces at Michael.

"Damn you! You'll pay for that!"

Reaching behind her, Katy grabbed the chair and shoved it at Michael, striking him in the knees. He winced, kicked the chair out of his way so that it toppled on the floor, and lunged at Katy. The force of his weight against her drove the air from Katy's lungs. The cry for help that had hovered on her lips remained unheard.

Liam O'Shea spotted Logan first. Excusing himself, he stepped away from the counter where a clerk was demonstrating a sewing machine, and raised his hand to catch Logan's eye.

Logan took the hand that Liam extended and shook it briefly. "I take it my wife's here," he said.

"Upstairs. What's happened?"

Taking the photograph out of his pocket, Logan showed the detective a piece that was not too revealing. He also showed Liam the note. "I received it this morning. Anonymously." He glanced around, dropping the note and picture back in his pocket. "Can we talk on our way upstairs?"

Liam nodded. He led Logan to the staircase at the rear of the store. It was separated from the shopping area by a pair of doors. Liam pushed through. "Your wife always uses the employees' stairs when she's here. Old habit, I suppose, from when she used to work here."

"Where is she shopping?" The stairwell was empty and his voice echoed eerily.

"I don't think she is. I wasn't far behind her when she walked into the store. She didn't look at anything on the main floor. She went straight through the store and up these stairs. I watched her from down here. She walked to the fourth floor before she opened any doors. I gave her a minute or so, then I went up. Mrs. Marshall wasn't anywhere in sight." He held up his hand, stopping

Logan's imminent interruption. "It's all right. I found out that she had gone back to the offices. She's with Michael Donovan."

Without a word passing between the two men, they quickened their pace on the stairs. "I couldn't stay up there with her without giving myself away. You told me just a week ago that she was suspicious of me again."

"It's probably nothing," Logan assured him. "You did what you're supposed to do. I haven't been thinking clearly since I got this garbage in my mail. I'll feel a whole lot better when Katy explains it all to me."

Their steps slowed when they reached the landing between the second and third floors. A clerk opened the door below them but took the stairs down.

"Still," said Logan, drawing out the word as other thoughts continued to trouble him. "I can't imagine why Katy would want to see Michael. She's never shown the least interest in him." He recalled the evening he'd gone backstage at Wallack's to Katy's dressing room. Michael had been there and Katy certainly hadn't been welcoming his attentions. Unsure of himself then, he had goaded her about Michael. "Remember at the cemetery? She refused to ride in the carriage with him."

Liam remembered. He remembered something else as well. "The day that Victor died, Mrs. Marshall had some words with Michael. He followed her out of Crestmore's onto Broadway, and when she tried to ignore him, he put his hands on her."

"You've never mentioned that before."

453

"I was working for Victor then. Honestly, I'd forgotten it."

Logan's steps quickened again. Michael backstage. Michael on Broadway. Michael at the cemetery. Had it been Michael at the Chesterfield Hotel? It explained Katy's reluctance to talk about who had accosted her. She would have been protecting Victor. That was Katy's way. Logan wondered if Katy thought she was protecting him now. *I'd never do anything to shame you.* Her voice echoed in his mind. Logan and Liam were running by the time they reached the fourth floor landing.

Katy held up her arm to deflect Michael's blow. It helped. She only fell backward against the desk, catching her hip on the corner. "Oh, God, Michael," she begged, choking on the words, "don't hit me again. The bruises . . . Logan will see them and—"

Although Katy was blindly hobbling backward, trying to put the desk between them, Michael was stalking her. "Shut up." His voice was a snarl. "I don't want to hear anything about Logan Marshall. We had an agreement."

Katy pressed on. "I came here to tell you I couldn't go through with it. Then you threatened me with the pictures again and I thought I could get them. I didn't even know you had them here." She held out both hands this time as Michael swiped at her with the letter opener. It cut across her palm. Blood beaded along her heartline.

The blood frightened Michael more than it did

454

Katy. He tossed the letter opener against the far wall. It clattered to the floor a second later. "You owe me, Katy. After the hell you've put me through, you owe me!"

She barely heard him. She was holding her wounded palm against her breast, nursing it with her good hand. When Michael grabbed her wrists and flung her toward the divan, she cried out. She had wrestled out from under him once before. Katy didn't think she could do it again.

"Let me up, Michael!" She pushed at him, bloodying the shoulder of his jacket. One of his hands was pushing the hem of her gown toward her hips, the other circled her throat. His mouth covered hers, smothering her pleas and curses. Katy bit his tongue as it probed at the barrier of her teeth.

Michael jerked away from her, holding one hand over his mouth. He tasted his own blood. He stared at her over the top of his hand for several long seconds—then he struck.

Standing on the other side of Michael's office door, Logan and Liam heard a muffled cry that they both recognized as Katy's. They abandoned their intention to knock. Liam twisted the door handle and discovered the door was locked. He backed out of the way and gave Logan first crack at it. The heavy oak door reverberated under Logan's shoulder attack but the lock didn't give. Liam tried next and met with failure as well. They alternated, using their bodies like battering rams. At the end of the hall a small group of employees looked on curiously, afraid to interfere once one of them recognized Logan Marshall.

The wood around the lock splintered on the fifth try, propelling Logan into the room. Only a step behind, Liam took in the same scene as his employer. He shut the door, keeping out prying eyes, and leaned against it. He did nothing to hold Logan back.

Katy was pushing hard at Michael's chest. Her face was averted as much as the hand over her mouth would allow. His knees separated her thighs so that all attempts to kick him were futile.

Michael was startled to feel the hands that caught him by his shirt collar. Anger had made him deaf to everything, including reason. He felt himself being lifted and he knew his adversary was strong. It wasn't until he saw the odd mixture of relief and fear in Katy's eyes that he knew he was going to face Logan Marshall.

"Your wife is the one who—"

Logan wasn't interested in hearing anything Michael had to say. His fist caught Michael across the jaw. Michael staggered sideways, knocking over one of the Chippendales.

Before he could recover, Logan's fists smashed into his middle and then just under his chin. He brought up his arms to protect himself but Logan found an opening.

Michael reeled, falling backward onto the desk. Papers scattered, littering the floor. Michael rolled off the desk and took refuge on the other side. Logan climbed right over its top to get to him.

The force of Logan's jump sent both men to the floor. Michael's chair skidded toward the window, cracking one of the panes.

The desk was blocking Liam O'Shea's view. He casually walked to the other side of the room to get a better look, and ignored the appeal in Katy's eyes asking him to stop the fight. Logan wouldn't thank him for his interference.

Katy wrapped her wounded hand in a handkerchief as she moved from the divan. She winced, jamming her knuckles against her mouth to keep from crying out when she heard Logan groan.

Michael had finally leveled a blow at Logan's chest. It wasn't enough to impair him. Logan responded with three quick jabs that immobilized Michael. He reared back to attack again, when he heard Katy's soft voice saying his name, begging him to stop.

Logan got to his feet. Michael rolled away so he was face-down on his Chinese rug. He lay very still, and except for an occasional moan, he was quiet.

"I'm all right," Katy said as she became the object of Logan's study. His pewter eyes darkened as they swept over her, taking in the swollen redness of her lips, the torn collar of her gown. Katy did not lift her hands. She didn't want him to see they were shaking.

"Really, Logan, I'm all right," she repeated softly when his attention strayed to Michael again. She had only seen the expression in Logan's face once before—when he attacked her stepfather. She thought he might kill Michael Donovan now.

Katy stepped between Logan and Michael's prone and unmoving body.

For a moment Logan stared right through Katy. A small shake of his head cleared his vision and brought Katy to the forefront. "Oh, God, Katy," he said quietly, raising his arms to reach for her. "I've never been so—"

"I know." She gave herself up to the warmth of his embrace. He held her so tightly she could scarcely breathe. *I know.* Katy closed her eyes, blocking out everything but the security of Logan's arms.

Liam O'Shea backed out of the room quietly, shutting the door behind him. He waited in the hallway with the small group of employees who had gathered there. His presence was enough to keep them from interfering.

Logan set Katy away, looking her over again to reassure himself. He examined her injured hand and rewrapped it with his own handkerchief, then he kissed her bruised knuckles.

"I have something to show you," he said. He reached in his pocket and pulled out the quartered sections of Katy's picture. "This came to me at the paper this morning."

Katy paled when she realized what he held. She averted her face, eyes lowered, until Logan cupped her chin and raised it toward him.

"I don't care about the photograph, Katy. I only care that you didn't trust me enough to tell me about it."

Michael was beginning to stir on the floor. Logan placed his foot squarely in the small of Michael's back and shoved him hard. Michael groaned once, then was silent.

"This came from Michael?" he asked.

She nodded. "He said he wouldn't show it to you if . . . if I . ." She couldn't finish. Instead she pointed to the torn photographs which littered the floor. "There were others. I only came here to—"

"We don't need to speak of it now," he said.

A faint, tentative smile lifted the corners of her mouth. He brushed his lips to hers, stood back and surveyed the color that had returned to her cheeks, then dropped to his haunches and began picking up the torn photographs.

"Get Victoria, Katy, and we'll leave."

"Victoria's not here. I left her with—"

"I didn't send that photograph."

Katy and Logan turned in concert toward Michael. He was on his knees now, breathing shallowly as he nursed his ribs. There was a trickle of blood at the corner of his mouth. "I didn't send that photograph," he repeated, grinding out the words as if they pained him. "After Katy threw it away, I never touched it again. In fact, I forgot about it."

"Like hell," said Logan.

"I swear it." Michael backed away awkwardly as Logan stood and approached him. He held one hand up to ward Logan off while continuing to protect his ribs with the other. When Logan extended a hand, Michael flinched. It took Michael a few seconds to realize there was a slip of paper dangling between Logan's thumb and forefinger.

"Are you telling me you didn't write this?" he

demanded.

Michael's eyes focused on the single word. *Whore*. A superior, insufferable smile crossed his face as he recognized the spidery scrawl. "That's Ria's hand."

"Liar!" Logan raised his arm to knock Michael back, intending to force the truth out of him. It was Katy's two-handed grip on his forearm that stopped him. She held him until she felt him relax, then she took the slip of paper from between his fingers. "Katy, don't—"

The word seemed to leap out at her, vicious and ugly. All she said was, "This isn't Michael's handwriting."

"I'm telling you," said Michael, "it's Ria's. She must have found the photograph."

Katy's fingers tightened on Logan's arm as panic laid an invisible weight against her chest. "Logan, Victoria isn't with me. I left her with Ria."

Logan hauled Michael to his feet and yelled for Liam. When the detective came in the room, Logan pushed Michael at him. "Help this bastard down to the street and hail us a cab. He's going to make certain we find his wife or so help me God, I'll kill him."

"But, Logan—" Katy began.

Logan shook off Katy's hand and took her by the shoulders. "You don't understand. I was at the Donovan house before I came here. Ria wasn't there."

"Oh, God." Somehow Katy managed to remain standing even while it felt as if the entire floor was shifting beneath her feet.

"I'm sending you home."

"No!"

"Katy." He gave her a small shake, wanting to force reason upon her.

"I'm going with you. It's my fault she's with Ria now. I can't wait at home, wondering if you've found her."

Logan realized she would follow him. He saw it in the set of her mouth, in the way she held herself so stiffly when all she wanted to do was crumple at his feet. "Very well," he said finally. He quickly straightened her torn collar as best he could and picked up her bonnet, shoving it into her hands. "Liam's waiting for us."

The interior of the hansom cab was quiet. Outside street noises did not penetrate the individual thoughts of the four occupants. Michael spit on his handkerchief and raised one corner of it to his mouth. He scrubbed at his bloodied lip while staring resentfully at Logan in the opposite seat.

"Don't think I'm going to let what you did to me pass," he said. "I'll own that damn paper of yours by the time my lawyers are finished."

"Really?" Logan asked softly, raising one eyebrow. "Then you'd better hope we find my daughter quickly, because I'm not going to consult any lawyers. I'll own your hide without anyone's help."

The force of Logan's implacable stare pushed Michael back in his seat. "For God's sake," he complained sulkily. "You're making too much of this. Ria's probably taken the baby out for a walk."

"Let's just hope that's the case."

But it wasn't. When they arrived at Michael's house, Duncan reported Ria had not returned. He

461

knew nothing about Victoria. Liam kept Michael in tow as they searched the rooms for the baby. None of the servants interfered or took any opportunities to summon the police. Michael's humiliation in front of his staff was complete.

Back inside the cab, Logan clenched his fists to keep from going for Michael's throat. "You'd better start thinking, Donovan," he said, biting out the words. "You have to know something about where your wife's gone." Out of the corner of his eye he saw Katy turn away and stare blankly out the carriage window. He reached for her hand and slipped his fingers between hers, squeezing gently. His other hand was still locked in a white-knuckled fist. "Think, Donovan."

"How the hell should I know! She's been flitting here and there for years now. I don't keep track of her social calendar. She's gone most every afternoon. Maybe she's with Mrs. Franklin. They're planning some sort of—"

"No, she's not," Katy said quietly. "She's not with Mrs. Franklin or any other of her friends right now. It's Wednesday. She's gone to Madame Restell's."

"Restell's?" Michael was incredulous.

"Katy, are you sure?" asked Logan.

She shook her head. "I can't be certain."

Liam called out new directions to the hack driver while Katy explained to Michael where she'd chanced upon Ria. When Liam confirmed the story, Katy realized for the first time that she'd been followed that day and probably every day since then. She glanced sharply at her husband.

"You said he wasn't in your employ any longer."

"I lied," he said without remorse.

There was nothing Katy could say to that. She wasn't even certain she was angry with him. How could she be, when he was only trying to protect her? "It was Michael who came to my suite at the Chesterfield," she said.

"I realize that now."

"I was afraid to tell you."

"Because of the photographs."

She nodded. "He would have used them to hurt Victor back then. Later he would have hurt you." Katy stopped, seeing the muscle working in Logan's cheek. This time it was she who squeezed his hand gently. No one said anything during the remainder of the ride to Madame Restell's.

The notorious abortionist's brownstone resembled nothing so much as a fortress. It was a large, rectangular residence, solidly built and uniformly dull. The windows were evenly spaced on each floor, the drapes closed for privacy. An occasional balcony broke the home's monotonous facade.

It surprised all four of the visitors that the front door opened readily to them. They were shown to a richly appointed parlor, furnished in royal purple and gold, where Madame Restell joined them almost immediately. She was a slender woman who carried herself with a stately air that lent her height and consequence. The pale skin of her face was engraved with fine lines, especially around her mouth, where they underscored an unfaltering and sour expression. The clear, sharp eyes were frankly assessing, wise, and shrewd.

463

"Which of you is Mr. Donovan?" she asked, going straight to the heart of the matter.

Michael stepped forward. "I am. I've come about my wife."

"I know why you've come," she said, cutting him off. Madame Restell fingered the jet beads at her neck. "And you're not any too soon. I was prepared to send for the police. I wasn't certain if you knew your wife was coming here or what she wanted." Michael's confused expression confirmed her suspicions. "I thought as much."

"Dammit, woman," he snapped. "Don't talk in riddles. Is my wife here or not?"

Madame Restell didn't blink at Michael's tone. She stared him down, then calmly went to the side table where several liquor decanters rested and poured herself a drink. She did not offer one to anyone else. "Mrs. Donovan has locked herself in one of the bedrooms upstairs. She did it when I tried to take the baby from her."

Katy sagged against Logan. Victoria was here! "Please, Madame Restell, the little girl is ours. I don't think Ria means her any harm. Surely you have a key for the room. Let us get Victoria now."

"Wait." Madame Restell held up one beringed hand. An emerald flashed. "I don't pretend to know all that's going on here, but then neither do any of you. I don't believe Mrs. Donovan means to harm the baby, but she doesn't want to give her up, either. She's been coming here for several months now—" she looked pointedly at Michael "—to arrange for the purchase of a child." Ignoring Katy's soft gasp, she continued "It's not such an unusual request but I'm able to discourage most women from coming here for that purpose. I have the privacy of my patients to consider."

"We all know the nature of your business," Logan said tautly. "And I don't give a damn about that now. I want my daughter. Are you going to give me a key or do O'Shea and I have to break in our second door of the day?"

"Hear me out," she said. "You can't conceive of Mrs. Donovan's attchment to that child. A few weeks ago I thought I had a baby for her. When the mother delivered, it was a boy. She wasn't interested. It had to be a girl, she told me. She had a name already picked out — Victoria. Is that really the child's name?"

Logan and Katy nodded. Katy's arms covered Logan's as they slipped around her from behind.

"My wife's last baby died shortly after the birthing," said Michael. "She was named Victoria Anne after my parents."

Madame Restell finished her drink and set the glass aside. "I thought it might be something like that. Your wife came here to show me the child, Mr. Donovan, to tell me that she found a baby without my help. This was none of my doing and quite frankly I'll be happy to have her gone. This is not the sort of practice I engage in. Now, knowing that she will not give up the child easily, you have my blessing to take her and the baby from my house. I do not need my home to be mired in this sort of scandal." She turned then and led them up the stairs to the second floor. "She has the only key, I'm afraid. I'll send you a bill for the door."

With that, Madame Restell retired to her own rooms.

Michael twisted the door handle first. "It's no good," he told Katy and Logan. "I could call Ria from now until next year and she wouldn't come out for me."

Logan swore under his breath. "God, man, she's *your* wife!"

"Let me try," said Katy. "Ria! Ria, it's me—Katy. Will you let me in?" There was no answer from Ria, but Victoria, recognizing her mother's voice, began to cry. Tears sprang to Katy's eyes. She swiped at them impatiently. "Please, Ria, let me in."

"Whore!"

The voice on the other side of the door bore little resemblance to Ria's soft, melodious tone. The word was hurled into the air and repeated in a staccato rhythm. Katy recoiled and raised helpless eyes to Logan.

"Step aside, Katy," Logan said. As soon as she did, he put his shoulder to the door. The door held, but Logan's shoulder did not. It hung at an odd angle, dislocated at the joint. "Don't look." He jammed it back into place on his second lunge at the door, swearing forcefully to take his mind off the pain. He stood back then and let Liam try the door.

It took more than a minute, an eternity to those in the hallway, before the lock gave way under the force of Liam's repeated kicking. The door flew open, banged against the wall, and started to close again. Liam caught it and led the way into the room. When he saw where Ria was standing with the baby, he caught Logan's eye, indicated his intention silently, and backed out of the bedchamber.

Cradling Victoria in her arms, Ria continued her retreat onto the balcony just beyond the widely arched bedroom window. A breeze blew at the ivory drapes, causing them to billow into the room and cover Ria's escape for a moment. When their view was clear again, she was pressed against the balcony's stone balustrade. The scene paralyzed Katy so that she could barely draw a breath.

"Don't come any closer," Ria warned them. "No one is going to take my baby away from me."

The drapes billowed again and this time Michael grabbed them, yanking them down. The crash frightened Victoria and her plaintive crying became a scream. Ria rested one hip against the stone railing and turned as if to begin her jump.

"What the hell do you think you're doing?" Logan asked Michael under his breath. "Don't say or do anything! Not a thing! Do you understand, Donovan?" Out of the corner of his eye he saw Michael nod. "Ria?" he asked softly, his voice nearly carried away by the wind. "We've come to see your baby, not to take her away."

"You're lying." She mouthed the words over Victoria's head. Her bright green eyes narrowed as they rested on Katy. She raised her voice. "I know you're lying to me. I thought you were so gentle and kind when you came to live with us as Victor's wife. Well, I was wrong about you and he was wrong about you. Michael always knew what a whore you were. He told me and I didn't believe

467

him. But then I didn't know you were *his* whore! Did Victor know, Katy? Did Victor know you were his son's mistress?"

"It's not true, Ria," said Katy. Her voice trembled. The ache she felt to hold Victoria in her arms was a physical pain. "I was never Michael's mistress."

"I saw a photograph that says differently. That's why you came to the house today, that's what you were looking for. There are more of them, aren't there? And you wanted them so I wouldn't suspect what a deceitful bitch you are." Her chin jerked in Michael's direction. "He made me have a baby because you were pregnant! I had to suffer his rutting when all he really wanted was a legitimate heir. That was your fault! It's only right that I should have Victoria now. She's mine! You owe me that!"

"Ria." Michael spoke her name impatiently, as though she could still respond to reason—or anger.

Her upper lip curled as her fever-bright eyes rested on her husband. "It was all for nothing! You were such a fool. Look at her!" She raised Victoria up, supporting the baby's head with her palm. "She's not Victor's daughter. Katy was playing you for a fool even as she was cuckolding your father. This is Logan's child! She has his hair, his eyes. Can't you see?" She held Victoria out, which made her own balance precarious.

Logan felt his heart simply stop beating in that moment. He expected Ria to reel over backward and take his daughter with him. "I received the photograph this morning, Ria," Logan said, drawing her attention back to him. "You were right to send it to me. There were so many things I wouldn't have known if you hadn't sent it." He inched forward, his palms lifted upward in a gesture of appeal and helplessness. He gauged the distance to Ria as too far to lunge and bring back Victoria safely.

Michael's blue eyes darted between the baby and Logan. "It's true," he said suddenly. "She's not my father's child." He turned on Katy and caught her by the wrist, yanking her toward him "You *bitch!* You let me think—all this time you let me think she was Victor's child!"

"Take your hands off her," Logan said quietly, carefully enunciating each word so that his meaning could not be missed.

"My pleasure." Without any sign of his intention he pushed Katy hard in Ria's direction. She stumbled on the hem of her gown and was propelled forward as she tried to catch herself. Ria screamed and lifted Victoria out of the way, dangling the baby over the balustrade so Katy couldn't reach her daughter. Victoria's slight weight, levered outward at an unmanageable angle, was enough to tip Ria's small frame over the stone rail. Katy's arms flailed, her fingers grasped Ria's skirt, then one ankle. She held on with a strength she had no idea she could summon.

Logan leaped forward to help Katy hold Ria. Panicked, Ria fought them and her grip on Victoria began to weaken. "Let her go, Katy," he ordered tightly. "I'll hold her. Try to reach Victoria." Ria's knees were hinged over the wide railing and

469

Logan sat on the balcony floor, holding her by the calves and ankles. The heels of her shoes pressed hard against Logan's injured shoulder as she tried to raise her torso. He groaned and rapped out the order to Katy again.

Katy leaned over the balcony and extended her arms as far as she could. "I can't reach her, Logan! *Oh, God, I can't reach her!*"

Chapter Fifteen

I can't reach her! Katy's impassioned cry for help hung in the air for several seconds before it was obliterated by Ria's agonized scream. Katy saw Victoria slip from Ria's nerveless fingers, then the baby was falling . . . falling.

Katy came awake abruptly. In real time, Victoria's descent took a mere heartbeat. In Katy's dream the fall was agonizingly slow, pulling Katy into the same vortex that imprisoned her daughter. She always woke before she hit bottom, always woke before she saw Liam O'Shea step out from beneath the balcony and catch Victoria in his outstretched arms.

Sitting up on the settee, Katy pulled a few pins from her hair and let it fall freely about her shoulders. She massaged her temples with her fingertips. A few moments passed before she realized she was not alone in the dimly lit front parlor. Logan was standing just inside the room, leaning against the closed door, a folded newspaper under his arm.

"I didn't hear you come in," she said. Raising the back of her hand to her mouth, she stifled a yawn. "What time is it?"

Logan glanced at the clock on the mantel. "A

few minutes after midnight." He pushed away from the door and went to the settee, dropping the newspaper on an end table. "Don't bother with the lamp," he said when she reached to turn up the wick. He took Katy's hands in his. "Are you all right?"

"Hmmm," she murmured, nodding. "Fine. Just a bad dream."

"Victoria's sleeping soundly," he said. "I just looked in on her. You're the one I was worried about. Why aren't you in bed?"

"I was waiting for you. I didn't think I would fall asleep."

Logan slipped one of his hands free of hers and cupped the side of her face. His thumb traced the curve of her cheek as he studied her. There were pale violet shadows beneath her eyes that spoke of too many restless nights. Only a week had passed since Ria dangled their child over the stone balustrade at Madame Restell's. Waking or sleeping, the memories were always there. Pain lingered in Katy's brown-gold eyes. Logan bent his head and kissed her gently on the lips. "Thank you for waiting," he said. "I hadn't meant to be so late, but," — he reached behind him and picked up the newspaper — "this story broke. I wanted to see it in print before I left the building." He handed her the first copy of the morning edition of the *Chronicle*.

Puzzled, Katy accepted the paper and opened it up. The headline drew her attention just as Logan meant it to: FRAUD IN THE HOUSE. Katy raised her head sharply and looked at Logan. "The colonel?" she asked.

"The *congressman*," he corrected. "The last damning piece of evidence came to our attention today. I decided it was time to let the rest of the country know about Richard Allen."

"He's aware of this?" she asked, lifting the paper.

"Not yet. He'll have an opportunity to deny his involvement soon enough. I have little doubt he'll do just that. Allen's not the only one named in this corruption scandal, but I think he may have the most to lose. He had set his political goals quite high."

"He may sue the paper, especially when he realizes you're behind this."

"Let him try. There's nothing in there that isn't true." Logan stood and went to the sideboard. "Would you like a drink? I feel as if I owe myself some small celebration. This day's been a long time coming."

"Nothing for me."

"Jenny and Christian already abed?" Logan splashed a crystal tumbler with whiskey. The house was quiet. After the noise and excitement of the press room, the silence was welcome.

"Just a little while ago. They're probably still awake if you want to show them this."

"God, no. They've had more than enough to take in since their return. Christian still can't believe Katy Dakota is Mary Catherine McCleary and that I'm married to both of them. This business with Richard Allen can definitely wait until morning."

"Your brother's been very understanding," she said. "And Jenny's right, you know, you could have

473

cabled them *some* news. They arrived home to find you've married and fathered a child and done none of it in the acceptable order."

Logan laughed softly. "Christian was more disturbed by the fact that he'd painted your eyes the wrong color." He shook his head, smiling ruefully at the memory of Katy's formal introduction to his brother. Christian didn't say hello or even extend his hand. He simply stared at Katy's face, studying her eyes as though nature had made the mistake, and said, "They're supposed to be green."

"Yes, well, Christian's agreed to change the portrait and leave my own eyes alone," she said dryly. Katy smoothed the newspaper in her lap. "Now, if you'd let me . . ."

"You don't have to read it this minute."

"I want to." She adjusted the oil lamp so she could see better and curled into one corner of the settee.

Logan sat beside Katy again, sipped his drink slowly and watched her read the three-column piece, gauging her reaction by the sighs, frowns, and soft, incredulous ahhs. When she was finished reading, he removed the paper from her lap and dropped it on the floor. He offered her his drink.

Katy took the tumbler and raised it to her lips. One swallow seemed to blister her insides and bring tears to her eyes. She gave it back hurriedly, making a face. "You know I don't like whiskey."

"You looked as if you could use a drink in spite of that fact."

"That's quite some story. Your reporters are sure of everything?"

474

"Everything."

Katy was silent a moment. "It wasn't just for revenge, was it?"

"No, not just for revenge. In the beginning, perhaps, but revenge didn't sustain me. I pursued this story because it was a national scandal, not for personal reasons. Your stepfather probably won't see it that way, but it's true. You taught me a lot about revenge, Katy. Sometimes I wonder why I've been so fortunate, when it all could have ended so differently."

Katy was in his arms then, her head against the curve of his shoulder. He held her closely and allowed the shudder that went through her to pass into him. He remembered the look in her eyes when she first woke. "You went to see Ria today, didn't you?" he asked.

"She didn't even know me," Katy said softly. "She sat there in her room, staring out the window, and never acknowledged my presence. She holds her arms cradled in front of her, just as if she were holding her baby, and she rocks back and forth even though her chair doesn't move."

"She'll get the best care at Jennings Memorial." Logan knew it was small comfort to Katy. It was little comfort to him as well. He thought he could very well have killed Ria if Liam hadn't started shouting from below that he had Victoria safe in his arms. With his child unharmed, Logan was able to pull Ria to safety. She fought him, cursed him, and screamed at him to let her go. Logan might have done exactly that if he hadn't realized her intention was to throw herself off the balcony.

475

In the end Katy helped him restrain Ria while Michael looked on dispassionately.

"I know," said Katy, bringing Logan's thoughts back to the present. "It seems so unfair, though. I wanted it to be Michael sitting there, locked in that room, alone and quite mad. I want him to be here now so you can hit him again."

A small smile lifted the corners of Logan's mouth. Rarely had he known such satisfaction as the moment when Ria's strength was exhausted and he could give his complete attention to Michael Donovan. Logan's powerful right hook caught Michael unaware and laid him out cold. At the time Logan had regretted the accuracy of his blow. He would have liked an excuse to knock Michael down again. "Say the word and I'll find him."

"No," she said. "I don't want his head. I want as few reminders of Michael Donovan as possible. I'll never hold Ria as responsible for what happened as I do him. He pushed her toward madness. I think he would have been grateful if we'd let Ria fall."

Logan was certain of it. Like Katy, he felt nothing so much as pity for Ria. He was not as sure they shared similar feelings about Michael. Katy wanted to forget him and Logan still wanted to hurt him. It would be some time before Logan knew he could come around to Katy's way of thinking. "Are you going to sleep on me?" he asked when he felt her suppress a yawn.

"No."

Sweet liar, he thought. "In that case . . ." He stroked her hair. He held the weight of one honeyed curl in his palm, balancing it carefully as

476

though it were water and he were a thirsty man. He touched the silky curl to his mouth.

"What are you doing?" she asked sleepily.

"Drinking." He let her hair slide off his palm. His fingers whispered across the back of her neck and he drew her hair to one side and let it fall over her shoulder. Her head was tilted now, the elegant line of her neck vulnerable. He kissed her there, just below her ear. Her breath was warm on his cheek. She stirred against him and Logan realized he had definitely engaged her interest.

"You're a provocative woman," he said.

"You must mean provoking."

He smiled and kissed her again, this time at the curve of her neck and shoulder. He could feel her hum of pleasure against his lips. "That, too."

The touch of him sent a delicious mixture of languor and excitement through her. "We shouldn't." Katy's hand fell on Logan's shoulder. "You haven't forgotten we don't have the house to ourselves."

"Shhh. I locked the door."

"Oh." Katy sighed as his lips moved to the underside of her jaw and his fingers began to twist at the buttons of her gown. Her hands slipped under Logan's jacket and eased it over his shoulders. Their arms tangled as he worked her buttons and she worked his. Katy's mouth opened under his, tongues touched, teased. Once they moved in the same direction at the same moment. Their noses bumped. They reared back, startled. He smiled a little sheepishly, she a little shyly. The moment had an endearing sort of awkwardness that made them think back to a certain hayloft and another time.

477

"How young I was," she said a shade wistfully. "How young we both were."

She nodded. The centers of Katy's eyes were darkening. Desire flushed her cheeks. Placing her palms on either side of Logan's face, she leaned forward and brushed the tip of her nose to his, then kissed him full on the mouth.

Logan eased them off the settee and onto the floor. He kicked a stool out of their way. It fell on its side with a soft thud that neither of them heard. They shared a growing sense of urgency that made them reluctant to take too much time with tiny buttons and stockings and studs. They took off what they had to and pushed aside the rest.

"You're very good for me," she whispered against his ear. She was filled with him. Her thighs cradled him, her arms embraced him. His skin was warm against hers and she knew the shape of her body by the contrast with his. The musky male scent of him was tantalizing. The moist suck of his mouth raised a response wherever it touched her.

"Right now, I'd rather be very good *to* you."

There was no question of that and Katy told him so, then she returned his every expression of love.

The floor only seemed uncomfortable in the aftermath. "I suppose we could move to the settee," he said.

Katy noticed he did not make any move in the direction. Instead, he was lazily rubbing his foot against hers.

Except for righting the clothes they hadn't discarded, Katy and Logan stayed precisely where they were. Katy's head rested against Logan's outstretched arm. Her hand lay on his chest inside his open shirt. His heartbeat filled her palm.

"I do love you, Logan Marshall."

He turned a little then to see her better. "I hope you never come to your senses," he said, half-teasing, half-meaning it.

She smiled. "I came to my senses a long time ago. Don't think I didn't. I know you for what you are, Logan, and I love you because of it."

"Warts and all."

Katy thought of her frog prince. She kissed his cheek. "Oh, darling, you have no idea how true that is."